ALSO BY SARA FLANNERY MURPHY

Girl One

The Possessions

The
WONDER
STATE

MCD · FARRAR, STRAUS AND GIROUX · NEW YORK

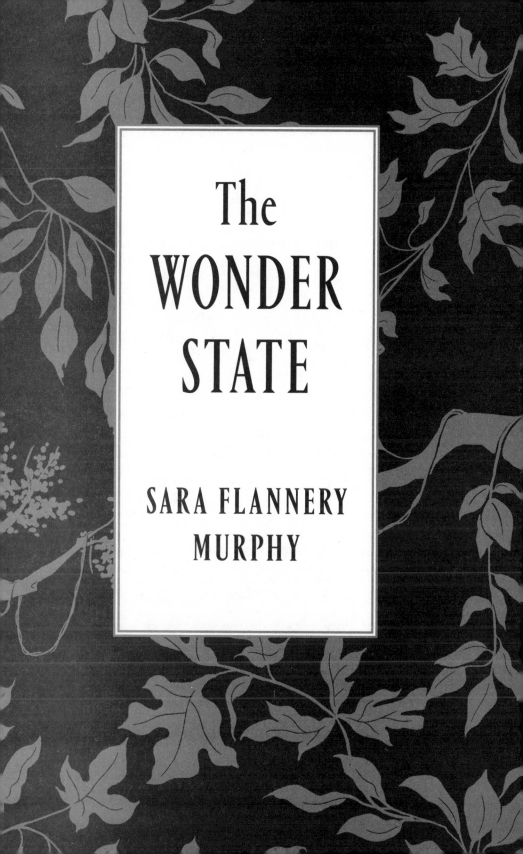

The
WONDER
STATE

SARA FLANNERY
MURPHY

MCD
Farrar, Straus and Giroux
120 Broadway, New York 10271

Printed in the United States of America
First edition, 2023

Title-page art by June Park.

Library of Congress Cataloging-in-Publication Data
Names: Murphy, Sara Flannery, author.
Title: The wonder state / Sara Flannery Murphy.
Description: First edition. | New York : MCD / Farrar, Straus and
    Giroux, 2023.
Identifiers: LCCN 2023002256 | ISBN 9780374601775 (hardcover)
Subjects: LCGFT: Gothic fiction. | Novels.
Classification: LCC PS3613.U7549 W66 2023 | DDC 813/.6—
    dc23/eng/20230210
LC record available at https://lccn.loc.gov/2023002256

Designed by Gretchen Achilles

Our books may be purchased in bulk for promotional,
educational, or business use. Please contact your local bookseller
or the Macmillan Corporate and Premium Sales Department
at 1-800-221-7945, extension 5442, or by email
at MacmillanSpecialMarkets@macmillan.com.

www.mcdbooks.com • www.fsgbooks.com
Follow us on Twitter, Facebook, and Instagram at @mcdbooks

1   3   5   7   9   10   8   6   4   2

*To Miles and August: may you always explore freely
while knowing home is waiting*

*And to everyone who grew up secretly hoping that
every ordinary doorway would lead to magic*

The
WONDER
STATE

1

MAY 3, 2015

NOW

Brandi Addams is finally leaving Eternal Springs. She's been planning it under their noses for months, and nobody suspects a thing. After thirty-two years, Brandi is as much a part of Eternal Springs as tornado season, or the springs that burst fever-warm from the ground. She was born in this town; everyone expects her to die here. She's a homegrown cautionary tale: the girl who squandered her entire future before high school graduation.

But she's leaving, and she's going farther than any of them.

There's only one more thing left to do. Which is why she's trudging through the Ozarks forest, fifteen miles outside the city limits, in the thorny wilderness that sometimes requires search parties to retrieve hikers from its depths. It rained last night, and the rocky downhill slope is slick with mud. Brandi's fallen twice, a scrape seething under her jeans. She keeps going. She hopes to god she's not wrong about this. She's been wrong about so many things in her life, but she'll accept every mistake and heartbreak if she can be right this one time.

Brandi's looking for a house, but the question is whether the house wants to be found. She scans the tree trunks until her eyes hurt, seeking that glimpse of a rooftop or the gleam of a window. She's avoided the Forever House for so long now that maybe she's missed her chance. Or maybe it's withdrawn into hiding, scared away by growling ATVs and hungry bulldozers. Even a wilderness this deep is getting invaded. But Brandi's got to try. She trusts that the house can sense the bright beacon of her need.

Her legs are growing tired. She asked Amber to drop her off miles back, near the old Asher Lake trailhead. There are no markers on a map that point to her true destination anyway, so she invented a cleaning job at the Motts' vacation home. In truth, the Motts aren't even in town, the expensive views of the lake wasting away in those picture windows. Ms. Mott used to follow her from room to room, jawing about how they'd never considered vacationing in Arkansas before Eternal Springs *came up in the world*. The Motts are the new type of tourists, thronging in to *revitalize, reinvigorate,* other shiny verbs that hide what they intend to do. *Replace. Remove.*

When Amber dropped Brandi off, she rolled down the car window to call after her, "Don't go raiding the liquor cabinet, hear?"

During the fifteen years she's cleaned houses, Brandi has never swiped any stray benzos or watered down the pinot noir. Not once. It's been her own uncrossable line, and Amber knows that. But looking behind the joke, Brandi saw that Amber was just worried about her. This latest sober streak is Brandi's personal record.

"Promise I'll be good," she'd said, overcome with tenderness for Amber, who was already in her work uniform. Black button-up forever smelling of grease and spice. And Amber smiled.

One thing Brandi never realized: how easy it is to be generous when you're about to leave. No wonder the others looked so free before they left town, everything bad already in the rearview mirror.

4

Overhead, the sky is a washed-clean blue. Brandi's close. She can feel it, that shift in the air. Birds quieting. Breeze stilling. Her heart swells with cautious hopefulness. She wouldn't blame the Forever House for rejecting her. Brandi's not the girl she was the last time she came here, that's for damn sure. But—but—

There, between the trees. Russet siding, peeling shingles. She picks up her pace.

There's a buzzing in her pocket. She fumbles her phone loose, tilts the screen so that she can see the display behind the starburst crack. Roy's texting her. *I wish you'd tell me.*

Brandi pauses to type. *Not til tonite. Its a surprise.*

Have I mentioned lately that I hate surprises?

She sends back a single heart. The ellipses bounce for a second, then vanish.

The house stands across a low gully, joined to the forest by a wooden bridge. Near the center, a fallen branch merges with the wood, as if the bridge is devolving back to its source. The house is in the same disrepair as the bridge. Roof slumping in spots, windowpanes missing. Even so, it's beautiful: a two-story log structure, a high gable roof.

Brandi stands on the other side of the bridge, echoes falling into formation around her as she remembers the first time she saw the house. The triumph they'd felt, brave explorers, the world coughing up its best-kept secrets just for them. Jay bent over her sketchpad, like she couldn't handle such wonder without a buffer. Iggy bouncing with excitement.

It's the first time in a while that she can think about the others without pain. After she first found out, their betrayal turned her favorite memories sour. Like she couldn't even be happy in retrospect. But Roy's helped her let it go. Forgive; forget; all that church-basement sobriety bullshit that finally makes sense.

The front door is unlocked, as always. Behind her, a startled cardinal rises from a branch, wings flutter-sharp. Brandi steps inside.

Instantly she feels time settle into her bones. Even the sunlight looks different through these windows, honeyed, thicker. Outside, the cardinal is no longer a quick flash of red, but is hovering in mid-air, wings fanned to show the white. Like flags of surrender.

The place looks centuries older than when she last saw it. The wallpaper sheds in strips, the wall beneath speckled with mold. A settee, back curved like the prow of a ship, sags with age. Brandi remembers the oil painting over the window blooming with color, the scarlet apple skin, the pebbled gem of a tangerine. The paint is cracked now, the apple palest pink. She spots the shriveled shell of a left-behind juice box on the floor. She remembers Jay sprawled across the settee, the rough slurp the straw made when the juice box was almost empty. That noise made them laugh till she had to pee. The ridiculous memory glows until she blinks away tears.

Upstairs, the windows show sweeping views of the forest, still as a photograph. From up here, the cardinal is a stark, unmoving burst of red against the trees. Brandi moves directly to the room at the end of the hall.

The child's bed is frosty white, the canopy a tattered ghost. In spite of herself, Brandi's heart gallops nearly out of her chest. Going to the closet, she reaches high on the shelf, groping around for a wooden box. There. Still safe, still untouched. Her hands shake with anticipation as she lifts the box down. She prays the house is looking out for her, that Theodora still favors her. Because everything that comes next could undo fifteen years of hurt.

Please let me be right, Brandi thinks. She sifts through the box's contents. A class ring, mint-green with oxidation. The white pellets of baby teeth, a braid of pale hair. Letters, letters, so many letters, thin and brittle. And—and yes, there it is, an antique key, simple and gold-plated, unadorned. So small that it's taken her all this time to fully appreciate it.

Brandi lets the relief hit her in one precious wave. She slides the key into her pocket and gives it a little pat. *Now.* Now she has everything they need. She can leave Eternal Springs for good, knowing that she's done her best, that she's ready.

"Thank you," she whispers to the house, hoping its creator will hear.

Back downstairs. If the bird's wings have moved, it's by a fraction of an inch. Brandi remembers the hold of this place, the way it feels like she's getting away with an amazing trick. But she knows better now.

As she crosses to the front door, her foot hits something. It rolls a few inches, leaving a clean trail through the dust. Everything else in the house has been exactly as she remembered. This—this is new, unaccounted-for. Easy to miss at first. Someone's been here.

Brandi looks around, pulse kicking up. Her eyes catch on the unassuming door that leads down to the cellar. She tries the doorknob. Locked. When Brandi slides the bolt, the door falls open as if it's been waiting a long time to release. It takes her a moment to understand the nasty feeling in her gut. The wood around the doorframe is scratched: a crosshatch of marks, gouged deep in some spots, growing thinner at the edges.

The stairs are steeped in darkness, cool air rising like icy water. She should leave. If she was watching herself in a horror movie, she'd be rolling her eyes, muttering, *Get out, lady, just go.* What had Roy told her recently, all love and exasperation? *You've always made other people's problems your own, and it's going to kill you one day.*

This isn't her problem. She's gulped down enough bitter guilt to last a lifetime. Here she is, on the brink of escape, and she has every right to leave and never look back.

Old memories stir, rise. Brandi shakes her head as if that will scatter the growing awareness of what she has to do. Doesn't work.

She knows the right choice, in a clear-eyed way that would shock everyone who's watched her make nothing but wrong choices. She can't leave town without knowing for sure. She's come too far for that.

And so Brandi Addams descends the cellar steps.

2

MAY 17, 2015

NOW

The vigil's nearly over by the time Jay shows up. She spotted the flyer stapled to a telephone pole right outside her motel, like a bad omen. Hot-pink paper, no-nonsense details scribbled in Sharpie. A candlelight vigil to bring Brandi Addams home, held at Thermal Park, six o'clock. In a daze, Jay stole the flyer off the pole and stuck it to the corner of the motel mirror. She's not helping Brandi much, hoarding this information all for herself, but then that fits with the overall pattern of the past fifteen years.

There's a photo. Brandi's xeroxed grin is so oversaturated that it could belong to anybody. That hasn't kept Jay from staring at it, willing it to explain exactly what she's supposed to do now that she's bought a last-minute, one-way ticket to Eternal Springs, only to find her old friend missing. Gone.

Jay spent the entire plane ride preparing herself to see Brandi again. Wondering what she could possibly say. Practicing apologies and excuses and justifications, the ones she's carefully crafted in her head for years, varying with the ebbing levels of her shame and regret. Maybe, she let herself think, Brandi has put everything behind her. Maybe this could be an overdue reunion. Jay was so worked up by the time she arrived in Eternal Springs that she was scarcely breathing, and then—*then* she saw the flyer, and all that hope and anxiety collapsed together into complete confusion.

So. No reunion, no forgiveness. Just a vigil and a xeroxed face and the one-line, two-word letter that drew Jay here. *You promised.*

The worst thing? In a horrible corner of her mind, Jay's relieved that she doesn't have to face her friend just yet.

Walking to the vigil, Jay looks around, marking the differences in her hometown. Eternal Springs has changed quite a bit since she left town on the heels of her high school graduation. Earlier today, on the hour-long shuttle ride from the regional airport, she noticed whole patches of forest stripped bald, making room for chain restaurants and boxy McMansions. The changes have even crept into downtown. New storefronts, expensive and sleek. Gleaming park benches and streetlamps.

It should be a kind of relief. Like each felled tree and refurbished building erases more of Jay's history here. But no. The memories only press in tighter.

At the entrance to Thermal Park, she stops to check her phone one more time. Still no reply. She swallows disappointment. With Charlie and the twins, she's not sure she has the right numbers. Iggy's silence, though . . . that hurts more.

Thermal Park is stubbornly unchanged. It's less a traditional *park* than a rising forested bluff in the middle of town, wound with stone steps. The hot springs are cordoned off into little pools, bottoms glittering with coins left by wish-makers. These springs are responsible for turning Eternal into a town in the first place: back in the late 1800s, they drew travelers hoping to cure their edema, restore their eyesight, mend their heartache.

It's nearly seven-thirty. Only a few people linger. Jay accepts a candle from a teenager she doesn't recognize. The muddy dusk hides her as she climbs the steps, pausing behind a cluster of older women. They pop up in her memory with disconcerting ease. A classmate's mother, the librarian who was always nice about overdue fines.

"I'm telling you, it's no coincidence. That girl's past finally caught up with her."

"I'm not even clear on what happened," the librarian says. "Is she missing or . . . you know?"

"Dead?"

The cheap foil candle holder scalds Jay's fingertips. *Dead?* The world tilts unsteadily, but she makes herself listen.

"Who knows," the classmate's mom—Ms. Suarez—goes on. "Amber dropped her off to clean some vacation house weeks ago, Kathy said."

Kathy. So Brandi was still employed by the same boss who hired her when she was eighteen. Still cleaning the same houses. It's as if these past fifteen years have moved differently for her than for Jay.

"Amber hadn't heard from her and got worried enough to go by her trailer. Found blood everywhere. No sign of Brandi since. They combed the woods."

"At least with Gene, they had a suspect," a third woman says. They all seem to realize the implications of this; the librarian laughs strangely, changing the topic.

"Jadelynne Carr?" The voice ambushes her from the opposite direction. Jay turns, heart hammering. Amber looks like she's about to poke Jay to make sure she's real. "What the hell are you doing here?"

"Uh. Jay. I still go by Jay."

"I ain't seen you in years and years. Your dad don't even live here anymore." Amber's face flickers in and out of familiarity, her teenage and adult versions colliding. This is the first time Jay's encountered anybody from high school in the flesh. It's not like she attended the reunions; those invitations went directly into the trash.

"You came all this way for Brandi?" Amber asks. "That's real decent of you."

Jay realizes she's braced for a fight. Part of it is muscle memory. Amber Penske has never been Jay's biggest fan—or Brandi's.

"Remember how the kids would call you two Bradelynne?"

Hurrying past the pain of that nickname, Jay gestures at the lingering dots of candlelight. "Who arranged all this?"

"I did. She don't really have a lot of people around here. I can't get hold of her mom, no surprise there. I'm not sure how else to help, but I gotta do something. Brandi's my best friend."

The surprise hits Jay in a gut punch. Amber and Brandi, friends. This feels wrong, like Jay's memories have been replaced behind her back. "You were the last one to see her?" she asks, repeating what she overheard. When she glances over her shoulder, she sees the women have moved down the hillside, out of earshot. "Do you mind explaining what happened? I'm confused."

"Well, I'm not sure I understand myself. I dropped her off about two weeks back, then had to get to my shift at Francesco's. After that, life got busy. She stopped answering my texts. I reckoned she was just busy with her own stuff. It took me over a week to go by her place. I should of gone by sooner, I should of noticed something was wrong. I've replayed it a thousand times in my head. If I'd known . . ."

The raw guilt in Amber's voice tugs at something in Jay's chest. "I'm sorry."

"Hey, not your fault."

It's something polite to say. Amber doesn't mean anything by it. But Jay's stomach churns. "Do you think—does this have anything to do with Brandi's . . . addiction issues?"

Jay instantly regrets that. *Addiction issues.*

Sure enough: "What do you care about her 'addiction issues'?" Amber asks, mimicking Jay's awkward cadence.

"Uh. It could . . ." Jay feels every year she's been gone, all the

time she spent whittling down her Southern accent, dissolving the
h in *what* and *why*, shortening her twangy, wayward vowels. She
runs her tongue over her newly straightened teeth. *You don't belong
here anymore, Jay; don't worry, this is just temporary.* "It could help
narrow down what happened to Brandi."

"You reckon she's in trouble because she's just some junkie?"

"Whoa. Hey. I would never call her—"

"Sure you wouldn't." Amber sighs. "Look. I won't sugarcoat it.
She's been in and out of rehab, in and out of jail. Some real tough
times."

So everything that started back then has just kept growing. Jay
outran it; Brandi didn't. How do you outrun anything when you're
stuck in one spot, trapped in the very trailer park where your whole
life went to hell in the first place?

"The funny thing," Amber goes on, "is that, before she left?
Things seemed a lot better. In fact—" But then Amber's eyes slide
beyond Jay and her gaze hardens. Her inner calculations happen
swiftly, and Jay feels the coldness slip between them. "Sorry, Jadelynne," Amber says. "Didn't mean to keep you from your *friends.*"

"What? No. I'm here alone."

"Sure about that?"

Jay turns. Down the hill, near Thermal Park's central fountain.
Three of them, sleek as a flock of ravens among sparrows, mate-
rializing out of the dusk. Hilma, Charlie. Iggy. They haven't seen
Jay yet, and for a second she's paralyzed. Everything she's been
squashing down tight since she last saw them—anger and yearning
and the pain of losing them, and, *god*, the swift joy of seeing their
faces—all blooms inside her at once. She half convinced herself that
they wouldn't show up, that this was between her and Brandi, the
original duo. Now here they are. And no wonder Amber's pissed.
Jay coming back alone was generous. Jay coming back as part of the
group, the whole gang reuniting in the wake of Brandi's sudden
disappearance?

That's trouble.

Amber slips away, and Jay knows that news of their return will spread fast now. She squares her shoulders back and descends the steps toward them. Her old friends.

Hilma wears a long black jacket with a high collar, her hair—still blond, dusted with premature gray—piled into a topknot. In the harsh candlelight, her lipstick is a red slash. A diamond sprouts from her ring finger; Hilma, married. Jay feels a quick, disoriented surprise, as if they're still eighteen. Beside Hilma, Charlie wears a slim-fitted suit, tortoiseshell glasses flickering with reflected flames. He seems like he's settled since she last saw him, without a hint of the twitchy anxiety that kept him in constant motion as a teenager.

And Iggy. Jay looks at Ignacio Nieves the way she gazed sidelong at the sun as a kid, defying every good reason not to. His dark hair isn't down to his shoulders anymore: it's shorter, but still tousled. His teenage ranginess has solidified. A thousand memories zip along Jay's nerve endings.

"Bluejay," Hilma says, unsurprised. "You're here." Charlie nods a terse greeting. Iggy meets Jay's eyes and offers a quick, unreadable smile.

"So are you." She's not sure whether to mention that they've been collectively ignoring her calls, or that they've shown up together. At least Max is out of the loop, too, by the looks of it.

"When did you get in?" Hilma asks, like all this is normal. She holds a candle carelessly, casually.

"Uh, just today. I came as soon as I could. I wanted to be here for Brandi. Of course."

"Oh, of course," Charlie echoes, the sardonic note easy to miss, except Jay finds she still speaks his language. "Anything for Brandi."

Before Iggy can chime in, Hilma lets out a bright, hard laugh. Around them, above them, along the rising steps, the silence deepens. Jay's acutely aware of how they must look.

"Cut the bullshit," Hilma says, mercifully lowering her voice.

"We aren't here for Brandi. We swore an oath. The only reason the four of us are standing in a park in fucking Eternal Springs fucking Arkansas is because we *have* to." Hilma drops her candle onto the grass, and Iggy tamps out the flame with the sole of his shoe. She yanks up her sleeve, revealing the pulsing red scar, a jagged line two inches long. "Brandi Addams called us," Hilma says. "We had no other choice."

3

1999

THEN

Jadelynne. Sorry—*Jay*. What are you doin' after school?"

Brandi and Jay had been eating lunch apart from everyone else since the start of senior year, hunkered down on the concrete barrier wall behind the school library. Out here they were surrounded by the greenish light fractured through the leaves, the perfume of milkweed. The librarian left the casement windows open, and the muted roar of the cafeteria felt pleasantly distant. Like Jay was already looking back on everything. In biology, Jay had learned about caterpillars in cocoons: melting themselves into genetic soup, rebuilding from scratch. She was taking this spirit into her senior year. She was a floating collection of imaginal disks, just waiting to become something new.

Brandi leaned closer. "How'd you like to go to the AIR House?"

Jay finally noticed Brandi's suppressed excitement. The AIR House was reserved for big-shot artists, luring talent to Eternal Springs with the promise of a state-funded fellowship. It was technically the Edward Payson Washbourne Lodge, but locals referred to it as the AIR House, short for artist-in-residence, short for the out-of-towners who dropped into their lives for one calendar year and left no trace behind. Jay had only ever known the AIR House as an inaccessible presence, perched high on the bluffs, huge windows reflecting the sky.

This year's guests had already proven unusual. A whole family moving in. Yet more surprising: instead of being shipped off to private school in Fayette, the younger Garnets attended the local public school. Jay still couldn't get used to Hilma and Max, sitting there every morning, larger-than-life, glaringly blond, clothes scavenged from more fashionable eras. Jay hadn't spoken to the twins since they started school three weeks ago, only observed them—sketching their profiles quickly, secretly, as if she could absorb their golden confidence by committing their cheekbones to paper.

Brandi smiled shyly. "Surprise."

"What? How?" Jay dropped her tray, grabbed Brandi in a hug. "Oh my god. You know how long I've wanted this."

"Gene's got a job with them," Brandi said, voice muffled against Jay's shoulder. "They wanted to hire local. He's going to work on the AC, it's busted." It was topping ninety degrees every day lately, the humidity dense as a wet quilt. "The Garnets ain't home right now, they went to Fayette for some artsy thing. Gene said we could come along."

Jay's excitement briefly faltered. Brandi's stepdad (the shorthand they used, easier than "absent mother's boyfriend") wasn't naturally generous. Gene being this nice meant he'd done something that required an apology. His kindness was always transactional, and temporary. But the idea of actually entering the AIR House had taken over Jay's brain, and she could tell how excited Brandi was to offer her this unexpected gift.

———

The long, remote road that led to the AIR House was even steeper than the typical Eternal Springs streets, jackknifing back and forth. Through the open windows of Gene's pickup, the cicadas' buzzing could've been emitting from the heat itself, a teakettle's whistle. By the time they pulled up at the house, Jay's T-shirt was gummed to her back with sweat.

Gene got out of the pickup and adjusted his hat. His skin was waxy in the direct daylight, but Jay was familiar with the signs of his hangovers. He winked at her, fully into his role as the doting stepfather. "You gals be careful, keep your hands to yourself. You know how these folks are." He whistled, *cuckoo*. "They'll notice anything out of place."

Jay couldn't answer. There it was, looming right in front of her, the AIR House. She'd never been this close.

"We won't touch nothing, sir," Brandi said.

"That's my girl."

The two of them followed Gene, slow, cautious, holding hands. Jay couldn't quite believe Gene Stippley had the keys to a place like this. The massive porch was level with the tops of the pines, like a treehouse. The interior was even bigger than Jay had imagined, all of it intricately constructed. The bottom floor sprawled open, kitchen leading to living room leading to dining area. The stone fireplace was big enough to stand in, flanked by low leather couches, flawless white, like nobody ever actually sat on them.

After Gene vanished to the back of the house, Jay and Brandi circled the perimeter of the ground floor, biting down giggles. With the AC broken and all those floor-to-ceiling windows, it was greenhouse-hot this late August afternoon. Three separate spiral staircases led to lofts; from below, Jay caught glimpses of the upstairs nooks, the sloping eaves, the edge of a bed. It was a home that flaunted its lack of privacy. Anything you did here would be visible to everyone. So different from the low popcorn ceilings and cramped, carpeted hallways of her own house. Jay's hands itched to capture this wide-open feeling on paper so she could revisit it again and again.

Brandi squealed. "Jay. Look."

An easel stood in one corner, a speckled dropcloth pooling beneath. A painting of a naked woman, grinning wide and proud to show crooked teeth. Jay never saw people with bad teeth in magazine ads or on TV, and seeing a smile that resembled hers was a shock, like she was looking in a funhouse mirror. *Me: not me.* The woman stared out of the painting like she'd been waiting for Jay to notice her. She sat naked, crossed legs hanging loosely open to reveal the soft, startling folds of her labia. The inside of the woman's vagina was lined with identically crooked, off-white teeth, a sideways smile beneath her real one.

Jay became conscious of the teeth in her own mouth, the overbite they didn't have the money to correct. The orthodontist in Fayette had explained that the overbite would give her jaw pain and tooth decay, then asked for four thousand dollars to fix it. He may as well have asked for a human sacrifice. Jay started bringing her hand up to hide her mouth when she laughed. The Ozarks version of braces.

The initial in the corner was abstract. *J&HG.* "Which one is the artist, again?" Jay asked, resisting the urge to touch the still-damp paint. "The dad or the mom?"

"Both of them," came a voice from nowhere.

Jay felt herself gaping, a slack-jawed yokel. Then she looked up and saw Hilma Garnet staring down, yellow hair swinging on either side of her face. Like she'd somersault over the railings, land right on them. Hilma pushed herself backward, vanishing; a second later, she descended the spiral staircase, slow now, regal as a lioness.

Jay and Brandi stiffened, caught red-handed.

"Both my parents," Hilma said, "are artists. They collaborate." Hilma reached the ground floor. She didn't look like the upwardly mobile of the Ozarks, who had blowouts, veneers. Her hair had the kind of watery natural blondness passed down like an heirloom. She was what kids at school called "husky," and nearly six feet. Some of the tall girls Jay knew slouched, compressing themselves downward and inward, but not Hilma. She wore a peacock-blue brocade dress, the type of thing Jay's mom wore in old photos.

"Who the hell are you?" Hilma asked.

So Hilma didn't remember them after spending two weeks in the same cafeteria, passing the busted equipment back and forth in chem lab. Of course she didn't.

"I—I thought you were in Fayette," Brandi said.

"I didn't go, I have cramps," Hilma said. "How do you know my family's gone?"

"You okay?" Brandi asked, like she was about to fetch a Midol.

"Nobody's explained why you're in my house."

The easy way Hilma said "my house," it might've been her ancestral manse. Jay knew she and Brandi were the intruders. But for a second the fact that Hilma Garnet had arrived here a month ago and claimed this piece of Jay's hometown was a thorn stuck deep inside.

"My stepdad works for you."

"The handyman is bringing his kids along? Is that typical in Arkansas? My parents are always trying to be so open-minded, hiring locals, but this is totally unprofessional."

"No. Hey." Sweat beaded Brandi's upper lip. "Please don't tattle on Gene. He's—it's—"

"It was me," Jay said loudly. "I asked to come here. Begged. I've always wanted to see this place. I love houses." She acknowledged Brandi's agonized, grateful stare with a quick squeeze of her hand. Hilma's eyes darted to where their hands met.

This half lie wasn't out of loyalty to Gene. Jay had seen inside Brandi's cabinets—the ramen noodles with orange price-reduced stickers, the canned green beans from the food pantry, edging on expiration. What happened to Gene happened to Brandi. He needed this job.

"You love houses," Hilma repeated. It could've sounded insulting, a mocking echo. But she narrowed her eyes thoughtfully. "Do you know a lot about the houses around here?"

"Sort of. Like, I'm not an expert or anything," Jay stammered, thinking of Jessie Suarez's mom, a real estate agent.

"Does the name Theodora Trader mean anything to you?"

"Who?" It did sound familiar, but only vaguely. "Wait, was she like—some old-time—"

"Do you know of any strange houses in the area?" Hilma asked, moving on.

"Strange? Like how?"

"Haunted?" Brandi whispered.

Hilma shook her head. "Houses that make things happen. Houses that feel different."

This house, Jay wanted to say. But Brandi's distress had evaporated, and she spoke up, puppy-dog-eager. "We do know a house like that. The Truth House. It's this old empty house out near my place. When we were little, we used to sneak out there and play. It was the weirdest thing, but you couldn't tell a lie when you was inside it. Everything we said was the whole, entire, God's honest truth." She crossed her heart.

Jay glanced at Hilma, ready to be angry on Brandi's behalf. It was a fierce protectiveness she'd felt since elementary school. Brandi hadn't changed much since those days, still all sharp elbows, gangly legs. Wide-set brown eyes that she smudged with blue eye shadow from the dollar store. Brandi's eyes looked so open that Jay worried for her, like she let in too much of the world.

"Just a game," Jay said quickly. "We were only in second grade."

"Sounds fun. Why'd you stop playing?"

Brandi faltered as the rest of the memory filled in. Jay took over.

"We asked some asshole from our grade to come with us. We were just trying to be nice, but it didn't work out."

"Amber Penske," Brandi supplied.

"Did the house work the same way on this Amber?"

"I mean, she would've told the truth no matter what," Jay said, remembering Amber's cruelty. *My mom says you're trash and we can't hang out with you no more.* "Anyway. Amber told everyone about it, kids made fun of us. We stopped going. The end."

"But it was magic," Brandi said stubbornly.

Above their heads there was a sudden creak and a hum, and they all jumped. A drift of cold air touched the back of Jay's neck. Gene must have fixed the AC, then.

"I'm Hilma Garnet." It seemed wildly generous of her to pretend the other two didn't know.

"Uh. I'm Jay. This is Brandi."

Hilma gave a shrewd look. "Not Jadelynne?"

"I go by Jay now." She said it as if she went by Jay to crowds of people and not just to herself, her dad, and Brandi. Then she caught up: So Hilma *did* know her name. She bloomed with pleasure.

"I get it. Your eyes are the color of a blue jay's feathers. You're more Jay than Jade. We go to school together, don't we?"

"I think so." Her nonchalance was only a little shaky.

"About this truth-telling house." Hilma turned businesslike. "I need you to take me."

Jay could feel Brandi's matching spark of excitement. "Yeah. Of course."

"Great. Tomorrow. Max can drive us. I don't have my license. Stupid written test is so boring, I can't make myself do it. You know where to find me," she said, and without a farewell, Hilma ran up the staircase in a flurry of her brocade skirt. It seemed like the fabric would get caught on the steps and send her plummeting, but she vanished safely at the top.

"Oh my god," Brandi whispered on their way out, her face brimming with everything Jay felt too. Adventure dropping down into their laps, unexpected and unbeckoned, all theirs, when usually anything exciting took so long to develop that it barely seemed worth the wait.

4

1999

The Truth House was a small pink bungalow at the edge of town, the embarrassing part, right where the effort of being picturesque gave way with a sigh to foil-covered windows and cars propped on cinder blocks. Tourists only saw this side of Eternal if they got lost, or if they were seeking rustic displays of Ozarkian poverty to show the folks back home. Jay had to admit the area had its own peculiar beauty. She loved the way the trees grew together so thickly here that you could remember that humans were the interlopers. She even liked the old yellow school bus perched back from the road, and the abandoned sheds and barns with soft, buckling roofs, like giant toadstools. But she was nervous today, seeing the town through the Garnets' eyes.

Jay had settled on one of her mom's paisley button-ups. It hung too loose, highlighting the ways Jay hadn't grown into her mother's long-gone silhouette. She fixed her hair—finely wavy, brown in most lights, auburn on the sunniest days—into a ponytail, the style that was easiest to ignore. She wore only one piece of jewelry, half of a friendship necklace that Brandi had bought with hard-won babysitting dollars in fifth grade. A heart, with BE FRI. Brandi wore the ST ENDS side of the necklace.

Jay worried the Garnet twins would laugh at them, a couple of hicks falling for their prank. Or worse: Jay and Brandi would show up at the AIR House and Hilma wouldn't even remember who they were.

But Hilma was waiting for them like she had nowhere she'd rather be. Max shook Jay's hand formally, flashing his toothpaste-ad smile. Then he'd turned to Brandi, grabbed her hand, and kissed it. Jay stared at her friend's hand in a new light, the broken mood ring, stuck on the murky green of *mixed emotions*.

"You look like Leo," Brandi blurted.

Max laughed, easy. "Hey, I've always preferred Michelangelo."

Jay didn't think he looked like Leonardo DiCaprio, anyway. His edges were harder, his yellow hair messier. But she knew why Brandi said that. Max had a famous quality to him, like he was being projected in front of you, three stories high, while you ate popcorn in the dark.

"Come on, weirdos," Hilma had said. "We're wasting time."

Inside the Truth House now, the dust tickled familiarly against Jay's nose. The rooms were as empty as when they were kids. Max was already bounding through the house, floors shaking under his weight. "I'm not seeing any signs," he called.

"The signs aren't always obvious." Hilma looked at Brandi and Jay, who were trying to catch up without admitting they were behind. "We have to test it out. See if it does what these lovely ladies claim it does."

Jay bit down the defensive impulse to point out that they hadn't *claimed* anything. They'd shared a story about a game, that was all.

Hilma reached into her leather bag, producing a spiral-bound notebook. "I came prepared. I wrote some lies down beforehand."

She opened it to reveal her handwriting in blood-red Sharpie. *I AM NAMED MICHELLE*. Hilma, enunciating carefully, read, "I am named Hilma." She laughed, cleared her throat. "I am named Hilma. I am named Hilma, I am named Hilma."

"Okay, Jesus, we get it." Max turned to Brandi. "Hilma's named after this weird Swedish lady who talked to ghosts. She begged my mom to rename her Michelle. You know, as in *Full House?*"

Jay smiled nervously, comforted the same way as when her dad laughed during a suspenseful scene in a horror movie to soothe her and Brandi. Just a joke.

Hilma turned the notebook page. *I AM THIRTY-FIVE YEARS OLD.* "I am seventeen years old," she said, staring at the page. "I am seventeen—I am—I am seventeen—I'm—" Her mouth worked for a moment, noiseless as she tried to read the words written on the page. "Fine. Screw it. Let's try some questions. Do you believe this house is magic?" she asked Brandi.

"Yes."

She turned to Jay. "Do you?"

Jay opened her mouth to say, *I'm not sure.* "Yes," she said, compulsive as a hiccup.

"See, that's the truth," Hilma said. "It embarrasses Bluejay. Look how red she is."

Jay pressed a hand to her cheek. "You *are* red," Brandi observed.

"As a tomato," Max said. "Looks good on you." Before Jay could react to this, he whipped around to his sister. "What's the capital of Kyrgyzstan?"

"I wasn't expecting a geography quiz."

Max bounced on the balls of his feet. "Say anything. This place will *make* you say the truth, so you'll always be right."

"I have no idea. Uh. Kabul?"

"Bishkek. I looked it up." He scuffed the floor with his shoe. "Doesn't work. Too bad, how sad, boo-hoo."

Jay made herself speak up. "It doesn't work like that. It's the truth as you know it. It's not the—like—objective truth, you know? When we were kids, Brandi said my favorite thing was playing with Barbies, but it wasn't. She *believed* it was, though. Until she knew better."

"It's drawing," Brandi piped up. "Jay's favorite thing is drawing. She's an amazing artist." They exchanged smiles. Being here with Brandi reminded Jay of being flat on her belly on the sun-warmed floor as they talked for hours, no lies between them.

"So it's what you individually see as the truth," Hilma said. "Not on some big cosmic scale. Okay. A truth house, not a fact house. What we need to do is ask tough questions. Questions we don't want to answer." She turned on her brother. "Did you leave the back door unlocked that time we were robbed?"

"Yes," Max said. Jay's heart leaped at the surprise on his face.

"If Jodie and Harold knew, they'd *never* let you stay home alone again," Hilma said. Jay put together that Jodie and Harold were the Garnet parents. The *J&HG* on the corner of the paintings. She couldn't imagine calling her dad Doug. "Were you drinking when it happened?"

"Yeah." Max recovered with a grin. "You know me."

"You idiot," Hilma said. "They spent all that time on the lawsuit against the security company for the lost work, when it was you."

"Please don't tell, sis." He drawled it as a joke, but when he added, "I'm so scared they'll take away my graduation trip," anxiety colored the words. Jay wondered if it was the truth.

"You'd deserve it," Hilma said.

She was about to go on, but Max lifted his voice. "Wait. Time-out. We could all be doing this on purpose. Like idiots moving the Ouija board thingy and pretending it's a ghost?" Max swirled his fingertips over an invisible surface.

"That's why we're going about this the scientific way," Hilma said.

"Ouija boards can work," Brandi added. "Jay tried it with her mom at a sleepover and her mom said, 'Hello, honey.'"

"That was me." Jay should've been embarrassed, but all she felt was a funny sadness, remembering herself crouched inside the shed, pretending her mom was talking through this piece of plastic they'd found at the thrift store.

"Your mom's dead?" Hilma asked, as if she'd known Jay for years and Jay had withheld this. "How did it happen?"

Brandi squeezed her hand, a reminder she didn't have to say anything. But Jay answered anyway: "Suicide."

The word seemed to hover in the air, an imprint. Jay tried to remember if she'd ever said *suicide* aloud before. Her dad always used euphemisms, so that Jay had to put it together slowly, like a reflection coming into focus in a foggy mirror. When she'd finally worked up the courage to tell Brandi in sixth grade, her friend had wrapped her in a silent hug, and Jay had realized that she'd already known.

"Damn." Max looked at Jay with something like respect. "It'll be hard to top that. Congratulations, anything we say will sound dickish now."

Jay laughed, embarrassed. She'd changed the whole tenor in the house. Max studied her face for a moment, as if he could read those thoughts. Then he spoke to Hilma without turning toward her. "Did you sleep with Tripp?"

The spotlight of their collective interest swung onto Hilma. "No," Hilma said at last.

"So you're a virgin?"

Her mouth worked, tongue at the roof of her mouth, about to form an *n*. "Yes." Hilma's skin was marbled. "Why, Max? Asshole. You could've asked anything. Don't start with—"

"I knew you'd lie about it in front of them." He jerked his chin. Brandi squeezed Jay's hand again, and she got the message: Hilma Garnet cared about what *they* thought. It was surreal. Like Jennifer Aniston choosing her red-carpet gown specifically to impress them.

Max focused on Brandi. "How about you, young lady? Are *you* a—"

Jay cut in quickly. "No. Our turn. Did you two want to come to Arkansas?"

Hilma said, "Of *course* not. Too easy."

Jay tried to think of a worthwhile question. When she was a kid, the truth had felt like a gentle protective spell, shielding them from all the lies adults peddled. Then Brandi invited Amber, and the whole house became a reminder that the truth could sting. Now the Truth House felt . . . important. As if one right question could make everything, anything, happen.

Brandi turned to her with a determined set to her mouth. "Jay. Did you really hate going to that arts camp?"

This was one question Jay didn't want to answer. Over the summer, Jay had finally saved up enough allowance to attend a summer arts camp in Kansas. She knew that Brandi didn't have the money to go along with Jay, but Brandi had given Jay her blessing, and so Jay had spent a full week with strangers, taking life drawing courses, relishing the expensive oil paints and dual nib markers at her disposal. Mostly, she missed Brandi. But there was something intriguing about being surrounded by strangers with pierced tongues and rainbow-splashed hair. Jay became a stranger herself, and it was scary, and it was . . . intoxicating.

When she came home, she told Brandi that the camp was boring, no fun, not even worth talking about. She'd sensed that Brandi picked up on the lie of omission, but now she was tongue-tied. She didn't know how the words would come out, filtered through this house's sticky, tricky magic. Jay hadn't realized it yet, the way she could usually say anything at all and figure out later whether it was the truth or not.

"No," she said at last. "I didn't hate it. It was fun, it had some good parts."

Brandi nodded, not mad, but unsurprised, which hurt more.

"But I missed you so much, Brandi," Jay said, and it was a relief to put it into words. "Nothing was the same without you."

"Well, I didn't go nowhere. I'm still right here."

"When we leave town? Together? It's going to be amazing, Brandi. There's so much out there," Jay said.

"Oh god. That was beautiful, you two," Max said, fluttering his fingers under his eyes.

"Shut up, Max," Hilma said. "It *was* beautiful."

"I know. I couldn't lie if I wanted to." Smiling to himself, Max wandered outside.

Jay eyed Hilma, belatedly aware that the twins had witnessed something intensely personal. The Truth House had peeled them open, exposing more than they'd intended to show. "Why did you want to visit this house, anyway?" she asked Hilma.

"Because it's magic. Right here in this little town nobody's ever heard of." Hilma lowered her voice. "And because if I find the rest of Theodora's houses, I'm going to escape."

From outside, Max called for them, and Hilma immediately turned and left.

"Other houses?" Brandi whispered. "What's that mean? Who's Theodora?"

Jay was more focused on the word *escape*, cool and bejeweled, the way Hilma's whole face changed when she said it. For the first time, Jay had seen an echo of herself in Hilma Garnet. It had to be the truth: Hilma wasn't faking it, not in the Truth House. "I'm not sure," Jay said. "But I want to find out."

Outside, they found the twins knee-deep in the weeds, crouching low to examine the house's foundation. Jay automatically thought of snakes, ticks, poison ivy, but that didn't stop her. While Brandi hung back, Jay edged closer, curious about what had excited the Garnets. At first she only saw dingy brick. Then she spotted the words in the concrete, a mosaic fashioned of glossy stone shards.

TRUTH IS MORE OF A STRANGER. The word *truth* embedded in the Truth House. Jay's stomach fizzed.

Hilma noticed Jay and stood, impatient but polite, like she was about to dismiss her with a tip. It was an abrupt change from the intimacy they'd just shared, and Jay's heart sank. Was Jay already at the end of her usefulness to the Garnets? She wasn't sure she was ready to step outside of this excitement they'd stirred up in her.

"There are other houses around here that are weird," Jay blurted.

It worked. Hilma's eyes lit up. "Weird like this?"

The houses Jay had in mind possessed a more garden-variety strangeness: a bungalow painted an ugly purple, the abandoned place where the cool kids gathered to get high. Jay weighed the truth in her mouth. "Yeah," she said. An easy lie; the house had released them the moment they stepped out the door. "Weird like this."

Hilma gazed at her. Maybe, like Jay, she was recognizing exactly how unstable the world felt now, the truth once again capable of taking on any shape it wanted. Lies could dress up as the truth and nobody would ever know the difference.

"Okay, Bluejay," Hilma said. "We'll be in touch."

5

2015

NOW

Jay sticks to the shadows, ducking behind trees when headlights wash up the road. To her relief, most of the old shortcuts are still intact. The stone staircase that curls behind the Big Pitcher Hotel. The alleyway, edged on one side by an unlit stretch of forest. All around her are the familiar, deafening sounds of the Ozarks at night, cicadas and tree frogs and bullfrogs, whippoorwills and owls, their half-remembered songs.

The four of them are meeting in an hour. Hilma wanted them to split up after the vigil and reconvene, as if that would throw the rest of Eternal Springs off their scent. Jay assumed they'd meet at a hotel room, but Iggy said, "We'll meet at headquarters." After hearing Ignacio Nieves say *headquarters*, Jay couldn't argue, although she'd agreed—they'd *all* agreed—to never use the houses again.

Before that, though, there's somewhere Jay needs to go. She trudges along this back road alone, not far from Brandi's trailer park. It's a route Jay took a thousand times as a kid. She's trailed by a thin ghost of the happiness she used to feel after school or on sleepy Saturday mornings, on her way to the shed, everything right with the world.

When Jay got the letter in the mail a week ago, she opened it with shaking hands. *You promised.* And after she'd stared at the words, numb one moment, panicking the next, Jay had peeked inside the envelope, and a photograph fell out, landing at her feet. A Polaroid of a house she recognized at once. Small, faded pink, covered in ivy. The Truth House. The very first one they'd found.

Jay's been puzzling over the photo for days now. She's rolled it over and over in her head. Why the Truth House? What's Brandi saying to her? *You promised*: the Truth House.

Well. Here's the truth. Jay has ignored Brandi for so long that she can't interpret her anymore. It's a secret message that belongs to another timeline, one in which the two of them stayed friends.

Jay's close now. Just around the corner. There's the old barn, the oak tree. Jay hurries around the bend, her heart hammering hard. And there—

No. Wait. This is all wrong.

The house is gone. Vanished.

Jay moves closer, slowly now. None of the other changes in town have prepared her for this. A blank space where one of Theodora's houses stood. For a second it's like the structure never existed. Jay feels a panicky responsibility. Maybe she wipes away more of her past every time she tells a white lie about her high school years, or lets gallery owners believe she's from some other city (Colorado Springs, Palm Springs), or allows people to assume she's never seen a dead body. This is the end result of all those untruths.

Then Jay's muscles unclench slightly. The house hasn't been fully erased from the landscape. The growing darkness just hid the evidence. As Jay walks up, she can see a scarred tangle of charred boards and insulation, cordoned off by the blackened lines of the foundation. The Truth House has been burned down.

6

1999

After their trip to the Truth House, the Garnet twins didn't approach Jay again all week. They were polite. They smiled, said hello. That was almost worse than if they avoided her outright, which would at least acknowledge that *something* passed between them.

Over the weekend, Jay gratefully retreated to Brandi's place at the edge of town. Brandi called her place a *mobile home* and not a *trailer*, though it felt especially immobile to Jay. Gene's presence hung over the whole place, surly and booze-scented one day, manic the next. Brandi's mother had been gone for months—in Tuscaloosa with her sister, last they heard—and Brandi was left with this provisional relationship, her mother's long-term boyfriend becoming her default guardian. Jay joked that Brandi was like one of those babies in fairy tales, adopted by wolves. "Ain't those wolves usually *good* parents?" Brandi had asked doubtfully.

Jay stood in Brandi's bedroom, watching as her friend jimmied her window open and hoisted herself up. She stuck a leg out, bridging the foot-long gap between her bedroom and the garden shed that stood in one corner of the trailer park. Jay followed, out one window and through the other. A Budweiser can winked up from the weeds.

They'd been using the shed as a two-person clubhouse for years. Fifty square feet, with a single window so dusty it was privacy glass. The window's little keyhole was defunct, filled in with spiderwebs: they were able to easily glide the window up and down in its frame, their own private entrance. The shed was a moldering wooden thing, prone to splinters, a single unused rake shoved in one corner. The walls were papered over with Jay's drawings, developing from her early sketches of the Arkansas landscape to the more elaborate pieces she'd been working on lately, fantasy worlds, sci-fi cityscapes. Scattered throughout were Brandi's photos of the two of them together, Jay grinning wide in a way she never grinned into her own mirror, uneven teeth on full display.

"Mind if I take some photos?" Brandi asked. "For the portfolio thingy."

Jay nodded. Ms. Hart, the art teacher who smoked during lunchtime, had them all creating final portfolios that would *embody your unique time at Eternal Springs High*. Jay had scribbled out a few sketches of her classrooms. They were uninspired, refusing to channel the spirit Jay wanted. Complicated by the fact that Jay didn't know what kind of spirit to channel. When she thought of her time in Eternal, she was overwhelmed by the tapestry of ordinary details, the deer that picked their way through the undergrowth, the hot sparkle of fireflies against the dusk. Jay trying unsuccessfully to tan with Brandi, legs extended on bathroom towels, slick with baby oil. Mostly, lately, she thought of Eternal as a place that she was already remembering—a jumping-off point for what came next.

"Hilma and Max want us to meet up after school tomorrow." Brandi aimed her disposable camera at Jay, snapping right as Jay's face opened in surprise and relief. "Max told me in the halls today."

"And you said yes, right?" When Brandi was quiet, Jay pressed, "Brandi? You said yes?"

Brandi lowered the camera. "Well, just feels like . . . with Gene working for them and all? I don't want to get Gene in any trouble."

"Is there any way we can hide it from him? He still doesn't know we went to that art house movie in Fayette." She was used to helping Brandi obscure their minor transgressions. The movie had featured French without subtitles and also nudity, two qualities Gene would definitely disapprove of.

Brandi brightened. "We can try."

"Do the Garnets want to go back to the Truth House?"

"Nah, some place near the library."

Hilma Garnet had found another house without them. Jay's urgency flared; she knew that she had to make herself necessary to the twins. Somehow, some way. She wanted back into the glow of their circle.

"We'll tell Gene you're at my place." When she saw doubt lingering in Brandi's eyes, Jay scooted closer on the cobwebby floor, leaned her shoulder into Brandi's. "What is it?"

"It's exciting, sure, but . . . remember what happened with Amber and the Truth House?"

"I don't think it's the same. Hilma has her own plans." *Escape*; goose bumps rose along Jay's arms. "And hey. If the Garnets do anything rude? I'll fight them for you."

Brandi buckled with a laugh. She had nice teeth, naturally even. "Yeah? What are you gonna do? Draw ugly pictures of them?"

"Maybe," Jay said, laughing too. "I'll ruin their self-esteem." She remembered those paintings, the overlapping teeth, and sobered.

"Okay, I'll go. But don't tell Gene, he gripes about the Garnets all the time. He says they ain't like us."

"What, because they're interesting? Because they've seen the world beyond Arkansas?"

" 'Cause they're only here for a year."

"Well, so are we. Graduation's in less than a year. You turn eighteen in March, me in April. After that? We'll be famous artists together. Take on the whole world." But even as she repeated the vague plan they'd been embellishing since middle school, Jay felt her attention divide. For now, she was excited about exploring the streets of Eternal Springs, her ordinary little town turned into something new.

As they approached the house Hilma had specified, Jay felt a sinking worry that maybe Brandi was right and the Garnets were just toying with them. The address was too obvious. If you were trying to think of a strange house in Eternal Springs, this would be the first suspect, so unimaginative that Jay had glossed right over it.

The house was haunted. Supposedly, allegedly. The place just *looked* the part: gray paint skinning off in patches, windows blinded over with boards. An ostentatious stone turret rose to the exact same height as the gnarled oak tree beside it. "That place was built to be haunted," her dad joked once. "Do you think it came with the ghosts already inside?"

Jay was jumpy. Destiny Lautner had passed them in her Camry on their way here, Kenny and Amber in the back seat as they drove in slow, leisurely loops, looking for something to do. Jay had insisted on doubling back and taking a shortcut to throw Destiny off the scent, but she still kept checking over her shoulder.

"We don't have to go if'n you're scared," Brandi said, holding Jay's elbow as they eyed the turreted house.

But Hilma had spotted them. She raised one hand in a languid, parade-float greeting. *Escape*—that word glittered through Jay's brain again. All Jay had was a half-baked plan to live with

Brandi in one of the cities they'd seen on TV; what was Hilma planning?

The twins had unexpected company. Charlie Olowe examined them coolly as Jay and Brandi approached. Seeing him out of the context of the school library was disorienting. As always, he was dressed formally: a fitted button-up, tortoiseshell glasses. He had a Clark Kent look, like he was underplaying his power through style choices alone.

"I invited Charlie. He's the smartest kid in your school," Hilma said, as if they didn't know him.

"Hey," Max nudged. "Tell the girls what you scored on the SAT."

Charlie rolled his eyes but obliged: "I got a fifteen-eighty."

"Wow," Jay said. "Congratulations."

"I'm retaking it."

Jay always saw a potential kindred spirit in Charlie Olowe, though she was too shy to do anything about it. She wondered if a Black kid found it difficult to live in the Ozarks. Charlie did spend a lot of time alone, but it seemed intentional, like he was on the cusp of something bigger, biding his time. And yet, the Garnets had managed to lure him out. Jay wondered what would've happened if she'd ever actually approached him.

"Charlie reads in four languages," Hilma said. "It's amazing he's even in this small town. But as long as he is, we're borrowing his genius."

Uncomfortable, Jay wondered what Hilma had told Charlie about her and Brandi. They were only here because they'd broken into the Garnets' house.

"My parents raised me not to go to second locations with strangers," Charlie said. "This is already on my 'potential regrets' pile."

"I don't waste anybody's time." Hilma tossed her hair, split ends majestic as a horse's mane. "But before I explain anything, someone has to go in there." She pointed at the house.

It was ridiculous, high school seniors daring each other to go inside a creepy house, like something out of those tattered Choose Your Own Adventure paperbacks from elementary school. Still. Stupid as it was, no one volunteered—they stood in a knot, barely breathing. Jay eyed the house, taking in its sheer size, the shadowy slivers of glass peeking through the bandage-like boards. The place felt more like a rumor than a home, but maybe somebody actually lived here. Jay tried to remember if she'd ever seen anybody going in or out. She might've once seen a car pull up. Maybe.

"Okay, I see what this is," Charlie said. "You two are playing at being the Bobbsey Twins, but you're too scared to do the dirty work."

"Who are the Bobbsey Twins?" Hilma asked.

"Why don't you two go in? There's zero chance Pell will arrest two rich white kids for breaking into some abandoned house."

Max kicked at the ground, and Hilma appraised the front door. Jay worried that any minute now Brandi would step forward. Brandi never could bear an awkward silence. But *arrest* wasn't theoretical for Brandi. Jay knew she'd been in the police station before, arguing with the cops, trying to post bail for her mom despite being a minor and also broke.

"I'll do it," Jay said, and watched as Brandi's shoulders lightened with relief.

"Brave," Charlie said, half approving. "And stupid."

Jay glanced at Hilma hopefully. Did Hilma think she was brave, stupid, both? Hilma gave a smile that flared in Jay's chest as she started toward the house. She'd knock, that was all. Easy. She was painfully aware of the others watching as she approached this front door like a Girl Scout or a Jehovah's Witness. It felt so stupid. She'd have more success knocking on a headstone. But at least the Garnets would see her try.

With the softest part of her fist, Jay knocked. The door was surprisingly beautiful at close range. Inlaid panels. The kind of darkly gleaming wood that seemed indestructible. She tried again, using her knuckles this time. Imagining her knock reverberating through the empty rooms gave her a lonely thrill.

Jay felt the others' stares resting between her shoulder blades. She waited for what felt like an eternity. No sound from inside. Carefully, she tried the knob: no give. She should have been relieved to have an obvious excuse to turn around, but Jay was annoyed. She was right on the verge of impressing the Garnets, she couldn't run now. Jay's eyes caught on the window next to the door, boarded up only halfway, a foot of dusty glass revealed. She could slide her body through the window without too much effort. She had experience.

Jay didn't let herself overthink. She stepped off the porch, the shrubs in the abandoned flower bed clawing at her legs. "Jay," Brandi called, "what are you doing?" But Jay didn't hesitate as she pulled the window frame upward. The frame resisted, then gave, screeching, and Jay pitched herself forward, knowing she was inelegant as she wormed her way through the open wedge of window, legs and butt poking out, but not really caring.

She was inside. The house was cool, a contrast to the day's muggy heat. A dusty smell enveloped her—rich and ethereal, like incense. Standing in the entry hall, Jay was startled to see her own face staring back at her, blue eyes wide over her sharp cheekbones, frizz-wreathed ponytail bronzed by the afternoon sun. Jay was a different girl in this mirror. Brave. Anointed.

Then she took stock. Mirrors. Everywhere, mirrors. More of them than Jay had ever seen collected in one spot, and she was dizzied.

From outside, a muffled shout. "Bluejay? What's happening?"

"Hold on," she yelled back. Moving cautiously, like somebody might pop out and yell, she went to the front door and unlocked it. The other four were on the stoop, Hilma in front, Brandi and Max bunched behind her, Charlie unable to hide his curiosity as he peered inside.

"I don't think anyone's home," Jay said.

"Perfecto," Max said, pushing his way past her. Jay watched as he walked deeper into the house with his bouncy, long-legged lope. The rooms were large and shadowy, with high ceilings. The mirrors chopped the space into smaller, brighter pieces. Max stared around, sunny hair rippling in the surrounding reflections. "Well," he called, "whoever lived here was a serious narcissist."

As she walked inside, Hilma nudged Jay. "Good job, meddling kid," she said, and Brandi caught Jay's eyes and beamed at her.

7

1999

"Who was Theodora Trader?" Hilma stood at the front of the room like they were kids playing schoolhouse and she was the teacher. Jay surged with excitement. Finally, Hilma was going to explain.

Their voices echoed in here, strange and too loud. The interior of the house wasn't what Jay expected; it was well furnished, tasteful if old-fashioned. Victorian couches, silent grandfather clocks. But the walls were suffocated with mirrors. Everywhere, every inch. Massive ovals, tiny round mirrors, ornate frames, mirrors that were cracked and tarnished with age. They covered the backs of the boarded-up windows. They even glittered on the ceiling. Jay glanced up to see her own shrunken face, high above, like she was at the bottom of a vast ocean looking toward the surface.

Their group had settled in the large living room, the floor coated in velvety rugs.

"Well?" Hilma pressed.

"The name sounds familiar," Charlie said cautiously. He was keeping a distance, like he might duck out at any moment. "I've seen the name Trader around town here and there. She was one of the earlier residents, right?"

"Very good," Hilma said. "Anyone else?"

"Ooh, pick me. I know, I know," Max called in an unenthused monotone. "You want to know *how* I know?" He swiveled toward the rest of them. "Because Hilma hasn't shut up about *Theodora* for the past two months. My parents gave her a big stack of books to bribe her into coming to the Ozarks. They wanted to get her excited about the hiking and the pretty landscapes and shit, but of course she finds a spooky dead lady."

"Theodora Trader was born in New York City in the 1880s," Hilma said, undeterred. "As an adult, she studied architecture. Barely any women were getting degrees back then, let alone in architecture. She tried finding work, but it was difficult, and when she did land jobs, Theodora wasn't exactly a model employee. They'd ask her to draft a post office, and she'd add in a room that didn't connect to the rest of the building. Or she'd work overnight and make upside-down archways where there should've been doors. Now, Theodora may have originally come to Arkansas because of the sanitarium, but her move ended up being a perfect opportunity."

"Excuse me, but you buried the lede," Charlie said. "She was in the sanitarium?"

"Patience," Hilma said, obviously enjoying herself. "Theodora claimed to be a 'traveler'—meaning she traveled to different worlds—and she was imitating the buildings she saw in these places. Her influential family got sick of this crazy woman who was working in a man's field and acting totally cuckoo on top of that, so they shipped her off to a nuthouse in the most godforsaken spot they could think of."

"The Arkansas Ozarks," Max supplied.

Hilma nodded. "Back at the turn of the century, Eternal Springs was famous for—"

"For its healing springs," Jay jumped in. She knew this part, at least. "People used to come here for the thermal springs. They thought it cured anything. Tuberculosis, hysteria."

"Hysteria?" Hilma repeated. "Should've been more worried about curing sexism."

Charlie and Jay laughed. Brandi smiled uncomfortably, as if she didn't quite know what the joke meant. Jay leaned over to explain, but Hilma was talking again.

"At the sanitarium, Theodora was on her best behavior. She convinced the doctors she was cured. But Theodora didn't go back home when she was released. Eternal Springs was booming in the late 1800s. It was the second-biggest city in the state. There was a new railroad and they were building new hotels and homes like crazy to keep up with demand. It was the perfect chance for an up-and-coming architect. Theodora was designing and slapping up houses all over town. They looked ordinary on the outside, and most of them were. But Theodora wasn't always using ordinary materials. She was bringing things back from these other worlds she visited. That way, select houses would have magic inside them."

Jay's mind spun in circles, giddy to skeptical, back again. She knew the basic history of this town— the Osage people who'd made a life among these towering bluffs. Early settlers seeking solitude, Victorians who'd made the arduous trek for the healing waters, hippies who'd come here as part of the back-to-the-land movement, building and then gradually abandoning their communes in the 1970s. But magic?

"Theodora continued building houses until the 1930s," Hilma said. "After the boom died down, her services weren't needed as much. She kept mostly to herself—people knew she came from the sanitarium, which wasn't the greatest icebreaker. She was known as a 'peculiar yet harmless hermit,' which, by the way, is exactly what I want to be when I grow up."

"Me too," Brandi breathed.

"She died in 1939, it was a little weird. She went hiking and got lost and by the time they found her, she was only teeth and finger bones. But her houses are still standing. And our mission—"

"Should you choose to accept," Max cut in.

"—is to find those houses. Every last one. By my calculations, there should be eight."

Eight. The houses of Eternal Springs, spread up and down the twisting, winding hills. The houses perched too close to the freeway, the bungalows tucked on side streets. The places Jay walked by or biked past every day, barely registering them anymore.

Charlie spoke up. "If we're going to break into houses looking for magic powers, I need more evidence. No offense, Hilda."

"Hilma, and none taken. How about this, then?" Hilma reached into her backpack, producing a book. It looked old, burgundy fabric cover, bindings molting like snakeskin. "This is Theodora's journal. My dad bought it for a steal, two thousand dollars. The book dealer is a friend, he brought down the price for us."

"Two *thou*sand?" Jay repeated without thinking, scanning Hilma's face for a joke. She looked again at the book, weighing it against the finicky transmission in her dad's Chevy, the braces she couldn't afford.

"It's handwritten," Hilma said, as if this explained the cost. Charlie gestured for the book, and when Hilma passed it to him, he began leafing intently through the pages.

"I have a question," Max said. "What if Theodora was writing down total BS because she was—oh *yeah*—totally crazy?"

"Max, you *felt* it already. You couldn't tell a lie inside those walls."

"Okay, but that house was lame. Telling the truth?" Max blew a raspberry. "What I want is a house that gives me superpowers. How do we find that one?"

"Well, hey, I want that one too," Brandi said.

"I called dibs."

"Theodora always left signatures," Hilma said. "Phrases that hint at each house's powers. *Truth is more of a stranger*, and the house invoked honesty in anyone who entered."

"What's *invoke* mean?" Brandi asked Jay, sotto voce.

Max answered first. "It means the house makes people honest. Ignore my sister's two-dollar words."

"You mean two-*thousand*-dollar words." Brandi's grin was shy as Max high-fived her, his hand dwarfing hers.

"How will we find them all?" Jay asked. This was the first time Eternal Springs had seemed like a large town to her. "Does she have a map or something in that journal?"

"Bluejay, I'm so glad you asked," Hilma said, mock-formal. "Theodora was worried about what would happen if her book got into the wrong hands. So, many parts are written in code. We can work on deciphering it, but we also need to think about any houses that're likely suspects. Abandoned places, weird houses, places that nobody seems to actually *live* in. Every neighborhood's got a house or two like that."

Jay could do this; she knew this town. This was how she could be indispensable, a part of the team. "How about places where people move out too quickly?" she asked.

"A house that makes you late on rent?" Max joked, and Brandi flushed.

"Not funny," Jay said without thinking, and Max lifted his hands, looking embarrassed. "I meant more like . . . people don't stay long? There's this place near me and I know five people who moved out after a year, and they never explain why."

"That's exactly what we're looking for," Hilma said.

Charlie snapped the book shut. "This looks authentic. Theodora refers to Thermal Park as Basin Springs. It was 1925 when they changed the name. And the handwriting follows the Palmer

Method, not D'Nealian. But all that suggests is that the diary is old. I've lived here my whole life. If there were . . . *magic houses* . . . don't you think I'd know about them? Why do you assume that residents who've lived here for decades would overlook that?"

"Because," Hilma said, "go look at the first few pages again, Charlie. Really read them." He shrugged before acquiescing, adjusting his glasses on his nose. As he read silently, Hilma translated for the others. "Theodora's houses affect each person slightly differently. There must be people who can live inside her houses for years and make excuses for every strange aspect. It'll be different for us, I imagine, because we have her direct words, and we'll be looking for the effects. But for most people who enter those houses? It's a roll of the dice."

"Like, people just ignore magic?" Max asked, skeptical.

"It's not unusual, really. Jay and Brandi were playing games right inside magic and nobody else paid attention to it. But the two of them knew."

Jay felt shy as the others turned to examine her and Brandi. It was true, though. They had been right inside Theodora Trader's legacy and even *they* had let it become a joke, a weird anecdote, a game. How many other people around Eternal Springs had done the same thing, in different ways?

"I always knew it was magic," Brandi piped up, matter-of-fact.

"See?" Hilma said. "There will always be those who listen to Theodora's message. Like our friend Brandi here."

Brandi grinned, and Jay bumped her shoulder, congratulatory.

"Okay," Charlie said. "But do we really think Theodora imported building supplies from alternate universes? The multiverse is a complex theory. It's been puzzling physicists for decades. If I could get to an alternate world, I wouldn't use it to create real estate in Arkansas."

"Why not?" Hilma asked at once. "Theodora was an architect. This was her language. She understood what it was like to not have a place in the world, and so she built these houses as an invitation to anyone willing to listen." Standing in front of that fireplace, Hilma looked like Joan of Arc, a rallying cry in the flesh. Jay memorized her expression so she could draw it later.

"Yeah, that's pretty," Charlie said. "You should send it to poetry-dot-com or something. But I'm not convinced yet, sorry."

"What would it take to convince you?" asked Hilma.

Jay tuned out as they argued, distracted by the hallway—that long, mirror-glittered passage. Without thinking, she rose and drifted closer. In her home, there was a mirror over the bathroom sink and one fastened to her closet door. She saw her own reflection in two easily avoidable spots, which suited her fine.

These mirrors were different. Not functionally, not even decoratively, but they were strangely alive. Jay remembered some of the rumors she'd heard over the years. A runaway kid who'd gone missing, not so much as a knuckle bone ever found. Teenagers who'd snuck into the house to make out and been chased away by rapping in the walls. These had seemed like stupid sleepover stories when Jay was younger. Now—

When Jay nervously glanced over her shoulder, she saw there was something strange in the big square mirror right behind her. She jumped. All these reflections were short-circuiting her eyes, that was all. Too many Jays, too many Jadelynnes. But she could swear that her reflection turned around a fraction of a second too late.

"But what's the proof?" Charlie was asking stubbornly. "Wall decor isn't magic."

"If you want proof," Hilma said, "then we need to go to the turret."

8

1999

THEN

The four of them followed Hilma up the staircase. It twisted in on itself, a corkscrew so narrow that Jay felt like she was running into the same wall over and over. The stairwell was hung with mirrors too, their reflections stalking them. Charlie's neat dark curls, Brandi's camo jacket, the twins' sunbursts of hair.

"How do you even know what's up here?" Max asked.

"I've done my reading," Hilma said, though her confidence sounded a little brittle.

"This is unusual, actually," Charlie said, half to himself. "You aren't supposed to hang mirrors facing each other, many cultures share that belief. Two mirrors reflecting each other supposedly allow ghosts to pass through."

Ghosts. Jay tried not to look too closely at the mirrors. Once, it appeared that Jay's reflection was facing the wrong way, a confusing flash of her ponytail. On the next turn up the winding staircase, her mirror-face was briefly smiling when she was actually frowning. She touched her own mouth, uncertain.

"Is it just me, or is this staircase longer than it should be?" Max asked. "This is a workout I didn't need."

"This place is our new headquarters," Hilma said. "So get used to it."

Headquarters. Even in this strange moment, Jay liked that term, the way it brought a whole future along with it.

Finally—finally—they reached the top, tumbling into a small room with a high, pointed ceiling. These windows weren't boarded up, and the sky outside was the creamy orange of a late summer evening. There was only one mirror up here. Jay breathed easier, freed from all those reflections. The mirror was full-length, a frameless oval suspended on the wall.

Charlie pointed upward. "I assume this is one of Theodora's 'signatures' that you mentioned?" The words were engraved along the top of the wall, worked into the plaster. ONE MUST LIVE UNSEEN. "Descartes, I think."

"Descartes comes before the horse?" But even Max sounded hushed.

One must live unseen. A phrase that reflected the nature of the house, just like the words worked into the Truth House's base. It felt like Theodora's spirit was in the room with them, confirming Hilma's wild theory.

The four of them drifted around the small room. Jay paused in front of the mirror, both relieved and disappointed to see that it was normal enough. There she was. Jadelynne Louise Carr. In her favorite gray jacket, wearing her friendship necklace. Without warning, her mom's face glanced through her mind, as high above her as the sun.

"What do you see?" Hilma asked, startling Jay by appearing at her elbow.

"I—it's a mirror? I see myself, I—"

Downstairs there were sudden voices, a laugh, the pattern of nervous footfalls. Jay's adrenaline kicked in hard. Charlie tensed; Max moved toward the doorway as if to guard it. Brandi had gone white. Everyone seemed to be remembering the invocation of ghosts, remembering that this house was haunted. Then Jay imagined people, flesh and blood. Her anxiety took a different turn, growing stronger.

"Oh," Hilma said. "Company. Perfect timing." She lifted her voice: "Hey, we're up here."

Silence, then a renewed rush of footsteps hammering through the house.

"What are you doing?" Jay whispered, frantic.

Casually, Hilma strolled to the oval mirror. She lifted it off the wall, dipping as she adjusted to its weight.

"Careful, that's like seventy years' bad luck," said Max.

Hilma turned the mirror around. The opposite side was mirrored as well, but darker glass, tarnished and speckled. Hilma carefully hung it back on the wall, shifting to find the nail.

The voices were rising. They were climbing the stairwell, toward the turret. Brandi moved closer to Jay, and Jay felt her hot shiver of panic. "Let's go," Brandi whispered to Jay. "Please, we gotta go."

Jay recognized the voices, and her jaw went tight. It was Amber and Destiny, along with Kenny, who always wore novelty "hillbilly" teeth on Halloween. Hilma stood calmly, and Jay realized she'd invited the others. She drew them here. Amber, the very one who'd ruined the Truth House for Jay and Brandi. It couldn't be a mistake. This was the conclusion of trusting Hilma Garnet. She was just going to embarrass them and abandon them.

"I'm so sorry," Jay whispered to Brandi. "I messed up."

The only way out was the same narrow stairwell that currently held their enemies, laughing, shrieking.

Hilma whispered, "Don't move, and shut up."

The five of them shrank against the walls of the small circular room. Amber stepped into the turret first, looking around with a mix of contempt and trepidation, while Destiny jokingly clung to her, wearing a sparkly Bebe T-shirt. Kenny, hair stiff with gel, came in last.

"Hello?" Destiny called. She locked eyes with Jay. "What's going on?"

Jay was on the verge of answering, flustered, defensive, when Kenny replied, "I swear I heard something up here."

"Please, it's a prank," Amber said. "I knew that bitch was tricking us."

Something bizarre was happening. The three newcomers didn't seem to see them at all. They weren't surprised to spot Max, towering in a corner; they weren't sneering at Brandi, who was twisting together clumps of her pale brown hair. Their eyes passed right over Jay. For a moment Jay thought *she* was the one being pranked, but there was no suppressed laughter, no darting glances. The confusion and annoyance on Amber's face were genuine.

Jay felt Brandi's breathing slow, like she was falling into a trance. Charlie was stiff with shock. Amber passed so close to Jay that she nearly touched her, the smell of her Sea Spray lotion ripe in Jay's nostrils. Jay could see Amber's freckles beneath their layer of thick powder.

"Can they not see us?" asked Brandi, amazed.

Destiny turned and looked in Brandi's direction, and Jay thought it was over, the joke was falling apart. Destiny's face betrayed no hint of recognition. "Did you guys hear . . . ?"

Hilma started talking, her voice loud, casual. "I learned about this mirror from Theodora's journal. She described it as the mirror that 'reveals you to yourself, while hiding you from others.' I didn't know it would work this well, though."

Kenny and Amber and Destiny didn't react at all. They couldn't hear her.

"What if it hadn't worked?" Charlie asked.

"I knew it would."

For a moment everyone waited for something to happen. Kenny reached out to pinch Destiny's lower back. She screamed and laughed, twisting away, highlighted blond hair swinging.

"You asshole," said Amber, visibly shaken. "There's no one here."

"Can we go?" asked Destiny. "This place is creepy. You know people have died here?"

Jay was right across from the tarnished oval of the mirror, but it had taken her all this time to fully recognize the truth. Her sub-conscious mind balked at the evidence in front of her: she couldn't see herself in the mirror anymore. She could see Amber, right in front of her, but behind Amber, there was only blank window. The disconnect was an eye-blink, a blip in Jay's prefrontal cortex. And yet it was everything.

After a small eternity, Destiny and Amber and Kenny, dissat-isfied, confused, began filing out of the room, grumbling. It wasn't until their voices faded that the five of them breathed again, a col-lective exhale. Charlie fell into a crouch. Brandi surprised Jay with a huge smile.

"I know," Hilma whispered, delighted. "It's magic."

Jay had stopped believing in magic years ago. Since second grade—the year Santa vanished, the year the Tooth Fairy stopped leaving quarters—every birthday held a piece of melancholy tucked in with the boxed-mix cake. Over time, Jay's sense of reality had hardened. And now? Now she felt how much it was going to hurt. Like a bone breaking and being reset. But she welcomed the pain. In exchange for the new shape her life was about to take, she embraced it.

Because here it was, right in front of Jay, right in front of all of them. Proof.

Here was magic.

9

2015

Jay's winded from running all the way from the destroyed Truth House to the Mirror House. One and a half miles, the steep streets ripping her lungs to shreds. She's terrified she'll find the Mirror House gone too. Burned, rebuilt, reduced to rubble. What if *none* of Theodora's houses are left standing? What if Jay's left in a world that's been stripped of the impossible?

When she crests the hill near the library and spots their old headquarters still standing, massive turret and all, Jay's so relieved that she almost collapses.

She approaches cautiously. The Mirror House is dark, silent. Maybe the others lost their nerve. They aren't kids anymore, they can't talk their way out of breaking-and-entering. Jay can't imagine explaining any of this to the gallery owner. Right on the brink of professional success, she's run back to Eternal Springs, Arkansas. Which is more suspicious, anyway: running away as a teenager, or returning fifteen years later to the scene of the crime?

Jay hovers on the steps. The memories of the house pull at her, and she's rocked by them, seasick. There's a reason they promised never to return here.

The front door opens. "Bluejay, stop fucking around," Hilma says, and drags her inside.

All those mirrors still shine, dizzying. Maybe they've been rearranged. It's hard to tell. Charlie and Iggy are pacing the living room floor, stalked by their reflections. Iggy catches Jay's eye and unguarded relief passes over his face.

"We thought something happened to you." Hilma passes Jay a bottle of scotch, which she gratefully drinks from. "You're late."

Lowering the bottle, Jay becomes aware that she's sweat-soaked, wild-haired. "The Truth House is gone," she manages, still out of breath.

Charlie stops pacing. "Gone?"

"Burned down. Nothing's left. Just the foundation."

It's not until she sees the loss on their faces that she feels it fully herself.

"You're absolutely sure—" Charlie begins.

"Of course, I'm sure," Jay says. "I saw it."

"Look, it's been a long time, it's not as if we still remember every location."

But Jay does. She can mentally trace the way to any of Theodora's houses as easily as the route to her apartment in Albany.

"Charlie's right, it has been fifteen years," Hilma says, clearly trying to stay calm. "Accidents happen. It'd be more bizarre to find this place exactly the same, right?"

"Still," Iggy says. "Feels bad."

"Why'd you go to the Truth House, anyway?" Hilma asks.

"Uh. Brandi sent me a photo." Jay fumbles to retrieve the letter and the Polaroid from her pocket, hands them to Hilma. "Brandi didn't explain the photograph. Just: *You promised.* Did you all get the same thing?"

Hilma examines the Polaroid closely, turning it over. Jay can't interpret her frown. But then Iggy reaches into his jacket pocket and produces a letter. He shakes it open and shows it to the room. Even in the dim light, Jay can make out the words. *You promised.*

So Brandi sent the exact same message to Iggy. Jay should've known the message wasn't for her specifically. Charlie sighs and extracts an identical letter from his messenger bag, and Hilma grudgingly follows suit. *You promised, you promised.* Echoing around the room, caught in the mirrors. Brandi calling out to them from . . .

From wherever she is.

Jay has the sudden crawling certainty that if she looks now, she'll see Brandi peering at her from the nearest mirror.

"I tried to ignore the letter," Iggy confesses. "I, uh, hid it in a desk drawer, way at the back. I considered throwing it out or burning it. Obviously, that didn't work. I thought I'd have to go to the ER and try to explain to them why a fifteen-year-old scar wouldn't stop bleeding."

"Same for me," Jay says, queasy.

"It ruined my best suit," Charlie says. "Italian. I went through two rolls of gauze, I had to tell my boyfriend I'd come down with food poisoning to keep him from visiting me."

"My scar didn't stop bleeding until I bought the ticket," Hilma says.

They all nod, acknowledging the similarities in their stories: the wounds reopening simultaneously, as fresh as the day they created those marks. A flash of grudging wonder passes around the room. After every magic-less day they've spent outside of Eternal Springs, this place lassoed them by the throats and yanked them right back.

"And the Polaroid?" Jay asks. "Did she send you guys photos of the Truth House?"

Hilma hands the Polaroid back to her. "No. Just the letter for me."

Iggy and Charlie shake their heads, all of them tense, uncertain.

"None of you?" Jay asks. "So the Truth House was just for me. What does it mean?"

"Maybe you're supposed to figure out who vandalized it," Hilma says.

"A scorched building could be a—a warning," Charlie says.

"You think Brandi's warning me specifically?" Jay asks. "About what?"

"One of those terrifying old Ozarkian superstitions?"

"Maybe," Iggy says gently, "it's a special reminder for you, Jay. That house was important to you and Brandi."

The fact that he remembers this glows painfully inside Jay's chest. "Maybe."

"Well, we'd better figure this little puzzle out quickly," Hilma says. "My hotel reservation is only for two nights. I don't plan on extending that."

"Don't even worry about hotels," Charlie says. "We'll be in prison soon enough, getting tortured by the *Hills Have Eyes* cast."

"Whoa," Iggy says. "Calm down, man. Who said anything about prison?"

"Don't be naive, *maaaan*," Charlie says, imitating Iggy's new California drawl. "Brandi's missing. Signs of foul play. Just like last time. In the middle of this, who shows up out of nowhere?" Charlie pretends to think, head cocked. "Oh! Right. The four of us. The ones who were here the last time everything went wrong."

"But they don't know," Iggy says. "Nobody else knows what happened last time." It's half a question, he's looking for reassurance.

"And nobody knows why we're here now," Charlie shoots back. "If anybody had suspicions, we've confirmed them with a glaring neon sign. You saw the way they were looking at us. Like we're"—his voice catches—"murderers."

Around the room, a distinct ripple plays across the mirrors, like shades of their younger selves are passing through.

"Do you know what I've accomplished?" Charlie asks. "I left

57

this miserable little state, and I made my place in New York City. I'm an independent curator now. I work with brilliant artists, I've organized shows for the Met, the Guggenheim, MOMA. I'm not going to lose that. Not for anything."

The Met. Jay visited once, wearing her nicest Anthropologie dress, walking reverentially through an exhibit of Max Ernst and imagining her own art hanging there one day. That was in her twenties, when she still had the constant painful impulse to turn around and talk to Brandi about their teenage dreams.

"I shouldn't be here right now," Charlie continues. "I'm on the verge of the biggest accomplishment of my career. There's a singer—I can't say her name, but you've listened to her, trust me, you probably hum her songs in the shower. She's also a visual artist, and she's been hinting at an exclusive showing of her paintings. It would be a complete coup to be the one behind her show, and she's interested in me. I've visited her penthouse. Now I'm supposed to just vanish to Arkansas with no explanation?"

As if this is an invitation to outline their respective sacrifices, Hilma speaks up. "I run my own company now. Geminist. We uplift entrepreneurial girls who need a business loan or a marketing boost. Geminist's my baby. I haven't taken a proper vacation in two years."

"Is your husband worried about where you are right now?" Charlie asks, nodding toward her ring.

"He thinks I'm on a wellness retreat," Hilma says with a small smile. "So does my staff, for now. How about you, Igs? You and Ellen are engaged, right?"

The room tilts. All right, then. A fiancée. Jay sensed this other presence in her conversations with Iggy, his omissions sketching out a silhouette. Jay has no right to know. She's been chatting with Iggy, that's all. She kept up a little ritual of checking her old Yahoo email address, *dayafterjay*. Just in case. One day, an unexpected new email from *iggy.football.82* popped up. A link to a *New Yorker* piece about the midnight sun phenomenon. She replied. He replied again. Emailing him became the best part of Jay's week. Through unspoken agreement, they've avoided the more painful details of the past and the present—suspended inside the purest part of their friendship, like it was never interrupted. It seemed like it might go on that way indefinitely. Until the letters.

"Elle," Iggy corrects Hilma. "She's been my rock."

"Cozy's must be going well," Hilma says. "I heard your jingle on the radio."

"Yeah. Yeah, it's been amazing to build this whole thing with my family. Eleven locations now. We just opened a new location in Salt Lake City, one in Fresno."

For a moment they're old friends, laying out their lives and tallying up the changes. And it's Jay's turn. At least she's had practice with seemingly endless statements of purpose and fellowship applications, boiling herself down to her best qualities, for all the good it does.

"Oh, I've done okay. It's tough to break into the art world, but I finally have a solo show lined up." She pauses as Iggy claps, a quick starburst of applause. "I mean. Just a newish gallery in Albany, it's not—not a huge deal or anything, but it's a start. I've had some commissions and I've sold a few prints. Otherwise, I'm doing admin stuff at the local college until."

It takes her a moment to realize they're waiting for her to finish. In Jay's mind, *until* has become its own beast. Until. Encompassing everything out there, the indefinable moment of satisfaction or success that Jay's been chasing, each new milestone ringing empty in her palms once she clasps it. Jay hesitates, wondering if she can ask her old friends about this. Because, more than careers or zip codes or relationship status, Jay wants to know if they've carried this with them too. The *until* that she can't ever shake off.

"Well, look at us," Hilma says, gesturing at their fractured reflections. "Our little teenage selves would be proud. Iggy's an entrepreneur, Charlie's in New York City bumping elbows with artists, Jay's got her own show, and I'm running the world, of course. The only thing that would confuse us is the fact that we're currently back in Arkansas."

"Right." Charlie sighs. "As it turns out, explaining to my boyfriend why I was traveling to *Arkansas* wasn't any easier than explaining the bleeding. He thinks I'm visiting my parents in Bluffville."

"I'm scouting a new location for Cozy's," Iggy offers.

"Family emergency." Jay didn't have to make excuses to a partner; her only friendships in Albany are collegial but distant, the way she prefers. Still. It will look bad if she's not home in time for her show—Jay knows another offer won't be coming if she messes this one up.

"Where's Max?" Charlie asks. "He's notably MIA."

Hilma rolls her eyes. "Lord, who knows? He's always too busy for me. It's completely like him to dodge out and leave us to handle this mess alone."

"Maybe he's the one who got the actual instructions," Charlie suggests dryly.

They consider this, and Hilma sighs. "It's just so . . . unsubtle. Isn't it? *You promised.* No details, no explanations. The most obvious thing she could've said to drag us back."

"Drag us back?" Jay repeats.

"You know what I mean."

"I know Brandi's in trouble," Jay says, not hiding her sharpness. "Maybe *You promised* is all she could safely say. She's missing. There was blood everywhere in her home . . . I know none of us want to be back in Arkansas, but aren't you at all worried about her?"

It's a reminder to herself as much as to them. The atmosphere pulls tight with the memory of violence. The rusty tang of blood, the space where a person used to be and now wasn't. Jay feels the floorboards under her feet, the chill pressing through her shoes' thin soles. She thinks of what lies down, down, down—and it flashes through her head that Brandi is gone. *Without a trace.* She shakes the idea away, unable to face it. In the mirror across from her, Jay's reflection looks a thousand years old.

Hilma says, "Listen, I'm worried as anyone, but here's a question for you. Under normal circumstances, if you heard that a high school friend was in trouble, and you hadn't seen that person since graduation, would you drop everything and fly back to the sticks?"

"Yes," Jay says, when nobody else volunteers. She's not sure it's the truth.

"Oh, bull*shit*. Who does that? You'd donate to a GoFundMe and forget about it by the next day. The four of us catching the first flight to Arkansas is—well, it's fucked up, and everyone's going to notice in this one-horse town. So how do we get out of here unscathed?"

"It's pretty simple," Jay says. "Brandi wants us to find out what happened to her." It didn't exactly seem simple until Jay said this out loud.

"Aren't we a little old to run around being the Mystery Gang?" Charlie asks.

"Should we do this more officially? Speak to the authorities?" Iggy asks.

"I doubt Pell will be much help," Jay says. She's not exactly keen to run into Officer Pell again, not when she's right back to the uncertain footing of her teenage self. "I have a better idea."

"Fine," says Hilma, and Jay wonders if it's the first time she's ever willingly let Jay take the lead. "Then what do we do next?" Her voice holds a hint of a challenge.

Jay takes a deep breath. She can do this. She knows Brandi better than anyone. *Knew*, anyway. "If we want to figure out what's happening, we start by going to Brandi's home."

10

1999

I don't like this," Brandi insisted. "We can't go in there."

They were standing in front of what would be their third house. Charlie, Brandi, Jay, and the twins. An actual group now. The Mirror House, as they'd nicknamed it, had bound them together, galvanizing and accelerating their newly budding friendship. Usually Jay never got past the first tentative steps in befriending other people; anyway, it had been her and Brandi Addams for so long, and who else did they need? But the five of them had seen magic together. They'd stood inside it, they'd crossed from one paradigm to another. (*Paradigm*, a word Charlie had taught Jay.)

This new house was powder-blue, two-story, with a sloping roof and empty window boxes. They'd approached with keen optimism, but now Brandi was having doubts. Jay stuck close to her friend, trying to be supportive.

"God, you're jumpy," Hilma said. "You know, Gene said you were like this. He was fixing the vents in my room and he talked about how you're always hiding from him. Like a 'scared cat.' Don't worry, kitty. We'll protect you.'"

Jay looked at her, surprised and disturbed by the fact that Gene had been gossiping about Brandi. But Brandi didn't even notice. "I'm telling you. That house ain't empty."

"Are we sure it's the right place?" Jay said, not wanting to see Brandi stressed.

"It's definitely the place." Charlie opened Theodora's notebook to a particular page. "Theodora oversaw the construction of a house at the very end of this street." The quickly sketched diagram showed the unmistakable curl of Dogwood Lane. A string of *x*'s representing ordinary homes, and at the end, a star. Marking this blue house.

Now that he was convinced of the magic, Charlie had tossed himself into house-hunting with full-hearted excitement. He said he felt like Champollion, translating the Rosetta Stone. Jay helped when she could. She loved handling the journal: the pages' spicy, musty smell, Theodora's fading cursive. The best parts were the sketches. The infinitely detailed blueprints of interiors, exteriors. A gable, a window, the angle of a roof. For the first time, Jay saw the connective tissue of houses, as if they were organic things. Muscle, bones, veins; mortar, brick, lumber.

Theodora was frustratingly vague about her houses. She hadn't left a conveniently marked map, just as Hilma had said. Besides, it had been at least sixty years since she'd filled these pages. Things had changed, neighborhoods had been rearranged, houses rebuilt, even in a town like Eternal, which had an entire downtown area on the National Register of Historic Places. It was going to be a "process of elimination," according to Charlie. Cross-referencing clues from the journal—a distinctive window, a wraparound porch—with the current layout of the town. The only foolproof way to identify Theodora's houses was to go inside.

Which was how they'd found themselves here.

"Don't worry. It's . . ." Max checked his watch. "Two-forty-five on a Friday. This is the time of day when most homeowners are away, which is the perfect time for break-ins."

"It's truly terrifying that you'd know that," Charlie said.

"We were burgled at night when Jodie's paintings were stolen," Hilma pointed out.

"Still throwing that in my face? Okay, enough. We're going in," Max said, and marched toward the house, the rest of them following.

The place definitely looked occupied, and a scent of perfumed fabric softener hung near the dryer vent. But Max was already bent over the doorknob, working at it quietly. "No need for Jay to break-and-enter this time. Look." He triumphantly wiggled the now-loose doorknob. "I've been practicing."

"Again, terrifying," Charlie said. "Why would a rich boy know how to pick locks?"

"Please, Charlie. We aren't that well-off," Hilma said, and Jay made a quiet note of the distinction between the terms, the way *rich* sounded childish and *well-off* sounded sophisticated.

Max purred a drumroll against the roof of his mouth as he swung the door open. At once, it was obvious they'd made a mistake. The house was furnished, a wallet and keys scattered on the table, a coffee mug with a fresh stamp of lipstick. A steady beep emitted from a blocky keypad next to the door.

"Don't panic." Hilma brushed past Max and punched the numbers: one-two-three-four. "Nobody's original enough to come up with anything better." A second of silence made Jay's stomach dip in relief. Then a shrieking filled the air, pulsing all around them. Charlie took off running. Brandi, hands over ears, followed close behind. Hilma and Max were yelling—or, no. Jay realized the twins were laughing, clutching at each other as they ran.

Jay glanced over her shoulder. A police cruiser inched its way up the hill. The five of them were hidden in the narrow service alley that ran behind the houses, but it wouldn't take long before they were spotted.

If they made a break for the trees, they'd have to run right in front of the cop car. Which most likely held Pell and his brushy mustache and thick eyebrows, neck boiling up over his collar. Not a fan of Brandi Addams or, by extension, Jay. And Jay knew that the patch of nearby forest wasn't as inviting as it looked. It went downhill fast, steep and rocky.

Then Jay noticed something strange. The back door of the next house over was open, and Ignacio Nieves was gesturing frantically to Jay, as if he'd been doing it for a while, waiting for her to notice. They locked eyes. *Hide here*, he mouthed.

Typically, Jay would've been too flummoxed by the sight of Iggy—floppy-haired, sloe-eyed star quarterback—to respond at all. But the urgency kicked aside any shyness, and she checked on the cruiser. If they ran now, they might make it to safety.

Jay hunched low and, sweeping her arm in a follow-me gesture, she ran. The screaming alarm almost felt like cover, like it could hide them. She prayed the others were trailing after her, *please-please-please*. Iggy kept his eyes on hers, reeling her in like a tractor beam. She reached the door and fell into a shadowy room. Iggy was still holding open the door when the others piled in behind her, crying, laughing.

Iggy slammed the door shut.

Next door, the alarm cut out and the sudden silence was filled with anxious breathing.

Outside, footsteps approached. Crunching through the gravel, steady. The cop—had to be Pell—must've seen them. He was taking his sweet time. This afternoon was supposed to be magical, and here they were, standard-issue juvenile delinquents about to get caught.

The footsteps came right up to the door. They all stared at the doorknob. Awaiting their fate.

"Kids?" It was Pell. Beside Jay, Brandi inhaled tightly. "Kids, c'mon out now. This ain't funny."

Nobody spoke. They didn't move. *Go away*, Jay thought. *Go.*

Instead, the doorknob turned, slow and experimental.

"Y'all still have a chance to make this right," Pell called. "Just come out now."

His shadow pressed against the window next to the door, looming large and wavery. They all drew back instinctively, just an inch. Jay thought she might throw up. She wished they could be inside the Mirror House's turret, hidden in plain view, safe.

There was a sudden crackle and spit. The police radio. Slowly, the doorknob turned back into position. After a long, unbearable moment, a distant door slammed, the engine started.

"He's leaving?" Charlie asked. "Just like that?"

"Lucky. Shit." Max half collapsed, before exploding upward in a leap. "You should've seen your faces."

"Don't," Charlie said. "You have no idea how bad that could've been."

Max reached for him, trying to ruffle his curls: Charlie deftly sidestepped him. "*We're* on your side," Max said. "Nothing's going to happen, Olowe."

Now that the threat had passed, Jay became intensely aware of Iggy, who was grinning at them, waiting for an explanation. Jay pushed her hair behind her ear, awkward. She tried to see herself with an artist's eye, appreciate her good qualities. Her thick commas of eyebrows, her cheekbones. But sometimes—sometimes, god, she wanted a more obvious beauty.

"You're my hero, man," Max said, high-fiving Iggy. "You saved our asses."

"Is this your house?" Hilma asked, too formal. "It's lovely."

It wasn't Iggy's house, and it wasn't lovely. But he laughed. "You caught me. This place's been abandoned for years. But I kinda like it. Nobody comes looking for me here." He winked. It landed on Jay, maybe accidentally. "Well. Usually."

It surprised Jay that Iggy would ever want to be alone. He always seemed at the center of things. The football team, the popular crowd at school, his family. When Jay and her dad went to Cozy's on special occasions, Jay would watch Iggy joke around with his brothers or give his mom a quick hug around the shoulders as she passed.

"What are you getting up to here?" Max asked him.

"I like some space for my thoughts. This place feels nice. It's . . . I dunno. Lucky?"

The room went still. "Lucky," Hilma repeated. "Charlie, do you remember that Latin word we found next to the map?"

"*Felix*," Charlie said in a hushed voice.

Iggy's gaze darted from one face to the other, surprised by their reaction. Jay noticed that the air smelled heavy with furniture polish, the chemical scent of new upholstery. It didn't match the tattered exterior of the house.

"Hey, hold on," Iggy said. "I'll show you." He pulled aside the heavy curtains, and light flooded the room.

The space was small but wildly, sumptuously furnished. These items didn't have the same effortless luxury as the AIR House. They were the sorts of things Brandi's mom would've picked if she won the lottery. A massive red pleather couch, outfitted with so many footrests and cupholders that it resembled a small vehicle. A marble coffee table squatted next to a flat-screen TV that was nearly as tall as Jay. A four-tier fondue fountain was still wrapped in plastic.

Max whistled and grabbed a knockoff Fabergé egg, tossing it from palm to palm. "It's like a *SkyMall* threw up in here."

"A what?" Brandi asked.

Hilma smiled, indulgent. "Sorry, Max forgot this is fly*over* country. *SkyMall* is—"

But Max yelped, fumbling with the egg. It toppled from his

hands, arcing so that it hit the bearskin rug, missing the hardwood. The egg lay there, unbroken, glittering.

"See what I mean? This place is lucky. Hey, look at this." Iggy retrieved a quarter from the tray of a full-sized slot machine. "Watch this. It's wild. Heads." He flipped the coin neatly into the air. It landed in his open palm, and Jay scooted closer. George Washington's profile, curly wig and all. "Heads," Iggy repeated. George Washington reappeared. "I'm telling you. Anytime I flip a coin in here? Like magic."

"Charlie?" Hilma asked. "What are the odds of flipping heads ten times in a row?"

"I believe it's, uh, about one in a thousand."

"May I?" Hilma asked, taking the coin without waiting for Iggy's answer. "Heads."

Max whispered the countdown under his breath. "Ten—nine—eight—" Each time, Washington appeared, smug, his face seeming to say: *You knew you were dealing with magic.*

On the last spin, as the quarter reached its peak, Max yelled, "Tails."

The quarter hopped off Hilma's palm, landing on the floor next to Max's sneaker. He plucked it up and showed it off, beaming like a game show host, the eagle's wings spread wide.

"Look up," Charlie whispered.

The ceiling was burnished copper, square tiles like a giant chessboard. A shamrock was imprinted in one corner, a horseshoe in another; over there, a delicate rendering of a rabbit's paw.

"There's something written." Max bounded up onto the red couch, touching the ceiling with his fingertips like he was reading Braille. " 'Oh, I am fortune's fool.'"

"I get it now," Charlie said. "I should've looked for older maps. The blue house is the last house on the street today, but in the 1930s? It didn't exist. Which would make this house . . . the last house on the street."

"Ladies and gentlemen," Hilma said. "We have found our Luck House."

"Our *felix homicilius*," said Max proudly.

Charlie groaned. "That's not Latin, that's just—no."

"Luck House?" Iggy repeated.

They turned, meeting the expectant beam of his smile. What were they going to do with him? Iggy wasn't a fellow misfit, like Charlie. He had actual friends. He'd dated half a dozen girls, always breaking things off amicably. If Iggy decided to tattle, even the protective shield of Hilma and Max wouldn't save them from the fallout.

"Do you know a lot about houses?" Hilma asked him.

"Sure, I explore abandoned houses around here," Iggy said. "After practice or work."

"Where do you work, again?" Max asked. "The Mexican place?"

"Nah, Honduran. It's my family's. We moved to Eternal when I was a little kid." Jay liked the way his face changed when he talked about his family. She'd heard the story about how Cozy's got its name, from a toddler Iggy mispronouncing *cocina*, and it fit the Nieves family: there was a warmth to them she envied.

"Anyway," Iggy said. "This town has a lot of cool secrets if you know how to look for them. I'd be happy to show you."

"You seem like a good egg, Ignacio Nieves," Hilma said. "Can we trust you?"

Iggy didn't even hesitate. "Sure. You can trust me."

So Hilma told him, and Jay used the moment to watch Iggy's face closely. He didn't look skeptical; he didn't laugh. She saw the way he smiled, his pupils dilating, as if the wonder he felt were a physical change in the light.

11

1999

THEN

They explored all afternoon. The Luck House was larger than Jay's home, but the expensive, dust-coated junk made the space feel cramped. Over by one window, a massive treadmill had a reproduction of Michelangelo's *David* propped on it like he was about to start running. In another room, a waterbed was piled high with a shining tangle of jewelry. Hilma and Max kept laughing over items, but Jay saw Brandi's eyes linger on the VCR player still in its box. For most people around Eternal Springs, luck was synonymous with money.

Hilma plopped into a giant massage chair. It rumbled to life, her voice wavering when she spoke. "We need to set some ground rules."

At first no one responded. A sudden flurry of beeps came from one corner of the room. Iggy was intent on the paddles beneath the coffin-shaped glass of a massive pinball machine. Jay tried not to watch the easy way his muscles shifted as he played. Next to Jay, Max shuffled the cards he'd found in a closet.

"My thoughts are: First rule, don't take anything," Hilma said. "We respect what we find in these places. Second, we never tell anybody else about the houses. This is between the five—sorry, the six of us. Don't go telling your little boyfriends or your moms. Lie if you have to. And third, you *must* tell all of us when you find a new house. No keeping secrets."

Brandi and Jay nodded, and Charlie gave a reluctant dip of his head.

"Quarterback?" Hilma called. "You're part of this now, too."

"Sure, no secrets," Iggy said.

Max bumped Jay to make sure she was watching. He flicked five cards onto the floor. With great ceremony, he turned them over. An ace; a jack; a king; a queen; a ten. All hearts. A royal flush.

"Most importantly," Hilma said, raising her voice, "we have to agree that we'll tell each other *everything* we do with these houses. Group decisions only."

"I don't like that," Max said at once. "What if we want to do something private with these places? Uh, personal?"

"What 'private, personal' things are you thinking of?"

"I dunno. What if there's a girl I like, and we end up here, and I ask her on a date?" Max turned five cards over. Another royal flush, spades.

Hilma huffed. "We've only been here like six weeks. Who can you even ask?"

"Her name's Destiny. Which is fitting, because she's mine."

Brandi threw Jay a wide-eyed glance. Destiny Lautner. Amber's friend, part of Iggy's general crowd. Barbie-pink lipstick, sunny blond hair. The one who, last year, had started a rumor that Gene was Brandi's boyfriend. Lately, Destiny had been bragging about leaving town, going to Hollywood, making it big. Jay was preemptively jealous.

"I know Destiny," Iggy piped up. "She's cool."

"Iggy, my man. I already like having you as part of the team."

"Why do boys walk among us like human beings?" Hilma sighed. "Wait till our parents hear you're in love with a Destiny. That will teach them to move their children to Arkansas."

"How is that worse than a Tripp? Anyway. You're saying that if I take the lovely Destiny to this house and ask her out to a . . . a hoedown, or whatever the mating rituals are around here—I have to run it by you virgins?"

"This isn't your personal dating service. Theodora wove a lot of power into these houses. We're going to respect that."

Brandi leaned her chin on her hands, looking more serious than Jay had ever seen her. "I agree. We respect Theodora."

"Can I add a rule, then?" Charlie said. "Will you stop talking to us like we're stupid hicks?"

The words were met with a surprised silence, except for the left-over tinkling of Iggy's pinball machine. For the first time since Jay met her, Hilma didn't have an immediate reply. There was a wash of vulnerability on her face.

"You look down on us," Charlie continued. "But I was the one who translated the Latin in that journal entry. Jay broke into the Mirror House. Brandi . . ." He faltered for a moment.

"Brandi found the Truth House when she was just a little kid," added Max. "She's Theodora's biggest fan."

Brandi blushed with pleasure.

"And Iggy saved us literally two hours ago," Charlie concluded. "All you've really done so far is own a book that doesn't truly belong to you. We're partners in this."

"Yes, but the book is vital. I mean, how else would—" But Hilma stopped and turned away, staring at a corner of the room for a mo-ment, gazing unseeingly at the Thighmaster. When she turned back, her expression had a purposeful resolve. "Okay. Look. I'm sorry if I offended you all. I just want to make sure we don't fuck this up."

"If it helps, she's like this with everyone," Max said. "She doesn't have any practice at being a friend." Hilma tossed him a death glare, but her perfect mask had dropped for a moment. It was strange for Jay to imagine Hilma Garnet being lonely.

"You're right, Charlie," Hilma said. "We're partners. Let's make a—a charter, okay?" Reaching for a gaudy pen, Hilma opened Theodora's journal, the book purchased for two thousand dollars of her parents' money, and started writing on an unused page in the back. "What rules did we propose, again?"

"No taking stuff," Jay said.

"Don't tell anybody about the houses," Charlie said.

"But *do* tell each other if'n we find one," Brandi said.

"Tell everyone before we make big decisions," Max said, rolling his eyes. "Boring."

"Lastly, we treat everyone with respect because we're all valuable members of a team," Hilma said. "Any other amendments? Anyone?"

"We should always take our major decisions to a vote," Charlie said.

"Okay, then. Let's take our first vote. Do we agree to these rules?"

Hilma called out their names, one at a time, and they agreed to the rules.

"Will the luck last?" Brandi trailed her hand longingly over a dusty stack of boxes printed with the As Seen On TV logo: a George Foreman grill, a Rejuvenique face mask. "Once we leave this place?"

She addressed Iggy, who shrugged one shoulder, abashed. "Uh, well. I'm not sure about all this—all the magic stuff. But yeah, the luck's only inside the house, you know? Once I leave, I get heads when I want tails." He flushed as Max laughed.

"That seemed to be Theodora's goal, to trap the magic inside the walls," Charlie added. "That's something we'll have to explore."

Hilma lifted her voice. "Full disclosure, then. There's one house in particular that Theodora describes. Her masterpiece, the final house she built. Every other house is just a stepping-stone. It'll be the trickiest house to find. Theodora doesn't give many hints about the location. It's a large house, and it took years to construct, but that's all I've figured out. Plus, you can't use this house without first visiting the others. Theodora didn't want just *anybody* stumbling across it; it can only be somebody who appreciates her work."

Jay sat taller, feeling a surge of resolve. She would be worthy, no matter what it took.

"That's why I'm writing down every saying we find," Hilma said. "We might need them all if we want the final house to work. We have three houses so far. We're nearly halfway there."

"So, finding these houses is like a quest," Iggy said. "Cool."

Charlie asked, "Isn't that a little . . . Harry Potter?"

"Harry who?" Max asked, but he didn't wait for an answer. "What I want to know is: What does this final house even *do*? Is it better than this one? 'Cause I could probably just stay in here forever and call it good." He spun out a third royal flush.

Intensity came over Hilma's face, like the sun appearing from behind a cloud. "Yes, Max. The final house is better than this one. It's better than all of them combined. If it does what I think it does? This house is going to change everything for us."

12

2015

It's dawn, the chill just starting to crackle into humidity. The trailer park is quiet at this hour, only a few windows lit. Jay picks her way through the snarled chickweed. Iggy follows at her elbow. As she approaches, her heart catches. Brandi always kept her trailer as nice as she could, fussing over the miniature rosebush out front, Windexing diligently. Now the trailer's vinyl skirting peels away to reveal cinder blocks, and the rosebush is a tumbleweed of dead leaves. Yellow caution tape droops across the door. It hurts to see Brandi's home decaying into a stereotype.

Jay passes right by the trailer's front door.

"Wait," Iggy whispers. He insisted on coming with her, while Hilma and Charlie are at the hotel, combing through newspapers for clues. "I thought we wanted to check inside her house?"

"Not there. You'll see."

Jay's never approached the garden shed from this angle before, always coming at it through the window, secretly. It's so small. Jay can barely believe this rickety thing used to hold her and Brandi, all their teenage hopes and dreams.

The shed door locks from the outside, a fact that never worried Jay when she was a teenager—she and Brandi didn't care if they were stuck, as long as they were together. Now she's grateful that it makes things easier as she slides the bolt aside.

When she opens the door, the photos and drawings flutter in the sudden movement, faces staring out like abandoned pets waiting for rescue. Jay braces herself and steps inside.

Iggy follows and shuts the door carefully behind him. "Remind me what we're looking for?" he whispers.

Jay scans the wall, hoping she hasn't lost credibility already. Her only idea is to crawl back to her old hideout like a kid retreating to a pillow fort. Then Jay sees it, and her doubt dissolves. "We're looking for that."

Three photographs are stuck to a corner of the shed wall. Simple Polaroids, the same style as the Truth House photo that Brandi sent Jay. Houses. The High House has been repainted a stylish gray. The Forever House is barely visible behind a crosshatch of branches; that photo looks older, as if it's one Brandi took a long time ago. And there's the AIR House—still, in her mind, the Garnets' home, though they haven't stepped inside for years. In one corner, a shot of Brandi's trailer is ordinary against Theodora's houses.

"Is that a map?" At Iggy's question, Jay tears her eyes from the photographs. It's a simple Google Maps printout of Eternal Springs, several pieces of paper taped together, crooked at the seams. The gray-scale streets are dotted with red pinpricks of marker. Iggy traces the lines with his finger. "Wait. Brandi was recording the houses' locations? Anyone could've found this."

There's a noise from outside. A screen door opening, creaking shut. Jay waits for the footsteps to go the other way before she rips the maps down, shoving the pages into her bag. "If Brandi was still using, we don't know what risks she took."

It's the first time Jay's acknowledged Brandi's addiction with one of the others. Iggy inhales. They've all been dancing around this fear: that the Brandi they knew has been changed by years of rehab, pills, alcohol, stints of sobriety, more pills.

"Anyway, nobody else knew what this shed meant to her. Not even Gene." His name's another stumble. Jay's surrounded by memories, crunching underfoot every way she turns.

"Gene knew more than he let on." It surprises Jay to hear Iggy speak so openly. "What do you think these photos mean?"

"No clue. I don't understand why she's only included these houses," Jay says. "Which ones are missing?" She makes a mental note: the Luck House, the Oath House, the Duplication House, the Truth House, the Mirror House. It's amazing how easily they come back to her. She looks more closely: there are gaps between the photos, the nubby gray of tape residue on the wall. Some photos have been removed.

"Maybe the police took some as evidence?" Jay asks quietly. But something knits together at the back of her mind. Brandi sent her the photo of the Truth House. There are five missing photographs.

Which exactly matches the five of them, Brandi's friends who left Eternal and abandoned her to Arkansas.

Before she can point this out, Iggy speaks up. "There's something that's bothered me. When you heard that Brandi vanished, did you think . . . that maybe she's gone to . . . ?" He doesn't have to complete the sentence.

The answer is yes. Yes, of course she's *thought*, of course she's *considered*. Brandi is missing. There's one place that Jay's mind went to instantly, the second she saw that flyer and realized that Brandi had vanished. But Jay's purposefully ignored that theory, because she can't do it again. She can't make herself vulnerable to the bone-deep disappointment that she's only just started to overcome.

"Let's worry about that later. First, look and see if there's anything else here. Could you search the drawer, maybe?" She takes the Polaroids down one by one, antsy, moving quickly.

She's almost finished when the shed door rattles. Jay freezes, and Iggy's breath catches. Nobody followed them. Jay watched the rearview mirror the whole drive from the hotel. The rental SUV is parked a quarter of a mile back. They should be safe.

A shadow hovers under the door. Jay presses backward into Iggy, instinctively, and they could be teenagers again, trapped and inhaling mildew and dust.

A click. For a moment Jay thinks the door will swing open, and she scrambles for an excuse that will make this all look less incriminating. Maybe it's Hilma, or Charlie. Maybe it's—

Jay doesn't realize she's mouthing Brandi's name until Iggy's hand is on her shoulder.

The shadow withdraws, but they don't move. Jay's palms are sweat-slick as she clutches the photos and the map printout. Iggy's so close she can feel his heartbeat. The silence stretches on, until Jay can't withstand the suspense a moment longer. Iggy steps forward and presses at the door, attempting to open it slowly. Jay's pulse is skittering, half fear, half wild and stupid hope.

Iggy tries. Tries again. He turns back to her, offering a strange, one-sided smile. "Well, sit tight," he says. "We're locked in."

13

2015

NOW

Jay's too old for this. She's stiff and clumsy, her joints hardened. As she stretches across to Brandi's bedroom window, she notices that the weeds below are a waist-high jungle now. Grappling, she manages to raise Brandi's screen, which glides up easily. So Brandi was still using their old window-to-window system. Jay slides one leg across, wincing at the pull in her muscles. "It's not as bad as it looks," she whispers to Iggy, who's eyeing the gap skeptically.

Jay has no idea who locked them in the shed. Was it a well-meaning neighbor, is someone on to them? Either way, she hates to think what would've happened if she hadn't known about the window, always unlocked despite its keyhole.

As Jay slides into the stale air of Brandi's trailer, she has a sudden sensation of slipping backward through time. A physical chill passes over her, disorienting and delicious. She's eighteen, seventeen—fourteen—ten. A kid again. She's Brandi's best and only friend. She's never ruined anything, the whole world is ahead of her, unknown and precious.

"Sorry," Iggy says, stumbling as he maneuvers his long body through the window. "It's been a while since my quarterback days."

Finally they're standing in Brandi's old bedroom, which is just the same, as if Brandi has been living in a makeshift version of 2000 for her entire adulthood. "We need to get out of here," Iggy says gently, but not hiding his tension. "I don't know if anyone's still out there, or if they've called the cops. But we're standing inside what could be a crime scene."

"Yeah. Let's go out the side door."

They creep through the still, silent rooms of the trailer. The walls feel so insubstantial around Jay, the floorboards shaky, the whole thing ready to cave inward. Nearly every spring in Arkansas, people die or lose their homes when tornados snap their trailers like twigs. Iggy is quiet as they pass the nook of a bathroom and the flimsy fiberboard cabinets. He's never been in here, Jay realizes. Their brief, vivid friendship, the year of the Mystery Gang, took place almost entirely in Theodora's houses, not each other's homes.

Jay thinks of those Polaroids in the shed. The map. What was it like for Brandi to live in this tiny trailer, when she could visit Theodora's houses every single day? Jay couldn't do it. It would whittle her down, that proximity to magic. Even thousands of miles away, the houses still haunt her imagination.

They're near the side door. Jay prepares herself to step outside and face . . . whoever or whatever might be waiting. But she stops. The morning light illuminates the shotgun layout of the trailer, giving her a view directly into the living room, which is marbled with blood. On the carpet, on the walls, blackish plumes. Blood slashes across the ugly plaid curtains that Brandi never replaced. It soaks the couch cushions. Brandi's blood. It feels unreal, somehow, like paint, like stage blood.

It's not the first time Jay's seen direct evidence of death, but the true impact of what happened to Brandi wraps around her throat and squeezes. *You promised you promised you promised.* Jay looks down at the small, uneven scar on her arm. Not so much blood, in comparison.

"Come on, Jay," Iggy says, and he pulls her out the trailer door and into the morning, which is empty, quiet, nobody waiting for them.

14

1999

A month after Jay met the Garnets, her dad eyed her in the kitchen one morning. He had a habit of examining Jay as if she wouldn't notice, searching for an incipient trace of the sadness that had overtaken her mom. "What's going on with you lately?"

"Why? Is something wrong?" Jay was a little embarrassed.

"Not at all. You seem happy."

Happy felt true enough. Jay woke up every morning and instantly had purpose. Magic had come into her life. Or . . . she'd walked right into magic, because magic had a physical address on a map. Multiple addresses.

When Jay had first heard about the eight houses—only *eight*—she'd thought it couldn't take long to locate them. But Theodora had been a haphazard note-taker, almost mischievous. She wrote in dialect or made-up languages sometimes, inventing fussy, intricate codes and then abandoning them by the next page. "She was traveling to different worlds," Charlie pointed out. "You can't expect her to just write everything down straightforwardly. Her brain was working entirely differently from ours."

The six of them had been retreating to the Luck House to speed up the process of decoding the journal, but the whole process felt uncertain. Jay was aware of the Garnets' limited time here. Already it was turning into autumn. By next summer, their parents' residency would be over, and they'd vanish back to the Northeast.

"What if'n you can't use Theodora's own houses to find out her secrets?" Brandi asked one afternoon, curled in the massage chair. "Like a . . . like a rock too big for Jesus to carry?"

"The omnipotence paradox," Charlie said, looking surprised. "Let's hope not."

The Luck House had also become their go-to for exams. Max's idea. If they studied in the Luck House, huddled up with all that luxurious junk, the pages of their worn-out textbooks always landed on the details that made their way into the exams. Holden Caulfield wondering what happened to the ducks in wintertime; a clear explanation of Punnett squares. Even though she was more distracted than ever from homework, Jay found her grades nudging higher.

"The Luck House likes you more than the rest of us," Hilma said to Max at school. Midterm grades were being handed back, a group project. "Brandi got a B minus when you *know* she wrote most of that paper. You stole her A."

"Nah, it's okay," Brandi said. "I'm no good at spelling."

"The Luck House recognizes that I'm its equal," Max said, "so I get double the luck."

Jay looked around to see if anybody overheard. At school, people had noticed their new arrangement. The Garnets, miraculously, sat with them now: Hilma plopping next to Jay during English, Max eating lunch with Brandi and Jay behind the library. Charlie abandoned his solitary study sessions and gravitated to them instead, eager to share new clues he'd found. Jay and Brandi had been a twosome for so long that it was exhilarating to be part of a *group*. To have *friends*, plural.

Iggy was the lone holdout. At school, he operated as normal—friendly but remote, always so surrounded by friends and teammates that Jay couldn't even share a smile with him without an audience. She felt like she knew two versions of Ignacio Nieves. The cheerful, inaccessible quarterback she knew at school. And then the boy who'd show up at Theodora's houses in the evenings or early mornings, curious, serious. She'd shown him her sketchbook at his request, and he'd stayed bent over her work for half an hour, asking questions, noticing details, as if he actually cared.

Jay and Brandi struggled to carry the armchair over the threshold. It was satiny white, boxy, and expensive-looking, and Jay was sure she recognized it. "Is this from the AIR House?" she asked suddenly.

Hilma had recruited Brandi and Jay to move furniture into the Truth House. They'd been scavenging items here and there. A rusty lawn chair from the trailer park. Candleholders imprinted with saints that Iggy nicked from his mom. The place was starting to feel cozy, though they didn't spend as much time in the Truth House. It was less interesting now, like the Truth House was a beloved toy Jay had outgrown.

"Yeah, I figured nobody would miss this chair," Hilma said. "It's so ugly."

The furniture in the AIR House didn't belong to the Garnets, not any more than it belonged to the other out-of-state artists who'd streamed through those rooms over the years. Jay considered saying something, but it felt hypocritical when they were breaking into houses constantly.

Also, they were inside the Truth House. Jay wasn't sure that her words would come out sounding polite. "Why couldn't Max stay and help after he dropped us off?" Jay asked instead, rubbing the bruise on her leg where the chair had banged her.

"He has some errand he's running, some scheme to win over Destiny," Hilma said.

"Is he gonna use the Luck House to ask her out?" Brandi asked wistfully.

"He knows the rules. Someone like Destiny could ruin everything." Hilma sat on the stolen armchair and stretched her long pale legs. "Although . . . two people inside our group might be a different story."

Brandi startled, but Hilma was looking at Jay. Her expression was knowing, eyes catlike and sly. Jay shrugged, uncomfortable.

"Ugh, don't play coy," Hilma exploded. "You get all moony-eyed whenever the quarterback's around. Just *say* something to the boy. If you need to flirt with him in the Luck House, I'll bend the rules for you. I'll play Cupid."

Jay couldn't answer. If she spoke, her truth would be right there, and Brandi would know for sure, and Hilma too. Worst of all, Jay would have to admit to herself that she liked Iggy.

She hadn't dated much. There had been a couple of boys who'd asked Jay, via ambiguous mumbles, if she'd like to go out sometime. Drive around Eternal at night, pulling into gas station parking lots to roll down the windows and talk to classmates on similarly aimless excursions. Jay found the whole thing both underwhelming and overwhelming. She wasn't saving herself in the same way as the ultra-Christian girls, with their purity rings, but she always assumed her first time would be at college, far from Eternal's shallow dating pool. A smart and ironic stranger, someone who'd wear dark flannels and see her Arkansan roots as a funny anecdote to share with the other shiny new people in her life.

Falling for a football player, a jock, a hometown hero—that was a cliché. Not for her. If she'd ever considered him, Jay had been protected from a crush on Iggy by the fact that they moved in entirely different circles. Now, though, their circles were overlapping, and Jay's imaginary future boyfriend was disconcertingly fading around the edges, insubstantial next to Iggy's strong, shining lines.

"Ooh, I know. Let's play a game of truth or dare," Hilma said.

"She don't have to tell you anything if she don't wanna," Brandi said, and Jay smiled gratefully.

"Are you worried Bluejay won't love you anymore if she has a boyfriend?" Hilma asked Brandi, sounding genuinely curious. "Gene mentioned that you two are girlfriends. Is that it?"

This wasn't the first time there'd been a rumor about the two of them. Jay loved Brandi more than pretty much anybody else; she knew how Brandi breathed when she slept, knew how she looked when she cried, had a mental map of her scars and freckles. But Jay was annoyed when outsiders presumed to know the secret shape of their friendship.

"Nope," Brandi said, simple and plain.

"Gene shouldn't be talking about stuff that's not his business," Jay said.

"But getting all the juicy stuff is *my* business." Hilma leaned forward. "God, come on, truth or dare. You already know what I'm going to ask."

Jay was realizing there *was* something she might get out of Hilma. "Okay, fine, I'll go with truth. But," she added, as Hilma clapped her hands, "only if you choose it too."

Hilma was distracted, already tossing herself into the game. "Yeah, sure, I'm in. Do you like Ignacio Nieves?"

A fire burned in her belly. "Yes," Jay said evenly. "A lot."

"Are you going to ask him out?"

"No."

"Why not?"

"Because if he says no, then I'll never get to imagine it's possible again," Jay said. Brandi caught her eye, smiled at her, encouraging. *He'd be lucky*, she mouthed.

Hilma blinked. "Okay. Wow." She didn't seem skeptical or amused now; there was a glimmer over her face, turning her younger. "But do you—"

Before she could go on, Jay raised her voice. "It's my turn now. Truth or dare?"

"Truth," Hilma conceded.

"What's the final house?" Jay asked.

Hilma hadn't revealed any details about the final house yet. She seemed to enjoy withholding the surprise. It became a game to guess what the house would do—print free money (Brandi), turn them into deities (Max). But Jay remembered the word *escape* and she knew it was something much bigger, better. Hilma had carefully removed the passages of the journal that referred to the final house, saving that section for herself, away from even Charlie's eyes. She insisted that this didn't count under the "no secrets" clause of their agreement since she was going to tell them all anyway.

Hilma stared at her now, silent. Jay thought maybe the house wouldn't work on Hilma: she was too defiant, protected inside her permanent membrane of good fortune. Hilma could refuse to answer.

But when Hilma smiled, she looked like some part of her was glad Jay had asked. "The final house is worth a thousand of the others. Theodora made the final house into a portal, so that anybody who entered could experience what Theodora herself did. It was . . . like her ultimate gift to the people of earth."

"The people of Eternal Springs," Brandi said, but Hilma didn't seem to hear.

Jay's heart was beating so hard she felt dizzy. "So—"

"That's right. The final house," Hilma said, "leads into another world entirely."

15

2015

Jay remembered being intimidated by the Thermal Park Hotel, the monument of Eternal Springs' heyday, velvet-draped windows and ponderous wall sconces. Now, when Jay walks into the lobby, she fights the impulse to check that she's in the right place. The exterior is still turn-of-the-century limestone, complete with demurely perching gargoyles, but the inside has been scrubbed of Victoriana and outfitted with purplish recessed lighting and plastic snake plants.

"What happened?" Jay whispers.

"Red Art." Iggy points at the small logo crouched next to the new Thermal Park Hotel sign gleaming above the front desk. "Some kind of . . . real estate developer group. Did you see all the billboards on the way into town?"

Sultry electronica bounces overhead, exhausting this early in the morning. Jay catches a flash of yellow hair at the front desk. Hilma. No: "Max?" Jay calls.

She rushes forward, and he turns. Instinctively, Jay steps back, nearly running into Iggy now. Max looks terrible, his skin pale and glassy, though expensive-looking aviators shield his eyes. He holds his arm close to his side, swaddled in an invisible sling. His hand is swollen, bruised in maroons, purples, sea-green.

"Jay Carr," Max says, and breaks into a brilliant smile. "Igster? God, I've missed you two." With his free arm, he pulls Jay into a hug. "What the hell are you doing here in Eternal?"

Jay can't tell if he's sincerely surprised—if he, like Jay, thought Brandi's summons was just for him—or if he's putting on a show of innocence for anyone watching. The tourists milling around the lobby won't see anything interesting in the three of them together. But Jay locks eyes with a passing woman in a housekeeping smock and recognizes her as the sister of an old classmate. They're being observed, their presence filed away. She and Iggy are still rattled by being locked in Brandi's shed. The drive back to the hotel was silent, bristling with the shock of the blood-splashed trailer, with the shadow beneath the shed door.

"Max, we need to talk," she says quietly. "Somewhere private."

Max has embraced each of them: slapping Charlie vigorously on the back, nearly making Hilma lose her balance with his one-armed hug. "So glad the prodigal twin decided to finally show up," Hilma says. But Jay can tell she's relieved.

"Me? I'm just here for a nice Ozarks vacation," Max says. "No idea I'd see you four. *Quelle* coincidence."

Jay can almost pretend that the Garnets will take the lead now, fix this mess, as if she's never seen evidence to the contrary. They're in Hilma's beautiful suite, the windows showing a sweeping view of Eternal, hills and streets glazed with sunlight.

"So Bran reached out to all of us?" Max asks, sobering.

In response, Jay rolls her hoodie sleeve up to reveal her still-angry scar. Charlie quickly flashes his own, and Hilma and Iggy follow suit. Their explanation, their calling card.

"Aww, poor guy," Hilma says, as Max processes this. "You thought you were the knight in shining armor, when really you're just the last to show up."

"I dropped everything when I got the letter, but this was the earliest I could manage. If it makes you feel better, I fucked up a major acquisition to get here."

"Are you okay, man?" Iggy says. "You don't look good. You're—"

"Brundlefly." Max yanks his own shirtsleeve up. The nubby gauze on his lower arm barely hides the reopened scar, his veins darkened and swollen. Jay's stomach drops. "No way am I explaining this voodoo shit to my doctor, so I've been roughing it. There was a point I—hell, I thought I wouldn't make it. Coughing up blood." Max pulls his sunglasses off. His eyes are bloodshot, silver-blond lashes a pale fringe against the bruises. "I thought I'd die in the restroom of a charter jet. Worse ways to go, but still."

An uneasy silence descends over the room.

"My god." Hilma reaches an unthinking hand toward her brother. "You're late to Eternal Springs by one day, and this is what happens? What are we supposed to do? If we leave, we're going to be killed by this fairy-tale curse."

"Not a curse," Charlie says at once. "An oath."

Hilma turns on him. "Is this the time to be a know-it-all?"

"No, no, hey, Charlie's right," Max says. "It's not a curse keeping us here. Brandi's our friend, we promised we'd come when she called." He looks at each of them in turn, pulling them together with his gaze. "So, the gang's all here. What's the plan?"

"We've been looking through the local paper. Absolutely nothing useful, they didn't even mention her. Before you showed up, we were waiting on these two to share with the rest of the class." Hilma gestures at Jay and Iggy.

Haltingly, the two of them take turns explaining what they

found in Brandi's shed. When Jay pulls out the photos to show the others, the images of Theodora's houses have the same impact on her friends that they did on Jay. Their best and worst teenage memories all lined up. Charlie winces. Hilma turns away, hand at her throat.

"Five houses are missing from these photos, I think. Well. Four, if you don't include the Truth House," Jay says.

"Should we worry that Brandi mapped out the houses?" Charlie asks. "Does everyone in this town know about Theodora's houses now?"

They exchange helpless glances, everyone waiting for somebody else to weigh in. All of them are outsiders now, Jay realizes. None of them know anything about what's happened in Eternal Springs since summer of 2000.

A headache nibbles at the back of Jay's skull. "We can't figure this out alone," she says. "We have to talk to folks."

"That's exactly what we're *not* doing," Charlie says. "No engaging with the locals. You two got locked in a trailer park. What's next?"

"That was probably an accident," Iggy says. "If somebody wanted to hurt us, they had every chance."

"There are just too many things we don't know," Jay goes on. "What Brandi's emotional state was like before she vanished, what she was doing, who she spent time with . . . whether she told people about the houses. People around here have fifteen years' worth of information that we don't. I hate it too, trust me, but—"

"But it's the right thing to do," finished Iggy, and Jay knows that seeing Brandi's home has transformed this situation from abstract to real for him.

Jay continues, "I was actually talking to Amber. Amber Penske? At the vigil."

"Who?" Hilma asks.

"Destiny's friend, right?" Max asks.

"Yeah. We should talk to her again. She's best friends with Brandi." Jay registers Iggy's and Charlie's surprise; they still have memories of Eternal's old social hierarchies, then. "Like I said, a lot changed. Maybe we can catch Amber at work. She mentioned a shift at Francesco's."

Max inhales, and Jay's surprised that he remembers the significance that restaurant holds for him and Brandi.

"Good for her," Iggy says, impressed. "I could never afford to eat there as a kid."

"So we get lunch at Francesco's," Hilma says. "I'll choke down some microwaved calamari if we get information out of it. Bluejay and I will go, we'll see what Amber can tell us about Brandi Addams."

"What about me?" Max asks. "I'm perfect for lunchtime schmoozing."

"You look like a *Walking Dead* extra," Hilma says.

As they argue, Jay gazes at the photo of the Truth House, which she laid out on the plush hotel carpet with the rest of the photos. *Truth is more of a stranger.* She still can't grasp that it's gone, burned down like any ordinary house, susceptible to bad wiring or stray cigarettes. There must be a reason Brandi included this photo.

"Are you sure that you didn't get any photos with your letters?" she asks the room at large. "Because that would make a lot of sense. Five missing photos, five of us."

The others fall silent. Charlie's face closes off, like a door slipped shut; Iggy won't meet her eyes.

"What's this about photos?" Max asks.

"With your letter," Hilma says. "Bluejay got a photo of the Truth House."

"Huh," Max says to Jay. "No photo for me. I feel left out."

"The Truth House burned down, right?" asks Charlie. "Maybe while Jay and Hilma talk to Amber, the rest of us can check on the other houses and make sure they're still standing."

Jay nods, but she notices that he's deftly ignored the question. And in that moment, it's as if the entire concept of *truth* is extinct. Like Theodora hoarded the world's honesty in that one house and it's all been burned down and scattered to ashes. Because even though it has been years since they've been together as a group, Jay knows for certain that her friends are lying to her.

16

1999

H ey, Bradelynne. Wait up."
Jay and Brandi paused in the school parking lot, caught by the unthinking authority of Amber's voice. They were on their way to house number four. This new house Charlie had located was exciting not just for its own purposes, but also as a step closer to the eighth house. Because the revelation of the final house—the Portal House—had lit a fire under all six of them. Another world existed, a trapdoor had opened in the known universe, and the entrance was somewhere in their very own town.

For now, they were still on earth, and they shared it with Amber Penske and Destiny Lautner. "What's up with you two lately?" Amber asked as they approached. Her hair was highlighted harshly, brown and blond stripes. "Why are you always with the rich kids?"

"Study group," Brandi blurted.

Jay winced; the cover story sounded stupid outside of their bubble, even though it was sort of true.

"So," Amber said, zeroing in on Brandi. "The Garnets hired your dad, and now they're taking pity on you? They're obsessed with trailer trash over there."

"Don't y'all like the Garnets?" Brandi asked.

"Those two walk around like their shit doesn't stink," Destiny said. "Nobody asked them to come here."

"The state pays them to be here, so *somebody* asked," Jay said.

"Okay, kiss-ass," Amber shot back. "Don't you think that money could go to someone else? Like Destiny. Her family's broke, can't they use it? Or does it have to go to someone who's not already here?"

"We aren't broke," Destiny snapped, unconvincing.

Jay wasn't sure what to say. From her perspective, the Garnets had brought a newness to Eternal, breathing adventure into every corner, but she couldn't think of a way to frame this to Amber, and anyway, Amber had a point, which was unusual enough to throw Jay off.

"I just mean," Amber said to Destiny, "that money could help with your hospital bills, or—"

"Quit it, Amber," Destiny said.

Jay knew that Destiny's health was an issue. There'd been a few months where Destiny came to school every day looking exhausted and crumpled, like she was carrying an invisible weight on her shoulders, and she'd fainted in gym class once.

"You should give the Garnets a chance," Brandi said. "They ain't bad people."

"Well, your weird dad was talking at the bar," Amber said. "The other night? He was talking about the creepy pictures they have in their house. All these naked ladies. Be careful, they're probably going to, like, human-traffic you. He said y'all are always running around together and hiding and shit."

"You don't know what you're talking about." Jay tried to sound withering, even as blood roared in her ears. She thought they'd been so careful to cover their tracks and never mention the Garnets in front of Gene.

"Just saying," Destiny said, "watch your backs, because those rich assholes will turn on you fast. You think they're your friends, but they aren't. I've seen it a thousand, thousand times."

"Max," Hilma said. "You cannot bring that thing in here."

"Her name is Lucky."

"Oh, well, if it has a *name*." When Max ignored her, Hilma sighed and pushed open the door. "Do not let it loose in here, I swear to god."

Lucky was a ball python. She had a condition called leucism, Charlie explained, a milder version of albinism, and she was beautiful, coiled around Max's shoulders, white scales shimmering like alien pearls. Brandi petted her head with one finger, cooing like Lucky was a fluffy lapdog.

"You couldn't get a nice cat or something?" Charlie asked.

"I got her at that reptile trailer by the freeway," Max said. "You'd never see a trailer full of snakes in Massachusetts. May as well have the full Arkansas experience." He pronounced it phonetically, *Ar-CAN-sis.*

"He's trying to prove he's an animal lover so Destiny will notice him."

Brandi's finger, stroking the back of the snake's head, faltered, and she exchanged an anxious look with Jay, who subtly shook her head. No need to bring Destiny and Amber into things.

Inside the fourth house, they clustered together. Jay had seen the journal entry. Theodora had scribbled ominous symbols, morphing along the margins. Crescent moons twisting into strange infinity symbols. It was Charlie who remembered seeing those shapes engraved in the eaves of a house on Sycamore Circle, close to his own home.

The place had been converted into a shop at one point, and the front still featured a big display window, papered over. Inside, metal shelves were knocked askew, scattered with leaves, cobwebs, animal droppings. The cash register was on the floor, drawers gaping and empty.

"What kind of store was it, again?" Hilma asked, kicking aside a discarded coat hanger.

"A thrift store." Jay had gone there with her dad a few times as a kid, combing through strangers' discards to find jeans Jay could *grow into*. Every time they went, they found different versions of the same ugly sweatshirts, as if the store had an unlimited supply of factory discards.

"Cool," Hilma said casually. "Love vintage."

When the main floor proved to be a disappointment, they headed downstairs. Jay scanned the walls for Theodora's signature. Max had promised whoever found it first a fresh fifty-dollar bill, and she'd already mentally spent it on a case of new markers. Fifty dollars for only ten colors, a ridiculous luxury.

In the basement, Jay spotted an ordinary-looking door, paint chipped. The shelf shoved haphazardly in front of the door caught her attention. Houses were different now, to her. Even the ordinary ones thrummed with potential power. She paid attention to the details, the doors with loose knobs, the faulty wiring in the dining room. She was learning houses' silent language, and the more un-inhabited they were, the more clearly that language came through.

"What's that lead to?" Jay asked, pointing.

"Nothing to do but find out." Max shouldered the shelf aside and opened the door, revealing yet another staircase, descending into a lower level. A swampy smell floated up.

"I've read about this," Charlie said, as they cautiously walked down the stairs. "There was another town built beneath Eternal. There used to be such a problem with flooding that they raised the buildings to avoid the runoff, and those old buildings are still just trapped down here, abandoned. There are entrances all over the city."

"Oh yeah," Iggy said. "When I joined the team, they made the new guys stay the night in some of those old tunnels. Spooky." At the bottom of the staircase he stopped, and Jay ran into him, feeling a slowed-down second of Iggy's warmth against her hips. "They scared me," he said. "Thought they were real."

Mannequins. Three of them, blank faces, smooth-crotched bodies the color of putty, pressed against one dank stone wall like a chorus line, next to a humped and grimy dropcloth that seemed hastily tossed over something large. There was a nest of silver high-heeled sandals against the opposite wall, a pile of pink blouses. The end result was that it appeared as if the mannequins had suddenly stripped naked. It was a stone cellar, a small nook, damp and strange.

"Don't tell me them things come to life," Brandi said.

"Now, now," Hilma said, walking into the sub-cellar. "It's not a *Twilight Zone* episode."

Max hummed the theme song, frenetic and off-key. Goose bumps popped up on Jay's arms. The mannequins' smooth, egg-shaped faces were tilted toward them at a curious angle.

Hilma paced back and forth, calculating. "What do you think? Spot anything weird?"

"They're naked mannequins," Charlie said. "Of course they're weird."

Jay moved closer, trying to find some pattern in the thrift store debris. Cautiously, she ran her hands over the gritty rayon, a moth-ball odor rising up. All five blouses were Pepto Bismol–pink, size M. The first two blouses were identical; the third one was flawed, one sleeve gone. The fourth blouse had the same missing sleeve, plus the collar was jagged and oversized. And the final one: the buttonholes were missing, the buttons melted clumps of plastic.

Jay remembered those morphing symbols along the edge of the page. Hair rose at the nape of her neck. Brandi knelt next to the sandals. "Hey. They're all left shoes."

She was right. The first two were normal, budget prom queen

gear. The third one started going wonky, the straps too thick, and the fourth shoe had a ten-inch heel jutting beyond the sole. Impossible to walk in, more like a sculpture of a shoe. The fifth had too many buckles, strange scribbles of metal, like somebody had tried to imitate a buckle and then gotten frustrated. Without thinking, Jay pressed her finger into a sharp tip.

"Hey, careful," Iggy said, reaching for Jay's hand. He lingered, holding her wrist carefully. Jay felt her heartbeat right where he touched her.

"It's like a game of telephone," she said, covering her fluster. "Remember that? When we were kids? Each one gets weirder and weirder."

From the corner, Charlie swore loudly. "The feet. The mannequin's—its *feet*."

The other two mannequins had the typical arched Barbie feet, toeless and tiptoed. The third mannequin, though. Its legs transformed into a set of hands, glossy fingers spread wide and groping at the end of its plastic ankles. Nausea ribboned Jay's throat.

"Shit, man. That is truly sick," Max said, delighted. "Are there more of them under here?" And he yanked away the dropcloth, conjuring a dusty glitter.

The fourth mannequin had melted-looking arms, trailing down past its knees, clustered all along their length with tentacle-like fingers, plastic nubs. The final mannequin was the worst. Multiple hands extending from its ankles, a new hand sprouting relentlessly from each smooth plastic palm. A stack of hands bent upward into stiff, curling loops.

Hilma walked up to the mannequins, stroking their lifeless cheeks in a show of bravery. "What do we think? The house copies them?"

"Sure seems so," Iggy said.

"Isn't this amazing? Back in Theodora's time, they didn't have Xerox machines or cut-and-paste on a PC. They still hadn't had the Industrial Revolution."

"Um, they were far beyond the Industrial Revolution," Charlie corrected.

"This is fucked up," Max said, still jubilant. "Like, does it duplicate everything? Is it gonna duplicate us?"

Jay imagined a version of herself limping out from the corner, a warped doppelgänger—four arms, a neck as long as a giraffe's, blank dead eyes. Her skin crawled, and without even thinking, she edged toward the stairway. Iggy appeared at her elbow, and she couldn't tell if he was guarding her or if he was worried too.

"This house seems weirder than the others, doesn't it?" she asked, realizing how far beneath the surface of normal life they'd sunk. "I mean, did Theodora know what she was doing?"

"Theodora wasn't building these houses just to be nice," Hilma said. "We can't assume all of them are fun and games. She was a complicated person."

"An evil genius," Max said.

"I don't reckon she was evil," Brandi piped up, and she was adamant enough that they all took notice. "Theodora wasn't an angel or nothing, but she also wasn't bad. She knew what she was doing. There must've been a reason for her to build this."

"You think so?" Hilma asked, looking intrigued. "Like Theodora was . . . what? Planning out these houses for specific people or something?"

"Why else would she build here in Eternal?" Brandi asked.

"Well, because she was institutionalized here." Hilma, very patient, was about to launch into her explanation of Theodora's escape into the anonymity of a boomtown. But Brandi was shaking her head, trying to explain what she meant:

"No, no, it's just—it's—I reckon Theodora chose to live here 'cause she wanted to help people. She must've made friends, right? She must have cared about Eternal, to stay here."

"Are you finding this from the journal?" Charlie asked. "Because I'm not seeing that."

"I mean, no, just—just thinking about the town. The way people know each other 'round here." Brandi shrugged, uncomfortable with the attention. "Anyway, I found the signature. Right there." On the ceiling, the words were rendered in dark brown tiles that matched the brick: *Hypocrite lecteur,—mon semblable,—mon frère!*

"Uh, it's—it's Baudelaire," Charlie said. His lips moved silently for a minute. "'Hypocrite reader, my . . . double, my brother.'"

"Who's Theodora calling a hypocrite?" Max joked. But Brandi was smiling at him, and he seemed to remember their bet. "Good job, Bran. Fifty dollars for you, madam." Max dug into his pocket, pulled out a crumpled bill, and tossed it to Brandi. "Catch."

Seeing the way Brandi shone with relief, Jay forgot all about the art markers.

"I've got a better idea than giving her fifty," Hilma said shrewdly. "What if we left that bill here? Next time you come back, you'd have a hundred dollars. The house will double it for you."

Jay watched Brandi waver, comparing the immediacy of the fifty-dollar bill with the uncertain promise of twice as much. "What do you think, Jay?" she whispered, and Jay shrugged, torn.

"Stop confusing her, Hil," Max said.

"It's sound financial advice," Hilma said. "Girls need to look out for each other."

Making a decision, Brandi knelt and tucked the bill beneath the closest blouse. "Do we just . . . wait for it to cook? Like it's a casserole or somethin'?"

"Let's come back every week and check," Hilma said. "That should give the house enough time to do whatever it's going to do."

"Okay, but I'm not giving you another fifty if somebody nicks this one," Max said. "Hilma's teaching you a financial lesson, so am I. Risk and consequences."

17

1999

THEN

A shadow fell across Jay's table, and Jay pulled the sketchpad closer, startled and protective. She'd been working out a rough sketch for the Duplication House picture. A self-portrait with six eyes, lining her face like a spider's.

She'd finally figured out her portfolio. The images came, and she drew until her fingers cramped, a pain she relished. It *should* hurt to create. In the Truth House, Jay drew herself with her mouth half open, the hot, hovering moment right before speaking. In the Mirror House, she was naked, one hand over her breasts, framed inside the gleam of a mirror, strangers crowding behind her without looking. In the Luck House, Jay wore a perfect white grin like a beauty queen's tiara. Jay liked to think she was tapping directly into what Theodora had left behind. Not just the magic, but Theodora's thorny creativity, the stubborn audacity of mixing worlds together.

"That's good," Charlie said. "Are you familiar with Leonora Carrington? Your work reminds me of hers, a little."

"I love her." Jay was embarrassed by how pleased the comparison made her.

Charlie sat next to her at the library table, and Jay showed him the rest of the sketchpad, her shoulder blades tingling with the quiet joy and terror of being looked at. When he reached the page with the naked self-portrait, Jay paused, uncertain. "Oh," Charlie said, amused. "Well. I love your shading here, but maybe don't show this one to the other boys."

So there was a small delineation between Charlie and the *other boys*. Jay, understanding that he'd just offered her a glimpse of the self he usually guarded, smiled at him. Then she imagined Iggy seeing this image; she went hot everywhere.

"Are you going to make a career out of this?" Charlie asked.

"I mean, yeah. I want to—to go to art school."

"RISD? Brown?"

For a moment she didn't even realize they were the names of schools. "I hadn't thought about it that much. Brandi and I just want to be artists, that's all."

"You're graduating in May, it's already October. You can't snap your fingers and get into a good school. Even if you could, it's expensive. Thousands and thousands, I mean. Sorry," Charlie said, noticing her expression. "But around here, it's not an expectation that people leave for college. You've got to advocate for yourself."

Jay's own face gazed back at her from the sketchpad, as if to say: *Am I enough to get you out of here?* After a second, though, she remembered that her future was rearranged, that college applications were part of another timeline, maybe a lesser one. The life in which she'd never met the Garnets and had no idea that another world waited for her somewhere. Her panic eased.

"Ask Hart," Charlie said. "She'll tell you about some scholarships."

"But, I mean, does it even matter? Because . . . you know."

"What?"

"The final house. The Portal House."

He straightened, looking around. The library was quiet at this time of day. A tenth-grader slept with his head between his crossed arms; on the walls, sun-bleached posters of Kim Basinger and Phil Collins implored them to read. "What are you saying, Jay?"

She dropped her voice to match his. "All this stuff, applying to colleges and moving away from Arkansas, it doesn't seem as important now that we can visit another world."

"Okay, but even if there is a portal, this world isn't going any-where. Theodora was a traveler, not a settler." He tapped the table-top. "This world will be waiting for us when we return."

Jay noticed that he used *if* to leave, but *when* to return. "Yeah. I guess."

"I'm not withdrawing my college applications. Those applica-tion fees nearly bankrupted us. My father would follow me to an-other world just to lecture me."

"But what if we want to stay? What if it's amazing there, or what if time moves differently, or what if—what if *we're* different there? Better people."

"What, like in Narnia? You think we'll be crowned royalty by the magical commoners?" Charlie was teasing, but a faint yearning was strung along his words. "Sorry, but look. If we find this Portal House at all, chances are we haven't been prophesied or foretold. We're not going to battle some ancient evil that can only be over-come by boring human teenagers. We'll take a look around and we'll come back home. Maybe we'll be gone a day or two. A week."

Jay was still unconvinced. For so long, she'd seen leaving Eternal Springs as the natural outcome of her teenage years. *Escape* seemed like something that would descend on her automatically. All the protagonists in the books she read, the movies she watched, got out of their tiny towns, made something of themselves. *This* could be Jay's true destiny. Not just escaping Arkansas, but slipping into a world she couldn't imagine yet.

"Anyway," Charlie said, "Theodora was only in Arkansas because of the sanitarium."

Jay balked. "If you still think she was crazy—"

"Not like that. I mean, we don't know what all that traveling did to her. The last house we found was . . . strange. Maybe some of them will be dangerous. Don't count on the Portal House as your escape until you know more about Theodora Trader and what she was doing with these houses."

Jay nodded silently, knowing he was right, resenting him for it a little.

"This is why Hilma shouldn't have told us about the final house yet," Charlie said, sighing. "Just . . . talk to Ms. Hart, okay? Just in case. Keep your options open, Dorothy Gale."

18

2015

NOW

"You've been here before, right?" Hilma asks as they settle at their table. They're by the window, a prime spot in the Francesco's dining room, the sunlight glancing across the glass.

"Just once." Jay's father had taken her to Francesco's as a graduation treat, but she'd been too numb to enjoy it. That was in late May of 2000, right after everything happened. All she could taste was blood; she'd chewed her lip to shreds, sprouted canker sores from the stress. Her dad had weakly attempted to talk up Jay's *fresh start*, and Jay could only silently obsess over everything she'd lost.

Now she examines the restaurant with new eyes. The soft, cracked oilcloth table coverings, the unlit candles inside red glass holders. The greenery outside the windows is rich enough that it takes away the need for elaborate decor. Jay should enjoy this. Once again, though, Brandi is all she can think about.

"Don't be nervous, Bluejay," Hilma says. "Pretend you're back in

Eternal to remind everyone that you got out. Like your own little high school reunion. That has to feel good."

Jay smiles stiffly. "Yup. I got out, all right."

"You have a solo show coming up." Hilma rests her chin on her hand. "Maybe I can get you an interview or something. Hook you up with my media contacts."

"No," Jay says quickly. "Your family has already done so much for me. I mean, the scholarship and everything."

"You haven't told me anything about your work."

"Just my standard stuff." Not precisely a lie. She hopes that Hilma will back off rather than admit she never paid much attention to Jay's work. Jay's not ready to discuss her show yet.

"Well, I'm impressed that you pursued art. It's a tough field to break into."

"How are your parents doing, anyway?" Jay asks, unable to resist.

Hilma smirks. "I'm paying you a compliment, Bluejay. When I last saw you, you weren't exactly in the mood to take on the world. But look at you. You have your career, your art. You're fine. Right?"

For a second, Jay almost comes clean. But she spots Amber over Hilma's shoulder, entering the dining room. When Amber sees their table, her automatic customer-service smile falls away and Jay sees a naked flash of worry. Then the mask is back, resting uneasily.

"Welcome to Francesco's, ladies," she says, approaching, apron in place over her black button-up. "My name's Amber, I'll be your server today. This your first time in Eternal?"

Hilma laughs. "I don't remember you being so funny. I'll have a Pellegrino. Oh, and Bluejay has some questions for you. About Brandi."

Amber's already suspicious, and if Jay starts babbling about photos and maps, she'll only make things worse for all five of them. "I was hoping you could tell me more about Brandi. You know, what was going on in her life before she—uh—vanished." Jay swallows under Amber's steady glare. There's a barrier between them now, genuine in a way that would shock her teenage self. Jay understands she was never really an outcast before; *this* is being an outcast. Really and truly separate from Eternal and all its tributaries of gossip, rumors, common knowledge.

"What about that guy she was seeing?" Hilma asks, leaning forward.

Jay's startled. Hilma hasn't mentioned anything about a *guy Brandi was seeing*.

Amber seems surprised too, her guard dropping. "You mean Roy?" she asks. And then she seems to realize, at the same time as Jay does, that Hilma was bluffing.

"Roy," Hilma repeats. "Right. How long has she been seeing him, again?"

Amber bites the inside of her cheek, a quick indent. "No idea. I'll get those drinks out to y'all." She turns and leaves, not looking back.

No idea. Too quick, too definitive. Almost certainly a lie. God, Jay misses the Truth House. Maybe Charlie knows the name of this paradox: when the very thing you need is the one thing that's been taken from you.

"She was chatting away with you before, wasn't she?" Hilma says. "Why so tight-lipped now?"

"That was before she knew all of us were back."

"Well, I'm not any happier about returning to Eternal than Amber is to see us. But don't worry, little Bluejay. We'll get her to open up."

When Amber returns, she sets down the water glass so hard that it splashes onto Jay's wrist. "Why do you care about Roy, anyway?" Amber asks, in the same tone she might ask for Jay's lunch order.

"All we want is to help Brandi." Hilma has shifted to a confiding, no-bullshit whisper. "The police around here are assholes, you know that. Brandi's friends know the real story."

"Uh-huh. Well, we can help Brandi just fine on our own. Thanks anyway."

"Understandable," Hilma says, reaching into her bag. She extracts her wallet, unclasps it, lays it on the table like a place setting. "In that case, I'll have the osso buco."

"Not on the menu. The special today is the lasagna sampler."

"Sure, why not? Two lasagna samplers. You've been so helpful, Amber. We're really grateful," Hilma says.

Amber's eyes move to the wallet, and a muscle in her cheek twitches. Jay catches on slowly. Lying inside the wallet, two hundred-dollar bills, green as new buds. So Hilma's found the exact spot where her interests converge with Amber's.

When Amber slips her order pad away, Jay spots the tattoos beneath her sleeve. Muddy-looking cursive names along with dates, ending in 2008, 2014. Kenzie and Jaxon. Amber has kids now.

"I'll have those samplers out to y'all in a jiffy," Amber says, and then adds quietly, "I can take my break out back. Five minutes."

Out behind Francesco's, the air is herbed with fresh garbage. Amber paces in front of the dumpsters. The slope of the forest rises upward from the thin alleyway, so steep it's almost vertical. It feels like this wall of greenery could smother them, a landslide of limbs and vines. Jay breathes deeply, distracted by Eternal's beauty for a surprising moment. She forgot how stunning this place can be. She's briefly irritated at her teenage self for assuming this beauty would always be hers for the taking.

"So. Roy," Hilma says, getting right to it. "Tell us what you know, Amber."

Amber scuffs the concrete with her white clog. "Hell, I barely know nothing about the guy. She seemed happy with him. Other'n that? He may as well've been a ghost."

"She was dating him?" Jay asks, focusing.

"Yup."

"Was it typical for Brandi to hide her relationships from you?"

"Nah. Usually we told each other everything. I was—I *am* one of her only friends."

"Why hide Roy, then?" Jay asks.

"Hell if I know. Maybe it was his idea. He seemed fucking weird."

Roy could be a lead; Roy could be somebody important.

"What about other boyfriends?" Hilma asks. "Was Brandi seeing anybody before Roy?"

"Why?" Amber shoots back. "You want her whole dating history?"

"Please, you can never trust an ex," Hilma says. "Nine times out of ten, a vanished woman can be traced right back to some misogynistic loser."

Amber considers this grimly. "She, uh—she'd broken up with Kenny a year or so ago."

"Kenny Stringer?" Jay asks, surprised. "He went to our high school. He worked at the Pizza Hut," she adds for Hilma's benefit.

"The Pizza Hut," Amber says, and laughs. "Sure, that's where he worked like ten years ago. That's never where he made his money, though."

"Oh, the dealer," Hilma says. "Okay. Go on. They broke up?"

Amber nods. "Kenny always reckoned she'd go back to him. They were off and on all the time. But when Roy came along, Brandi ended things for good, and Kenny was pissed."

"Have the police questioned him already?" Jay asks.

"First thing. He's over in Fayette now. Said he hadn't been back to Eternal all month."

It's a leaky alibi. Fayette is only a forty-five-minute drive; plenty of people commute that distance every day. "How can we get in touch with him?" Hilma asks.

A longer pause. "Shit. He might be at the party tonight," Amber says at last. "Kenny'll never turn down a party. You could try to talk to 'im there, but I'm telling you, be careful. People ain't happy to see you back. Don't tell anybody I'm the one who told y'all."

Jay thinks of the shadow beneath the shed door; her breath feels trapped for a second.

"Where's the party?" Hilma asks.

When Amber gives the address, Jay recognizes it at once, and Hilma must also have it memorized, because she smiles, knowing. "In that case, we'll definitely be there," Hilma says.

"I've told y'all everything I know," Amber says. "I gotta get back to my shift."

"You've told us about an ex-boyfriend who might be at a party, and a current boyfriend who's a 'ghost.' We need more than that," Hilma argues. "Have you seen anyone suspicious around town?"

"Yeah, I've seen some suspicious folks around. All five of you came crawling back. Anyone can see it ain't a coincidence."

"You're right. It's not a coincidence," Jay says, a burst of desperate honesty. "But we're here to help our friend. That's all."

Amber gazes back into the forest as if asking the trees to bear witness to Jay's stupidity. "Help? Now? Where were you when she got thrown in jail, or when she ODed, or when she dated assholes who treated her like garbage? Why weren't you here when she—"

"All right," Hilma says, "thanks for your help, but spare us the lecture." She hands Amber the money, and Amber flicks through the bills, her face hard with yearning and shame. Hilma turns to leave.

But Amber says, "Jadelynne. Can you wait up? Without her." She sounds grudging, like she'd rather not do this. Jay glances wordlessly at Hilma, who nods her approval and then vanishes back inside.

Without the bracing presence of Hilma, Jay feels exposed. Small and uncertain in all the ways she was as a teenager, with a new layer of adult weariness.

Amber stares her down. "You look different. Your teeth."

Jay smiles, close-lipped. She waits for the point.

"You never even called her," Amber says, voice fierce now, low. "I guess Brandi wasn't good enough for you anymore. You were running off to your fancy life, you couldn't let folks know you were best friends with a junkie murderer from Arkansas."

"I—it's—people fall out of touch with their high school friends," Jay says, ignoring her racing heartbeat. "I mean, have you stayed in touch with Destiny Lautner?"

"She has her own shit now," Amber says gruffly, and Jay knows that Destiny's in Los Angeles, or New York, struggling to keep track of her old dreams, and Arkansas is a distant relic of her past. "She always knew she'd get out."

"See? It happens to the best of us," Jay says.

Amber sniffs. "Y'all are asking about Roy and Kenny when *everyone* in this town knows that you had something to do with this. I know it. The five of you."

There it is. The accusation overturned between them, sticky and staining. Jay stays calm, with effort. "Amber. How is that even possible? We haven't been back to Eternal Springs since 2000, we couldn't have hurt Brandi—"

"You've been back," Amber interrupts. "Not you, Jay. But some of y'all. Like the blonde's creepy brother. I've seen him skulking around. Can't miss him, he's nine stories tall."

Max. She means Max. Here in Eternal Springs. But he would've mentioned. He would have said something. Of all of them, he and Hilma had the least reason to be back in Eternal Springs. It must be a mistake.

"He didn't tell you?" Amber presses, examining her face. "Of course he didn't. Don't waste your time askin' me questions, Jadelynne. Ask your little friends."

19

1999

Jay stood on the sidewalk, cowed. The house pounded with music, distorted to pure bass, vaguely recognizable as Christina Aguilera's "Genie in a Bottle." It would be easier to walk into another world than join this afterparty. The house had a roof that sloped over each of the front windows, like dozing eyelids. Beneath that, each window glowed a dull red with Halloween string lights.

Jay had never gone to homecoming before. When Iggy invited them to the party, Jay assumed he was joking. "Are you allowed to go to the afterparty if you don't go to the dance?" she'd asked, and Max had repeated the word "allowed" and laughed, and Hilma had explained that this was the *only* way to observe homecoming without losing self-respect.

Jay wore one of her mother's peasant dresses, embroidered black flowers crawling along the neckline. The girls brushing past wore body glitter, plastic butterflies nesting in their hair, and Jay felt old-fashioned, a dark splotch. At first she fell back on the soothing vision of her future in New York City or Los Angeles, surrounded by people who'd appreciate her idiosyncracies. Then she shifted, saw herself somewhere farther away, wilder, weirder. A world so unfamiliar that she'd be remade too.

"There you are." Hilma bumped into Jay, jolting her back to reality. "Gene gave me and Brandi a ride here. And I managed to nab a little bonus from my parents." Hilma produced a bottle of bourbon from her coat pocket, waggled it.

"Gene knows you're friends?" Jay looked at Brandi, startled.

She half expected Hilma to correct her. Such a plain, vulnerable word, *friends*. "Of course he does," Hilma said, as if it would never not be true.

"Wish you'd come with us, Jay," Brandi said.

"Oh please," Hilma said. "You two can be apart for half an hour, it won't kill you."

"Where's Max?" Jay asked.

"Going solo. He doesn't want us embarrassing him in front of what's-her-face. I hope he brought protection. The last thing we need is Max leaving a love child in Eternal."

Iggy and Charlie approached. Charlie looked like he was being led to a guillotine. "You better have a damn good reason for dragging us to this party," he said to Iggy. "You've never been bullied by these people."

"They won't bully you," Iggy said, amiably confused. "I promise, guys, this is going to be fine. Better than fine."

"Whose house is this, again?" Jay asked. She knew it was the party house, a place she'd never really considered visiting, a place she'd never been invited to.

"Kids just come here when we want to drink and stuff. Not my scene."

Jay examined Iggy as he pushed his curls off his forehead. He was bright-eyed, almost feverish-looking. He still hadn't acknowledged any of them in a public setting. Was he going to walk into this house and immediately pretend he didn't know them?

Iggy plucked Hilma's bottle out of her hands. "Nah. You won't need that, trust me."

"Ugh, don't go straight-edge on us," Hilma called after Iggy, but he was running up the long stone staircase that led into the mouth of the house, vanishing through the door.

Jay was braced for dirty looks the moment they walked in, a record-scratch of contempt, but the kids closest to the door merely nodded at them, so friendly she turned her head to see if a more popular group had followed them in.

Hilma wrinkled her nose. "Love that eau de cat pee."

It was a ripe pit of odors, including what Jay nervously suspected was weed, a scent like the mulchy forest floor. The house was even less furnished than Brandi's trailer. A premature jack-o'-lantern had an unlit cigarette dangling from its mealy grin. Everywhere, bottles—some half-full, some doubling as ashtrays. There was a palpable neglect hanging in the air, something Jay recognized from Brandi's home. A pervasive, electric sense that no responsible adults would intervene in whatever happened.

It seemed to take a long time to get to the kitchen, the hallways narrow, people pushing in on all sides. Jay stumbled into the kitchen, finally, the light here harshly fluorescent. Somehow, they'd lost Iggy. There was a crowd, people perched on the countertops, sitting cross-legged in the nook where defunct fridge hookups sprouted from the wall. Max towered over Destiny, whose blond ringlets wilted along her shoulders. He was showing her some card trick, but he was fumbling. An ace of hearts fluttered to the floor.

Amber leaned in one corner, her cobalt satin dress exploding into feathers. Her date was Kenny, who homed in on Jay. "Nice dress," Kenny yelled, twitching Jay's skirt. "Like a hot Wednesday Addams."

"God, Kenny. You'd hit on anything." Amber burped delicately into her fist.

"This is our last chance to party. It's all ending after this, baby."

"What do you mean?" Jay asked, feeling glossy and blurry, like her brain had been dipped in Destiny's body glitter. She thought maybe Kenny meant the Portal House. Maybe *everyone* was heading into another dimension, an Eternal Springs field trip.

"Y2K," Kenny said. "It's the end of the world as we know it. Don't be on a plane at midnight. You hear they're all gonna crash out of the sky?" He mimed a dive, an explosion.

In Jay's other ear, Destiny scoffed. "No way. I'm not dying at seventeen. I'm getting the fuck out of this town. If I gotta die on January first, I'll die in California."

"We have a vacation home in Laurel Canyon, you're welcome at our place," Max said, his voice at a weird, unsteady volume. Jay wondered how much he'd had to drink.

"Do you know any famous people?" Destiny asked him.

"Faye Dunaway bought one of my parents' pieces," Max offered. "In the eighties." When Destiny stayed blank-faced, he went on. "Um, my parents know Ida? Ida Applebroog?"

"Are you making shit up?" Destiny demanded. "No. How about, like, Freddie Prinze Jr. or that Van Der Beek guy or something? Someone who can actually help my career."

The room swirled, tilted, righted itself. Usually Jay would've been closing herself off, frantically boarding her walls against potential cruelty: instead, she was flinging her windows open. "You're going to be so good, Destiny," she said, magnanimous. "You're going to be the best."

Destiny blinked rapidly. "Uh. Okay. Thanks? I guess." Her eyes roved over Jay. "You—you look nice tonight."

"Thanks," Jay said, flush with goodwill.

"She's stunning," Max said, though he was smiling down at Destiny.

"Wow, a little lovefest." Amber's voice was too loud, pitched all wrong. "Is that why y'all are always hanging out together, Jadelynne? You're his girlfriend?"

"We're just friends," Jay said. Again, she picked up on the crackling awareness that anything could happen. It tilted back and forth between warm and dangerous.

Brandi tried to step backward and stumbled; Amber pounced on this. "Oh my god, little Bradelynne's totally soused," Amber said. "Following in your daddy's footsteps, huh?"

"Gene's not my dad," Brandi said.

"Oh yeah. 'Cause he's your boyfriend, huh?"

"Leave her alone." Jay was about to point out that Amber had been drinking too, but then she saw that a little plastic butterfly was sliding along one of Amber's tendrils of hair, wavering right over the petals of her mascara-stiff lashes. It struck Jay as so funny that she began laughing. Everyone was staring, but she couldn't stop, clutching at the countertop for support.

Where was Iggy? Why had he brought them here?

Charlie leaned over, clutching his stomach. "I'm going to—I'm going to be sick."

"I got you, man," Max said. "Take deep breaths."

"Someone's spiked our drinks." Charlie stared around the kitchen, wild-eyed and ashen. "This isn't right. We've been—it's fluni—"

For a moment everyone stared at Charlie. Kenny gave him space.

"It's flunitraze— We've been drugged," Charlie managed.

"But," Jay said, the thought emerging slowly, "we don't even have drinks."

Charlie stared down at his empty hands. The truth of it spread across his face. Jay felt increasingly light, like she could skid away, bop against the ceiling like a balloon. She dropped to the floor, hugging her knees to her chest to root herself.

"Why are y'all even *here?*" Amber asked, something new in her voice, a hot glitter like broken glass under the words. "You think every house belongs to you now? 'Cause Kenny saw y'all walkin' out of that house near the library. You've been breaking-and-entering, and I know why."

"Leave it," Destiny said half-heartedly.

Jay's pent-up laughter hurt now, like it would snap a rib if she didn't let go soon. But she sensed that Amber was out for blood. Could they know about the houses?

"Y'all are trying to find a new home for Addams," Amber said, "so she can finally move out of the trailer park."

Charlie and Brandi and Jay, Hilma and Max, looked at each other, a quick Morse code. Jay laughed in a helpless burst, her face too close to the dingy kitchen tiles. Theodora's houses were still their secret. Theirs. Always. She didn't quite know why she was laughing: Relief? Shock? But she couldn't stop herself, and didn't want to—

"How is that funny, Jadelynne?" Amber asked. "You can hang out with whoever you like, but you're still trash like the rest of us. Your drawings ain't gonna save you."

"Hey. Stop it."

The room went quiet as Iggy came into the kitchen, his hair ruffled. His walk was off-kilter, but his face was determined. He dropped next to Jay. "You okay?"

"Yeah." She realized too late that her cheeks were wet. She tried to explain to Iggy that she'd been crying from laughter, that the tears weren't real.

Iggy helped Jay to her feet and looked around the kitchen. Destiny stood unsteadily, grabbing at Amber's arm for support. "What are you doing, Iggy?" Destiny asked, voice soft with surprise. "You know her?"

"We're friends." No hesitation.

"Friends." Amber's gaze skipped across both their faces. "Is this what you've been doing? That's why you've been ditching us."

"We miss you, man," Kenny said, mock-wistful.

Here was Iggy's chance to realign himself with his old life. Easy, familiar, just waiting for him. "Yeah, well, things change." Iggy turned away, still holding on to Jay. "I have to show you something, remember? It's upstairs."

He didn't have to explain who he was addressing. The others watched as they broke off, one by one: Hilma, Max, Charlie, and Brandi, their new grouping, public for the first time. Jay held on tight to Iggy.

They moved in silence through the dreamlike, red-washed rooms. Iggy led them upstairs to a bedroom. The noise dimmed up here. The designation "bedroom" was mostly due to a saggy air mattress, a flotsam of condom wrappers and cigarette butts against the baseboards. A makeshift tapestry of shabby tie-dye sagged across one wall.

Iggy rose onto his tiptoes, grabbing one end of the tapestry and tearing it down. A gritty cloud of dust rose, and all six of them coughed, swatting the air. When Jay felt safe opening her eyes again, faint words swam on the newly revealed wall. She blinked. The words were real, engraved into the brick. "'I taste a liquor never brewed,'" Jay read aloud.

"Emily Dickinson," Hilma said. "Yeah, I beat you to it, Charles."

Something broke through Jay's fuzziness. "Is—is this one of Theodora's houses?"

"That's why I took you here. Kids come here because they want to get wasted. These parties get you blackout-drunk after, like, two hours." Iggy stumbled, as if proving his point. "One time, I came just to hang, not drinking or anything. I had a big game the next day. And I *still* woke up the next day with a hangover. I was pissed at Kenny for days, I thought he'd slipped me something."

"Did you check the journal?" Hilma flopped onto the filthy air mattress. Jay stared. Normally Hilma would sooner have crawled face-first into poison ivy than sit there.

"Yeah. Charlie let me take a look the other day." Iggy aimed a high five at Charlie, and Charlie wobbled away, seasick. "Theodora wrote about a house that can make you—what was it? 'Overcome.' I thought that was a weird word, *overcome*. I was looking at her sketches of the house, trying to figure out where it was, and she wrote that the house had a 'jerkinhead' roof. I researched it at school. This place has a roof with that shape."

"Like sleepy eyelids," Jay supplied, remembering the front of the house.

Iggy grinned at her. "Totally. I thought, hey, maybe this place is one of Theodora's? Maybe it makes you 'overcome' by whatever you're smoking or drinking."

"Or not drinking," Max added. "High on life, baby."

"At the turn of the century," Charlie offered, "*overcome* could mean 'intoxicated.'"

"Listen to our resident nerd," Hilma said from the air mattress. "Even drunk, he's a walking dictionary."

"You're amazing, Iggy," Jay said impulsively, and he beamed. "You're like a detective. This is our fifth house. The High House. More than halfway there."

"I reckon we should get out of here," Brandi said. "I don't like a house that makes folks forget what they do. Can we go?"

Through her haze, Jay peered at Brandi, struggling to identify the look on her face. She wasn't flushed or glassy-eyed or grinning like the rest of them. Brandi looked resolute, chin lifted, eyes sliding away from Jay's attempt to meet her gaze. It took a moment for Jay to pinpoint it. It was the look Brandi got when Gene'd been drinking, the look she got when her mother was in town and flurrying with anger or trying too hard to be the fun mom. Brandi was trying to disappear.

"Yeah," Jay said. "Yeah, we should go."

As they filed back through the living room—the press of bodies, the bone-rattle of the bass—Jay felt a cresting swell of amazement.

This was the first time she'd been inside one of Theodora's houses with people who didn't realize they were caught in its power. These guinea pigs, laughing, flirting, vomiting, brains fattened with dopamine from another world.

For a moment she wondered about the thrift store owners who'd left town, and the previous owners of the Luck House. Where they went; what happened to them. Brandi's insistence that Theodora must have built the houses with a specific purpose burned hot in Jay's mind, but she was too spun-around to make anything of it.

When they were almost to the door, there was a sudden shout. Destiny zeroed in on Iggy. "Ignacio," she called. "Is this why you gave up being homecoming king? Really?"

He didn't answer. They were outside, in the clean night air. A headache popped up behind Jay's eyes, her giddiness crumbling at the edges.

"Homecoming king," Hilma repeated. "No. Our Iggy isn't a homecoming king. That's for people with no imagination and no way out. He's the king of home-leaving. The king of away-going." Standing on the step above him, she brushed his curls off his forehead, looking down like she was laying a sword on a knight's shoulder. "Stick with us, kid, and you're going to be royalty in a place those idiots can never imagine."

20

2015

NOW

The house is visible from a block away, the same as their high school days. But as they move in a pack past the other houses, Jay notes the changes. The houses of her memory are swapped for charcoal-gray exteriors, boxy shrubs. Generic. These houses could be picked up, dropped anywhere in the country, and make roughly as much sense.

Max stops them a few doors down. "Let's go in with a plan. Be friendly, but don't reveal too much. Ask more questions than you answer."

Jay examines his broad, handsome face, looking for a sign that he's hiding something. She can't stop obsessing over what Amber Penske told her about Max being back earlier—a lie, a mistake, or is he hiding something?

"People won't make trouble," Hilma says. "Anyone who's partying on a Monday night in Arkansas is going to be too drunk to care."

"You've never met a mean drunk?" Iggy asks.

"That's why we keep things as friendly as possible," Max says. "Kenny is the main point. Whoever spots him first, get him alone, okay?"

Jay catches Iggy silencing a call. Elle's face briefly fills his screen, caramel-soft highlights, sweet smile. She looks like a kind person. A normal person. How much has Iggy told his fiancée? Is Jay just a *high school sweetheart*? An *ex-girlfriend*? Somehow, what existed between them was both too small and too big for those terms.

"How do we keep from getting messed up ourselves?" Charlie asks.

"Keep your head about you," Max says. "And be quick."

Inside the house, the narrow hallways are emptier than Jay remembered. People are chatting amicably enough in different corners. Most guests are in their thirties now. Jay doesn't see any high schoolers, which is one small mercy. People look at the five of them with a vague curiosity. But there's none of the distrust and fear Jay bumped against at the vigil.

This will be fine. Fine. The High House will protect them, in its twisted way.

Jay hesitates in the front room, afraid to walk alone among these not-quite-strangers. She already feels the tug of the house's influence. She didn't realize she was so tightly coiled until her body unwinds against her will. Charlie smiles wanly at a woman with a septum piercing, who pantomimes for him to follow her down a hallway. Hilma and Max have already vanished. The bass quivers beneath her soles. Jay bumps into the edge of a couch. She attempts to focus: *Get answers. Get out of here.*

"Jay." Iggy's voice at her elbow. Turning, she sees him at her side, his deep brown eyes intent on hers. She has a sudden, vivid memory of the first time they were in the High House together, and the way he claimed them, *her.*

"Can we stick together?" he asks. "I'm not looking forward to this, honestly."

"Yeah. God, of course."

Jay can feel the High House trying to upend her, like an incoming tide tugging gently at her ankles. In unspoken agreement, they head into the crowd, merging slowly, brushing cautiously against people, making eye contact that feels nervous at first until it becomes more natural. Faces pull in a bright string through Jay's mind, half-remembered, people who've been playing bit roles in her dreams and memories and fears all this time. Old classmates, tangential friends. So many have stuck around town. When they see her, there's sometimes a flicker of recognition, and Jay knows she's stayed in their memories as well. The role she's played has likely been darker, stranger.

Iggy's being hailed left and right. Jay's not sure why he was nervous about coming. Everybody seems glad to see him. The hometown hero returning, the local boy who made good. *Igs, Iggy, Igster*, a chorus trying to snag his attention. Jay pushes through the blurriness to remember their purpose here.

Kenny. That's who they need.

Iggy ducks into a circle, and suddenly they're part of something. It's a group of people Jay kind-of, sort-of knows. No Kenny. Jay double-checks before she forgets again. But the conversation closes around them as if this group has just been waiting for Jay and Iggy. Iggy keeps his arm around her, and Jay leans into him. This is fine, good. Someone must be fighting for control of the iPod, because it's switched from Maroon 5 to Robert Smith crooning that heaven knows he's miserable.

"Just like old times," Iggy says. "God, it's a lot of the same old crew, huh?"

"Yeah, we didn't let the kiddos take this place over," someone says casually. Judd? Jay thinks it's Judd; she sat next to him in middle school, watching him create gum stalactites beneath his desk. "They tried, but we were like, nah, man, get your own place. This is *ours*." Before Jay can process this, Judd is saying, "Jadelynne Carr! We were asking if you're a hotshot artist yet."

"Not yet," Jay says, good-natured. "I'm working on it."

"Remember us when you make it big."

The conversation goes careening toward all the Eternal Springs residents who've done things in the world. Someone who played football for Oklahoma State. The girl who worked for Mike Beebe. The tone swings between admiring and contemptuous. They bring up Charlie: nobody here understands exactly what he does, but they know he's in New York City, a feat in and of itself.

"I'm always looking for Destiny," a woman with choppy bangs says. "On commercials and whatnot. She was so fucking pretty. How is she not Jennifer Aniston yet?"

"She was so pretty," Jay agrees.

"God, everybody leaves this town," the woman says. Jay half remembers her: Casey? Carey? "It's not such a bad place, is it? It's kinda special."

"Now you sound like Brandi," Judd says. Jay recognizes it as an inside joke, and though she joins in the laughter, she realizes that everyone here knows a side of her former best friend that she's never seen. The room shivers like a living thing.

"Why? What did Brandi say?" asks Jay.

"That this place is fuckin' magic."

"Magic?" Iggy speaks lightly, but his arm around Jay's waist tightens.

"I mean, she's crazy as hell," Judd says. "But, god, she has an imagination on her. She makes you believe in things. Like you can just reach out and grab magic out of the air." He mimes snatching at Jay, palm nearly touching her hair, and she laughs. *Magic.* Absurd.

"What kind of magic?" Iggy asks.

He's more pointed now, but nobody else seems to notice. "Oh, you know," Judd says. "Weird shit. Like—like you can only tell the truth."

This is bad, wrong, but Jay's too fuzzy-headed to stop the conversation.

The woman—Caroline?—points at Jay. "Didn't y'all used to play a game like that?"

"Yes." Jay's charmed that this almost-stranger remembers. "Our little game. God, that was a million years ago."

"You two were always off doing something crazy and not letting anyone else join you."

"I used to get Brandi and you mixed up," Judd volunteers.

"Yeah, we got that a lot," Jay says. "I mean, we were best friends. Bradelynne."

Judd and maybe-Caroline exchange quick glances. It's enough for Jay to realize that she's been outmaneuvered; in her dozy state, she's walked right into a trap. But it's true that she and Brandi used to be best friends. They used to wear necklaces that said so.

"You ran the moment you turned eighteen." Judd makes a sound effect that reminds Jay, hilariously, of Wile E. Coyote racing off a cliff. "I've always wanted to ask: What really happened during senior year?"

Here it is. This is what Jay's feared. But the magic is too powerful, the music plucking her attention away. "What do you mean?"

"Do you think Brandi really did it? Really killed Gene?"

"Oh god," Casey-or-Caroline says, her voice long-suffering. "He's going to tell you his conspiracy theory."

"They never found his body, okay?" Judd says, getting into this, stepping back and holding up his hands. "And now Brandi disappears, same as him? Brandi'd never leave town. Not ever. That's what makes this all so fucked up."

The empty trailer, striped with blood. Brandi: gone. For a second, the horror of it grabs Jay by the neck, and then the tipsiness rushes back in.

"There's something real weird about how Gene vanished," Judd says. "Something they aren't telling us."

"*They?*" Iggy repeats.

"Her stepdad never showed up?" Judd says, ignoring him.

"Never-ever? Not any sign of 'im. Brandi swore up and down she didn't do it. But Gene's never come back. Seems awfully weird to me, that's all."

Iggy tenses against Jay, a twitch.

"What it makes me think," Judd continues, "is that Brandi didn't do nothing to Gene. And whoever did . . . maybe they came back for her? Because she was going to squeal. Does that sound crazy?"

Iggy doesn't answer. The silence stretches.

"It really does," Jay says, and somehow, she and maybe-Caroline are laughing together until Jay's eyes flood with tears. "It sounds so crazy."

Judd leans forward, pupils enormous. "My two cents? If we can get to the bottom of what happened to Gene, we'll find Brandi."

"You and your stupid conspiracies," Casey-or-Caroline says. "We all know that Brandi killed Gene. And we all know he deserved it."

Jay's pulled under by a warm, slippery wave of hysteria. She's had nightmares about this exact scenario, she's woken up sweat-drenched and screaming, but now she doesn't know why she was ever afraid. She could just tell them. Right here, right now. Yell out: *I know exactly what happened to Gene.*

She opens her mouth—

"All right," Iggy says. "We need to mingle." He backs away, pulling Jay with him.

They're moving down the hallway, bouncing against humid bodies. Hands grazing Jay's ass, maybe-accidentally. A woman in a red dress emerges from a bathroom, and Iggy seamlessly pulls Jay in behind him, locks the door. "Listen," he says, his voice loud in the sudden quiet. "This is worse than we thought. Brandi told people."

"About—about Gene?"

"About the houses."

In the mirror above the sink, Jay's cheeks are stained with brightness. She's standing so close to Iggy, whose curls are damp against his neck. He's becoming less of a memory and more of a reality by the second. Their hips brush as Jay leans back against the sink basin.

"You think she'd do that?" The music purrs under the door, seeking them out.

"She was talking about magic," Iggy says, slowly, like he's trying to remember. "We have no clue who else knows about Theodora's houses. And Judd's theory about Gene. What if they start looking into—"

"Hey. Shh." Unthinking, Jay interrupts him with a finger over his lips.

Energy moves between them, a hard zap. Who cares if people know? Who cares, who cares? She's here with Iggy, and he's between her legs, his body pressed against her thighs, and she's not sure who starts it, but she's pulled into the kiss. Somebody pounds on the door, and his hands are in her hair, and the past fifteen years are nothing, gone. An illusion, a mistake.

It lasts forever. It lasts no time at all. The equation of their bodies has changed since they were young, more assured and more hesitant at once. Some raw sweetness swapped out for a polish and confidence, and Iggy is tracing her inner thigh, and her hand's cupping the back of his neck—

He pulls away first. "No, wait. That wasn't supposed to happen."

She tries to remember why she can't kiss him, but everything is swirling lights. She's drunker than she's been in a long time, her whirring anxiety slowed to a delicious sludge.

Iggy leans close again, breath stirring her hair. "Jay? We need to get out of here."

They split up. Leaving the bathroom, Iggy veering to the left, Jay to the right, splitting apart physically as if that will break the connection between them, as if it's ever been that easy. Jay's not sure if it's been minutes or hours since she set off into the crowd alone. She's damp with her own sweat, other people's sweat, spilled drinks, her smell yeasty and ripe and sweet. Jay scans the blurry, smiling faces rippling past, hoping one of them will remind her of what she's supposed to be doing here.

"There you are." A hand on her shoulder as she shoves sideways through a group. "Jay, we gotta get out of here. Abort mission. Do you know where the others are?"

Max. He's flushed pink, blond hair damp, eyes in constant motion over her head. He tugs her closer, protecting her from the tidal pull of the crowd.

"The others? No, I—no, I was—"

"Kenny isn't here," Max says, tilting his head to speak directly into her ear. "He found out we were coming and he decided not to show. I think we've been set up."

Set up. Looking at Max Garnet, Jay's reminded of something else. She's alone with him, and her inhibitions are stripped to nothing. "Have you been back in town?" she yells.

"Sorry? What?" Max squints. "Did you hear what I said about Kenny? We—"

"I'm asking, have you been back in Eternal?" Max shakes his head, and Jay can't tell if he's denying it, or if he can't hear her, so she screams it right at him, "Amber said she saw you here in Eternal. Before Brandi's disappearance."

Max straightens, and his whole face changes, fear tightening his features. "Fuck," he mutters, staring past her. "Fuck fuck *fuck.*"

Slowly, she turns.

A police officer stands in the doorway, stiff and formal against the crowd. Pell. Jay feels a rush of nostalgia that's almost friendly, at the sight of his stern eyebrows, his steady squint. When he sees her with Max, Pell edges forward. He points at them. "You," he calls, his voice traveling over the music. People are noticing now, dancers stumbling to a stop, conversations falling quiet as Pell cuts a path through the bodies. "You're needed at the station."

Max places a hand on his chest: *Who, me?*

"Max," Jay whispers, staring up at him, his pale hair red in the lights, "oh, Max, what the hell have you done?"

"Hey. Hey, I'm talking to you." And it takes Jay a strange, suspended moment to recognize that Pell doesn't care about Max at all, that he's looking right at her.

21

1999

THEN

The moment of truth," said Hilma. They stood in the Duplication House basement, the warped mannequins watching them like they were all old friends now. Brandi knelt, lifting the edge of the blouse. Jay almost couldn't look. Discarded money didn't usually last around here; in the Ozarks, you held on to something when you got it.

But the money was there. Still safe. Brandi beamed.

"Well?" Hilma nudged. "Is there another one?"

Jay had almost forgotten that the second bill was the whole point. Brandi reached deeper under the pile of blouses and extracted another fifty-dollar bill, identical down to the same faded marker stripe near Grant's cocked eyebrow.

"I have a hundred dollars. A hundred. Jay, you should take half," she said, turning around impulsively.

"Brandi, no," Jay said. "It's yours."

"Well, neither of you should spend it yet. Max and I were talking. What if people can tell it's counterfeit? We could get caught, they'd ask questions, someone would squeal, blah blah. Then this whole thing would be over before we ever find the portal. It's not worth it."

Jay imagined the manager at the 7-Eleven running an ultraviolet light over the bill. It was hard to picture how someone like Jay's dad or Officer Pell would react, but adults had the power to control all kinds of impossible, intangible things. Sex, hope, freedom: magic would go the same way.

Slowly, Brandi tucked the bills back under the blouse. "Yeah. I don't wanna ruin anything. If there's some pacific way they can tell." Hilma flicked her eyes to Jay at Brandi's mispronunciation, her smile conspiratorial. Jay smiled back, automatically pleased at Hilma's attention, before she caught herself, guilty.

Brandi was silent as they ascended the stairs, back to the main level. "Cheer up, Brandi," Hilma said. "Is this about the drama with Gene?"

"Drama?" Jay repeated. "What drama?"

"Oh, I forgot to tell you," Brandi mumbled.

Jay was startled at the idea of Hilma and Brandi having secrets that Jay didn't know about. For most of Jay's life, her knowledge of the world had lined up perfectly with Brandi's.

"Gene killed the Chinese holly," Hilma volunteered. "My parents had to dock his pay."

That explained Gene's sour mood lately, hanging over the trailer like a poisonous fog. "I'm sorry," Jay said to Brandi, who smiled at her. Jay resolved to pay more attention.

"Why?" Hilma asked. "It's not her fault."

There was something about the way Hilma said it, her confusion so straightforward. How could it be Brandi's problem if it wasn't her fault? Jay had seen that alchemy happen a dozen times, the way the slights that Gene absorbed from the world would manifest, a few days or weeks later, in Brandi getting yelled at, punished. But for a moment, Jay let herself be pulled in by Hilma's confidence: maybe it was true, maybe Brandi didn't have to be involved at all.

22

2015

NOW

The police station is the same, right down to the pattern of dust on the artificial ficus. Sitting in a pebbly plastic chair, Jay could be eighteen again. Officer Pell seemed so old when Jay was a teenager, but now she realizes he can't be more than sixty. Which means he was only in his forties the last time Jay sat in this room and made a decision that cracked her world in two. She wonders if he's remembering the same thing. There's definitely a self-satisfied look to him, like he always knew it was only a matter of time before she was back.

Max offered to come with Jay, but she refused. It's nine at night, and the High House's high is wearing off with a jackhammer force. Jay feels gray, shaky. All she wants is to be curled up on a hotel bed with an ice pack and a handful of ibuprofen.

Pell clears his throat. "I'm sure you can guess why you're here. Brandi Addams. Sad business."

Jay can't imagine his relationship with Brandi improved much over the years. She takes a sip of gritty coffee.

"It must be strange being back," Pell says. "Been a long time."

God, she can't throw up here. She eyes the distance to the wastebasket. Pell is speaking conversationally, but anything she says in here potentially turns into a trap.

"When's the last time you were in contact with Bran—with Miss Addams?"

"Uh." She focuses. "Um. Not for a while."

"But you're here now. Nice of you to fly all this way."

Jay shrugs. That's her, all right, the nicest friend that ever there was.

"So why did you come here to Eternal? If you don't mind me asking."

"I heard that an old friend was in trouble," Jay says.

"Heard from who?"

From Brandi herself. "Uh, I heard it on the news."

"See, that's the thing. The only thing that strikes me as funny . . ."

Is that you would come back to see a girl you haven't contacted for fifteen years. Jay's so prepared for what Pell will say next that she's startled when he says something else.

"I'm sorry?"

He repeats himself, unsmiling. "I'm wondering how you all got here so early. We didn't go to the press with these details until just today, but you all arrived Sunday morning, I believe. Yesterday."

Jay doesn't move. How did all of them miss this? She replays it in her head. Arriving here with only the letter, the photo, the scar. Hilma and Charlie didn't find any new details in the newspaper. All their information has been scavenged from conversations with locals. In all the stress of being called back home, Jay hasn't looked at it from an outsider's perspective. No wonder everyone's suspicious.

Pell is waiting for an answer.

"I'm still in the loop," Jay says, keeping her voice steady. "I hear things."

"All five of you, though? Jadelynne Carr. Max and Hilma Garnet. Ignacio Nieves and Charlie Olowe. I had no idea all of Brandi's old friends were still interested in our little town."

"We keep in touch." The obvious doubt on his face stings. "Look, am I being detained? You called me into the station because—what? I was too punctual? Is that a crime in Arkansas?"

"No, Jadelynne, you're not being detained. I called you to the station to ask you about something we found at Miss Addams's home." Leaning across the desk, Pell hands Jay a plastic baggie.

Jay accepts it, her headache throbbing. A necklace lies inside the evidence baggie, cheap silver. The pendant is half a heart, designed to look like it's torn in half. BE FRI. Shock blooms through her.

"Any idea why Miss Addams would've had this in her home? Why it would've been right in the middle of the . . . scene of conflict?"

"No idea," she manages. "Should I recognize it?"

"I would hope so. This belongs to you."

Jay's mouth is dry, but if she swallows, the sour panic will choke her. "Hmm, I don't think so." He can't remember her teenage fashion choices that clearly. It's absurd. Just as absurd as the presence of this necklace in this police station, when Jay knows for a fact that it shouldn't be here. It should be sixteen hundred miles away, tucked into the bottom of her sock drawer.

"Turn it over," Pell says. When she does, he points to the letter J scratched haphazardly into the back of the necklace. Jay's dizziness increases. "Isn't that your initial?"

"That random scratch?" The initial does look distorted, a half inch too long, more like a fishhook than a letter. That's good; plausible deniability. "Nope. Sorry."

"I know that Miss Addams wore the other half of the necklace."

"What, when she was a kid? A million years ago?"

He blinks at this. "Miss Addams never stopped wearing it. I saw it on her every time we talked. 'ST ENDS.' She joked it meant Saint Ends. We didn't find her side of the necklace, though. Only yours."

Jay can't get lost in the implications of Brandi still wearing their pendant, while Jay hid hers away. "I'm sorry I can't help you. Did you run any fingerprints?"

Pell doesn't answer, but the twitch of his mouth tells Jay they haven't found any matches. Even so, it makes her blood run cold. Jay subtly glances at the other evidence baggies Pell has lying on his cluttered desk, pushed mostly out of her view. A glint of black catches her eye. A phone. It has to be Brandi's. And instantly Jay knows she must get her hands on it.

"I'm disappointed, Jadelynne. I know you can be real helpful when you want to be."

Jay doesn't rise to the barb. She's too distracted by that phone. She blurts, "Have you looked into Brandi's ex-boyfriend? Kenny-something?"

Pell blinks. "He's not a suspect at this time."

"What about a—a Roy? Does that name mean anything?"

"Should it?"

"I want to know that Brandi's disappearance is being taken seriously. This is a tiny police department. You don't want national attention about botching this case." Jay doesn't want that either. God, no. Investigators swooping in, kicking around in the dirt. But she *does* want to needle a reaction from Pell, and here it comes—

Rising, Pell goes to the door and shuts it. Jay takes the opportunity to reach out a hand, snake-strike-quick, and grab the phone. She slides her hand into her jacket just as he turns. Adrenaline kicks through Jay's bloodstream. It's been a while since she's felt like this, the furtive little thrill of being a criminal.

Coming back, Pell pitches his voice low. Jay can barely hear him over the rush of blood in her ears. "Let's be honest: Brandi has a reputation. She's been in and out of here for years: possession, intent to sell, public nuisance. It's not a story that's gonna tug at people's heartstrings, I'll tell you that much. If you don't help me out, Brandi may never get justice."

That outlaw bravado is still chugging through Jay's adrenal glands. "There was blood all over Brandi's trailer. Did you test it?"

"Testing isn't magic. It can take up to a month. Maybe two weeks, if we're lucky."

"That's a long time," Jay says without thinking.

"What's wrong? Do you think the results will upset you and your friends?"

Abruptly, Jay rises, praying the evidence bag will stay concealed inside her jacket. "Am I free to go?"

"I'd like it if you stayed around town. The five of you. We'll need to talk later." He leans forward. "Maybe when I'm able to prove that necklace is yours."

She turns, heart hammering, her urgency colliding with her hangover. When she's almost at the door, Pell calls her name. Of course she wouldn't get away with this, her lifetime supply of luck has been burned through already, she can't take dumb risks—

"Do you think Gene Stippley is involved in this?" Pell asks.

That name hits her like a fist.

"We never did find out what happened to him," Pell continues. As Jay's adrenaline fades, she suddenly, uncomfortably sees the scene not as a rebellious girl defying a small-town cop, but as two tired, worried adults. "He wasn't good to that girl. I can't help thinking, what if he came back? What if this is revenge?"

Images slide, slimy and heavy, through Jay's brain.

"Yeah," she says. "I wouldn't rule Gene out."

But that's a lie, a lie so shameful that she thinks of the photo of the Truth House and wonders if this is what Brandi meant by it— that Jay's a liar, through and through. Because Jay knows Gene has nothing to do with this.

Gene Stippley has been dead for fifteen years.

23

1999

THEN

Jay tapped on the doorframe. "Ms. Hart?" Brandi hung at her elbow. She'd insisted on coming along as moral support, and Jay was happy to have her. It was proof that this little rift she'd noticed between her and Brandi, splinter-tiny, wasn't an issue after all.

Ms. Hart didn't put out her cigarette when she saw them. Jay thrilled at the idea that her art teacher trusted them with this adult secret. "How are those portfolios coming along, girls?"

Jay had come here reluctantly, a *why-not*, a *may-as-well*. They'd stalled on finding the sixth house, Theodora's descriptions too cryptic even for Charlie. And the High House was a disappointment. It didn't belong to the six of them, not the same way the other houses did, the rooms always occupied by people they didn't want to run into.

So she was thinking of Charlie's advice, the way he encouraged Jay not to give up on this world just yet. "I actually was wondering about schools and stuff?" Jay said. "Like scholarships. We both were."

This made Ms. Hart stub out her cigarette in her coffee mug. "Oh, Jadelynne, really? You're a shoo-in. I had no idea you were interested."

"Yeah, well, I've always wanted to be an artist. Both of us," she said, gesturing at Brandi.

"Jay's the real artist," Brandi demurred.

"You're more of an artist than me," Jay insisted. "If I go to art school, you're going too. It won't be any fun without you."

Brandi smiled, though there was something sad in her eyes as she bent to examine the bouquet of stiff-bristled paintbrushes sprouting from a mason jar.

"Well, you're both very brave." Rising, Ms. Hart turned to shuffle through her filing cabinet. "Look, I won't sugarcoat this, girls. No matter how much you care about your art, so few people around here can turn it into a living. But that doesn't mean you shouldn't pursue it."

Jay's optimism faltered. "What about the Garnets?" Brandi asked, straightening.

"Who?" Ms. Hart asked.

"The artists-in-residence," Jay explained.

"Ah. Them. Different situation, isn't it?"

"They're making a living from it," Jay pointed out.

"So I've heard."

Jay thought of the Garnets, the elusive parents she still had barely glimpsed except via their paintings. The woman with the crooked teeth between her legs had been joined by sisters, different versions of them, evolving on canvas every time Jay dropped by. It occurred to her that the Garnets—Jodie and Harold—could help her and Brandi with their artistic aspirations, more than her under-funded public school could. The elder Garnets could be their guides to the intricacies of this world the same way Hilma and Max were their guides to the other one.

As if Ms. Hart could hear Jay's thoughts, she spoke up. "Did you know that most artists living here in the Ozarks make their biggest sales outside of the state? We have such wonderful artistic talent here, but it's a lonely thing, to feel like the people around you can't—"

"Can't appreciate what you make?" Jay asked. She understood that.

"Maybe they can't *afford* to appreciate it."

Jay considered this, a melancholy growing in her. In a way, Eternal Springs was wound into nearly everything she'd created. The first time she'd drawn anything, it was the forests around her house. She'd noticed the way the leaves almost but didn't quite touch at their tops, the shape the sunlight made as it cracked through. Brandi's photos too: the shed was filled with images of their town. Jay had known for a while that they were going to leave, but Ms. Hart's words still made her feel inexplicably sad.

Jay tried to shake it off, embarrassed at imagining what the twins would think if they saw her getting all nostalgic over Eternal.

Ms. Hart sat back at her desk with a sheaf of papers. "Now, you both have parents or guardians to help you fill these out? Because that's a big part of it, I'm afraid."

Brandi's cheeks flamed. She was looking at her feet in their knockoff Uggs, the ones that Hilma said looked like casts.

"I can help Brandi," Jay said. "I mean, my dad can help us both."

Ms. Hart looked from one of them to the other, seemed to realize something. She nodded. "Of course. And listen. Don't let me discourage you. You're bright young women, you're going big places."

24

2015

When she leaves the station, she finds Iggy waiting for her. Jay slides into the rental SUV and brings her forehead down to her knees, letting out a single, gasping sob. It takes her a moment to realize that Iggy is squeezing her shoulder. She can't help leaning into his touch, and he slips his arm fully around her. "Iggy," she says, keeping her head down in the dark SUV. "Why did you contact me? Why did you get back in touch?"

"Do we need to have this talk now?"

"You didn't tell me about Elle. You didn't tell me you were engaged."

"I was waiting for the right time. I didn't want to be one of those guys who mentions his fiancée every few sentences. Like, *How's the weather over there, oh great, me and my fiancée are enjoying the sunshine—*"

"You know what I mean." When he doesn't answer, Jay goes on.

"We agreed it was for the best not to talk to each other again. After we left town."

"We made a lot of agreements that aren't going great."

"Does Elle know about any of this?"

Iggy's laugh is pained. "What do you think, Jay? No. Have you told your boyfriends about us? Or about where we first kissed? Or about why we—"

About why we can never let go of each other.

Jay doesn't feel any inclination to talk about the people who've passed for *boyfriends* in her life, the anemic substitutes for her first love. "You're going to marry her?" she asks instead.

"That's the plan. Yes. I'd like to have a . . ."

"A what?"

"A normal life, Jay. What do you want me to say? Wife and kids and all that. A house in the suburbs. A dog in the backyard."

"Sounds magical."

"You know what? We were kids, and we've never had a chance to process what happened between us." Iggy's voice shifts to a new register. "You *know* that it wasn't healthy, Jay. Maybe it could've been, eventually, but you didn't let us get there."

A week ago, she wouldn't have imagined being in a car with Iggy's arm around her, unearthing their beating hearts and attempting to dissect them. "Okay," she says, pulling away, embarrassed, angry at herself. "Just forget it, then. We should focus on Brandi."

"Fine by me." He sounds wounded; he sounds relieved. "Are you going to tell me why you were being interrogated by the cops? Do they know something about Brandi?"

"They found my half of the friendship necklace at the crime scene," Jay says.

Iggy's face falters between surprise and doubt. "How would that happen? Did you leave it there? Did you— Is it yours?"

"I don't know, I haven't been back in fifteen years," says Jay. Her dad moved to Kansas a while ago, and she's made a point of never crossing state lines into Arkansas. "Last time I checked, my half of the friendship necklace is in Albany."

"Then how—"

"I don't know," Jay repeats, anguished. "Pell is suspicious, of course. He won't go easy on us." Her voice shakes. "And our hands are tied, we can't explain any of this."

"Let's see what the others think," Iggy says at last. "Maybe they've found Kenny. We can't panic yet."

"We're fucked," Hilma says. "End of discussion."

Jay keeps glancing at the oval mirror in the corner. It's turned to the wall, tarnished side facing out, but she doesn't care if they're hidden. If she hears somebody enter the Mirror House, she's going to run. It doesn't help that they're in the dark, shadows all around.

"Is there anything else we should know, Jay?" asks Max.

"Not that I can think of," Jay lies. There are a couple of things Jay isn't ready to reveal. Amber's assertion that Max has been back in Eternal, for one. The longer she goes without saying anything, the bigger the accusation seems to grow. And she hasn't told them that she has Brandi's stolen phone.

"This isn't the end, then," Max argues. "What? Pell's got some stupid friendship necklace? They probably sell them for a buck on Amazon."

"We've got to take this seriously," says Charlie. "Amber must've directed Pell straight to us at that party. And no Kenny, either. We're idiots. Amber was obviously setting a trap."

He looks queasy. They all do. They're hungover, sweaty, and hunched.

"Did we find out anything useful at the party, at least?" asks Jay.

"A lot of people are upset with the developers," Charlie contributes. "A lot of people forced to live in Fayette or beyond because of that company. Red Art."

"Right," Jay says. "They took over Thermal Park, didn't they?"

"Gene," Iggy contributes, and everyone stiffens. "People think Brandi's disappearance has something to do with Gene. Or that they don't know the full story about his disappearance."

"Pell suspects that Gene came back," Jay says, feeling very tired.

"That's good," Max says. "We can use that. If they focus on him, we're off the hook."

"Are you serious? If they look too deeply into what happened to Gene, they'll find things we won't like," Charlie says, his voice holding an edge. "That's terrible news."

"Brandi's behind this," says Hilma. She stands, and there's something in her face that silences them all. They turn to her, sunflowers drawn to the glow of her misery. "The letters? The oath? And now your friendship necklace. It's too much. She's out for blood."

"Hey, now, setting us up is a huge leap," Iggy says. "That doesn't seem like Brandi."

Hilma shakes her head, almost violently, strands of gray-streaked blond coming loose. Reaching into her coat pocket, she pulls out a photo and tosses it onto the floor. "Shit. I got a photo, all right? Just like Jay." Jay leans forward, heart hammering, both stunned and not surprised at all because she *knew* it, she knew the others were lying to her.

The Polaroid echoes Jay's photo of the Truth House. A simple shot from the sidewalk, showing a massive house with a rising gable, weathered siding, and board-blinded windows. The Mirror House.

It's disorienting to see the photo version, while Jay's standing inside these walls. Like a twisted urban legend. *The photo is coming from inside the house.* Jay identifies the exact window that she's currently standing in front of and steps back, as if she can be seen, as if a tiny copy of herself will appear in the photo.

"She sent this to you, Hilma?" Iggy whispers.

"Brandi knows," Hilma says, and her voice breaks. "She figured out everything. I hoped it wouldn't come to this, but—fuck. We have to check the basement."

25

1999

THEN

October 31 was chilly, the air carrying the sharpness of wood-smoke, the breeze kicking up eddies of leaves. Nostalgia welled in Jay as she hiked toward the Mirror House. Five years ago, she'd still been trick-or-treating with Brandi. The pleasures of high school Halloween—animal-ear headbands, candy-flavored vodka shots—could never compare to the illicit magic of venturing into the dark, knocking on doors without knowing what waited on the other side. She'd never loved her town more than during those autumn nights.

Charlie was hesitant about going to the Mirror House on Halloween night. "It's a cliché," he argued. "Everyone will have the same idea. Every drunk Neo and Cartman is going to be in there." But Hilma insisted she had something new to show them.

Iggy answered Jay's nervous knock. He wore a glow-in-the-dark skeleton hoodie, and his face was painted like a corresponding skull, hollows around his eyes. But his smile was warm and familiar.

Jay knew he had better options for Halloween parties tonight, but he was here with them. With her.

"So what does Hilma want to show us?" she asked shyly, following him through the halls. The mirrors were quiet tonight, almost like ordinary reflections, which was somehow ominous.

"No idea. She's waiting for everyone."

In the living room, Max and Hilma were impatiently pacing, while Charlie, staunchly out of costume, sat and watched. Max wore angel wings, comically tiny on his broad back; Hilma had red devil horns nestled in her white-blond hair. "Where's Addams?" she demanded.

"I thought she'd be here," Jay said, surprised. "She wouldn't miss this."

"Well, it can't be Gene's fault," Hilma said. "My parents actually apologized to him after the misunderstanding over the Chinese holly, they gave him a raise to say sorry."

This didn't comfort Jay. She knew Gene's habits and patterns, and an apology payout from some out-of-state artists could go either way—celebration or umbrage. She fidgeted, adjusting the blue scarf and plastic pearl earring she'd worn as a half-hearted Vermeer nod. A few months ago, Jay'd asked her dad for a flip phone, with no success, but it hadn't mattered because Brandi was always right there, the only person she'd ever want to talk to. Now the distance between them felt vast.

From outside, there was a howl, distorted by the Mirror House's boarded-up windows until it sounded half-inhuman. Probably just a kid playing around. Jay's skin prickled anyway.

Sensing her agitation, Iggy grabbed for her hand. Warmth spread through Jay's body. She turned to smile at him. In the surrounding mirrors, hundreds of tiny versions of her lit up like candles sprinkled through the shadows. Then Jay saw it, and all the light died.

In the mirror—right behind them—a horrifying face hung over Jay's shoulder, bruised and bloated, coming right for her.

Jay screamed. She tripped over a side table, letting go of Iggy's hand. Hilma and Max swore, and Charlie dropped into an approximation of a fighting stance. Somehow, Iggy pushed himself in front of Jay. For a second their reflections scrambled in the same panic.

"What are y'all doing?" Brandi's voice, small and confused.

Brandi had painted her face in a hurry, mottled zombie colors, olive-greens and blotchy purples. Exaggerated circles scooping out the skin beneath her eyes. Jay's tension uncoiled, immediately replaced by confusion. Something about the painted face struck her as wrong.

"You're here," Hilma said, laughing. "You scared us. Oh my god, weirdo."

"Sorry. Just gettin' in the Halloween spirit."

Max cuffed her, his angel wings shuddering, and Brandi laughed as she sparred back. Jay peered closely at her friend, anxiety skipping higher. Something was off. In the mirrors that surrounded them, Brandi's face was always turned away, hidden from Jay, the back of her head frustrating as a locked door. She examined the real-life Brandi, and saw a dark softness around one eye, as if Brandi had used the face paint to hide something—something worse—

"All right, kids," Hilma said, adjusting her devil horns. "No more playing around. We're going down to the basement."

The basement stairwell was long and narrow, hemmed in by cool stone and mirrorless walls. As with all the dimensions in the Mirror House, it didn't precisely match the outside, extending down too far. Jay stuck close to the others as they moved down the stairs toward the door at the bottom.

"My skin itches," Brandi said, scrubbing her fingernails over her arm with a dry, irritating sound. Jay reached for her hand.

"Allergies? Dust?" Hilma suggested.

They finally reached the end of the stairwell. Max swung open the door, groped for a light switch. The basement was a large, square room. A hum came from somewhere; a water heater, a generator? On one wall, there was a massive mirror, concave and taking in the entire room, apparently embedded into the wall itself. The rest of the space was blank, a bare bulb dangling from the center of the ceiling. The space was identical to the turret, but dark where the turret was light-filled, buried instead of exposed to the sky.

"What dust?" Charlie asked. "There's no dust in here."

He was right. It felt . . . clean. A pins-and-needles sensation grew along Jay's arms.

"Are there bugs?" Iggy asked. "I'm being eaten alive."

There weren't any bugs. No mosquitoes or flies or spiders. Iggy's skin was clear and free. If anything, everyone's complexion seemed to be brightening, as if they'd been freshly washed.

Looking around, Jay yelped. On the opposite side of the mirror, pushed against the baseboards, lay a dead animal. A—a raccoon, or what'd once been a raccoon. It was a desiccated shell, body peeled open at the center, paws curled. The raccoon's insides looked pickled and preserved, barely recognizable as organic matter.

"It musta wandered inside," Brandi said. "Poor old thing." She let go of Jay's hand.

Something moved inside the raccoon. Maggots, Jay thought: she'd seen plenty of deer corpses and gutted possums by the side of the freeway. But her stomach roiled as she looked more closely. The edge of the raccoon's rib was shedding away.

"Its eyes are still intact," Charlie said, peering. "Usually insects would go for the soft part of the face first. It can't have been here that long."

"It's melting." Jay turned to look at the mirror, its muted metallic sheen. She swore that low, electrical hum was growing. "No. Not melting—dissolving."

"Oh shit." Max held his hand out from his body as if it had been infected, and something dropped from his fingertip. A fingernail landed on the floor. The tiny crescent sizzled.

The shrink-wrapped pressure prickled against Jay's skin. She imagined her teeth raining from her gums, her bones coming unglued. She looked again at Brandi; she was crying, Jay realized, but the tears fizzled to nothing the moment they slid from her eyes. Her face paint was shedding in specks, leaving her looking like a pointillism portrait.

Jay began backing away from the corpse, from the piercing hum in the basement—

"The mirror," Jay whispered. "That mirror eats things."

Jay felt a tickle on her arm, slithering. A long lock of brown hair slid free from her ponytail and landed on the floor. Max was molting costume feathers like Icarus. Without even having to consult each other, they retreated from the mirror's blind gaze.

"I don't like this place anymore," Iggy said as they walked up the stairs. They moved carefully. It reminded Jay of being a kid and forcing herself to walk slowly down unlit halls, not running, feeling the warm breath of *something* on her neck.

"Are you kidding?" Max asked. "This is great. Anything you don't want, drag it in here and you're set."

"I'm disturbed your brain went there," Charlie said.

"My brain goes where it likes," Max said. "Sorry. But come on. Think about it. You have something illegal? A little baggie of something? Just toss it, and voilà."

They reached the top of the stairs and dropped onto the floor like shipwrecked sailors. They heard Hilma and Brandi making their way up the stairs.

"Why—why would Theodora make a room like that?" asked Iggy.

"You guys," Jay said. "I'm beginning to think that maybe she didn't have our best interests at heart."

She expected Brandi to jump in and defend Theodora. She wanted it, almost. But reaching the top of the stairs, Brandi only said, "Same as every adult, then." And though the others laughed appreciatively, Jay could only see that Brandi looked very serious, very tired.

26

2015

NOW

They're smart, this time. They still remember the old ways of protection. All of them wear glasses, sunglasses, too many layers of clothing. Jay has her hoodie pulled tight over her hair, and Charlie wears his caramel-colored leather jacket. Even so, it feels like they're walking into radiation. Jay's skin itches furiously as she enters the Mirror House basement—an eyelash slides down her cheek. Her mind feels even less protected. The memories are impossible to escape, and they're so vivid she could poke a finger into the images.

Because Brandi knew. She knew, she knew. The thing that Jay's been dreading her entire adult life is here, and all the times she's constructed it in her head, fleshing out every detail, prove useless. The reality shoves its way in with a pain Jay couldn't have summoned.

What was it like when Brandi put it together? How long did it take her? Did it grow in the background for months, years, or was it one abrupt realization, some missing piece clicking finally into place? All Jay knows is that if she'd figured the same thing out—she'd be livid. Heartbroken.

She'd burn the fucking world down.

"I was going to tell you, but I didn't want the rest of you to panic," Hilma is saying to Max as they crowd into the basement. "I was trying to keep control of this situation—"

"Sure," Max says. "Right. Because you taking control has worked so well before."

"I run a company now," Hilma says tightly. "I know what I'm doing."

"Not when it comes to this town, you don't. None of us do."

Jay's throat cinches, thinking again of the way Brandi's gone without a trace. Gone, devoured. What will they see in here? What if she spots bone, blood, a single staring eye—moldering?

She won't be able to bear it. Anything but that. Anything.

"Well," Charlie says, voice brittle. "It appears someone was down here."

Jay forces herself to look. The space is so unforgivingly bare that the differences are immediately obvious. No human remains. She allows herself one moment of unfathomable relief. But here are the unmistakable signs that their return is no accident, that there are layers they can't understand yet.

Over in the corner, near the wall, roughly matching where they found the raccoon corpse on that first Halloween night: A book. What's left of it. A single spine, the eaten-away crusts of the pages ruffling outward, bone-white stubs.

Theodora's journal.

Charlie lets out a strangled cry, the most naked emotion he's shown so far, and dives for the destroyed journal. He kneels, leafing through the left-behind scraps of pages. A few stunted, cut-off sentences of Theodora's familiar handwriting are still visible, but so much is just gone. Jay remembers Charlie, young and bright-eyed, intent on those pages, a cartographer revealing the map to a new world.

"Why would she—how did this—?" Charlie asks.

"Don't get sentimental. The journal's useless now," Hilma says. "It was useless when we left it with her." But Jay can't tell if the uncaring shell around Hilma's voice is genuine or not.

"It was an amazing historical artifact, if nothing else," Charlie says.

If nothing else. Jay watches as Charlie carefully turns the leftover nubs of the pages. He pauses near the back, and Jay spots Hilma's handwriting, the ink from the bright fuchsia gel pen standing out. The rules—Hilma's rules, the ones she wrote that long-ago day, the ones they all agreed on.

Iggy inhales. His face is rigid, cheeks sunken in the grim overhead lighting. He's not paying any attention to the wreckage of Theodora's journal. He's staring at the floor, and Jay follows his gaze.

There are scratches in the concrete. Lightly gouged, but so many of them that they deform the smoothness of the floor, like animal tracks, like hieroglyphs. Jay forgets the painful itch on her skin as she drops into a crouch to get a better view. They're—they're words. Phrases. As if to compensate for the words destroyed in the journal. Scratched into the concrete, just beyond the glare of the mirror, the letters angular and rough-hewn.

It takes her a second to work out the first phrase, fitting the letters together. Or maybe Jay doesn't want to admit what she's seeing. Because: *Truth is more of a stranger* has been worked into the floor. And once Jay interprets this one, she can more easily decode the others. *One must live unseen. Oh, I am fortune's fool.* The Baudelaire quote, butchered French. And on, all of them. A giddy sickness fills Jay's sternum. Her eyes move to the final phrase.

And eternity in an hour.

"We have to figure out what's happening here," Iggy says, his voice laced with panic.

"Oh, I think we already know," Max says, and he sounds—terrified, yes—but also impressed, and Jay gets it because she feels it too. "We've walked right into a trap."

The upper story of the Mirror House feels luxurious after the basement, the air plump with oxygen. "All right, kids," Hilma says. Long strands of blond-gray hair shed onto her coat. "The days of pretending this is innocent are over. We're under attack."

"Under attack from who, though?" Charlie asks. He's kept the scrap of the journal, clutching it like a talisman. "Did Brandi do this? Do we really think she's capable?"

"If she found out about what happened? She'd be fucking pissed. I wouldn't blame her." Max's eyes are somber.

"Maybe that's what somebody else wants us to think," Iggy says. "We don't have any evidence that this was Brandi's work, not if she told someone else about the houses. Or someone else found out against her will."

"Jesus, don't say that," Hilma groans. "Brandi being behind this is the best-case scenario."

"Why, because you think she'll go easy on us?" Max says.

"I mean, Brandi was never vengeful," Iggy says, and the words sink in. Everything the five of them have done has been built on the knowledge that Brandi wouldn't seek revenge. But imagining Brandi orchestrating all this, wanting *revenge*, is a pain so deep and startling that Jay physically twists away from it.

"Where do we even go from here?" she asks.

"The eternal question," Hilma says.

"I didn't expect us to stay this long. I'm running out of excuses. It's a nightmare to not be able to explain anything to my boyfriend," Charlie says. "My client isn't answering my texts anymore."

Jay knows the others must be thinking of their families, their partners. Elle. So many people are unwittingly trapped in this situation with them.

"We need to find Kenny," Iggy says. "If he dated Brandi for a long time, he must know things. Whether or not he was involved in any of this."

"The fact that he's hiding from us makes that a bit difficult," Hilma says.

"Doesn't he still deal?" Max asks. "We could fake being interested in buying."

A pause as they all consider this.

"We're back in Arkansas for two days and we're already buying narcotics from my high school bully?" Charlie asks. "Wonderful idea, Max, especially when we have spies watching us in every trailer park."

"I'm just saying. If Kenny's still the same guy, he'd risk anything for a payday. How hard can it be to find his number?" Max argues.

Jay clears her throat. "Uh. It's probably easier than you think." She reaches into her jacket pocket and pulls out the phone, still sheathed in the crinkly evidence bag, so obviously illegitimate that everyone in the room freezes as if she's retrieved a weapon.

"My god," Charlie says. "You—that's—when you were at the police station? Jay. Jadelynne. They're going to notice that it's missing. Even an incompetent ass like Pell is going to see that a major piece of evidence is *gone*, coincidentally right after he spoke with a suspect."

"We can't get any more suspicious, can we?" Jay says, recklessly defiant.

Max gestures for the phone, she hands it to him. He rips open the plastic as casually as if it's a chip bag, removes the phone inside. It's an older iPhone, the screen a collage of webby cracks, encased inside a chipped case of pink camo print.

"Actually, we *can* look more suspicious," Charlie says. "Stealing evidence is concrete, Jay. It's a real-world crime. We can't rely on Pell not understanding the magic we're using."

"We'll get what we need from the phone and then we'll destroy it in the basement," Jay says. "They won't be able to prove anything."

She catches Iggy watching her, reevaluating her. Jay forgot the way that Theodora's houses alter her, as if the houses leave a trace of themselves inside her body, the same way she leaves her fingerprints and breath and skin cells inside their rooms.

"Well, it's hers, definitely," Max says, and turns the screen around. The lock screen is a photo of Brandi and Amber, faces pressed together, smiling broadly. Jay doesn't have any defenses up. She's not ready for the intimacy of a selfie. Jay can see the changes in her friend, the way her addiction made each year pull double duty. The wrinkles around her wide-set brown eyes, the deep circles beneath them. But there's an unguarded openness in Brandi's smile. It startles Jay, who's adopted a sleek uniformity since she left Arkansas. She's seen it as self-improvement, shedding her redneck roots. When Jay contrasts herself with Brandi, though, she understands that there are parts of her missing now.

"I can't get in," Max says, fingers moving rapidly over the screen. "Jay? You'd know her password better than any of us."

Jay focuses. "She used 'diamond' when we were younger. Because of the diamond mines." There'd always been a pride to the fact that Arkansas was known for its gems, delicate and priceless. Brandi had fixated on that. "Or maybe try her birthday? Uh, that's March third, 1982. Or try it backwards. Some variation on that."

For the next twenty minutes, Jay rifles through her memory for a useful scrap. Brandi's home address, her mother's birthday. Jay's forced to admit that she doesn't know Brandi anymore, and by extension, this phone is inaccessible. Her risk was worthless.

"No luck," Max says finally. "We're about to be locked out permanently."

The word—*luck*—sticks to the air. They all sit up straighter, taking notice, the old vocabulary coming back to them.

"Charlie," says Hilma. "What are the odds of guessing a six-digit passcode on a first try?"

He answers reluctantly. "One in a million."

"Easy enough," says Hilma.

"Is it safe?" Jay asks quietly, because now they know that there might be someone who understands the houses as well as they do. Someone who's left behind a trail of blood, destruction, cryptic clues. This whole town is dangerous, and Theodora's houses, their once-refuges, are the most dangerous of all.

Sure enough, Max clears his throat. "If you want to go to the Luck House," he says, "it might not be as easy as you think."

27

1999

The views from the AIR House changed in November. No longer green and lush, but alien and mournfully beautiful. Low-slung gray skies; stark tree branches. Banners of smoke curled from chimneys and bonfires, drifting upward until they were absorbed into the larger grayness. Jay took out her sketchpad, working quickly. She so rarely saw Eternal Springs from this angle. If she lived in this house, she thought the town would never stop surprising her, its beauty right here for the taking.

"And to what do I owe this pleasure?"

Jay stuffed her sketchpad back into her backpack guiltily, as if she'd been stealing the views. The woman who stood watching her was short, her hair silver. Physically, she was like a small ghost of her own children, but her sharp eyes stilled Jay at once. Jay had wheedled Hilma into letting her visit, hoping she could extract some insight from an actual successful artist. Now that she was here, though, Jay was tongue-tied.

Ms. Garnet extended one hand. "Let me see, sweetheart."

Jay handed the sketchpad over, nerves buzzing as Ms. Garnet flipped through the pages. From where she stood, her sketches looked flat and clumsy, like someone had replaced her work with amateur scribbles. Jay remembered too late that the houses were captured right there.

"You have talent," Ms. Garnet said at last. "Hilma has mentioned that you have an interest in the arts. It's inspiring to see young people transcending their surroundings."

"I like your paintings too," Jay said, relieved at *talent*.

Ms. Garnet smiled with a trace of indulgent irony that seemed directed at somebody else. "I realize our work may not be what you're used to. I hope you aren't too shocked."

"I was curious," Jay said, before she lost her courage, "how did you become an artist? How did you make your career?"

"I wouldn't call it a *career*. That's exactly the wrong word. A life immersed in the arts is a necessity, it's almost a curse. You're an artist because life gives you no other choice."

"Yeah, but—how do you make money?"

"Oh my god, Bluejay," Hilma said, bounding in from the kitchen, crunching on an apple. "What, do you want our tax returns?"

Ms. Garnet hushed her daughter with a hand to her shoulder. It made Jay feel worse, as if they were two adults handling a child. "Hilma, I'm honored that your friends are interested in us. Here I thought we'd be complete unknowns in the Ozarks." She addressed Jay. "If you're thinking about money, you're focusing on the wrong things, my dear."

So Ms. Garnet was offering her the same adult evasiveness Ms. Hart had, only from a different angle. "Yeah, but it's not about the money," Jay said, frustrated. What Jay wanted was to be part of things, to see and be seen in return. She wanted beauty in her life, some tiny pocket of control. But she wasn't sure how to put this into words.

"How did you find yourself here?" Jay asked at last, gesturing around at the AIR House.

Ms. Garnet's eyes flashed, her cheeks stained in two perfect red circles that reminded Jay of Max's blush. "In Arkansas? Well, I suppose some mistakes were made."

It took Jay a moment to figure out that Ms. Garnet was offended. "No, I mean—this house. It's so beautiful. I'd love to live somewhere like this, one day."

Ms. Garnet glanced around consideringly. "Ah. It has its charms, I suppose."

Jay wondered what Ms. Garnet would think if she visited Jay's home, the place that only looked decent via careful rearrangement: a couch placed to hide carpet stains, a picture over a crack.

"Well, Jadelynne, commit yourself to the artistic process and one day you could be in this house yourself."

"I can't live here," Jay said. "The artist-in-residence program is only for out-of-state artists." For a funny second, she remembered Amber griping about the money going to out-of-towners, not people like Destiny's family, not people like Brandi or—

"Then I suppose you need to find other opportunities, darling. Experience other countries, expand your awareness. See the world."

This, Jay could do. She could expand her awareness. She could see other worlds. For the first time during this conversation, Jay felt a surge of power. She was going somewhere Ms. Garnet couldn't imagine. For so long, Jay had seen her art as her escape hatch, the ticket she'd hand to the universe in exchange for an interesting life. But what if Jay wasn't meant to succeed in this world? When she thought of college, she panicked at the rules, the complications, all the wading into adult territory. So many new terms, *FAFSA* and *statements of intent*. Finding the portal was theirs, though. It belonged only to the six of them.

Jay imagined loosening her grip on any Plan B. It didn't feel frightening. It felt freeing.

"Thanks for talking to me." Jay grinned shyly, and Ms. Garnet's eyes drifted to her teeth. She wondered if Ms. Garnet was memorizing her crooked incisors, storing them away for a future painting.

Eager to get away, Jay started out the door, following Hilma. But Ms. Garnet reached out and grabbed her arm. "Jadelynne. I wanted to thank you, young lady."

Ms. Garnet spoke quietly, quickly. Jay automatically dropped her voice too. "For what?"

"For being friends with Hilma. I know my daughter won't say it, but we appreciate it. Your companionship has meant so much to her. Well, to all of us. Hilma doesn't always have the easiest time with her peers."

Jay mutely nodded, trying to look as if she knew what Ms. Garnet meant, as if it were even possible that she was the one doing Hilma a favor instead of the other way around.

28

2015

The old Luck House is gone. Not the same way as the Truth House, but the force of panic hits Jay so hard, it might as well be burned down. The falling-down house of her memory has vanished, the entire sprawling mess of it. This version has been painted a cold magazine-ad white. The waist-high swamp of weeds and flowers has been replaced by AstroTurf, an eye-hurting fake green stretched behind a literal white picket fence. Even the sound is different, though it takes Jay a moment to work out why as she sits in the rental SUV, window rolled down. The insects and birds are gone with the wildflowers.

Jay's bleary, this Tuesday morning. She spent a sleepless night in the hotel, waiting for a knock on the door. Pell coming back with reinforcements. In her insomnia, she brainstormed different passwords, gazing at Brandi's familiar-but-unfamiliar grin. Nothing. And now another blow. The Luck House, their deus ex machina, belongs to somebody else. All that luck is out of reach.

"See?" Max says, and behind his resignation, Jay catches the same sadness she feels. Theodora's houses aren't theirs anymore. "Not exactly accessible."

"Well," Jay says, "that hasn't stopped us yet, has it?"

"What, you're going to crawl in a window?" Max teases.

"Maybe. Why not smash a window?" she asks, getting reckless. "If it helps Brandi—"

"All right, all right, Nancy Drew. We don't have to go that far." And Max is out of the rental SUV and approaching the Luck House, walking through the gate like he's still a brash teenager, still instantly at home in other people's houses.

Iggy swears, looking around. Jay, making a split-second decision, hops out and runs after Max. It's dawn, the air cool and damp. Not many people are out at this hour, the cul-de-sac quiet, the surrounding windows dark or lit with embers of lamplight. Max goes around to the back of the house, where at least they're more hidden. "What are you doing?" Jay whispers.

Max goes to the back door and reaches up easily, brushing his fingertips along the top of the doorframe. "There's got to be a key somewhere. These little towns, everyone trusts everyone else."

"I don't think this is safe," Iggy says, following them. He's jittery. "We don't know who's out there watching us. I can't be locked up for breaking-and-entering."

"Relax, it's unoccupied," Max says, all confidence.

Jay has to admit that he's right. She hasn't lost her almost extrasensory abilities from her days of seeking Theodora's houses. She can always tell when a house is empty. Vacation homes, rentals, abandoned and foreclosed houses moldering on a street corner: they all have the same silence to them. A house without a human inside becomes its own watchful creature.

"Okay, but," Iggy says. "We know Pell is after us now. We can figure out the passcode some other way, we can—can go back to the High House, ask around."

But Max gives a cocky, triumphant whistle, ta-da, and presents the key he found tucked on top of a porch post.

Jay thinks of what Amber said. Max, back. Max, returning. "How did you know to look there?" Jay asks, the accusation strong enough that Iggy looks from one of them to the other, bewildered.

Max shrugs. "Just lucky, I guess."

The interior has been entirely cleared of its junk. The result looks shorn and desolate. The furniture looks like the waiting room of a mid-range dermatologist. Modular IKEA bookshelves without any books, chairs with neat gray upholstery. Neutral nothingness. All the old nooks and crannies and crawl spaces have been painted over and neatened out of existence.

Before she can catch herself, Jay's sad that the Luck House couldn't shield itself against this creeping standardization. She feels protective of Eternal—but then, what does Eternal owe her? She abandoned it.

Jay drops into a chair and pulls out Brandi's phone. "It's almost out of battery." She spots a glossy white phone charger in the corner. Jay's stomach tingles; she forgot how good this place can feel, the thrum of things going her way.

A sense of calm falls over Jay, a renewed belief. Brandi was always sentimental, always tucking hidden significance into everything. Even that friendship necklace had been her birthday gift to Jay.

Birthday. Not Brandi's, but Jay's.

Not letting herself second-guess anything, Jay types her own birthday into the phone: 041682. The screen trembles reprovingly, shaking her attempt off. Maybe Jay's forfeited any remaining right to luck. Maybe this won't work after all.

"It doesn't look like anybody lives here," Iggy says, emerging from a back room. "Are they transforming it into a business? Does somebody know what this place does?"

Max huffs. "Imagine what you could do with this place, if you were willing to capitalize on it. Imagine . . ."

"What?" Iggy presses.

"Well, we were kids when we found this shit. We used it for our homework. Imagine an adult finding it. You know?"

"Wouldn't they have to know about Theodora's magic? Believe in it?" Iggy asks.

"Charlie's the expert on all that. But if somebody made it work?"

Jay's only half listening. She types her birthday backward, 286140. The screen unfurls. She's in. It worked. The luck inside her fizzes, followed by the realization that Brandi was thinking of Jay, in some small way, every time she unlocked her phone. Jay guards against it.

There's a better view of Brandi's face, floating behind the little grid of apps. The phone is sparse. Default apps, mostly: the phone looks freshly scrubbed. Jay's hand is trembling. Where to first? She opens Brandi's texts. There are only a few threads, some of them obvious spam. Either Brandi deleted the incriminating ones, or she was a minimal texter. Just another side of Brandi that Jay's never seen, their separation spanning technological jumps.

One remaining thread is between Brandi and KaThY! Jay assumes this is Kathy Wheelehan, Brandi's boss. Jay recalls her as a tall, serious woman with hair the color of antique lace. Jay's heart catches as she reads a string of texts from Kathy, each one seen but not responded to, dating six months ago: *Brandi, we really need to talk. Please contact me.* Then, a day later: *Brandi, could you please speak with me in person before you go to the Clarkson house?? Thanks.* And on for several days. Finally, a simple, contextless text from Brandi.

does this mean Im fired?

And a terse reply from Kathy. *I'm sorry but yes.*

Brandi held that job for fifteen years. Kathy hired her as a not-quite-eighteen-year-old and kept her on during everything that happened next. It feels unsettling, ominous really, that Brandi lost her job and within less than a year has gone missing. As if that last tether snapping were enough to send Brandi hurtling into the unknown.

"Jay?" Iggy asks, and she realizes he and Max have fallen silent. "What's going on?"

Jay doesn't answer, too absorbed in the screen. She scrolls through the photos next. What if there's an image of the elusive Roy? What if there's a shot that—somehow—points to precisely what happened, that reveals everything the five of them have missed so far?

There are disappointingly few photos. Mostly selfies. Brandi pouting or smiling, the phone angled sharply downward. Brandi's eyes hold a haze that gives Jay a knot in her belly, recalling the blurriness that grew over Brandi like a cocoon in the months leading up to Jay leaving town.

The final one, though, is different from the other selfies, in a way so subtle that a stranger might not notice. Brandi looks alert. Like her old self. The face that Jay knew before she truly knew her own. There's a directness to Brandi's gaze that's intimate, challenging, like she's peering beyond the screen to lock eyes with Jay.

Iggy leans close, staring at the screen. "Wait a second. Look at that. The date. Can you check the location too?"

Jay blinks back her tears. The photo was taken on May 8. Five days after the last time Amber saw Brandi; only four days before she summoned them with her letters. "No location on the phone, but it looks like this photo was taken in the shed."

So it's proof that Brandi didn't truly vanish on the third, that she was still in Eternal. The realization blooms in Jay, changing the shape of everything they've uncovered. Brandi didn't vanish as long ago as the rest of Eternal Springs assumes. She was here, undetected. Doing . . . doing what?

The three of them exchange stunned glances, nobody willing to break the silence. "What does this mean?" Iggy asks at last. "Brandi was in Eternal, but she didn't talk to anybody? Was she hiding on purpose?"

"I hate to say it," Max says, "but Miss Addams is seeming less and less like a poor vanished girl and more like someone who knew exactly what she was doing."

Jay's breaths turn shallower. Brandi's eyes on hers are clear. Awake.

"Okay," Iggy says. "Whatever else is going on, Kenny can help us rule out whether this was all due to Brandi, or if she was working with someone else."

Steadying herself, Jay goes to Contacts. There's no Roy; she checks swiftly, disappointed to find him missing. Maybe deleted. Amber's there, and Kathy again, and—"We have Kenny's number," she announces.

Max springs into action, wasting no time. Pulling out his own phone—Brandi's looks like an ancient artifact next to his—he swiftly enters Kenny's number and hits *call*.

"This Kenny?" Max asks after a second. "Hey, man. We're in from out of town and Amber mentioned you're the person to talk to." He's altered his voice, uncertain but confiding. "Can you meet us somewhere around town tonight? I can promise it'll be worth your time."

Jay's not even sure if it's luck taking hold right now, or if Max is simply using his personal charisma. Whatever the case, Max's posture adjusts, his knee bouncing with anticipation, and Jay knows this is working. They'll talk to Kenny, and she feels everything inside her go steely, preparing for the confrontation ahead.

Kenny must know something. He might even have something to do with Brandi's disappearance—with the destroyed journal, the markings in the floor. Jay never got to see Brandi in a relationship, but she can only imagine that Brandi's loyalty extended to her romances. And if Kenny Stringer has continued being the boy she remembers from high school—opportunistic, hungry—then he so easily could have weaponized Brandi's own sweetness against her.

On the phone with Kenny, Max rattles off an address, and Jay recognizes it.

"He's already coming back to Eternal and selling?" Iggy asks, when Max hangs up. "Less than a week after his ex-girlfriend vanished and he was questioned by the police? That either means he's innocent—"

"Or that he's stupid," Max provides. "I was reading about some meth head who shot his girlfriend and was at a bar with the blood still on his shirt. For some rednecks, it's a badge of honor to return to the scene of the crime."

"Not just rednecks who do that, is it?" Jay says.

Max has the good grace to blush. He still blushes the same way he did as a teenager, two perfect circles. "What the hell, Jay?"

"Sorry. But you have to admit, the five of us aren't exactly in a place to judge." She moves on. "What are you planning on doing to Kenny? The Oath House seems like the last place you'd want to take him."

"Trust me," Max says. "I scoped it out earlier. It's a bed-and-breakfast now."

"God, all of Theodora's houses are changing," Jay says. But she's distracted. Looking at Max—big, leonine, supremely self-satisfied now that he's solved their latest problem—she can't help thinking about Amber's warning. Jay received a photo of the Truth House; Hilma had a photo of the Mirror House. In the shed, she found the AIR House, the Forever House, the High House, Brandi's trailer. That leaves several key photos unaccounted for. The Oath House, the Duplication House, and—

The luck thrums through her, quicksilver and seductive. "Max," she says, letting every second of exhaustion rise to her voice. "Could you grab me some water?"

"Yeah, Jaybird, of course." Max hurries out of the room,

whistling under his breath. Through the open wedge of the doorway, Jay watches him in the refurbished kitchen. He swings open the cabinet door, takes out a glass. Thoughtlessly, he moves to the fridge and fills the glass with ice. Every move is practiced, calm, with the automatic ease of routine. Maybe it's just luck. Maybe.

When Max comes back with the water, presenting it with a little flourish, Jay won't take it. She stares up at Max until he falters, looking around with showy confusion.

"Max," she says. "Remember what I said at the High House? Amber knows. She's seen you." Max freezes, his face going very still. This next sentence is a gamble, but after all, Jay's in the perfect place to follow a hunch. "Amber knows that you've been back to the Luck House."

His face stays so blank that she thinks she's made a mistake. Amber didn't say a word about the Luck House. But then, they aren't in the Truth House. Jay can say what she likes and hope to land a royal flush on the first try.

"What's Jay talking about?" Iggy asks, confused. "You've been back here? That seems like something you should really tell us."

And then Max smiles, slowly, wearily. Jay even notices a trace of relief, as if a guilty secret he's held like a stone has been taken from him, lightening his burden. Max reaches into his pocket, handing Jay a small Polaroid photo, bent and cracked. She unfolds it, and a strange sense of calm falls over her. She turns the photo around so that Max and Iggy can see the Luck House, in its current refurbished state.

"Yeah," Max Garnet says. "You got me. I've been back."

29

1999

As they walked through the forests, Jay let the twins' gentle bickering wash over her like birdsong. It was a chilly early December evening, but the cold was bearable, with the afternoon sunlight lancing through the branches. They should've been worrying about getting lost; it happened in these woods often enough. A stray camper or a runaway vanishing temporarily. These forests could swallow you up. But Jay felt okay, here with her friends. Ahead, Brandi chatted with Iggy. Charlie walked quietly alongside Jay.

Jay kept her eyes open for a house. There were structures scattered throughout the trees out here, sure, but they were typically the homes of hippies, the occasional meth lab, or else lavish vacation homes built in this rarefied privacy. People compelled to hide from society, or people who chose to avoid society. Jay imagined Theodora out here, far from normal life, building one of her creations, alone.

While they were seeking out unoccupied houses, Jay couldn't help watching Brandi. The bruises from Halloween night had faded. Brandi was so unwilling to talk about it that Jay had let it drop into a guilty corner, but she was vigilant around Brandi now, looking for some sign of how to help.

"Where's this Portal House, anyway?" Max asked.

Jay slowed, matching her pace to the twins' so she could better eavesdrop. The importance of the Portal House had only grown since her talk with Ms. Garnet. Jay had been especially involved in the process of locating these last two houses, helping Charlie work out the codes until they made her head hurt. Intricate symbols that reminded Jay of the games on the back of cereal boxes, only a thousand times trickier. The description of one house included details suggesting something unbreakable, something that'd hold them fast: Jay pictured being paralyzed, or confined. She wasn't looking forward to that. And another house was apparently buried deep in the woods, which was why they were here.

The eighth and final house, the Portal House, remained totally elusive. Jay wasn't too worried yet. She assumed that Theodora's final creation would only become obvious once they found the others. Everything she knew about Theodora Trader pointed to a particular and demanding soul, a woman who'd fought too hard to have her own way to give it up easily.

"Max, seriously." Hilma was in a bristly mood. Jay could tell she wasn't at home in these forests; it was funny to see her out of her element. "Let's just focus on finding the next two."

"These other houses are letting me down," Max said, grabbing up a loose stick, sending it hurtling like a Frisbee into a tree. "I left Lucky in the Duplication House overnight. Destiny's birthday is coming up, I thought we could have matching snakes. Cute, right?"

Jay forgot to hide her eavesdropping. "Is Lucky okay after?"

"Well, she's barely eating," Max admitted. "I'm going to take her to the vet."

"Does the Duplication House even work on living things?" Jay asked.

"I still only have one snake after twenty-four hours. If that proves anything."

"Y'all," Brandi called, and her voice, though soft, cut through their chatter. "If'n we want to find this house, you gotta be quiet. You're gonna scare it away."

"Scare the house away?" Hilma asked.

Brandi gestured at the woods spreading around them, darkly honeyed with the evening light. "This is where Theodora built her house," she said. "She wanted this house to be somewhere quiet."

"Oh, come on," Hilma said. "Are you pretending to have some mystical connection with Theodora? How do you know what she wanted or didn't want?"

"'Cause I live here too," Brandi said. She wasn't timid, wasn't defiant. Jay was surprised at the quiet assertion in her voice. "I know Eternal Springs. I reckon Theodora loved it too, at least a little. And if'n she built a house way out here in these forests? She had a reason."

"Didn't she die out here in the woods?" Charlie asked. "Didn't they find her remains out here?"

Max lifted one foot, looked down as if he expected to see a skull peering up at him through the undergrowth.

"Like I said, there's magic out here." Brandi placed a palm against a tree trunk, gazed upward. "So. Let's be quiet."

Everyone acquiesced, falling silent. The six of them kept walking, walking, losing track of time. Something loosened, embracing them, inviting them in. There were over a million acres in the Arkansas Ozarks, some of it old-growth forest, trees that had been left to evolve beyond the reach of most human eyes. Jay caught the glimmer of swimming holes, the rising ridges of the bluffs. She fell under a spell. The crunch of her feet through the leaves, the contrast of the sunlight's warmth with the sharp breeze. She and Brandi had loved coming out here when they were younger. The forest's vastness felt like their own backyard and like a whole unexplored world at the same time.

But despite their silence, they couldn't find the house. When they only had an hour of daylight left, the six of them retreated, walking through the quickly pooling dusk, the crickets singing loudly. They emerged near a dirt road, far from the Garnets' parked car. They'd been using the old Asher Lake trailhead as a convenient landmark.

"What does this forest house even do, again?" Max asked.

"It's something about time moving differently. Time standing still, maybe?"

Time standing still. Right now Jay didn't want that. She wanted time to keep moving steadily forward, hurry up if possible. Get to the part where they'd found the last two houses, found the portal, and slipped through to whatever waited next.

30

2015

Yes, I've come back to Eternal Springs," Max repeats. "How many times do I need to say that? I'm not lying, I have nothing to lose at this point."

Hilma and Charlie had arrived at the Luck House for Max's arraignment; Jay didn't feel right questioning him without the others present. He sits in front of them, hangdog but defiant. Iggy is still shocked, Charlie is annoyed, but Hilma is livid, pacing in tight circles.

"Just tell us this, Max," Jay says. "Do you have anything to do with Brandi's disappearance?"

Everyone tenses. The luck has gone dangerous in Jay's hands. Does it still count as *luck* if it forces her to accept something terrible about one of her old friends?

"Jesus, is that what you think? Hold on," says Max, more wounded than she's seen him. "You think I'm a monster? Yeah, I've been back, and no, I didn't tell you, because I knew it'd lead to a lot of unnecessary bullshit. Case in point." He gestures at the four of them.

Jay remembers Max as a teenager, those playing cards revealing one royal flush after another. All that luck hoarded into his fingertips. She wonders if it feels strange for him to be in this place with everything going wrong. "Why did Brandi send you a picture of the Luck House?" she asks.

"Because I've been using it," Max says wearily. "How do I explain?" He exhales, scrapes his hands over his face. "All right. Shit. Here goes. When I was twenty-three, I got a job at Spearhead, and I was struggling. I was raised by *artists*, I didn't have that same cutthroat quality that the MBA assholes had. I was barely hanging on as a junior banker. I lost faith in myself." He touches his heart, illustrating where the belief had seeped out of him. "I was drinking too much, and I kept thinking back to when I was eighteen. When I was king of the world.

"It was a moment of weakness, okay? I thought it'd only be the one time. I took a red-eye flight over the weekend, showed up, didn't say a word to anybody. I bunked out in the Luck House, stole a Wi-Fi signal from a hotel, and worked on my pitch book from here. Everything fell into place for me. Boom. Before I left, I got a call from a client and talked my way into a major deal, one far beyond my pay scale. It was so fucking easy. Then I get home, and within a month I'm drowning again. So back I go."

"You never told me," Hilma says, accusatory.

"You weren't exactly available back then. I worked my way up the ranks, snuck away on weekends when I could. I worked hard. Trust me, I worked *hard*, this job is all I have. But yeah, the Luck House gave me boosts when I needed them."

"You've been using Theodora's magic to affect the outside world," Jay says. "That's a pretty big betrayal. Maybe we need to bring back our charter."

"I've stopped, I swear. I haven't been back since—god, 2012." He hesitates. "Maybe 2013. I can't remember. I have stopped, though."

"Have you?" Jay demands, skeptical.

"Yeah, sure. I've already got my corner office," says Max, but his brashness doesn't last. "Or—shit, I stopped because I knew I was addicted. My girlfriends left me. All the lucky trades in the world couldn't fix that. It got ugly. When I wasn't in Eternal, I convinced myself I was running into bad luck, scared, paranoid. I was just as coked out as every asshole I worked with, only I didn't have any rehab, couldn't talk about it to anyone. I acknowledged I'd fucked up and weaned myself off the Luck House."

"Just an hour ago, you said you couldn't imagine what it was like for adults to find this magic," Iggy points out.

"I lied. Obviously. I *do* know what it's like to encounter Theodora's magic as an adult, which is how I know it's dangerous. Anyway, the last time I came, the whole place was different." He encompasses their surroundings with a sweep of the arm. "Someone bought it up and changed the whole look. That was as good a reason as any to quit."

"Red Art?" asks Iggy.

"Not sure, I never asked who owned the house I was breaking into," Max says. "Look, I just know that—if Brandi was addicted to magic the way I was—" His voice cracks. "I just want to help her."

"All right. Hey, it's okay, man." Iggy moves to Max, as if to embrace him. But it's Max who crosses the distance and folds his huge frame into Iggy's. "No harm done."

Jay's heart catches at the two of them together. It's the closest they've come to the intimacy of their senior year.

"But there is harm done. People saw you," says Hilma, and the men break apart, looking at her. "You're publicly connected to this place, Max. Do you know how hard I've worked to keep our names disconnected from Eternal Springs, Arkansas? And you come sneaking back?"

"You didn't exactly complain when Spearhead helped you out with Geminist. If I hadn't used the Luck House, neither of us would've gotten our careers off the ground."

"That makes it worse. I never would've agreed if I'd known where you got your luck."

"Hey. Hil. No, no, it's okay," Max says, his voice pained, gentle. "I've been a chump. But don't lose sight of the plan. Who better than me to talk to Kenny Stringer? I'll do all the dirty work. I'm going to fix this. I'm going to get all five of us the hell out of here."

31

1999

"Thanks for studying with me," Iggy said as he and Jay trudged through the dusk. They were taking one of Eternal's shortcuts, a rocky pathway that twisted behind houses, giving them a rare back view of familiar structures. The latticework of stairs and porches, the messy yards slouching behind picture-perfect front lawns. Holiday lights sparkled, oddly melancholy against the twilight.

"I mean, I love talking about art, I could do it all day," Jay said. She'd been avoiding Ms. Hart since the conversation about college applications, feeling guilty without quite knowing why. But Iggy had asked Jay for help on a unit about abstract painters. They'd gone together to the Luck House, the sky darkening in that all-at-once way of early winter as they sat in opposite La-Z-Boys, poring over Picassos. It was a throwaway assignment, and the knowledge that it was an excuse added to the shy enchantment of the evening. When Iggy pointed to a displaced eye and his hand brushed against hers, the luck was so potent Jay felt she could explode.

"You know Hilma is named after an abstract painter? Hilma af Klint. She was into creepy stuff. Ghosts and the occult."

"Yeah, she mentioned. Makes sense 'cause Hilma's pretty wild herself."

For a second Jay remembered the way Ms. Garnet had spoken about Hilma, as if Jay were doing the Garnets a favor by befriending her. She batted the unease away. "She's great."

"Totally. Yeah." Iggy hesitated.

"What, you don't think so?"

"I love the twins, you know that. Just, sometimes . . . they kinda remind me of kids like Kenny Stringer. My mom always tells me not to hang out with Kenny, and it's weird, 'cause the twins make me feel that same way."

"Oh my god. They're nothing like Kenny."

"Yeah, not in most ways. But they're a little . . . dangerous? It's not always a bad thing."

"Well, if you're going to follow them into another world, you better trust them."

As they broke out onto Jay's street, Jay spotted her dad down the block, standing in the open doorway, scanning for her. Her pulse jumped, and she picked up her pace. Was her dad worried about her? When he saw them, he rushed forward.

"Dad," Jay said, heat rising to her face. "It's not what you think. This is—we were studying—" She wasn't lying, anyway. They *had* just been studying.

But her dad lifted a hand toward Iggy, hasty and distracted. "Yeah, nice to meet you, son. Jadelynne, we've got to go. Your friend's in trouble. Brandi needs us."

"What?" Everything else fell away at once. Jay saw a vivid flash of those bruises. Beside Jay, Iggy went very still. "Is she hurt? Where is she, is she—"

"She's at the police station."

In Pell's office, the room was divided. On one side, Max, long legs extended out from the chair like he was perched in a child's seat. Ms. Garnet stood behind him, her hand on his shoulder. She looked around the grubby office with curiosity. To Jay, she had the air of someone transplanted from the wrong painting, a De Lempicka in a Rockwell. There was a man too, a familiar-looking stranger, medium height with rumpled white hair. Mr. Garnet. If his wife was vaguely contemptuous, he seemed to be holding back a laugh.

Next to this trio, all by herself, was Brandi. One knobby, pale knee drawn to her chest. She was chewing on her knee without thinking, a tic that Jay hadn't seen since first grade.

"What's the trouble here?" Jay's dad asked. Jay went to Brandi, hovering near her so she wasn't alone. She caught the edge of Max's wink as he tried to get Jay's attention.

"Well," Mr. Garnet said, before Pell could speak, "it seems our star-crossed lovers—"

"Harold," Max interjected. "No. Stop. Don't say *lovers*, gross."

"—have been caught committing the cardinal sin of American society, making a mockery of their capitalist economy."

"They stole from Francesco's," Pell said patiently. "Sat down, ran up a one-hundred-and-fifty-dollar check, then tried to pay with counterfeit money."

"*Counterfeit*," Ms. Garnet said. "What a histrionic word choice. They're children. They aren't running some operation here. They made a small mistake."

"Ma'am, it's a small mistake that carries up to twenty years in prison," Pell said.

Brandi hunched lower.

"Anything to feed the for-profit system, I suppose," Mr. Garnet said. "Listen, this is ridiculous. It's a waste of your time and of ours." Laughter twinkled under his voice, like they were all in on the joke.

Jay tried to understand. Brandi and Max went to Francesco's together? They paid with counterfeit money. She realized that the "counterfeit" had to be the bills from the Duplication House, the ones Hilma had made Brandi swear not to spend on rent or groceries. It surprised her that Brandi would use those duplicated bills, but not half as much as Max and Brandi together. She'd felt deliciously guilty, "studying" with Iggy, and meanwhile Brandi and Max had been brazenly sitting at a restaurant table with candles and cloth napkins.

Jay willed Brandi to look at her, but her friend was a tight knot.

"How do you know the money is counterfeit?" Ms. Garnet asked.

Pell seemed to have been waiting for this question, because he produced a handful of bills and fanned them out on his desk. "The waitress noticed a few telltale signs, unfortunately for these young people."

Jay leaned closer, heartbeat wild, wondering if Pell or her dad or the Garnet parents could possibly detect the magic at play. The bills looked convincing enough at first glance. It took Jay a second to realize that Grant was winking.

She suppressed a startled laugh and looked at the next one. IN DOG WE TRUST stretched across the Capitol spire. The third looked fine, but Jay reached out and touched it tentatively. The texture was subtly wrong, fuzzy as a new leaf.

"These are well crafted," Ms. Garnet said. "Surely that effort counts for something?"

Pell cleared his throat. "Using illegal tender is a crime, as I've said. Anyway, ma'am, I've seen fake bills before in this town. About as well crafted as these ones here."

"Brandi," Jay's dad said. "What is this? You're not like this."

It was the first time someone had addressed either Brandi or Max, and she jerked her head up. Her mouth left a wet pink imprint on the skin of her knee.

"I'm sorry about this," Jay's dad said, addressing every adult in the office. "Brandi's been my daughter's best friend for a long time. She comes from a difficult family, but she's been a good girl as long as I've known her. This is very surprising."

"Apples and trees." Pell fixed his gaze on Brandi, and Jay bristled.

"We knew our children would meet different types out here," Ms. Garnet said delicately. "I trusted that they'd be strong enough in their own convictions to not be unduly influenced. We've been glad that Max and Hilma have found a new group of friends, but—"

"Fuck, it was me," Max said loudly. "It was all my idea. It's not her fault that I paid with fake money, okay? She was just being a good friend. Throw me in prison, whatever, I don't care, but don't blame her." His eyes were burning. "She's innocent."

The office went silent. Brandi stayed still, like she couldn't trust herself to move. Pell looked down at his desk, shifting a pencil a few inches. "Well, young man," he said, "that's a very gentlemanly thing to say. I admire someone who can protect the less fortunate. Nobody would judge you for falling in with the wrong crowd."

"No," Max said. "It's me. *I'm* the 'wrong crowd.' Brandi did nothing wrong. And if you try to get her into trouble, I'll sue you. I'll sue this whole town."

Pell held up a palm. "All right, now. We're still figuring this out."

"Let us cover the restaurant bill and then some," Mr. Garnet said, with an air of finality. "We'll speak to the restaurant's owner, we'll make sure everyone is well compensated for the trouble. Kids will be kids. I'm sure we've all learned very important lessons about economic value. Use the slips of paper the Man says you can, no other paper will do. Ridiculous, isn't it? Our entire economy devalued by a single wink?" He gestured at Grant.

"I reckon that paying for the meal is the best course of action,"

Pell conceded, and Max bounced out of his chair as if the tension of the past hour had entirely vanished. "But you kids need to be careful from now on. We don't take lightly to people breaking the rules."

The shed was dark, but they lit a candle, sitting inside the circle it created. Jay was relieved to be in here again, just the two of them. Except for occasional sessions of drawing, or picking work for their portfolios, she and Brandi hadn't spent much time without the other four. Jay leaned in close, their knees touching as they sat cross-legged on either side of the candle.

"Oh my *god*," Jay said. "What happened? Max was breaking the rules, Hilma's going to *kill* him. Nobody voted on this or anything."

"It was my fault, no matter what he said, Max invited me out, and—and I wanted to go so bad. I wasn't thinking. At the end of dinner, I saw that check and I panicked, and—"

Jay burst out laughing. "IN DOG WE TRUST? Seriously?"

Brandi didn't join in. "Most of the time, people don't notice."

"What do you mean, *most* of the time?" Jay asked, growing serious, realizing that Brandi wasn't amused. When Jay reached for her hands, her friend's grip was light, restless.

"I been using the bills from the Duplication House to buy stuff."

"What kind of *stuff*?" Jay asked.

"Just things. I don't know. Toilet paper. Food."

"Can't Gene help with that? We know he has a job."

Brandi didn't answer.

"Hey. If you're in trouble, you can tell me. Always, Brandi. Come on."

There was a silence, and Jay realized that the very act of saying this was a fissure between them, proof that Brandi couldn't speak freely because they'd become almost strangers, even while they were sitting right next to each other. Her chest hurt with the loss.

"Don't tattle to the others," Brandi said at last. "Please." She freed one hand and dragged it under her eye, leaving a wet glitter of eyeliner. "I'm embarrassed, I don't wanna ruin this."

"I would never. I don't think Max will tell either. He was looking out for you." Jay caught Brandi's small smile, highlighted in the candle flicker, and grabbed on to this. "Hey. You two were on a date, huh? Your first real date?"

Brandi laughed then, shy and pleased. "Yeah, I—I reckon so."

"What did you talk about? What was it like? Did you—did he kiss you?"

"Jay," Brandi protested. "No. He wouldn't. I mean, he was being nice and all, but no. He's not—I don't reckon he'd like me when Destiny's around, you know?"

"That's ridiculous," Jay said forcefully. "You're perfect. Are you kidding me? Max would be so lucky. And look, Brandi, he's not asking Destiny to come to another world with him. He's asking you." Lightly, she touched Brandi's forehead with her fingertip.

32

2015

NOW

"This is so stupid," Hilma says, perched on the bed part of the bed-and-breakfast. It's ruffly white, a massive upholstered headboard rising behind her. "We're already potentially wanted for murder and now we're soliciting drugs in an Airbnb. Are we like those idiots in true-crime documentaries who bring it on themselves?"

Max has booked the honeymoon suite, the only room available at such short notice. Iggy and Charlie both bowed out of this mission, staying at Thermal Park instead, running damage control on their interrupted lives. Jay wonders if their absence also has something to do with the last two missing photographs. It's too big a coincidence, and finding out about Max's photo has only made it more obvious. Hilma and Jay and Max each have Polaroids from Brandi, why not those two? Pacing in front of the electric fireplace, Jay calculates which photos are still unaccounted-for. The Duplication House; the Oath House. The one they're in right now.

The rear of the house has a half-built shell of scaffolding, the place is in the middle of a paint job, but for now it's still recognizable as the two-story bungalow that they broke into that long-ago day. Jay's scar tingles; this is where the skin was first broken.

"On the other hand, if we get a confession out of this asshole, we could be out of here by sunset." Hilma looks from Jay to Max and back. "Do you think it will be that easy?"

Jay shrugs helplessly. At some point after she arrived back in Eternal, Jay thought fulfilling the promise could be simple, something from an episode of *CSI*. Find out what happened to Brandi. Solution, resolution, escape. But now that she's seen the vandalized basement of the Mirror House, the eaten-up shreds of the journal, it feels like there's more to this. Not just Kenny hurting Brandi in a tired, ugly brawl, but Kenny finding out about the houses, Kenny warping the magic into a cheap scheme. She remembers the way he once bragged about finding customers by hanging around the school counselor's office, and rage rises in her.

There's a knock, quick and confident.

Max opens the door. It takes only a second for Kenny's expression to change, his smile falling away: He jerks, tensed to run. But Max grabs Kenny by the collar and pulls him into the suite, shoving the door closed behind him with his hip. Hilma jumps to her feet. Jay's grimly glad that Max is on their side and taller than Kenny by half a foot.

Max pushes Kenny into the center of the room before barricading the door with his body. Kenny stumbles and rights himself. He looks the same, but skinnier, all his baby fat deflated. "Fuck," he says. His voice is the same, gravelly and twangy. "Hey. Listen. Listen, I don't want any trouble."

"What a coincidence. Neither do we."

"How'd you get my number? What'd you do?"

"Oh please," Hilma says. "You're not exactly a hard man to find, Stringer. You agreed to meet up with a total stranger."

"No, I thought you was—" Kenny shoots back, then stops, collecting himself. "I never agreed to meet up with *y'all*. What are you playing at, anyway? This is goddamn entrapment."

"You'll get out of here quickly if you do what we say." Max is infinitely patient.

Kenny's eyes bounce from one of them to the other, sticking longer on Jay. She stares back, unafraid. There's a rush of power in using Theodora's houses again, a feeling she hasn't found anywhere else. Most houses feel inert to her, hollow and lifeless. Finally, she's back inside houses that are alive, breathing, passing their power on to her.

"Jadelynne," Kenny says. "This is about Brandi, huh? Y'all know I didn't kill her. I didn't do a thing to that girl. You must've talked to the cops, you *know*—"

"Well, now you're going to talk to us," Jay says. "Okay? If you don't want the police to know you're here with the intent to sell."

"They already know about me," Kenny says. "What will piss them off is y'all, coming back here, making trouble, thinking you're above the law. As always."

Jay's stomach twists at his sanctimoniousness, though a deeper part of her wonders if he has a point. They are the interlopers now, the outsiders. She feels the full separation between herself and Eternal Springs. Here she is, aligned with the rich kids, exploiting someone like Kenny. It's a surprising and sudden self-doubt.

"Listen," Max says. "We aren't your enemies, Kenny. If you tell us what we need to know, we'll all walk away from this happy. We'll even pay you what we promised. I swear, man." The air shivers, like the whole house is inhaling. "But I need a guarantee from you too."

Jay watches Kenny. If he does know about the power of Theodora's houses, then he'll refuse. He'll probably understand what's at stake when you agree to something inside these walls. He's frightened, but his expression doesn't change as he chews this proposal over. "What kinda guarantee?" he asks finally.

"Nothing big. Just swear that you'll tell us the whole truth about Brandi Addams."

Kenny considers, then jerks out a nod. "Yeah, I can do that."

"Swear," Max presses. "Actually say it, man."

The genuine confusion on Kenny's face makes Jay believe that he doesn't know about the house at all. He doesn't understand the power being invoked here. Her theory that he's behind this flickers, uncertain.

"I swear," Kenny says, and at Max's keep-going gesture, he continues, "I—I swear I'll tell the whole truth about Brandi Addams."

Again, the air ripples.

Hilma wastes no time. "So tell me the truth. Did you kill Brandi Addams?"

"No," Kenny says. "I told you, I didn't kill her."

The three of them are quiet, watching, not sure what will happen next. They don't know how the Oath House will affect him without his own scar as a barometer of promise-keeping.

"Did you kidnap her?" Hilma asks at last.

"No," Kenny spits.

"Did you ever hurt her?" she presses.

"No, I fucking didn't."

Hilma's quiet. Jay realizes that they're all three waiting to see how this latest statement will pan out, whether it will meet the exacting standards of the Oath House. It takes only a minute; Jay thinks of the way her scar began aching by the time she'd read the entirety of Brandi's message. *You promised.* Already, Kenny's turning paler, skin draining of color, slick with sudden sweat. He tries to fight it. He puts up a good effort. But then he's sinking to the floor, clutching his stomach, groaning softly in an instinctive, animalistic way that makes Jay pity him in spite of herself.

The oath is working. He's a liar.

"Kenny?" Max asks conversationally. "Do you want to try again?"

Kenny's head jerks. He opens his mouth, and a thin splatter of vomit lands on the plush rug. Hilma steps back, wrinkling her nose. "Just tell us the truth, Kenneth. You promised to tell the truth. Did you hurt Brandi?"

"I've—I've hurt her in the past," Kenny says, speaking to the floor. "I have. Nothing big. Just . . . we fought, you know? When she was out of her mind, when I wasn't feeling good. I'd—I'd hit her, sometimes. Shove her. Nothing big. But I didn't hurt her this time, I swear it. We barely talked at all. She was always with that shithead. With Roy." His voice strengthens as he speaks, until finally he's able to straighten. "I—I don't know what happened. I'm . . ." He gestures, humiliated, at the vomit.

"Forget it," Max says. "Do you know where Brandi is?"

"I don't know. If I knew, I'd do anything to help her. I loved that girl. Still do."

"It doesn't exactly sound like it," Jay says. "You hit her." Her anger boils, low and hot. He had no right, no right to hurt Brandi. But then, it wasn't the first time Brandi got hurt by people who were supposed to love her.

Kenny holds her gaze, but at least has the decency to look ashamed.

"And now you don't know anything about what happened to her?" Jay asks.

"Not a thing. I've told the cops everything."

They wait. Nothing happens. Kenny stays standing. He's telling the truth. Hilma curses, wheels in a small circle. Jay releases a long breath. The knowledge that Kenny isn't behind Brandi's disappearance pushes them back to square one.

"Do you know who Roy is?" Jay asks, changing tack. "Did you ever meet?"

"Never. I don't even think that's his real name."

"Well, that's fucking convenient," says Max.

"He must've been some hot shit, though. She was obsessed with the guy. If anybody finds him, he has a lot to answer for, 'cause either he did this to her, or he doesn't care about her at all. He hasn't come forward. Coward." Kenny half lifts his baseball cap, an angry gesture.

Roy—or whoever he is—is starting to seem more and more like a ghost, something conjured just to baffle them. "Was he from around here?" Jay asks.

"Nobody knows." Kenny laughs grimly. "Goddamn if that's not the biggest joke that girl ever played on me, falling for some out-of-towner. She hated all these new developments."

"Progress comes everywhere," Hilma says, distracted. "Even to Arkansas."

A harsh laugh. "Yeah, that's what folks say. That we gotta be grateful for progress. Well, I lost my job because of places like Red Art. They all have their own crews. That's why I had to move to Fayette. Couldn't make an honest living here anymore."

"At least you can still make a dishonest one," Hilma chirps, and Kenny smiles.

"Red Art," Jay repeats, caught on that. "I've seen that name around town. They took over management of Thermal Park Hotel, didn't they?"

"Took over a lot more than that. They've been buying up everything. If you don't want to work for them, you're out of luck."

"Is that why Kathy fired Brandi?" Jay asks, remembering the texts.

He looks startled, suspicious. "How'd you know about that?"

Jay waits for his response.

Kenny glances at the ceiling as if asking for Brandi's forgiveness. "Kathy is good people. She put up with a lot, she was real nice about Brandi not always making her shifts on time. But Brandi finally fucked up for good. Kathy found out she was breaking into houses around town."

The world stutters to a halt around Jay.

"She was using her keys to get inside. It's shitty. Brandi *loved* that job. She said it wasn't about cleaning other people's messes, it was about making the 'space beautiful again.' I never thought she'd get fired, not even at her worst."

"What, was she stealing?" Hilma asks.

"Nothing was missing. That's what Kathy told me. Not even a box of Kleenex. But Kathy couldn't risk that shit, you know, people thinking her cleaners were stealing. Not when Red Art was ready to swoop in and take all Kathy's jobs."

"So what was she doing in the houses," Hilma says, but it's not quite a question.

"No," corrects Jay quietly. "What was she looking for?"

The artificial fire ripples, a strip of flickering, bruised purple. The significance of this shines against all three of them, as clearly as the reflected flames.

"Was Brandi planning a trip or anything?" Jay manages, throat gone tight.

"Uh. Well, now. One time I came by to grab some shit and she had a suitcase open on the couch. Didn't even know she owned a suitcase. I've never seen her go farther than Branson. I tried to guess where she was going, and she laughed me off. She said she was going somewhere I couldn't follow. I thought she was joking, but not a month later she's . . ."

Gone. She's gone.

"I reckoned y'all would know." Kenny's tone slips into darkness. "Wouldn't you? The six of y'all were always breaking into houses. I'd be biking around town and I'd see you breaking windows or hanging around some old dump. So I figured, maybe you know what she's looking for now. Maybe that's why . . ."

"Why what?" Max asks.

"Why y'all came running back, the moment she left."

The three of them are quiet. While he's been inside Theodora's house, bound by his oath to them, Jay's let herself half forget how much Kenny hates them. But there's no mistaking the fear and disgust in the look Kenny gives them right now.

"You said we'd all walk out of here if I answered your questions," Kenny says. "I've upheld my end of the deal. I got places to be."

The Garnet twins exchange glances over his head, and Hilma speaks up, as if they've prearranged a script. "Kenny, can you promise me you won't tell anybody we talked to you? Swear you won't share a word of what you said to us tonight."

He gnaws his lower lip. "You know what? Fuck you and your promises."

"How much money do you make in a night, usually? Here's double," Max says, gentle. He takes two bills out of his wallet, but when Kenny reaches for them, Max pulls them out of his grasp. "We were serious when we said we didn't want any trouble. We need your discretion right now."

Kenny huffs. But his subconscious—now having been tethered to Theodora's magic—must recognize the threat that falls over him. "I swear I won't say a word about this. Happy?"

"Very," Max says, moving out of the way of the door, extending the money with an exaggerated graciousness. "Pleasure doing business."

Kenny can bolt for freedom. He doesn't. He looks so furious that Jay feels herself become the monster, feels the house around her turn into a weapon. "I know you're hiding something," Kenny says, addressing all three of them, or maybe just Jay. "I'm just telling it to you straight. People ain't happy to see y'all back. And if you've hurt Brandi? We'll find out."

No, you won't, Jay thinks, very tired. *You haven't yet.*

Jay knocks, getting more frantic. She feels exposed out here in the glossy, refurbished corridor of the Thermal Park Hotel, but she needs all five of them to know about Brandi breaking into houses, Brandi and her suitcase. Brandi leaving town. This is what they're meant to discover. This is at the center of everything, she knows it, she knows it.

The moment they heard that Brandi Addams was gone—*without a trace*—they shouldn't have wasted time with other possibilities. It's so obvious what happened. But Jay needs to talk to Charlie. She needs his mix of cynicism and optimism, the way he can measure all possibilities.

"He's not here."

Iggy's in the hallway, his face drawn, very tired. "What do you mean?" Jay asks, moving back from the door. Another reason she's seeking out Charlie before Iggy: she doesn't trust herself to be alone in Iggy's hotel room. "Did he step out, or—"

"He left, Jay, he bailed on us." Iggy shows Jay his phone. A single text from Charlie, bright on the screen: *I'm sorry, but I've made other promises too. Good luck.*

33

2000

As long as we can see those lights, the world hasn't ended yet," Charlie said.

They sprawled in a close circle, limbs intertwined, reckless and giddy. All of Eternal Springs was spread out beneath them, a network of shining lights. They were at the Mirror House for New Year's Eve, with the twins' stolen bottles of champagne, which left bitter sparkles in Jay's mouth. They had been so wrapped up in the search for the sixth and seventh houses, and ultimately for the Portal House itself, that the panic over Y2K was a background buzz.

Jay felt bad for the people who were hoarding groceries or hiding in their tornado shelters. They only had the one world, after all. They occupied exactly one reality, and if anything happened to it, they were screwed.

"Almost time," Max shouted, springing to his feet. Lucky, curled around his neck like a boa, shifted lethargically. "It's eleven fifty-nine, everyone. The end of the world."

"In Tonga it's already 2000, we'd know if the world had ended," Charlie said, but he was drowned out by the twins, who started yelling the countdown.

Six—five—four—

Jay imagined their world gone, vanished, thrown into disarray. But they'd stay together, the six of them. They'd look for the remaining houses, their own private mission. It would be freeing, in a way, to have nothing left to leave behind.

"Happy New Year," Max shouted, and the lights outside were still shining, insistent on their own survival. Max was kissing everyone, kissing the top of Hilma's head, kissing Iggy and Charlie on the cheek. His mouth landed on Jay's, champagne-ripe, and a surprising flutter woke inside her. She watched as Max kissed Brandi next, his huge hands cupping her face, leaving her rosy when he pulled back, as if he'd transferred his own blush to her skin. Jay grinned at Brandi when Max's back was turned, and Brandi bit down an abashed smile.

"This is the problem with this town," Charlie said. "Nobody for me to kiss."

"I'll kiss you again," Max offered, "you're the best-looking one here," but Charlie pushed him away, laughing.

Then Brandi wrapped Jay in a hug, one of those ferocious embraces that nearly rocked her off her feet. "Happy New Year, Jay," she whispered. "What's your resolution for me, huh?"

Jay had nearly forgotten about their tradition. To come up with resolutions for each other, which always motivated them more than trying to stick to one of their own promises. Jay hadn't put much thought into this year, but then, she didn't need to think about it. "I resolve for you to be totally happy," she said, brushing Brandi's hair behind her ear.

Brandi laughed. "That's cheating, and you know it."

"It's what I want for you," Jay protested. "Okay, then. What's my resolution, Ms. Smartypants?"

But before Brandi could answer, someone tapped Jay's shoulder, and she turned. Iggy pushed his hair out of his eyes. His heartbeat was visible in his throat, and she had a sudden impulse to press her fingers there.

"Well, it's past midnight," Iggy said. "We're still alive."

"Yeah. We are."

Iggy's lips brushed the side of her mouth, and Jay didn't let herself overthink things—didn't let herself calculate exactly how many girls he'd kissed, divided by how few boyfriends she'd had. Instead, Jay hooked her hand around his neck, his skin feverishly warm, and she kissed him, full on the mouth.

When they pulled back, a little stunned, a little unsteady, Jay shrugged, her old shyness falling over her again, though her body was still buzzing. She'd kissed Ignacio Nieves and he'd kissed her back. Max whooped, clapped his hands.

"Happy New Year," Iggy said to the room at large.

"Happy new millennium," Hilma corrected. "This is the year we blow this popsicle stand for good."

And Jay felt it. Just as surely as she'd known that their lives wouldn't end at midnight along with everyone else's, she knew now that their lives weren't going to continue, not in the same way. Their lives were going to start anew, start all over again.

34

2015

NOW

After a sleepless night, the four of them have reconvened at the Mirror House. It's the beginning of their fourth day in Eternal Springs, Arkansas, and so far, instead of finding their sixth friend, they've lost another one. Charlie's blocked their numbers; the hotel clerk verified that he checked out of his hotel room, but couldn't say anything more. Jay is wild with worry. "Well, he's a grown man," Max says. "He handles artists for a living. As the child of artists, I can assure you, that makes Charlie tougher than you think."

"What does he even mean by 'promises'?" Hilma asks. "Should we be worried that he's going to sell us out?"

"I figured he meant promises to Ms. Blind Item," Max says. "The actress?"

"The singer," Jay corrects. "That's the most likely explanation." But she can't shake the fear that all of her friends are lying to her, that the missing pieces of this puzzle are tucked inside them, waiting to be diligently collected. Hilma was lying. Max was lying. Why not Charlie too?

"Maybe he meant promises to himself," Iggy says. "Promises to his loved ones. We've all got those." His smile is bitter, and Jay thinks of Elle, left behind and in the dark. How long before Iggy makes a run for it too? She imagines that one by one they'll leave her behind to clean up this mess alone.

It might not be the worst thing. When Jay thinks of her apartment in Albany, of the clean, well-lit gallery that will hold her drawings, it's all far away. Eternal feels incredibly present. Maybe it's because of the Portal House, that possibility reawakened.

"We never even got to tell Charlie," Jay says, realizing. "He doesn't even know that Brandi found the Portal House."

"No," Hilma says at once, flat. "She didn't find the Portal House."

Max and Iggy look back and forth between them, sensing the impending fight.

"What?" Jay says, confused. "Brandi was breaking into houses. She's gone now. Where else could she be?"

"She couldn't have, I'm sorry. We looked everywhere when we were teenagers. I was thorough. You know how much I wanted that. You know how much we *all* wanted that."

"You left her with the journal, Hilma," Iggy points out, and Jay's grateful to him for backing her up. "Brandi's lived in Eternal fifteen years longer than the rest of us. Why is it so crazy to think that she found it?"

Max watches them, head ducked, biting speculatively at a fingernail.

"You want me to say it? Fine. Make me into the bad guy, I'm used to it." Hilma leans forward. "I don't think an addict in Arkansas is capable of finding a place that all of our combined efforts couldn't."

"That's not fair," Jay says. "She was only an addict because *we* did it to her."

"Oh, I'm not playing that game."

"What game?" Jay demands. "It's true."

"Brandi's mother is an addict, wherever the hell she is," Hilma says. "Her stepdad too. I'd put down good money that her ancestors were addicted to something. So I don't blame myself." She pauses. "I don't blame *us*."

Jay's irritation at Hilma flares, this matter-of-fact summary that skims over so much of Brandi's family history, the knots and tangles of neglect and optimism and despair. At the same time, what if Jay could convince herself that Brandi's addiction isn't her fault? It's tempting to at least ease some of the shame she's been carrying.

"All right," Max says. "No need to point fingers. If Brandi did indeed find the Portal House—" He holds out a preemptively appeasing hand to Hilma. "*If* she did, then why bring us to Eternal? I mean, maybe Charlie has the right idea. We're free to go."

The photos, the message. *You promised.* The warped phrases carved into the basement of the Mirror House. The left-behind necklace, the blood splashed across Brandi's trailer. All this effort. But for what?

"Do you remember the last time Brandi wanted to go on a quest?" Jay asks softly.

The others' faces go very still. They don't have to answer.

"I think we're back on a quest now," Jay says. "Whether we like it or not." She stands, stretching, pacing, trying to find her way back to girl-detective mode. "Red Art," Jay says. "That name keeps popping up. I think we should look into them."

"What's your theory?" Hilma asks. "Brandi pushed back too hard against the developers? They retaliated against her, hurt her?"

"That seems extreme," Max says.

"Maybe one of them found out about Theodora's houses," Jay suggests. "Maybe they're going after those specific houses on purpose." She shifts her theory from Kenny Stringer to faceless real estate developers.

"How would we find out who's behind Red Art? The county clerk?" Hilma pulls out her phone, fingers flying as she researches. "Right, the county assessor. They're open today. If I give them a call from the Luck House, do you think I can pull off being an interested party? Maybe I'll get lucky, the assessor will be in a gossipy mood." She looks around. "So that's my task. Anyone else want to step up and be useful?"

"I'm going to the Duplication House," Jay says decisively. "Remember the necklace they found in the trailer? Maybe Brandi—or whoever—made a copy of mine and planted it. We need to see if there's anything else that could show up and hurt us." There's also the issue of the two photos that remain unaccounted-for, but Jay doesn't mention those.

Iggy chimes in. "We should be going to all of Theodora's houses. Look how long it took us to go to the Mirror House basement. We can't risk that again. We need to visit the Forever House too."

"Hey, I don't know," Max says. "Should we leave fingerprints inside every house?"

"Max, come on," Hilma says. "It's a little late to play that angle. You've been sneaking back for years. If anyone's endangered us, it's you."

"Fair point, madam. I'll take the Forever House, then." Max's eyes flick between Jay and Iggy. "I doubt either of you want to go there."

"If you can actually find it, that would be great," Jay says. She doesn't acknowledge the way something long-buried rears its head at the mention of the Forever House. "You know the Forever House is unpredictable, it won't just show up when you need it. Please don't get lost, Max."

"Don't worry about me. I'm a rich kid, remember? They'll call in the professional search parties, it'll be front-page news." He winks, but it doesn't dispel the tension. "You go with Jay, Igster. If somebody's using the Dupe House to fuck us over, she'll need protection."

Jay says, "I don't need a bodyguard. I defend myself just fine in the outside world, I can do it here in Eternal too."

"I'd like to go. Not to protect you," Iggy adds quickly. "But strength in numbers, right?"

He doesn't have much of a choice, Jay realizes. Either he comes with her, the two of their adult selves alone together, or he goes to the place that holds nothing but memories of them as teenagers.

As Jay's about to leave, trailing Iggy into the clean, sunlit morning, Hilma catches her elbow. "Bluejay. Listen. I was being shitty about Brandi and her issues, and I'm sorry." She sounds so regretful that Jay's surprised. "It's not entirely about Brandi, okay?"

"I know you've never liked Arkansas," Jay says. "It's fine."

"I'm nervous for you, lady. That's all."

"Nervous for me? I'm all right. Well. As all right as any of us."

"I don't want you getting obsessed with the Portal House. I don't want to reopen that wound. You've obviously managed to get your life together, and it's not worth it to blow that apart." With an incredible gentleness, Hilma smooths Jay's hair down. "It's safest to keep that door shut until we have more proof. Okay?"

Jay nods, and Hilma lets go of her, apparently satisfied. Jay's not sure that Hilma even realizes it, the way her own face was transformed with longing when she spoke, back to her seventeen-year-old self, yanked from the brink of a new world.

35

2000

THEN

I don't believe it," Jay repeated, as they hurried up the long, twist-ing hill that wound past the post office. Her breath came in silver puffs. January was the bleakest month in Arkansas, a never-ending stretch of gunmetal skies that could make you forget sunshine ex-isted. Jay's mom had called it *the great grayness*, apparently based on some old picture book, and that term came into Jay's head when-ever winter fell. But at least there was a ray of hope, because Brandi had found another house.

"If you keep saying that, I'm gonna be hurt," Brandi said, laughing.

"Sorry, but when did you find it? How?"

"I was in this house the other day, and I noticed something. I went and double-checked in the journal, and I reckon Charlie was reading one of those little maps upside down, sorta? 'Cause if'n you turned it sideways, it matched the house I was in."

"Wait, you were in someone else's *house*?" Jay asked. "Whose?"

Brandi's face took on one of these new expressions Jay couldn't decode, and it gave Jay that sudden sinking feeling. There was a guardedness to Brandi that Jay wasn't used to; it was as if she'd had a house key for years and then, one day, found all the locks changed overnight.

"You'll see," Brandi said.

The six of them stood in the living room. Jay saw her own confusion mirrored in the others' faces. Someone's coat was draped over the love seat. In the room was a Christmas tree, left over from the holidays, its lights unplugged. The air was itchy with artificial lemon. The place was clearly occupied. If there was any of Theodora's magic inside these walls, it had to be so gummed up behind the humdrum of ordinary life that it couldn't get out. Jay pressed her hand to a wallpapered corner, the texture faintly sticky.

"Brandi," Hilma said. "What makes you think this is one of Theodora's? I know we're all getting impatient, but have you even tested it?"

"No," Brandi said. "I waited for y'all. Of course." Her eyes darted uncertainly.

"Well, that's sweet, but if Charlie couldn't track it down, and I haven't found evidence of this house in the journal, it just seems unlikely that . . ." Hilma paused.

"That I found it?" Brandi finished for her.

"Does it matter?" asked Jay, hiding her own doubt. "We've been stuck for months. I think it's amazing that Brandi found it."

"Don't look a gift house in the mouth," Max said.

"Why do you have a key to this place?" Charlie asked Brandi, kind but skeptical.

Brandi bit her bottom lip, hesitating.

"Brandi, this really is very unusual," Hilma said. "Are we safe here? Is someone about to come walking in?"

"The folks who live here are out of town. I know because I've been cleaning houses," Brandi said in a rush. "That's how I found it."

Iggy nodded, unbothered. He worked late shifts at his family's restaurant all the time. But Max rubbed the back of his neck too hard. Jay concealed her surprise. They'd had summer jobs—babysitting, scooping ice cream, manning the dustier gift shops. But this felt serious. Like the kind of job that you got when you decided you were staying in one place.

"Cleaning houses?" Hilma repeated. "What for?"

"For money," Brandi said. "Rent."

"You live in a trailer, don't you?"

"It's lot rent," Jay jumped in, bracing herself against the Garnets' follow-up questions. "For the space to keep the trailer on, and hookups and things. Like septic tanks." Brandi shrank at the mention of septic tanks; Jay wondered if she'd gone too far.

"Okaaaaay, well, I didn't know about that," Hilma said, flushing, whether from embarrassment or annoyance Jay couldn't tell. "I figured if you were living in a trailer park, you at least didn't have to pay for it, that seems—"

"Don't," Jay said quietly. She couldn't stand the way Brandi looked right now, her pride drained away to reveal that sadness that always clung to her these days. "Leave it alone."

Hilma looked like she was going to argue, and then something shifted in her. "There's just so much that I don't understand about, like, not having much money. I haven't had many friends who are in that position."

"Or any friends, for that matter," said Max.

"Max—" Hilma began.

"Oh come on. They should know, Hil. We know so much about them. We're going into another world. The six of us will be each other's only friends there. Like, each other's only *anything*. We can't have secrets or—or be judging each other and shit. We have to be open."

Hilma stood next to the Christmas tree with its threadbare tinsel, the unlit bulbs like glossy buds among the stiff green branches. Jay didn't recognize the expression on her face: she looked unpeeled, the lines of an erased draft peeking through her more polished facade.

"What are you talking about, guys?" Iggy asked.

"There's actually been some trouble, back home," Max said. "Kids who are just total shitheads to Hilma. You should hear the names they made up. They'd invite Hilma out and then nobody would show up, somebody found her diary once and read it aloud to the class—"

"*Your* friends, Max," Hilma said, and Jay was relieved she'd cut Max off before they had to hear any more details. "Not just some kids."

"They weren't really my friends. Just acquaintances." But Max scratched one cheek. "Anyway. That's why my parents wanted us to come to Arkansas. Because of my sister. Like a 'fresh start' or a 'reset' or something. If it weren't for her and her issues, we'd be back home in Massachusetts. Fourteen hundred miles away, baby. That's how much distance my sister needs."

It was difficult to imagine Hilma Garnet being friendless, alone, unliked. It flew against everything Jay knew of this ferocious girl forged of brass. She imagined Hilma crossing state lines with Theodora's journal on her lap and becoming somebody else because she *had* to.

"I'm real sorry," Brandi said at last, addressing Hilma directly. "You don't deserve that."

Hilma's face crumpled before she caught herself. "I really am sorry too. I'm so sorry, Brandi, I was being horribly rude."

"You have us now," Jay said impulsively. "We're your friends, right? Always."

"Totally," Iggy said, and Charlie nodded, somber.

There was a muffled car horn, reminding them all that the outside world existed. Brandi walked to the closet next to the Christmas tree, clicking on the light. The shelves inside were piled with fleece blankets, board games, but Jay instantly spotted the words carved into the wall, near the ceiling. HIS WORDS ARE BONDS, HIS OATHS ARE ORACLES.

"Definitely looks like Theodora's work," Charlie said, moving closer.

"What do you think it means?" Hilma asked Brandi, an olive branch extended.

"Well, I reckon it's like a cross-your-heart-and-hope-to-die house," Brandi explained. "You make an oath to each other, and maybe this house'll hold you to it?"

She was wistful. Jay knew exactly how many broken promises were scattered across Brandi's life. Sometimes, lately, Jay felt like she too was letting Brandi down, even if she couldn't pinpoint exactly how.

"Yeah," Charlie said. "I suspected there was a house like this, Theodora mentions making promises to the people in her life, and she seemed to take those promises very seriously."

"See?" Brandi said. "I told y'all she had friends around town. Didn't I?"

Max turned to Brandi. "You're the one who found this house, my lady," he said, with a flourish of an imaginary hat. "So you're the one who gets to decide on our oath."

Brandi looked around, face alight. "Really? Because there is somethin'." She stopped, struggling. "I want us to always be there for each other. Like we are now. We should promise that, if'n we ever need each other? We'll come when the other calls. No matter what."

After a second, Hilma exhaled. "That's a huge ask."

"Nah, I like it," said Max. "Like the Bat Signal. Let's take a vote. I vote yes."

"It's perfect," Iggy said. "The six of us? Look what we've done together. We'll never have anything like this again. Yes."

"I agree," Charlie said, quiet but intense. He didn't seem to want to explain any further.

Jay was alive with a deep gratitude for the five of them and the way they'd rearranged her last year into something unimaginable. They'd shown her exactly what was beyond the reaches of Eternal Springs, pried open her future. "Let's do it," she said.

They were all looking at Hilma now. Wordlessly, she nodded once.

Brandi grinned shakily. "Okay, then."

"Can that vote be our commitment?" Charlie asked. "How does this work?"

"No," Iggy said. "Everyone knows you have to draw blood to make a vow serious."

"That's extremely unhygienic," Charlie said, but his protest was half-hearted. This house had shifted. It was no longer a family's messy home. It was a glowing temple: a place where vows were formed, sacrosanct, eternal.

Without wasting time, Iggy patted himself down and extracted a penknife. He made one quick stroke across the underside of his forearm, and blood rose in bright beads.

"Jesus, Iggy, I underestimated you," Hilma said.

"I tore my meniscus when I was in sixth grade. This is nothing."

Max let out his breath, shook his shoulders back. His slice was more hesitant, but after a second, blood welled, a hot line against his turquoise veins. Hilma closed her eyes, wincing, not breaking the skin for what felt like an agonizing eternity. Charlie was intent and precise, like a doctor.

When it was Jay's turn, she didn't let herself look at what she was doing. She dug in, and there was a second of breathtaking pain, and then it subsided into a lusterless ache. She passed the penknife to Brandi, who didn't flinch at all when she cut herself.

"All right," Max said, poking experimentally at his own smear of blood, "let's hurry, while this is still fresh. Addams? Your move."

"I promise," Brandi said at once.

"I promise," they echoed.

"That whenever my friends call me, I will come to them."

"That whenever my friends call me," they echoed, intertwined voices gone holy, "I will come to them."

The house was listening, the ceilings yawning taller, the windows vibrating with the sound of their voices. Their words slipped through the vents, cycled through the walls, and returned to the six of them, entering back through the slits in their skin.

"No matter where I am," Brandi added.

"No matter where I am." They stood in a circle in the strangers' house, their arms held outward like the petals of a flower, fists meeting at the center. Hilma's cut was barely a scrape, Brandi's was staining the cuff of her sweatshirt. The Oath House was just a house again, the TV screen reflecting their blurred shadows, and they were intruders. But Jay was hit with a deep and abiding comfort: No matter what, they would return for each other. Always, forever.

36

2015

NOW

The Duplication House is still standing, but the house next door has been gutted and fenced off, a banner trailing enticingly from the chain-link fence. CHANGE IS COMING reads a sleek modern font. RED ART. Jay thinks of Hilma, back at the Luck House, sniffing out who's behind this company that's been eating Eternal Springs alive. She says a quiet prayer that the luck is diverted to her, every stray volt channeled into the battery of Hilma Garnet.

The back door is unlocked, and Jay and Iggy slip inside. The interior still has that mothball smell. But Jay thinks of all the houses ringing the Duplication House, the back windows, the screen doors that hang open on this humid afternoon. She feels watched.

"I'm just thinking," Iggy says, as they descend the stairwell. "If Charlie gets out of Eternal Springs safely, he'll call us from New York, right? He'll let us know it's safe to leave."

"That would be great," Jay says automatically. The truth is, the idea of walking away from Eternal Springs no longer excites her in the same way. She thinks of Hilma's insistence that Brandi couldn't possibly have found the Portal House because of her addiction. *Hillbilly heroin*, she heard a college classmate joke once. It seems unlikely that Brandi could escape to another world when she couldn't even get out of Arkansas.

But if she could—if she did—

"I saw your show," Iggy says abruptly. "I looked you up online. Stalked you." He sounds like he's been practicing this, and it still comes out unnatural.

"Oh." Jay's heart sinks. "I'm sorry, Iggy. I meant to tell you, and the others."

"You don't have to ask our permission to draw the houses or anything," Iggy says. "They looked really good. You're talented, you always have been."

"You don't think I'm pathetic?" At his look, she explains, relieved to get it out. "I've lived in the outside world for fifteen years, I've traveled as much as I could. My teenage self couldn't even imagine the person I've become. But when I sit down to draw, it's always the same old places." She laughs. "Nothing else sticks."

Iggy smiles. "The outside world."

"What?"

"You still call it 'the outside world.' Everything outside of Arkansas. Outside of Eternal Springs, really." Before Jay can reply to this, he's pushing open the sub-basement door. "Anyway, Jay. It's funny because you were the one who wanted us to leave Eternal forever."

"What? That's not true." Even as she uncomfortably wonders if it was. "We made every decision together."

Whatever Iggy's going to say next ends up dropping off as they enter the basement. The mannequins are gone, and Jay feels a surprising loss. She'd been looking forward to seeing them. The basement feels emptier without their cool plastic faces. Jay shoves everything out of her mind but their purpose here: look for anything incriminating, make sure there isn't some other remnant of her senior year waiting to bite her in the ass here in 2015.

There's a stack of papers in one corner, haphazard and splotched with mouse droppings and spiderwebs. Jay holds her breath as she kneels to cautiously sift through the papers. These spiderwebs are wrong, some of them tacky as glue, others almost alive. She uses her jacket sleeve as a glove to push them aside. She doesn't want to catch hantavirus from mutated mouse droppings; she shakes off the first paper diligently before examining it.

It's an art print. The paper is too brittle, almost like it's been fried in oil. The image shows abstract shapes, pinks and browns and creams. A sort of wobbling rainbow, and scattered across it, globules like fleshy bubbles. Looking at them makes Jay's own skin feel itchy, nausea tightening the corners of her mouth.

"What is that?" Iggy asks.

"Uh, prints? This one looks like Hilma af Klint's work," Jay says. "But nothing of hers I've seen. It's like a bad imitation of her stuff."

She sifts through the remaining papers in the pile, Iggy joining in, the two of them working in silence. There's only the faint drip of moisture, that echoey underground ambience. The Duplication House hasn't gotten any better at imitating a simple sheet of paper, and the results are all off in some way. Downy, limp, ridged, sticky. A few sheets are so thin they crumble to dust at Jay's touch. Images shift in and out of focus. Picassoesque faces, half-melted, or sketches of bodies that become alien and twisted. More than anything, these prints remind her of AI-generated artwork, something coolly inhuman spinning out its own version of human significance.

"I don't understand," Jay says at last. "They seem to be copies of artists' works."

"Anything that could be traced back to you, Jay?"

"No. None of it means anything to me." She can't connect these images to their time as teenagers; it doesn't feel like evidence. But that only makes her disquiet grow. Someone's been down here.

Someone's been using this space. If not Brandi, then who? Maybe locals. Jay hasn't forgotten those weird sweatshirts she always found at the thrift store, the suggestion that the shop owners had used this basement for years, a simple and unspoken part of Eternal's ecosystem.

Or maybe it was Roy. The name keeps popping into her head.

Iggy straightens. He's holding a bizarre contraption, something that once had a passing relationship with a pair of glasses. The lenses are thick tubes, extending out six inches, like distended goggles.

"These could almost be Charlie's," Jay says, pulling them out of Iggy's hands without thinking. Sure enough, the pattern is Charlie's signature tortoiseshell. "Maybe a more accurate copy of his glasses is on its way to Pell?"

Jay feels all her suspicions and theories and questions propagating around her, turning more warped with each version. What if Charlie ran away because of this? What if he knows something they don't?

As they start back up the stairs, Iggy pauses. She follows his gaze into the far corner, and she instantly steps closer to him, needing to be near another human. The corner of the basement is damp with collected humidity. Jay has ignored it, assuming it's the usual slow leak from groundwater. But the wetness is too dark, the texture too thick.

"Is that blood?" Jay asks hoarsely, not really wanting an answer.

When they move closer, she sees that it's not exactly blood. It reminds her of something—of Brandi's trailer, the strange stains splashed along the wall—

"I'm starting to think Charlie was smart to get out of here," Iggy says.

37

2000

THEN

"This is on purpose," Hilma said, stopping dead. "It's hiding from us. I know it."

The day was a sun-soaked reprieve between late February's tornado sirens and overcast skies. Still, the six of them had been venturing through the woods for two hours, and Jay's shoulders ached, a fat blister rubbed onto her heel.

"Why can't we find it?" Hilma asked, spinning in wild circles.

Jay eased her backpack from her shoulders. Since Hilma was increasingly certain that this house had something to do with the passage of time, they were prepared each time they went searching, packing enough for an extended stay. Jay had brought four changes of clothes, plus a selection of nonperishables from the pantry. Tinned corn, granola bars.

"Well, the woods are like this," Brandi said. She was the only one who didn't seem perturbed. "They hide things from you. Always have."

"At the last minute, we're going to be screwed over by trees?" Hilma tilted her face upward, yelled, "Please let us find the house." The trees stayed stolidly silent.

Over a month had passed since they last found one of Theodora's houses. This was one of the many calculations Jay had going in the back of her head, the countdowns that had sped up since the New Year. If Jay was on edge, it was nothing compared to Charlie. After sending in over a dozen applications to universities, there was nothing left for Charlie to do in the real world but wait. He dived into Theodora's journal entries, looking for any excuse to stop thinking about rejection letters. Searching for the seventh house, and then the Portal House, had become his raison d'être. "The Portal House is my real backup school," he'd said. "Forget Duke." When Max had laughed at this, Charlie had said, a little frantically, "I'm not kidding."

Only two months until graduation. Until the Garnets' sabbatical was done, and someone else moved into the AIR House, some semi-famous portraitist or avant-garde sculptor who would never acknowledge the locals. The future was coming toward them too fast. Destiny was talking nonstop about leaving town, about the waitressing jobs in Hollywood that would afford her the best chance of being scouted. Even Judd had tentative plans to work for his uncle in Oklahoma. Everything was beginning and ending at once, and Jay wasn't sure where she fit anymore. These final two houses were her main comfort. If Jay focused on the quest, everything else fell away.

She'd applied to a handful of schools, just in case. Hendrix, RISD, University at Albany. She'd felt bad watching her dad write out the application fee checks, knowing she had other plans. Whenever she asked Brandi about her own applications, Brandi changed the subject.

The seventh house stood in the way of everything. Without it, they couldn't even use the Portal House. If Theodora Trader's aim

was to create a house as distant as possible from its neighbors, separated from the tight-knit solar system of Eternal Springs proper,
she'd succeeded too well. They spent hours in the woods every day,
and Jay came home striped with scrapes, leaves in her hair, shoes
squelching with mud.

"We'll find it next time," Jay said, reassuring herself as much as
anybody else.

"Actually, Max and I are traveling next week," Hilma said.

A jolt passed over Jay, even though she knew some of her classmates left town every spring break. "Seriously? Where to?"

Max replied, "Jodie and Harold are dragging us to Oaxaca. I'm
gonna work on my tan."

"Every year they kidnap us and bring us to the middle of nowhere," Hilma said. "They're obsessed with going to the most remote beaches they can find."

"You need someone to babysit Lucky?" Brandi asked, cheering
at the thought.

Max stared at his feet, crunching through the undergrowth.

"You haven't told them, Max?" Hilma demanded. "Lucky died."

The other four erupted into awkward mumbles of apology.
"Oh, don't be sorry for Max," Hilma said. "He treated it like a
Tamagotchi."

Max's cheeks flamed, but he spoke with a careful flippancy.
"Hey, now, please think of me during this difficult time. Without
Lucky, my chances of sleeping with Destiny are zilch."

"That's what you're thinking about?" Iggy asked. "Not your dead
pet?"

Brandi scuffed at the rocks with the toe of her sneaker.

"Okay, look, don't be like that. Lucky will be fine," Max said,
defensive now.

"Max," Charlie said patiently. "Not to put too fine a point on it,
but she's dead."

"I have my ways, kids. Don't worry."

Maybe because it was Max Garnet, his hair a burnished halo in the afternoon sunlight, or because she needed something to hold on to right now, Jay half believed that maybe nothing was fully beyond the reach of their six-person configuration, not even overcoming death itself.

On her way out of school the next day, Jay nearly stumbled over Destiny, who was sitting with her legs stretched out, ponytailed head tilted back against the brick wall. She held a purple juice box and it made her look young, like they were little kids again, ignoring each other across the crafts table. "Sorry," Jay said, then looked closer. Destiny's skin seemed clammy under her careful bronzer application. "Are you okay?"

"Just got back from the nurse." Destiny lifted her juice box in a toast. "I'm golden. Don't worry about me."

"Okay," Jay said cautiously. "Good. What's wrong? Are you . . . ?" She hesitated, not sure whether *sick* was the right term.

"Maybe she's born with it, maybe it's type one diabetes."

Jay blinked. She'd thought type 1 *was* the kind you were born with. Then she caught Destiny's small smirk, and realized she was joking. "Got it."

Destiny twirled the tiny straw idly. For once, she seemed open to Jay, curious even as she teased. Jay was quiet, sensing that if she said the wrong thing, the spell would break. Sometimes this happened: stumbling into a little pocket in time with another person where the old rules sloughed off.

"People think I'm selfish for wanting to get out of here," Destiny said. "Like, a bitch who only wants to be famous. And yeah, why not? I want to be famous. But I also don't want to be broke forever, you know? I don't have the choice to stick around here and not make money."

Jay thought of her own crooked teeth, the cost of fixing them, and wondered what it would be like if her dad *had* to pay that money. Not a discussion, but a necessity. "You're going to be huge. I've always thought so."

Destiny smiled. "Hey, thanks. You too. Your drawings aren't half-bad."

Jay nodded her thanks. The compliment would've thrilled her so much, once, and now she could only think that her plans were beyond Destiny's comprehension. She toyed with the idea of telling her—was it selfish to keep this information to the six of them?

"So you're dating Nieves now? Nice work."

"Oh. No. Just friends."

"Can I ask you something? Do you think Max is a good guy?" Destiny asked. "I know he's your friend. Or whatever."

"I think—I think he really likes you," Jay said, very conscious of the fact that Max was on the verge of leaving Eternal too. "He's immature, sometimes. But I think his heart is in the right spot."

"I mean, it's good to know I can attract guys who aren't from Arkansas, I guess." Destiny nodded her head backward, toward the nurse's office. "What's up with Addams?"

It felt like a shadow skipped over Jay's heart. "What do you mean?" Jay had eaten lunch with Brandi and she'd seemed fine then.

"She was in the nurse's office," Destiny said. "Not sure why."

"The nurse's office?" Jay glanced back anxiously. "I should go check on her."

"She already went home." Destiny rose, tossed her juice box into the trash can in a perfect slam dunk. "Nice talk. Good luck getting out of here and all. Let's make a deal, we won't speak again till we're both famous." She winked and was gone.

38

2000

Yelling, the voices cresting and breaking below her. Fighting.

Jay blinked awake, sticky-cheeked. She sat up, and for a moment she was floating in the treetops, cradled by branches. But—no, she was in the AIR House. In Hilma's bedroom, on her huge bed, up in one of the lofts. She'd come to look at the journal with the twins, hoping to decipher the tangled, elegant maps that Theodora had drawn along the margins of the journal, and all the exhaustion of the past few weeks of hiking and hoping and worrying had overtaken her, and she'd fallen asleep.

Hilma was sitting on the spiral staircase when Jay went to investigate. She was listening intently, knees drawn to her chest. When she saw Jay approaching, she pressed a finger to her lips. "Gene trouble," she whispered.

She said it like a joke, but Jay's heart jumped. She thought of the way Brandi had been pulling back subtly from their friendship.

Was *being* pulled back, maybe, carried on an inexorable tide. Jay sat on the step above Hilma, breath held; below, she saw the top of Max's head edging into the room, and knew he was eavesdropping too. The fighting filled the airy, open space, shrinking it.

Jay could pick out the rough edges of Gene's Arkansan accent, pushed up against the careful cadence of the Garnet parents. "What would you have us do?" That was Ms. Garnet. "Did you truly expect us to leave your daughter to suffer alone, merely to appease your pride?"

"I didn't 'spect her to get into that situation in the first place," Gene said. "But since she did get into trouble, you should've let me handle it. She ain't your charity case."

"Of course not," Ms. Garnet said. "She's a lovely young woman, and since our son was involved in the incident as well, we naturally wanted to help."

"What exactly is the issue here? How can we make things right, Mr. Stippley? Do you want us to return to the police station and insist that they press charges?" Mr. Garnet said.

"I don't want you acting like she's yours to take care of." This kind of anger cast the shadow of a much larger rage. This wasn't just about the counterfeit money. "I want you to stay away from Brandi. Why wasn't I called to the police station? She's my responsibility. I don't like hearing about all this from other folks. Strangers."

"We apologize. We should have contacted you, of course. I'm not sure why the local law enforcement didn't reach out to you, that's between you and them."

Jay knew exactly why the cops hadn't reached out to Gene. But she didn't know whether Mr. Garnet also understood: Was there something sharp tucked inside that magnanimous tone?

"She shouldn't be spending time with that boy," Gene said. "She's too young to be dating, and he's not looking out for her best interests."

Jay hadn't been aware that Max knew that she and Hilma were on the stairs, but he looked up at them, making his eyes cartoon-wide. Hilma shook with silent laughter.

"Maximilian isn't dating your daughter," Mr. Garnet said. "They're friends."

"And Gene, if I may, your daughter is an independent young woman," Ms. Garnet said. Jay hated the way they kept drawing that line between Brandi and Gene, *father* and *daughter*, the way Gene only claimed that title when it afforded him power. "She's eighteen, is she not? I don't think any of us have authority over our children's sex lives, that's not—"

"You implying that Brandi is a slut?" Gene's voice burned for a second, and the Garnets were left stunned. Cooling off, he retreated. "God, I don't want them spending time together. I don't know what you believe, but I'm Brandi's guardian, I look out for her."

"Liar," Jay whispered. She was so angry that she felt acid in her throat. Hilma shushed her with a hand to her knee. Gene had never properly looked out for Brandi, not in any way that actually mattered. Jay thought of Brandi in the nurse's office: What had happened?

"Fine," Mr. Garnet said. "Fine, we'll certainly have a discussion with our son. Hopefully we can put all this behind us and stay civil. We'd be glad to retain your services until the completion of our stay here."

It seemed like the end of the discussion. In a daze, Jay listened to the footsteps dispersing. But then Gene was speaking again, calling from the door: "And in case you don't know, those kids are up to no good. Running all over the town like wild animals, getting into all kinds of trouble. Trespassing and shit."

"Thank you for making us aware," Mr. Garnet called.

The moment the door slid shut behind Gene, the twins were converging on their parents, Hilma darting down the stairs and Max hurrying from the corner. Jay hesitated, uncertain whether to hide in Hilma's room or to sneak out, aware that she was intruding on a family moment. After a second, she trailed after the twins. The four Garnets together created a tight formation, Ms. Garnet stroking Hilma's hair, Mr. Garnet leaning against the table, the edges of his hands stippled with paint.

"Remind me again why we still employ that wretched man," Ms. Garnet said.

For a ferocious moment, Jay wanted them to cut all ties with Gene. Excise him neatly so that he wouldn't have access to this house's inner workings and private functions, and he wouldn't have any proximity to the six of them as they explored the town.

But . . . Brandi. Always Brandi. Jay's heart sank. Her friend was caught up in the oblique tangle of Gene's consequences. Gene knew it too. The way he'd talked to the Garnets today had been the way of somebody who knew he had leverage, however tenuous and undefined.

"You know why," Hilma said. "You don't want to admit to your friends back home that you couldn't hack it with the locals. Your humanitarian award will go to someone else."

Ms. Garnet swatted at her daughter without energy. "Oh hush."

"I'm not even *dating* Brandi," Max said. "He's paranoid."

"She seems just wonderful," Ms. Garnet said, too firmly, as if Max had suggested otherwise. "But do be careful, sweetie? You're not here long."

Jay leaned against the wall, the late winter sky a grainy, darkening blue all around them, highlighted through the windows. The harsh scent of turpentine razed her nostrils. She saw so clearly, for a second, the way Eternal Springs was only temporary for the Garnets. A little interlude that would launch them back into their actual lives refreshed and remade.

"Bluejay is here," Hilma said, a warning.

Like she'd been introduced in a play, Jay stepped forward, smiling awkwardly.

"Well, if it isn't the delinquent," Mr. Garnet said. "What's all this I'm hearing about trespassing?"

He was joking. He was joking, and his family was smiling—the twins had inherited their smile from their mother, a curl that rose higher on one side—but Jay couldn't make herself laugh along. She imagined Gene trailing them, watching them, and felt only a hard beat of panic.

"I don't blame you," Mr. Garnet said. Idly, he ran a fingernail under the crackling white scar of paint on his opposite palm. "This little town has surprised me. The architecture around here is quite astonishing. I wouldn't mind—haven't I been saying this, Jodie?—I wouldn't rule out coming back here at some point. Owning a little real estate, a vacation home. There's a unique peacefulness here that's deepened my work. The world moves so slowly."

"Oh, he's not serious," Ms. Garnet said, misinterpreting Jay's blank stare. "He tries to buy a vacation home everywhere we visit. Remember that 'villa' in Poitou-Charentes? We nearly contracted asbestos poisoning from that place."

Hilma ran with the topic, and Jay realized it was a deflection, a distraction, luring her parents away from the topics of Gene and houses and trespassing. But Jay watched through the massive kitchen window as Gene hauled empty potting soil sacks to his truck. His wolflike lope, the back of his neck a rough, spackled pink even in the winter months.

And Jay knew what she had to do. Her sense of purpose grew stronger. She was going to find the Portal House, no matter what, and she was going to take Brandi far away from here, out of Gene's reach.

39

2015

R ed Art," Hilma says, "has been outbidding the locals, cash-in-hand offers that nobody from the Ozarks can compete with. That assessor was thrilled to rant about it. I didn't even need the Luck House to open her up. They've been buying up properties left and right."

They'd come back to their Mirror House headquarters this evening, and Hilma was energized, taking the floor.

"I called up a few realtors, too. As far as I can tell, they aren't specifically targeting Theodora's houses, but they aren't avoiding them either. They already own the Oath House, and it looks like they may have bought the Luck House, too. Whether they're after Theodora's houses or not, though, they're on track to purchase most of this town. Property values are apparently 'skyrocketing.' The assessor told me how much one of those shacks on Mountain View cost. I swear, it went for nearly as much as an LA loft. Maybe a loft in Palmdale, but still."

"Kenny wasn't lying about the prices going up, then," Jay says. She wonders uneasily if her dad could even afford the simple one-story ranch she grew up in on Mountain View.

"We figured as much," Iggy said.

"Excuse me," Hilma says. "This from the kids who brought back some weird-ass goggles? If you don't have anything useful to share, let me talk."

Iggy lifts his palms, appeasing. The goggles aren't the only thing they found. There was that strange bloodstain in the corner, knitting itself together into a fine vein, like a rust-colored spiderweb. Iggy and Jay searched the Duplication House basement for any other signs of violence or trouble; Jay was antsy, expecting to stumble across a deformed finger with seven joints, a blinking eyeball. They didn't find anything but the maybe-blood in the corner. It could be nothing, it could be the result of some minor injury. They know that the Duplication House has strange effects on organic matter. But Jay can't shake her worry.

"The bad news is, the assessor doesn't know anything about who's behind Red Art. Not just because of privacy laws or blah blah, because, trust me, this woman seemed ready to throw anyone and everyone under the bus. But Red Art is an anonymous LLC."

"So it'll be tricky to figure out the man behind the curtain?" Iggy asks.

"Or the woman," Hilma says. "Usually multiple people."

"Where was it incorporated?" Max asks. "Is it local?"

"Delaware, apparently." Hilma looks at the others. "Does that mean anything to you?"

Jay and Iggy shake their heads, but Max swears, straightening. "That's no good. Anonymous LLCs file in Delaware to hide behind the state's privacy laws. When people go to this level of trouble to be anonymous, they typically want to stay that way."

An unsettled silence falls over the four of them, a feeling that reminds Jay of seeing a house from a distance: spotting the exact shape of it, but unable to access any of its rooms.

"Max, if anybody can sniff out a liar, it's you," Hilma says.

"I can try," Max says. "The first step would be reaching out to the secretary of state's office, but that'll likely be a dead end. Otherwise, our best options would be private investigators. I know a few guys who aren't afraid to get their hands dirty."

"How long would that take?" Iggy asks. "Weeks?"

"More like months," Max admits.

Months. Jay feels it around them, pinning them down. She imagines Charlie, probably already across county lines, maybe in the airport by now. He's proving them all wrong, refusing to let his promise in the Oath House devour the life he's built on his own.

Hilma clears her throat, eyes darting. "There's something else. I don't know exactly what it means, and I don't want you to panic. But the assessor said that somebody local was working with Red Art, because there's clearly insider information about houses going up for sale, stuff that an out-of-town corporation wouldn't know—"

"Roy," Jay supplies. Of course. "Whoever Roy is, he's clearly important to Brandi, and nobody knows who he is. There must be a connection." She's hit with a surge of hopefulness, pieces coming together, however loosely.

"No," Hilma says. "Not Roy. The assessor said that Brandi Addams was working for Red Art."

Jay can't fit this together. She stares at Hilma, looking for the joke. "Well, that doesn't make sense. Brandi hated the developers."

"Even so, Brandi is an employee of Red Art. Or was. Apparently, she was working for them for the past year. Which would mean she was working for them even before she was fired from that cleaning job. When she was breaking into houses, maybe it was on behalf of Red Art."

"Could she have been coerced? Like, somebody forced her?" Iggy asks.

"I'm sick of giving Brandi the benefit of the doubt," Hilma explodes. "What if Brandi Addams got tired of this town? It's not as if it's ever done anything for her. Maybe she got smart and capitalized off her knowledge of Eternal. Good for her."

"All right," Max says, careful, diplomatic. "Let's say Brandi has been helping Red Art. What happened? Did she get herself into trouble?"

A headache squeezes the back of Jay's neck. Brandi was apparently working for Red Art. It twists things to know this—it casts a shadow against Brandi's motivations. *You promised.* Was it a plea, a dare, a taunt? They've been here for days with no clear end in sight. Did Brandi expect them to move back to Eternal Springs for good? Will their lives remain suspended, held in stasis, while a childhood promise keeps them trapped in this Arkansas town?

It's the first time Jay's truly considered that the vagueness of those words, *you promised*, might be designed to ensure that none of them can ever walk away. She isn't sure how she feels about this. It should feel terrifying, oppressive, but by now Jay's almost relieved at the idea of letting go and accepting her punishment.

And anyway, she reminds herself, Charlie got out. He's been gone for nearly twenty-four hours now.

Hilma is talking. "Do you know I've been paying someone? For more than a decade. The best reputation management money can buy. I can't risk having our names connected to this place. Everything I've built—Geminist and my sweet husband, all the women I've helped and the businesses I've launched—brought down by a town in the Ozarks."

Brought down by you, Jay thinks. *Brought down by us.* Not the town.

Hilma looks directly at Jay, eyes fiercely damp. "Whatever Brandi wants, I'll give it to her. Does she want money? She's got it.

Does she want a ticket out of Arkansas? Of course. The best rehab facility, whatever job she wants. I have connections. Just tell me. Just tell me what to do so we can leave."

Hilma speaks with an intimate desperation, as if Jay can transmit this message to Brandi personally. Before anyone can answer, there's a distant sound against the front door. A knock, but not quite. A helpless thud, like a bird slamming against a window.

"Any of you expecting company?" Max asks tightly.

Together, the four of them move down the stairwell, into the entry hall. The door looks blankly innocent, but someone or something waits behind it. Pell coming with new evidence, ready to arrest them. Or maybe the mysterious Roy. Or—or it's Brandi.

Max opens the door, yanking it with a Band-Aid-ripping quickness, the humid loudness of the early evening air breaching the austerity of the Mirror House. Charlie falls inside.

He's bleeding badly, half-conscious, words slipping from him. Nothing that makes any sense. Iggy and the twins go into a grim triage mode, everything else falling away. They get him into the bathroom, and Hilma presses water to his lips. Charlie's wearing a bandage fashioned out of rough brown paper towels, already sodden, and Max unwraps it gently. Iggy cradles Charlie's head in his lap.

Jay knows she should be helping too. She knows it. But she's drawn magnetically to his discarded jacket, the wallet tucked inside. She slips it open. There, among the credit cards, the New York driver's license, is a tightly folded photo of the Duplication House.

40

2000

THEN

Hilma and Max left during spring break. Jay couldn't stop worrying that they wouldn't return—that once Arkansas loosened its grip on them, they'd never look back. Everything seemed to be crumbling. Charlie had developed a cold. Brandi was out of school for a few days leading up to the break, the trailer dark when Jay biked over. She knocked on the door and the windows, checked inside the shed. Nothing, no response. Jay hoped that Brandi was just toppled by Charlie's cold, or maybe that her new cleaning job was keeping her busy.

Because the other, less welcome possibility was that Brandi had picked up on the inevitable tension that Gene created. Ever since the overheard confrontation at the AIR House, the twins had been on edge. They led the group in circuitous laps around town, trying to throw an unseen Gene off their trail. They'd stopped sitting together at school. Max had gravitated instead toward Destiny, who was reciprocating his flirting lately, laughing at his jokes.

Jay knew that Brandi sensed the change in dynamics. She wanted desperately to explain—but she couldn't reveal the fight with Gene to Brandi. Brandi would be mortified if she thought she was jeopardizing the quest.

When Jay arrived at their usual meeting spot in the forest, she was braced to be alone in the search for the seventh house. Instead, Iggy was waiting for her, same as always. He held up a hand to greet her, and that simple gesture restored a little of the world's shine.

"You know what?" Jay called to him as she approached. "I have a good feeling about this. We're going to find the seventh house today."

There were only two houses left to find now, and both of them were proving difficult, nearly impossible. It wasn't just this seventh house. They'd also been puzzling over the Portal House. Turning their attention to Theodora's account of her masterpiece, her most carefully guarded treasure. She'd sketched this house in bits and pieces, and Jay tried to match the elegant bow windows and the cross gables to any structures around town. No luck. Hilma said it must've been remodeled, and she and Charlie had spent days at the library combing through records, but so far they hadn't found any perfect candidates. Jay didn't want to admit it out loud, but she kept thinking about what Charlie had said. About Theodora's time in the mental institution. What if these final two houses didn't exist at all?

She expected Iggy to respond to her optimism, but his dark eyes were serious. "So last night my parents told me they're thinking of moving to California," he said. "They might open a new location of Cozy's. It's a great opportunity."

"California? Wow." Jay hadn't expected this. "Congratulations, that's big."

"Yeah. But I thought, I don't know if I'll even be here when they move. Then I started thinking, can I even say goodbye to them before we go through the portal? How will I tell them where I'm going? And what if we—" He stopped, shrugged. "Thinking through all the logistics, it freaked me out."

"Wait, so you won't go through the portal?" Jay asked. She hadn't even considered this: that the six of them wouldn't be together.

"No, no. I want to go. I just—"

A crunch of a footfall, and Iggy and Jay both turned. It was Brandi, and at first Jay was guiltily disappointed that someone else was breaking into this private moment, but then she saw her friend, and the world went unsteady, everything shrinking to the pinpoint of shock. Brandi's eye was swollen, visible even behind her flimsy sunglasses. Her arm was in a sling, neon pink.

Iggy instantly ran to her. Jay stood for a moment, willing her brain to catch up with what had happened. "Did you fall?" Iggy was asking. "Were you in an accident?"

"It was Gene," Jay said. "Wasn't it?" Anger built under her skin, tighter and tighter.

"Her dad?" Iggy asked, half wondering, as if he'd never considered that a parent could be the cause of pain.

"Don't tell nobody," Brandi whispered. "It was an accident. I don't want trouble."

Iggy looked from one of them to the other, color draining from his face.

"No. You need to tell somebody," Jay said. "He can't get away with this." She'd been so naive to think they could hold on and just wait for the portal. She went to Brandi and, after hesitating a second to make sure it was all right, wrapped her in a hug, tender, breathing in her familiar smell of strawberry shampoo.

When Jay pulled away, Brandi hitched her backpack higher on her uninjured shoulder. She looked around at the forest, her face set in such dazzling determination that Iggy and Jay both stood back, awaiting her orders. "I just want to find this house.

Okay? Today's the day. That's why I'm here, and that's what we're gonna do."

"Can't you reach your mom? You could come live with my dad and me until you get in touch with her."

"I told you, Jay, drop it."

Jay couldn't. She was poking at it obsessively, the way she thumbed her scrapes or bruises as a kid. "You're not safe with him. Stay in the Luck House. Hide in the Mirror House. Tell Officer Pell." But already she knew these solutions were paper-thin. Pell wouldn't help without turning his assistance into another kind of punishment.

Brandi just shook her head.

"Well," Jay said, "what if I can get you away from him forever? What if I can find a place where Gene will never think to look?"

"You mean the portal?" Brandi asked, frowning.

"Exactly. What if you and I stay there, Brandi? For good."

"Leave Eternal?" Brandi asked. "Never come back?"

"We've been planning on doing that anyway," Jay reasoned. "We can be in a new world together, not just a new city."

Brandi glanced at the forest floor, biting her lip. "I'm not sure. Maybe."

"Think about it. Seriously."

"Forever?" Iggy asked. Jay had almost forgotten he was listening. "You'd do that? Like, not just visit this new place, but . . . stay behind?"

"Of course I would," Jay said. "For Brandi."

Jay understood the awed doubt in Iggy's voice, especially when he'd just expressed his own uncertainty. Their assured configuration, the six adventurers together, had been scrambled around. "But," she said to Brandi, "until then you have to find a safe place. Maybe the twins can help you with a hotel room or something."

"You really don't know?" Brandi asked. "The Garnets fired him. They reckoned he was stealing, some paintings went missing. He came home drunk and said I couldn't hang out with the Garnets no more. He called Hilma all kinds of names, called her a slut and a liar, said I was tryin' to get knocked up with Max." Her cheeks flamed, luminous with shame.

Jay was silent. She'd been so careless to think she could shelter Brandi from what happened in the AIR House that day, that it would stay restricted to those walls.

"The Garnets can't help. They're the reason Gene's angry in the first place," Brandi said.

"But if you—"

Brandi put out a hand, and Jay stopped, silenced. The house.

The house was there, only a few yards away. It gleamed in the sunset, the orange catching deep in the brown siding and shingles. If this exact building had been sitting on a neighborhood block, it wouldn't have stood out to Jay. An ordinary enough structure. Wood siding, shades of fading amber and mahogany. But out here, surrounded by miles of trees, no civilization in sight?

It was magical.

Jay groped for her sketchpad, hands shaking as she crouched and began drawing. Iggy's face was lit up; he jumped in the air like a little kid, releasing a raw-sounding whoop of joy.

"The house knew we needed it," Brandi said. "It came to us."

41

2015

I tried to get away," Charlie whispers, once he's feeling strong enough to speak. "I really did try."

"Yeah, no shit," Hilma says, not ungently.

Jay sits on the closed toilet seat. Here Charlie is, blood-soaked proof that Brandi's not done with them. They haven't helped her. Not yet, not enough, maybe never enough. *You promised, you promised.*

Charlie takes a long drink of water. "I have these dreams where I'm back in Eternal Springs, and I'm this shy kid again, and nobody cares about the things I care about, and everything is bottled up. I always wake up panicking, and I have to walk around my home and touch everything. The works of art my beautiful friends made for me, and the first edition of *Another Country*, and this spider plant that was the first thing I bought for myself when I came to New York. Then I curl up next to Damon to remind myself that I'm here, I'm here, and I found my own magic. No. I *made* it. I made my magic.

"This? It's like the reverse of that dream. Like I never left Arkansas, and everything that's happened since has been the hallucination." He lifts his eyes to theirs, irises darkly striking without his glasses. "I've worked so hard to find a place in the world where I belong."

Hilma says, "We all feel that way, Charles."

He ignores her. "So yes, I drove as far as I could. Twenty minutes, thirty minutes past the county line, I thought I was doing okay. I thought I'd call you all from the airport. Maybe from the apartment, once I got home safely. Or maybe never. But after an hour, my arm started hurting. Somewhere around Fayette, it started bleeding. I ignored it until I couldn't focus anymore—I was veering off the road."

Jay knows exactly how steep those roads are, labyrinthine and twisting highways, plunging into a sea of trees at all sides. To enter or leave Eternal Springs, everyone runs that scenic gauntlet.

"I started thinking, what will happen if I run off the road? What if I have to go into some shitty gas station where half the trucks have Confederate flag bumper stickers? I can't even seek help. I turned around." Charlie leans his forehead into his closed fists, shaking. "It's unfair. I was a naive kid when I made this promise, I had no idea what I was agreeing to. I deserve to grow beyond my childhood friendships without sacrificing everything I've created. Other people get that opportunity, don't they? They don't even see it as a gift."

"But the Duplication House," Jay says then, and hands him the strange, distorted goggles. "These are yours, right? You've been back."

Charlie turns the goggles around, looking at them from every angle. When he lays them next to his original glasses, the tortoiseshell lines up perfectly: strangers connected by one similar feature. "I must have missed these . . . There was a time I accidentally left my glasses behind. Always a dangerous idea, in that house. Listen.

It's not exactly easy to support yourself in New York City. I don't come from money. You know that. After a few years, I was starting to think I'd have to come home with my tail between my legs. I just couldn't cut it. Then I managed to get an internship with this overgrown trust fund kid. His grandparents had accumulated a personal collection I could only dream about. I guess having an 'intern' made him feel like he was doing something other than getting high in his brownstone every day. Meanwhile, he leaves me alone with a storage unit full of thousands of dollars' worth of artwork.

"There were original sketches by Dalí and Picasso and Lipchitz. Images I'd never encountered before." Charlie's eyes dart to Jay, knowing she'll understand the amazement of it. "The owner treated them like—like Anne Geddes greeting cards. I lasted about a month before I mentioned the sketches to somebody. Just as a joke, at first. I was in New York for the first time, and everyone was a thousand times smarter and cleverer than I was. These neglected Picassos became an anecdote I could tell at dinner parties or at bars. People loved it."

Charlie looks around to make sure they're all listening.

"Finally, a guy took me aside and asked if I could 'borrow' one. 'Borrow.' It was tempting. I was nearly homeless, and people were offering me thousands of dollars for a sketch the owner wouldn't miss. One day, I was holding this Dalí and I thought, god, what if I had another one—what if I could somehow draw a perfect copy . . . ?"

The rest of the story unfolds in Jay's mind. Those overlooked sketches: the ability to create convincing fakes. The desperation to make it in the world, the cost of sheltering dreams against the harsh winds of reality. Max needed success, Charlie needed money. Jay understands it, down to her bones—she just didn't expect it. It makes her feel like the only idiot who honored their unofficial agreement.

"At first I did it just to stay afloat, but you know how it goes," Charlie says. "I kept flying back to Fayette to see my parents, and each time I'd drive here first and go to the Duplication House and leave a few sketches. I'd return to a perfect copy. Don't worry, I've been careful. Nothing big or flashy, and I've never sold to my friends. Nobody's tracked me down so far."

"Congratulations," Max deadpans.

A haunted look shadows Charlie's eyes for a moment. Jay knows exactly how guilt can be more poisonous in small doses.

"I don't regret it," Charlie says, reading Jay's mind. "I saw it as a tax. Eternal Springs didn't give me what I needed to succeed. Arkansas didn't care whether I made it or not. So why not use Theodora's houses to make something of myself?"

"Now that you're a curator," Hilma says, "you could duplicate the works of emerging artists. Hold on to them and wait to sell."

"Artifacts," Max pipes up. "Wouldn't be so hard to pocket a Han Dynasty spoon or a de Kooning and pay your rent for the rest of the year."

"Christ, the biggest steal I ever pulled off was some unfinished Matisse sketch, okay? I turned in my resignation to that rich kid years ago. I'm supporting myself completely now. And I'm good at it. If it hadn't been for . . . all this . . . I'd be catching the biggest break of my life." Charlie's eyes are fierce, his vitality returning. "None of you pious assholes get to judge. Not you, Jay. Or Max, or Hilma. I can't have you looking at my life and thinking I don't deserve it when all of you've coasted along on luck you can't even see. Just because your luck doesn't come from one of the houses, don't pretend it doesn't exist."

They're all silent. But Jay's thinking about the probability that Brandi saw each of these returns—Max's, Charlie's. The Brandi in Jay's head has become complicated, evolving from the sweet, earnest girl that Jay befriended in a kindergarten classroom. Different from the person she said goodbye to, broken in half, stitched back together with a poisonous patchwork of oxycodone, morphine, whatever came after those lost their power.

This new Brandi knew about Max and the Luck House. She knew about Charlie duplicating his future, piece by piece. She knew about Gene and the Mirror House, its ugly secret. Brandi saw everything with a clarity that Jay hasn't had in years.

"Am I the only one who didn't come back?" asks Jay.

She addresses Iggy, and he instantly looks away, gaze bouncing off hers as if they're matching magnetic poles. This one is going to hurt. Iggy. Her high school sweetheart, the boy who'd defied time itself with her. But he's been lying to her. There's no escaping it now.

"Brandi sent us those Polaroids for a reason," Jay says into the now-quiet room. "I think she wants us to be honest with each other. No matter how painful it is. Iggy? You're the only one who hasn't shown us a photo yet."

"What about the Truth House?" Iggy says. "Your name was on that, Jay. You never explained that to the rest of us. We still don't know who burned down that house."

"Wait. You aren't saying that I . . ."

Nobody else steps in to help her out.

"Well? Did you burn it down?" Iggy asks, blunt and without warmth.

"Of course I didn't. I haven't been back to Eternal Springs since we graduated from high school. Unlike the rest of you, I actually stuck to that." Her defensiveness flares, then instantly breaks apart under their gazes. It's shockingly painful to be on the outside of this group. "Do you think my life would look the way it does if I'd come back here and used the houses?"

Still, they don't answer. She wants to list it out for them. The times she's priced flights to Eternal Springs. The times she's plotted road trips. Just one excursion to the Luck House to fix her flagging life. A single visit to the Forever House to produce a career's worth of work and then step outside, back at the beginning. And—and just to be back here, regardless of the houses. To breathe in the morning air, to listen to the crickets sing her to sleep. To meet the people she left behind as a teenager, maybe see them through new eyes.

And Jay hasn't given in, not once. That should count for something.

"All right," Jay says, feeling cold now, reckless. "If you have nothing to do with the Oath House, then come with me, Iggy. Max still has the honeymoon suite booked for a few days." Max, head ducked, nods affirmation. "Let's all go. It shouldn't be a problem for you."

"All of us?" Iggy asks. "Who's going to watch over Charlie? He needs to recover."

"Hey, I got it covered, chief," says Max. "I've had enough exploring for one day."

"Fine," Iggy says, and he finally meets her eyes. There's something burning there; when he speaks, she thinks he's about to confess, but: "You're lucky, Jay. Lucky that the Truth House is gone and none of us can hold you accountable."

42

2000

THEN

The house held an ancient smell, creeping from the corners, a sense of peace settling over Jay. It wasn't just the hammocks of cobwebs and spiderwebs, the old-fashioned furniture, but a cool, settled quality in the air. Like venturing into a cave, somewhere primal. All the windows were sheathed in thick curtains, and Iggy pulled them open slightly, letting the evening light crack inside. "Welcome home," he said.

Both Iggy and Jay had brought along timers. Jay's was a bright egg timer, swiped from the kitchen; she settled hers on the porch outside. Iggy's was a shabby stopwatch, black and red, which he set on the windowsill inside. The two miniature clocks faced each other across an invisible chasm. They seemed to be moving at different speeds already.

Jay put down her backpack. "Keep an eye on the timer outside," she said. "We don't really know how time works here. If I'm not back by tomorrow morning, my dad will freak out."

"My parents will have search parties combing the hills for us," Iggy said, tossing his bag onto the settee, sending up a cloud of gritty dust. "But it's what we need to do, right? We're testing the house. Maybe we spend one night here?"

Brandi was already circling the edges of the living room, examining the ceiling for any words. "We need this inscription," she said. "It's the last one."

Jay realized that nobody out there was waiting for Brandi. That everyone who'd miss her in the outside world was already here.

Iggy waited until Brandi wandered out of the room before he approached Jay. "Didn't Hilma say something about time 'standing still' in here?"

"I think so." Jay glanced again at the two timers, the way the one outside seemed to be stuck, while the stopwatch was still functioning.

"Maybe it's a good thing for Brandi," Iggy said, low. "It'll give her some space to heal. If this house works the way we think it does, she'll be able to get better and Gene won't even know she's gone."

Jay watched Brandi through the doorway, the sling bright and garish, her huge eyes holding that quietly haunted look. "We'll stay as long as it takes," Jay agreed in a whisper.

They explored the house, the three of them. Downstairs, an old-fashioned kitchen, a living room. Upstairs, a large bedroom. A simple closet, a bed, its covers smoothed over with a pattern of dust and sunlight. Other than that, the place felt scrubbed of clues as to who had lived here. "We don't even know this is Theodora's," Iggy pointed out. "Like, we haven't found an inscription yet."

"It's hers," Brandi said, entirely confident. "I can feel her here."

The basement door led to steep stairs, a shadowy darkness; they were too nervous to venture down there. The bathroom held stagnant but clear water in an ancient tub, plus a sort of rudimentary toilet that Jay didn't think about too closely.

Most surprising was a child's bedroom. Pinks, whites, creams. A canopy bed. A tiny pair of shoes, sitting as if just waiting for someone to step into them. Jay tried to imagine a child living out here, in this house in the woods that disappeared and reappeared at will. Was all this from a recent tenant, or from long ago?

It occurred to Jay how furious yet delighted Hilma would be when she found out they'd discovered this house without her. It felt strangely right, as if the particular equation of the three of them had unlocked the house.

They claimed bedrooms. A funny giddiness hit Jay, like they were having a sleepover. She chose the main bedroom; Brandi decided on the child's bedroom, which made Jay secretly happy. There was something comforting in its pastels, the hanging mosquito netting over the small bed. Maybe it would help Brandi heal more quickly.

Iggy volunteered to take the settee in the living room. At the bottom of the staircase, Jay paused, unthinking, watching as Iggy pulled his jacket off in one motion. His T-shirt rose, revealing a wedge of smooth stomach, the curves of muscle, and it was so intimate that Jay blossomed with something she'd never experienced. Not desire, but deeper: a feeling like she was arriving home from a long day and Iggy was here, and his body didn't surprise her anymore, but it delighted her, because he was hers, and she was his, and he was safe and known and home.

Home.

She'd never spent the night with a boy before. Her dad had forbidden it in middle school, back when it seemed like it might be a necessary rule. Jay turned away, aware that she was invading Iggy's privacy, but she was left with a lingering mix of excitement and nerves. There were no parents here, there was no supervision. Just them, and the forest, and this house holding them close.

Brandi had packed more supplies than either Iggy or Jay. A deck of cards wrapped in a rubber band. A dozen paperbacks from the library discard shelf. A flashlight. A box of tampons, rolls of scratchy toilet paper. Jay wondered briefly how Brandi had afforded it all, and thought of those contraband bills from the Duplication House. She hoped Brandi hadn't gotten into trouble, but she was impressed by the thoroughness of her friend's planning.

The three of them pooled their food, taking careful stock. Fruit Gushers, granola bars, beef jerky, juice boxes. The sink in the kitchen sputtered with water that ran dirty at first, then slowly cleared. "We could last a week, I bet," Iggy estimated. "But we're gonna be skinny at the end of it." He patted his taut stomach.

"What are those?" Jay asked, noticing the white at the bottom of Brandi's backpack.

"Oh, that? Nothin'." She hastily closed the bag. "Just medicine."

"Yeah, good idea, always be prepared," Iggy said. "I scraped myself pretty good on the railing out there. This place is old, watch your-selves." He held up his hand to show off the wound. But looking at Brandi, Jay felt an uncertainty pass over her quickly, there and gone.

"It's not dark yet," Iggy said.

Jay looked up from her spread of cards. According to Iggy's stopwatch, still perched safely on the windowsill, they'd been in here for at least a day. They'd already talked for hours, hypothesizing about the location of the Portal House, about Charlie's college acceptances, about what happened on *Roswell* that week. They carefully dodged around anything too serious: Brandi's injuries, the questions of who might go through the portal and how long they'd stay.

Brandi was dozing in the other room as Jay and Iggy split a packet of Sour Patch Kids, eating them slowly, biting their heads off first. Iggy saved all the blues for her. "They match your eyes," he said. He taught her conquian, a card game his grandfather had loved. Jay was terrible at it, Iggy beating her again and again.

And yet it was still late afternoon. As if not even an hour had passed. Jay looked around, evaluating, her circadian clock spinning wildly. The light moved weirdly in this place. Or rather, didn't move: an evening glow lay suspended against the windows.

Jay stood up and peeked out the slim crack in the curtains where their timers rested, separated by the glass. Her heart carved out more space in her chest. She pulled the curtains open wider. The egg timer's little plastic lever hadn't moved a centimeter. The forest wasn't moving. It was like a painting, a backdrop in a school play, a screensaver—but richer and more vivid than any of those, the world sustaining all its perfect depth. Jay had never seen everything stand still like this.

"It's frozen," Iggy said, at her elbow. His voice held the same awe she felt, giving it a shape. "Nothing is moving at all."

Days passed, or maybe they didn't.

The outside world faded from significance, even though they could see it from every window. The expanse of the forest around them, the trees moving with a kind of extravagant underwater slowness, the sunlight taking its time as it curled around each trunk, each leaf. Leaning her forehead against the windowpane, Jay felt like she was observing a different world entirely. One where the sunlight lasted for a hundred hours at a time, stretching on and on in its luxuriant goldenness.

Jay imagined her dad out there, miles away. Still inside the same hour as when Jay left home. Charlie, resting in bed with a book. Gene, knuckles bruised. Everyone caught in a single moment without even realizing that they were trapped, like the citizens who fell into an enchanted sleep alongside their cursed princess.

It was hard to guess at the time of day. Morning, evening, afternoon. Even though they had Iggy's stopwatch, it felt as if time had been unpicked from the usual methods, as if these little blocky numbers had become purely abstract.

Jay felt, though, that this was morning: a waking-up sensation, even though she hadn't slept much. She sensed movement behind her, and she turned to find Iggy. "It's weird that Theodora added so many windows," Jay said. "Don't you think it's worse to be able to see outside when the world isn't moving at the same speed?"

Iggy smiled at her, crooked. "Charlie told me about cities in, like, Sweden and Alaska where there's too much sunlight, or too little. It's not so crazy, maybe." He stepped closer. "It's kinda nice."

Jay kept her eyes on the nearest tree, feeling his presence right beside her.

"Everything's moving so fast now," Iggy went on. "So many choices. Graduation's coming up, college, jobs, moving away. In here, we can hide from all that. Like a—like a secret. Nobody will ever know that we've lived this extra time."

"The Forever House," Jay whispered.

"Charlie will fight you on that," Iggy said, only half joking. "It's not really a house that lets you live forever or anything, right? We're probably aging normally in here." He held up his hand, tapped his small scrape. "This has been getting better every day. It's just that we're on a different timeline than the outside world."

"But it feels like we could stay in here forever. I guess that's what I meant."

"Okay," Iggy said. "The Forever House. I like it."

Brandi was healing slowly. After a few sleeps, her eye was pale purple rather than the deep, burst-plum color it'd been when they arrived. She lost the hunted look she'd had. She smiled again. She laughed, cautiously at first, then freely.

It didn't take long for them to fall into their own patterns. Jay had never felt such a complete freedom. Not just from her home life, from school, from her dad, but from time itself. Iggy had it right. This was secret time, unaccounted-for, all their own. She'd brought her sketchpad, her markers. All the worries over college acceptance letters came fully unstuck from her fingers, and she drew freely, the images leaping from her imagination to the page. Self-portraits. Brandi, Iggy. The house itself, these rooms with the too-much-sunlight and ancient furniture.

Brandi seemed to feel the same effect. She'd brought her disposable camera, and she snapped photos of all of them. A self-portrait in a mirror. Iggy and Jay together, laughing over a game of go fish. Jay on the stairs. Jay lying in her bed, talking to Brandi about whether Destiny would ever be famous. "The light in here," Brandi said. "It's so beautiful, Jay."

Jay remembered all the times the two of them retreated to the shed, Jay with her sketchpad and Brandi with the little disposable cameras she had to diligently save up for. The way they could interpret the world more easily in that tiny space, fueled by their own creativity, by each other's encouragement. For all the magic that had entered their lives, they'd lost something too, when they stopped going to the shed as often.

"Do you mean it?" Brandi asked Jay as they lay on their stomachs in the child's bedroom, surrounded by the comforting pastels. "That you'll go into the other world for good?"

"Why wouldn't I? You and me. Together."

Brandi gave a funny smile. "It's just . . . you didn't even want me to come to art camp with you, that's all."

Jay felt uncomfortably exposed. She hated that Brandi picked up on those half-guilty thoughts, the ones that Jay had barely acknowledged to herself. The way their friendship sometimes felt confined to the context of the Ozarks. "That was stupid of me, Brandi. I'm an idiot. Anyway, this place will be new. That's the great thing. We'll both be weird. We'll both have to figure out the rules."

"I like the weird we are already. Here in Eternal."

"You're not even considering it, Brandi?"

"I am, of course, I just . . ." Brandi yawned, nestled closer to Jay. "Can we talk later?"

"Yeah. Of course. We have all the time we need."

They couldn't find Theodora's inscription, no matter how hard they looked. They spent hours—according to Iggy's stopwatch—going through each room methodically. Poking around window frames, peering under furniture. Knocking for secret compartments. It almost began to feel beside the point. Maybe they'd come here only to hide in this strange, evening-edged house. That was enough.

At some point, though, they had to acknowledge that their supplies were running low. It was the only real tie they had to the outside world. Jay felt the full constraints of her physical body. If they left for more supplies, Jay wasn't certain they'd find the place again. She sat on the edge of her bed, trying to accept the fact of reentering a world that felt unfamiliar now. She'd have to go back out there to where the sun raced in dizzy circles, never satisfied, pushing them forward and forward and forward—

A creak in her doorway. "It's going to be nighttime soon," Iggy said.

Jay looked at the brilliant orange that slanted across the floor. The change had happened so gradually and subtly, but it was undeniable now. This was the just-before-twilight evening sun, the last hurrah. And when nighttime landed, it would last for weeks inside this house.

"Have I ever mentioned that I kind of hate the dark?" Iggy asked.

She pretended to ponder. "I don't think you have, no."

"I say the night-light in our bedroom is for my little brothers, but it's really for me." He stayed politely in the doorway, not venturing deeper inside. "Plus, we're low on food."

"But we can't leave until we find the inscription," Jay said. "We won't get another chance."

"We can still try, even if we don't have much time."

It felt ridiculous—not having enough time—but it was true, even here. "I wish we had more." Jay became aware that she was talking to fill the silence, because otherwise she'd have no borders between herself and what was about to happen.

"Jadelynne." Iggy came into the room, sat on the edge of her bed. Her legs, bare beneath her white sundress, rolled against his in the indent he'd created. She didn't move away.

"Ignacio," she said, faux-formal, hoping he couldn't detect how nervous she was.

"Want to hear something interesting?"

"If it's about you being afraid of the dark, I already heard that one."

"So, Ignacio means 'fiery one.' My last name, Nieves, it means 'Our Lady of the Snow.' My name is, like, hot and cold."

"Fire and ice." Jay's stomach was fluttering so hard she could put her palm to her navel, feel its beat. "But that's not you."

"You don't think so?"

"No. You're not—you're not extremes like that. Hot and cold. You're always . . ." She thought of the way he'd become part of their six-person group, even though he had infinite other options. "You're warm."

He smiled to himself. "Hey. I thought you were going to say cool."

They were quiet. Soon this light would tip into darkness, and they'd have only twilight for company. But for now, they were part of the evening's amber, and they could do anything.

Letting herself be another girl, Jay reached for Iggy, wrapping her arms around his shoulders, and kissed him. A repeat of the New Year's Eve kiss, but this was different. No audience; no end to the evening, not yet. When they pulled back, they were both breathless. "You're sure?" he whispered, low, and she nodded.

She hadn't expected Iggy to feel shy. He had plenty of practice, as far as she knew. All those girls who once surrounded him, confident girls balancing on the verge of adulthood, while Jay was still trapped in her awkward cocoon. But when she looked at him after their next kiss, Iggy was flushed, his eyes soft with nerves. He was scared too, and she realized that what they were about to do was going to change them both.

The first time they had sex would always stay in her memory in gold-encased slices. Iggy sliding her dress off her shoulders. The light-bronzed gleam of his skin, the faded burn scars that etched a pattern on his forearms. How freely she could look at him. The wide-open feeling of his hands on her. His mouth, the taste of it; the way they laughed together when they lightly knocked foreheads, when Jay's dress was stuck around her waist.

And the way it felt when everything suddenly clicked, and she was both floating above her body and sinking into it, and every moment of trying to ignore her physical self was gone, because together, the two of them were condensed to this breathless point of contact.

"You know what? We'll get even better," Iggy whispered, after. At the promise of what would happen next, the future awaiting, Jay rolled against him, their skin warm and damp, his heartbeat tapping a Morse code against her cheekbone.

———

They did get better. They stayed in bed for hours, days. Who knew how long? Until the light faded, Jay kept telling herself. When it transitioned to nighttime, she'd stop, and they'd leave, and they'd return to their normal lives. But nighttime was so far away, and for now they had this bed, and this gorgeous secret of a house, and each other, and nothing else.

They used protection. Jay was careful of that, remembering the advice she'd scrounged through teen magazine columns, the woeful sex ed at her school. She knew that she didn't want to be pregnant, not at almost-eighteen. She'd heard the jokes, the way people assumed every girl growing up in Arkansas would be pregnant before graduation. Max had stuck a box of condoms in Iggy's backpack as a joke, and Jay burned with pride and embarrassment that they'd actually become useful.

There were times sex was clumsy, and times it was sweet and tender, and—once or twice—Jay would have to arrive back in herself afterward as if she'd slipped into a whole other dimension. They had to lie there, lulled and tired and happy, legs intertwined, fingers playing across each other's palms, until they could talk easily again.

Hilma had ranted, once, about how the concept of *losing virginity* was rooted in patriarchy. That virginity was not a tangible quantity that could be lost. Jay finally felt like she had the authority to agree with this. Because she felt like she'd gained something. She'd become someone who could be purely at peace with another person. With Ignacio Nieves, who was not hot, not cold, but warmth, a sunset that would last forever against her body.

Emerging from the bedroom for a drink of water, Jay stopped in the hallway, startled and then shy. She was worried that Brandi had overheard. Her friend was sitting in the hallway, back against a wall. There was a wooden box next to her, and she was bent low over what looked like a letter, her lips moving slightly as she read.

Jay smoothed the skirt of her sundress. In the lingering evening light, Brandi's features were hidden. She hadn't seen Jay yet. With a sigh, Brandi set aside the letter, grappled for a tiny white bottle. She brought her uninjured palm up to her mouth, and her throat moved as she swallowed. It was a gesture that looked practiced.

"What do you have there?" Jay asked, and Brandi jumped.

"Jay." Brandi hid the bottle behind her body. "Nothin'. The doctor gave them to me."

Jay paused. "Um. I was asking about those papers."

"Oh. Yeah." Brandi wiped her eyes, though there was no evidence that she'd been crying.

Jay felt the joy of their time in the Forever House faltering. She realized what it would've been like for Brandi these past few days, traipsing through this lonely, ancient place alone, having to contemplate what would come next. What would happen after. Gene and his cruelty might be held in stasis for now, but he'd be waiting. The Portal House was still too far away, its location a mystery. Even the inscription for this house was still hidden.

"Is everything okay?" asked Jay. "I know I haven't been around much."

"I'm happy for you." Brandi smiled; it didn't reach her eyes. "He's real sweet."

Jay thought of the rumors that swirled around her classmate Byron's older sister—the sports injury, the pills, the intervention—and she wondered if she should say anything. "Be careful with that medication. It's just . . . those pills can be pretty strong."

"Well, only if'n you're taking them for fun. These were from a doctor. I need them. I don't want to hurt all the time."

"Right. No. I get it." Jay glanced at the open box. There were more maybe-letters stuffed inside, a ruffled sheaf of them, and objects—a key, a curl of hair, a human tooth. "So what is all this?" she asked, eager to move on from the pills. "You found a little treasure chest."

"Oh." Brandi perked up. "Yeah. They were in the bedroom closet? Way, way up on the shelf. It's amazin', Jay, you should read some of them. They're letters. But . . ." Her face clouded.

"What is it?"

Brandi tapped her fingernail against her teeth, then spoke in a rush. "I reckon maybe this house makes people get . . . attached. Maybe too attached, if you know what I mean." When Jay shook her head, confused, Brandi went on. "Listen to this. 'If bonds made in heaven are sealed forever, then this house is a small piece of heaven.'" She read slowly, haltingly. "Don't that sound like trouble? 'Sealed forever'?"

"Is that—who wrote those?" Jay knelt, but Brandi pulled the letter away.

"I'm still workin' on putting it all together," she said.

"Okay. Wow, sorry."

From the bedroom, Iggy emerged, hair rumpled, shirt unbuttoned. He smiled a question at Jay. "Iggy," Jay said, excited. "Look what Brandi found. They're—"

"No," Brandi said, a stubborn whisper. "It's okay. You two don't gotta spend time with me. I can do this." She pulled the box of letters closer to her, protective.

"But this seems important," Jay argued.

Iggy looked at them both.

"Jay, I got it," Brandi insisted.

"Hey, I trust her," Iggy said. "She knows what she's doing."

He wanted Jay back to himself, she could tell. Her heart flipped just looking at him, the timer at the back of her head clicking away the seconds.

"Go on," Brandi said. "You two don't have to babysit me."

"I can stay. I can talk," Jay said. "If you need someone."

"Be with Iggy. I'm okay."

When Jay and Brandi were together in another world, soon,

they'd have so much time together. "All right," Jay said, relenting, and followed Iggy back into the bedroom.

They stood at the threshold for a long time, nobody wanting to be the first to leave.

Their time in the Forever House had finally come to an end. There was no more food; they'd lasted roughly two days without anything to eat, but Jay was hollow-gutted, dizzy, and anyway she didn't like the way Brandi looked. Pale-skinned and distant, her laugh loopy and just out of sync with whatever Jay said to her. She didn't know where that wooden box had gone. Brandi wasn't saying.

But when Brandi left the prescription bottle unattended, Jay had taken a quick peek. Generic for Percocet, sixty pills. Only one left. Jay didn't think they'd been here long enough to get through a month's supply, but maybe she wasn't calculating correctly. Still, it left her nervous.

Iggy reached for Jay's hand now. He squeezed it briefly, and she understood. Her throat hurt with tears. They were saying goodbye to their beginning. Through the windows, the sky was purplish, dusted with stars. The shadows in the house had deepened and lengthened. If it was a moonlit night, it wouldn't matter, but Jay wouldn't want to spend an eternal night with only a flashlight for company. She knew how feral the darkness could get out here in the woods.

"Are you ready?" Iggy asked them both.

No. No. Jay wasn't ready. She imagined never leaving, she imagined letting the world run on without the three of them. "Yes."

They stepped out of the Forever House.

Iggy closed the door behind them. Their deflated, empty backpacks hung from their shoulders. The noise of the outside world poured around them like water. The shrill, stunning songs of tree frogs, nocturnal birds, and insects. Jay laughed, gasped. Everything came rushing at her at once, nearly knocking her off her feet.

"Holy shit." Iggy was staring down at Jay's egg timer. They'd set it for an hour, the highest amount of time, before they entered. "Still eleven minutes left. We were gone for less than an hour." He exchanged looks with Jay, laughing helplessly. "It's like . . . when you go into a movie theater, and you come out, and it's so messed up that it's still light?"

"That, times a thousand."

Brandi reached into her backpack, grabbing for the pill bottle. When she'd retrieved the one pill, she winced in disappointment, and with horror Jay saw that her friend's eye was freshly bruised again, blooming with darkness as Jay watched. Jay grabbed Iggy's hand and saw that the scrape was back, vivid again.

"We lost all that time we spent in the house," Jay said. "We're back to the way we were when we entered." She felt the edges of her own hair. Shorter, less ragged.

"So where did all the time go?" Iggy asked.

Jay placed a hand on her stomach, like the time was curled up deep inside her. Weird to think that Charlie was still sick, that Hilma and Max were still in another country for spring break. Her dad was probably finishing dinner, washing up. Nobody knew anything about what had happened.

After they'd walked a few feet, Jay realized that Brandi wasn't with her and Iggy. She turned around with a squeeze of anxiety. Brandi had stopped a few yards from the Forever House, staring downward. "It's right here," Brandi said. "We found it after all."

The words were embedded into the forest floor itself, a mosaic of stones, half-buried beneath the leaves. Jay was gripped with awe as she stood in the twilight, Brandi's flashlight beam picking out the words in a slow sweep.

AND ETERNITY IN AN HOUR.

43

2015

In the honeymoon suite of the Oath House, Hilma gives Jay and Iggy their privacy, retreating to the small breakfast nook, furiously texting with her assistant.

Jay worries that she's all wrong about this. Maybe there aren't any new transgressions and the Oath House means nothing to Ignacio Nieves. She watches him take stock of the room: its hopeful gestures toward romance, the vanilla-scented candles and the basket of dessert wine. But a light behind his face snaps off. Without a word, he moves into the bathroom, and a second later Jay hears the intimate, unmistakable sounds of vomiting.

So she was right.

Jay waits for him. When he returns, he immediately lies on the bed, fully clothed, stretching his legs long. Jay has a funny vision of the two of them as husband and wife. If they'd stayed together, if they hadn't diverged. There are times Jay can't even remember why they did it. The duty of that long-ago choice has stayed, while the urgency has faded.

She lies tentatively beside him. They stare at the popcorn ceiling, the gilt-edged ceiling fan blades. Their long-ago promise is stitched into this very structure, an invisible line hovering between their scars and the walls.

"I came back to Eternal Springs," Iggy says. She thinks Iggy's crying, but he's dry-eyed. "I should've told you right away. I saw Brandi, actually. I've wanted to tell you."

"Brandi?" Jay asks, heart jolting. "When?"

"A year ago? I was trying so hard not to run into her, but we were driving by, and I looked out the window at a stop sign and there she was, waiting to cross. I don't think she even recognized me. She looked bad, Jay. Strung out.

"I've tortured myself over it. What kind of man turns his back on an old friend? I wasn't the person my parents raised me to be. Some wealthy asshole, staring at her out the window of a rental car. I've replayed it a thousand times. I could've helped her. I could've talked to her. Maybe if I'd loaned her some money, or told her how much we missed her. I could've done something. *Anything.* But I was scared. I drove away before Elle noticed her."

It takes a second to catch up with the full meaning. "Elle?" Jay repeats. "You brought her to Eternal Springs?" The betrayal is quick, sharp as a knife.

"I did," Iggy says, agonized. "Elle's been so curious about where I came from. I've given her the bits and pieces. Mostly before the houses. The quarterback and the prom king and the parties. Pre-you." He pauses. "Pre-us."

Jay's alternate past collapses, veering from the two of them as a long-married couple to them never being involved at all. Iggy dating Elle as someone with a normal high school history, nothing more regrettable than a bad date or failed math exam.

Iggy shuts his eyes, smiles painfully. "I want so much to be part of Elle's life. She's kindhearted and funny. There's absolutely no reason not to love her. That's what makes it so hard when I can't stop thinking of you instead."

Jay leans her forehead into his shoulder, closing her eyes.

"You're the one I compare everything to, Jadelynne. Everyone else, even Elle—it feels like I'll never get back to what we had together in that house."

The sunlight that would never end.

"It's not fair," Iggy whispers. "We were . . . what, seventeen? Eighteen? So young. I cared about you so much, Jay. Even before we were friends. I always noticed you, this girl lost in your drawings, or laughing with Brandi. I was curious about you before you ever noticed me in the Luck House. But if someone had asked me, *Do you want your obsession with this girl to last forever? Do you want to be in love with your high school girlfriend until the end of time, even when she insists that you can't be together?*"

"What did you do, Iggy?" Jay whispers.

"I brought Elle here. Just to show her the town, or that's what I pretended. She teases me about being from Arkansas. But she said Eternal was prettier than she expected. Quaint, cute. We had a nice time. I didn't plan it," he says, voice dipping to agony. "I didn't. It just hit me, in bed with her in the hotel room, at twilight, that if Theodora's magic had made it where I couldn't stop loving *you*, then couldn't it do the same for me and Elle?"

"Iggy." Jay almost can't stand to hear what he says next.

"I couldn't find the Forever House. We hiked the forests until I knew Elle was getting tired, but the house wouldn't show itself to us. Maybe it knew I had the wrong intentions. I almost gave up then. But on our last day, we came . . . here."

The Oath House. As if it knows it's being discussed, its rafters groan softly.

"It felt so perfect that it was a bed-and-breakfast, like it had been planned just for us," Iggy says. "I canceled our other room and booked this suite. I made it romantic. Champagne and rose petals, the whole deal. Elle was so delighted. I looked at her, this perfect woman, and I was so desperate to love somebody other than you, and I said—I made us swear to love each other, always. I made us promise."

She can imagine it, too clearly. Iggy standing here, using Theodora's power to inexorably force his future in a certain direction, against the grain of what they'd put into motion long ago.

"It's worse than what Max and Charlie did," Iggy says. "They were just trying to build their lives. They manipulated a business deal or—or a pile of drawings. Not the love of their life. I'll never know if Elle is with me because she cares about me or because I've forced her. And what will happen if she stops loving me, or if I stop loving her? Will she be punished? I'll never forgive myself for that. I deserve to be punished, but not her. Not her."

"Iggy," Jay says, broken by the guilt and shame in his voice. "You weren't—you're a good person. I know you." She intertwines her fingers with his, squeezes. "It's why I wanted us to stay away from Eternal Springs, all of us. Because otherwise we'll never know if anything in our lives is real."

"Bullshit," Hilma says from the doorway, making them both start. She's looking right at Jay. "Your whole life is built on this town's magic, Bluejay."

"What are you talking about?" Jay asks. Conscious of the way she's on the bed with Iggy, she sits up and lets go of his hand, but Hilma doesn't seem to care. "I haven't come back to Arkansas for years, Hilma. Before I got Brandi's letter, I stayed away. I don't know why I got the Truth House photo, I swear."

"It's not only about geography, is it? All I'm saying is, don't be so self-righteous. I've seen your show. You've been drawing the houses. Fifteen years later, and that's all you want to draw?" She pauses. "I also read your artist bio, Bluejay."

"Okay. You don't have to do this," Jay says, very tired. "Yeah, I had a rough patch. I spent a few days in the hospital. I'm proud of myself for managing to get better. The show is part of my recovery."

That's all she wants to say about that stretch of her life. She remembers it, of course. The darkness that clamped over her the moment she woke up, lingering until she fell into sleep. The world thinned and bleached, promising nothing. She felt how intangible it all was, and the awareness that there was something else out there, worlds shimmering out of reach, only deepened the darkness of the world she was stuck in. The one where she was the worst version of herself, in a way she was terrified she could never quite fix.

On the days when she couldn't rise from bed, Jay thought of two people. She thought of her mother. And she thought of Theodora Trader, institutionalized, alone, planning her houses, these little pockets of other worlds. Jay understood Theodora in a way she hadn't yet, and when she drove herself to the emergency room and then later checked herself into the outpatient program, she gripped that sliver of hope. The hope that she could come out on the other side of this and create something of her own.

"So it doesn't matter much that I avoided Arkansas and Theodora's houses," Jay says, "if it only landed me on suicide watch. Is that what you're saying?"

Hilma seems to be considering her next words very carefully.

"Bluejay. When I came to Eternal Springs in 1999, I was prepared to search for those houses alone. I didn't want to make friends in this town, not at all. I was supposed to be taking a break from socializing. My parents made me go to your shitty little public school and I figured I'd just keep my head down and focus on the houses. But then I met you and Brandi. You two—you had something. The way you were always together. I hadn't expected to find that in Arkansas. I wanted it for myself. Sometimes I've thought . . . that's why I asked all five of you to help me find the houses. That was behind everything. The two of you."

It's almost cruel for Hilma to say it while they're trapped in the rubble of everything Jay's lost. Whatever she and Brandi had as children seems to be long gone. In Jay's hands, their bond turned out to be a weapon, not a gift.

"I've been watching you, Bluejay. Watching what it's like for you to be back here. This is the first time I've been around you without Brandi Addams glued to your side, and it's . . ." Hilma hesitated, shook her head. "What I'm trying to say is that maybe what you're missing so much isn't the magic or the other world."

It takes a long time for Jay to be able to answer. "I do miss her," she manages. "Always. I know that. I've never not known that."

"But that's exactly why you're a hypocrite," Hilma says evenly. "You've been so proud of yourself for not coming back earlier. You've guilted Max, shamed Charlie, made Iggy feel like a real piece of shit."

"No, it's fine—" Iggy begins, but Hilma goes on, and Jay can see from her expression, calm and firm, that this is important to her. Jay accepts whatever she says next. She can handle it.

"It's not that you've avoided coming back because you're nobler than the rest of us, or because you respect Theodora's magic more, or whatever excuse you've held on to for so long," Hilma says to Jay. "It's because you're terrified to face Brandi Addams after what you did to her. It's because you're scared to see what you really gave up."

44

2000

THEN

A different version of Brandi emerged from that house in the woods.

The adjustment back to normal time was difficult for all three of them. For days, Jay felt like she was being rushed along; she had to take her dad's Dramamine to manage the nausea. Iggy handled it by napping too much. Weeks passed, and Jay and Iggy got better, back to normal, but Brandi couldn't seem to shake off the effects. Jay wasn't sure if Charlie or Hilma or Max noticed anything. Maybe Jay was making it all up, stewing in paranoia. The signs were tiny. Brandi's eyes were dazed. She'd seem suddenly, inexplicably chatty, and then would lapse into a sour drowsiness. Her hair was greasier, her skin sheened with sweat sometimes, a rashy red other times. Jay cataloged all these side effects, quietly searched on her school computer: *Percoset side effects. Painkillers too much tired. How long taking painkillers after injury.*

The websites only told her what to look for in an overdose, and none of that seemed relevant to Brandi, which gave Jay temporary relief. Maybe she wouldn't have to figure out how to help: that seemed so insurmountable that Jay was intimidated by it. But always, her relief would break and the fear would come back. A sudden flash of this other-Brandi.

At the same time, Jay's head was so full of equally pressing concerns. Now that they had found the first seven houses and had collected their inscriptions, their energy was channeled into the seemingly impossible task of finding the Portal House. They'd been searching every corner of town, hiking up steep hills, venturing through makeshift shortcuts. Jay had found new muscles in her legs. She came home late every night, telling her dad she'd been studying. "I've got to set a curfew for you, young lady," her dad joked. "Getting to be too smart."

He was right to be suspicious, because the other thing eating up Jay's time was Iggy. She missed the privacy of the Forever House. It was like Iggy and Jay had been adults together for a secret lifetime, and now they were, embarrassingly, teenagers again, scrounging for space. Iggy's house was a no-go. His family was large and happy in a way Jay envied, but it made finding privacy difficult. The idea of stifled sex with her dad watching reruns a few yards away was intolerable to Jay. Neither of them even owned a car, so there was no option of fumbling in a back seat.

They improvised. The Luck House on the abandoned waterbed. The Mirror House: Jay was brave enough, on a Friday night, to lean back against the turret window as Iggy kissed her, the mirror turned to hide them, and there'd been the sticky thrill of watching people pass by so close on the sidewalks below, never guessing.

Still, it took time away from her friendship with Brandi. Since spring break, Gene had been cheerful, expansive, and generous, mentioning nothing about Brandi's injuries. He'd been looking for new work, not even acknowledging the Garnets or his firing or the stolen painting that had exiled him from their rarefied world.

Jay's plan stayed firm. Brandi was going to be gone by the time anything else happened, encased safely inside a new world with Jay by her side.

The three of them had kept their secrets for each other. Jay and Iggy hadn't mentioned the real reason behind Brandi's injuries, letting the others accept her shaky cover story that she'd fallen on the hike home. And Brandi hadn't talked about Iggy and Jay. Sometimes Jay felt the secrets tightening among them, a precious bond. Other times it felt dangerous, these unseen fault lines coming between the six of them right when they needed to be strong together.

Jay paused at a small intersection, the wind tearing her hair into her eyes. She was only five minutes from the one place she was certain she'd be safe. The wind was working itself into a fury, trees bent nearly double. In the Mirror House with Iggy, she hadn't even noticed the storm clouds. Now the fuzzy lull of sex was replaced with panic as the sirens keened in the distance.

Tornado season was nearly over in Eternal Springs. This was the tricky time when people relaxed too early, shelters transformed back into shoe closets and basements. Jay had a healthy fear of tornadoes. They could spin themselves out of nothing, a sunny day turned dark, the shriek of sirens rising in an eyeblink.

Rain-lashed and panting, Jay stumbled, grateful, into the Luck House. All along the block streetlights were winking out as if they didn't want to be spotted. In here, the electricity still worked. Jay flicked on the overhead lights, listening to the furious knock of the wind and rain against the windows.

"Fancy meeting you here."

She spun. "Charlie. Oh my god. What are you doing?"

"I was here first, so I get to do the interrogating." He was curled up in the massage chair, face tense, but trying to sound casual. "So did you and Iggy make it official? Is that what you're doing out here? Because I saw him running past ten minutes ago."

After a moment, she nodded, blushing.

"Good for you two. I was wondering. All that free time in the Forever House; it was bound to happen sooner or later."

"So why *are* you here?" Jay asked.

He held up Theodora's journal, a rueful answer in and of itself. "The Luck House is busy today," Charlie said. "A regular Grand Central Station, Max has been in and out too."

"Max? Doing what?"

Charlie seemed to deliberate for a second. "I have to show you something." He got up, and Jay followed him through the Luck House, all the piles of treasure spotlighted by the lightning flashes. Charlie knelt next to a little crawl space, undoing the latch and swinging the tiny door open. It was shadowy in this nook, but Charlie flicked on a flashlight, pointed it at the interior. "This is what Max has been getting up to," he said.

Jay noticed a strange coil first. A limp, rubbery boa, a sickly grayish white, but unnaturally familiar. "Is that . . . Lucky?" Jay whispered, feeling queasy.

"The one and only. I guess Max tried to duplicate Lucky's body. As if it would magically produce a replacement snake after he let her die." Charlie rolled his eyes. "I'm not surprised that it didn't work on living creatures. I suppose it works on organic matter once it's . . . well, dead."

The replica of Lucky's body was uncanny, scentless and limp, mouth gaping open, pearly blue eyes clouded. Other than the snake, the crawl space was mostly empty, just a stack of what looked like typical Luck House fare. Easels and Tiffany lamps. "I was looking into previous owners of this place," Charlie said. "Several people lived here and moved out without any issues. But—do you remember that older guy who'd only come out in the evenings? He was always all wrapped up in a dozen coats? When we were little kids."

"Yeah," Jay says, surprised. "Brandi and I called him the Invisible Man."

"This place was his. He lived here for a long time, and he was obviously buying whatever he could from home shopping channels. I was asking my dad about it, and he remembers this man always hosting poker. He must have made a fortune."

"Wouldn't the other people get the luck, too?"

"It's possible the luck primarily goes to the person who owns the house," Charlie says. "But there's a catch. Outside of the house, my dad said this guy was the unluckiest man he'd ever met. Always falling down the stairs or being involved in fender-benders. He was destitute by the time he died. He rarely left the house."

"That doesn't make sense," Jay said. "I mean, he lived in the Luck House."

"Maybe he convinced himself that his luck was *only* in the house," Charlie said, contemplative. "Or possibly the world felt too unlucky when he went outside. I've wondered what it would be like to stumble across these houses without Theodora's journal. Never being sure if it was your imagination, never understanding the rules, either ignoring the magic or getting too obsessed with it. What if these houses take revenge on people who misuse them?"

"Are *we* misusing them?" Jay asked, anxious. "I thought we were on Theodora's side."

Charlie shrugged. "I wonder how her journal ended up for sale. Some of the phrasing in it sounds like she was talking to people directly. It feels like it should have been here in Eternal Springs all along."

A branch smacked into the window, and they both jumped, Jay's heart pounding in her throat. "That's scary, if the Luck House can use up your actual luck."

"Have you had any good news lately?" Charlie asked her, half joking.

"Um. Sort of? I—I got accepted to a school. In New York."

"State or city?"

"State."

"Well, that's amazing, Jay. See? You've had good news."

"But I didn't get any scholarship money, and my dad can't afford the tuition. I could take out loans, but my dad said they'd just hang over me, for something like art school where I won't get a job. It's not happening. It's not a big deal," she added quickly, dodging Charlie's pity.

"Well, I got an acceptance too," Charlie said, like he was daring himself to say it. "Several, in fact. Good universities. Very good, the best."

Jay didn't get why his voice was flat, like he was reading from a script he didn't understand. "Congratulations. Your parents must be so proud."

"They're ecstatic. Our relatives on at least two continents have been informed. I'm just not sure how it even works anymore," he said, panic peeking through the flatness. "Back in August, this moment was all I could imagine. It was what I lived for, getting into a good school and getting out of Arkansas. But now?"

Jay sensed that Charlie only needed her silence.

"I've been going over old deeds, old boundary maps, visiting the library, the historical society. I looked up old fire insurance maps. Nothing. It's frustrating because Theodora describes the Portal House more carefully than the other houses, and I know for sure it doesn't match any buildings in this area. Maybe it got torn down? Is it even possible to destroy her houses without consequences? Anyway. Right now, the Portal House doesn't exist. And it's all I want."

The next time lightning flashed, something caught Jay's attention inside the crawl space. She reached in deeper to examine the objects stacked up behind the grayish replica of Lucky's body. There was a canvas, turned the wrong way around, that looked subtly out of place. Jay pulled it loose and her stomach gave a dip. The woman she'd seen the first time she entered the Garnets' home, more polished now, shadowed and highlighted as if she could just step out of the canvas, those crooked teeth gleaming between her legs. Could this be the painting that had gotten Gene fired? Jay let the canvas fall back into place, confused.

Charlie continued, unaware of what Jay had found. "The Garnets are leaving in a month. If we don't locate this place soon, then I don't know what's going to happen to us."

45

2000

THEN

As she entered the school gym, Jay felt an unexpected wave of awe. The place was transformed for the Senior Ball, strung with a dangling disco ball and carefully crafted tinfoil stars. Even Matchbox Twenty spitting from the tinny speakers couldn't muffle the radiance. Hilma had, last-minute, invited everyone here for a "big announcement." It was the first school dance Jay had ever attended, and for a second she felt sad that she'd been missing out all this time. Maybe every dance had been just as magical.

Iggy adjusted the corsage on her wrist. "Thanks for doing the photos for my parents."

"They were really enthusiastic, huh?" she teased. After the Forever House, it had seemed surreal to pose and smile politely while Iggy's dad took innumerable photographs and his mom dabbed at her eyes, laughing at herself for crying.

"I'm the oldest, so I have to be the one to do all the milestones and get it out of the way for my little brothers." His voice softened. "You look really pretty tonight."

Jay was wearing one of her mom's old dresses, cream-colored silk, age-spotted on the hem but clinging to her in a way that made her feel more adult, deserving of being freshly eighteen. They watched their classmates spread out across the dance floor, swaying in awkward pairs and happy clusters. Jay's eyes caught on Destiny and Amber, who looked gorgeous in sequins and high heels.

Jay was shoved gently from behind, Hilma's perfume hitting her a second later. Hilma summed up the dance floor with one glance. "This is every bit as depressing as I thought it would be. One last normal high school event before the Portal House."

"Yeah," Jay said, though she felt a sting at Hilma's scorn, embarrassed at how entranced she'd been just a second ago.

The music switched to a thumping bass line. Hilma wore sweatpants, her hair in a half-hearted ponytail. Dressing up was beneath her. In contrast, Charlie's suit fit him perfectly, a black that veered into blue when the light hit it exactly right. Max pulled out a silver flask and took an unapologetic drink. Jay thought of that painting in the Luck House, wondering if she should bring it up with him. He caught her eye and winked, flicker-quick, as if he could read her mind.

"Does this mean you've found the Portal House?" Jay asked Hilma.

She gave a mysterious smile, lifting her eyebrows.

"My theory," Max said, bobbing his head in time to the music, "is that there is no Portal House. It's just Theodora's shitty trick to keep us trying—"

"No, the Portal House is real."

They turned. Brandi hovered at the edge of the circle, wearing a fluffy pink coat over her eighth-grade party dress, too tight in the chest, the plastic rhinestones shedding. Her eyes were glazed in the overhead lights. The pills, Jay thought at once, and looked around at the others' faces, a quick sweep, to see if they caught it too. Nobody had.

"Theodora went through that portal herself," Brandi said.

"What are you talking about?" Hilma said. "There's nothing about that in her journal."

"But there was this big old box of letters in the Forever House. I spent the whole time reading 'em. Letters to her, and from her."

"Letters?" Charlie asked. "Whoa, whoa. Brandi, those are primary sources, those would be an amazing insight into Theodora's life here."

Jay felt Iggy nudge her gently. She remembered the box of letters Brandi had been reading while she and Iggy were together, all those lonely hours Brandi must have spent in the house that wouldn't sleep. She'd been so distracted. It had slipped Jay's notice that the letters were actually Theodora's.

"We're getting to the bottom of this." Hilma gestured for them to follow her behind the bleachers; the air reeked of disinfectant, but the music dulled back there.

Brandi was talking, jittery, sped up: "I reckon Theodora had friends in town, just like I always said. I mean, the letters were real old, and I couldn't always read the handwriting, but I did my best. One guy, he was telling her that he had terrible luck all the time, just real bad. Another person was saying nobody ever kept promises to him and he was real tired of it. He wanted a place that would hold people to their promises, and nobody could ever get out of it, even if they tried."

"Wow," Charlie said, eyes alight. "So essentially they were describing problems that could be fixed by each of the seven houses?"

"Or problems caused by them," Iggy said, sounding worried.

"Brandi, why didn't you tell us sooner?" Hilma asked. "That's amazing."

They had to notice the swirly quality behind her eyes, as if somebody had dipped a fingertip into Brandi's pupils and stirred them around. "Listen," Brandi went on. "There were all these—all these cool, weird things. Like, the Oath House, the man pacifically asked Theodora to make sure nobody could ever destroy it."

Specifically, Jay corrected in her head, a blip.

"And one of the letters was from the woman who lived in the Forever House her own self. Her and her little girl. She was widowed, and she had this kid, a daughter who was sick. Doctors told her that her daughter would die by ten, and that was if'n she was lucky. That's why the woman had come to Eternal in the first place, for the healing springs."

Jay's heart throbbed painfully. The lights from the disco ball peppered Brandi's cheeks.

"Theodora built the house out in the forest for this lady and her daughter to live in," Brandi said. " 'Cause that way they could stay there for as long as they wanted, then walk out and all that time would be . . . just gone. Poof. They went right almost to her daughter's death, again and again, and then came back out of the house. I reckon they spent whole lifetimes in there. Living and starting over and living and starting over."

Jay remembered that child's bedroom, its sweet pinks and creams. It had been a prison and a paradise all at once.

"But it wasn't good for them," Brandi said. "Like, I was reading these letters and the lady was startin' to worry. She said that everything that happened in the house, it'd, like, stick to her head?" She patted her own skull to demonstrate. "And her little girl's. Each time they stepped outside the house and went back in, her daughter would change, like each lifetime was just staying and not going away."

"Did you bring these letters back?" Charlie asked, hungry.

"I'm not gonna take anything from Theodora's houses," Brandi said. "That's one of the rules. I ain't breaking the rules."

"Well, in this case—" Hilma began, but Jay interrupted, desperate to understand.

"Wait, what are you saying, Brandi? About things staying and not going away?"

"Oh, well, Theodora wrote that the Forever House couldn't take the time off their lives, but it got into them other ways. Like, whatever happened in there was scrubbed from their real-life bodies, but that meant it was stuck inside, got into their brains or whatnot. Hey, I wrote one of the lines down." Brandi fished in her jacket pocket for a slip of paper.

Charlie peered down at it. "'What happens here is written forever on the heart.'"

"Is there any way to fix it?" Jay asked Brandi, thinking of the pills.

"I don't reckon so," Brandi said. "Because . . . because Theodora built the Portal House for them. She went through it with this woman and her little girl. They all escaped into the other world together."

Jay tried to put it together, Aerosmith wailing thinly in the background.

"But Theodora died here in Eternal," Iggy said. "They found her body."

"They found parts of her body," Charlie said slowly. "Just parts."

"Teeth," Hilma said reflectively. "A finger."

"Duplicates, I reckon," Brandi said.

"Shit. Shit. Like she faked it?" Max asked.

Brandi nodded. "The lady knew this was her last chance to save her little girl, and Theodora went through the portal with them, to guide them along. It was the first time she ever shared that with somebody else."

"She wanted a fresh start," Charlie said. "I understand that. She didn't want the risk of people coming and looking for her. Or making trouble for her."

The dark, noisy gym vanished, and Jay saw Theodora and her

friend and this little girl who carried so many versions of a recycled life, walking into another world, beginning anew.

"So anyways, the Portal House is real," Brandi said brightly.

"It is," Hilma said, remembering her original purpose. "And I've found it. That's why I called you all here, actually. We have a date. Wednesday night."

Wednesday. Only four days away. Jay's spike of dread and excitement nearly lifted her right off her feet. After spending her whole life training to leave Eternal, the chance was right here, glittering in front of her.

"What should we bring?" Iggy asked.

"Oh my god," Max said. "I love you, Igster. We're about to venture into another dimension and you're worried about packing enough underwear."

"I asked you here to enjoy yourselves," Hilma said, spreading her arms wide. "So. Enjoy."

The rest of the night passed in a blur. Knowing how soon they'd be leaving gave Eternal a strange, pre-nostalgic beauty, steeped in its own impending absence. It seemed like everyone felt the same. Even kids who weren't leaving town were crying, embracing their friends tightly, aware that *something* was coming to an end. Jay ignored the stares and danced with Iggy, leaning her head against his shoulder, the dotted lights giving the room an underwater feel. She let herself enjoy Iggy's arms wrapped around her in front of everybody.

At one point, she glanced up to see Max and Destiny near the bleachers, Destiny, miraculously, smiling at him. "Maybe she knows he's leaving soon," Iggy whispered.

"How would she know about the portal?" Jay asked.

"Leaving Arkansas, I mean."

A slow song came on. Jay looked up at Iggy, his curls falling over his forehead, humidity-ruffled. His eyes were far away, and she wondered if he was thinking of his family, of the potential move to California, of saying goodbye to his brothers, his parents, without them understanding the significance of the farewell. Even if he was only going into the portal for a day, there were no guarantees. Selfishly, Jay was glad he'd be with her.

But on the other side of the portal, their own goodbye would be waiting. When Jay stayed and he came home. Her heart squeezed.

Every time they made a rotation of the dance floor, Jay's eyes automatically sought out Brandi, perched on the bleachers alone, burrowed into her coat. She looked blank-faced, but there was a melancholy stitched into her posture. Jay couldn't stop thumbing at the idea of the Forever House sticking to them, the house slipping inside their neural pathways for good. Brandi had been taking those pills nonstop. What if each one had lodged itself into a place even more permanent than the last? It only emphasized to Jay how important it was to find this new world and give her best friend a fresh start. The fresh start Theodora had intended.

The next time they made a rotation, Brandi was gone.

"Jadelynne?" her dad called, a shadow half rising from the couch. "You're home awfully late. Did you have a good time?"

"Yeah." She stood, knowing she was luminous in her mom's white dress. The lights in their house were off, except for the wonky bulb above the stove, the downcast orange that highlighted the grease stains they could never quite scrub away. Jay looked around at the ordinary lines of her home and throbbed with nostalgia, a tender fist inside her chest.

"You look pretty," her dad said, rising, yawning. "I'm glad you decided to go to one of these dance things. I always thought you'd have a lot of fun."

"I didn't think you cared if I went," Jay said.

"Of course I do. I always care."

She couldn't answer. It truly hit her what she was going to do in saying goodbye to her dad, to this little house, to Eternal Springs. To Arkansas. To everything. She caught him in a hug, and, wordless, he embraced her back, her mom's dress pressed between them.

46

2015

NOW

Jay leans her forehead against the cool glass of the turret window, staring at Eternal spread below. The weeping willows and the crepe myrtles, the little houses that have clung to their original shapes despite all the changes pushing in. Evening is spilling across the hills.

The other four are busy. Max is making a last-ditch effort to find the Forever House, Charlie is attempting to piece the vandalized journal back together, Hilma and Iggy are pursuing the anonymous LLC. But Jay just feels numb, quieted. She needs to be alone in the Mirror House and vanish from life for a moment.

The conversation with Hilma knocked something loose. Jay misses Brandi. Every day since they last saw each other, she's missed her. Being back in Eternal has been terrifying, yes, caught in this uncertain trap. Jay's pretended to be as eager as the other four to claw her way back home.

And yet. And yet. In the silent moments, Jay feels more awake in Eternal Springs than she has in a long time.

What if she had stayed? What if she'd never left, in 2000? Jay doesn't even know what her relationship with Brandi would look like now. So much of their bond was formed in childhood, rolling down hills until they got dizzy, playing ghost in the graveyard at twilight. Amber Penske became the friend Brandi needed. For all her thoughtlessness as a teenager, Amber grew up into someone practical, steady, a good friend. Jay tries to imagine the day-to-day Brandi and Amber built together, something she—with her lack of adult friendships—still doesn't quite understand. Was Brandi close to Amber's kids? She sees the two of them worrying over rent, sleeping off weekend hangovers, giving each other rides to work—

Jay straightens. She reaches for Brandi's phone, runs her fingertip over the cracked glass. Amber's number is in the Contacts. Jay punches the digits into her own phone, then hits the green button before she can second-guess. It rings for a long time. Amber must be at home now, maybe heating up a simple dinner or carrying out bedtime routines.

"Yeah?"

"Amber. It's Jadelynne." There's no point in small talk. "I have a question. When you dropped Brandi off to clean that client's house, where was it?"

"I, uh—it was the Motts', but they wasn't even home, I already—"

"But where is that? Like, where did you drop her off, exactly?"

"Why does it matter?"

"I just need to know. I think it could help, actually."

"Still playing at helping Brandi, huh? Y'all should be worrying about yourselves."

There's an ominous edge to this that's clearly meant to worry Jay, and it does, but she holds firm. "Amber. Please."

A sigh. "Out along the county road."

"Near the Asher Lake trailhead?"

"How the hell did you know?"

Of course. Of course.

"Thank you, Amber," Jay says, and she drops her phone, shaking, triumphant. Jay should've asked sooner. She remembers the shape of these woods, still. The significance of that trailhead—their old milestone—will always shine in a corner of her mind. Jay stands, her spark of curiosity reawakening. She needs to tell the others about this. Maybe Max has found the Forever House by now. Whatever happens next, she's going to get the other four out of Eternal, dispatch them back to their lives. They deserve that, no matter what Jay decides to do.

She starts toward the stairwell, then pauses. Footsteps are coming toward her, a rising staccato. The tread is heavy, tentative. All wrong. Jay freezes for a split second before she tiptoes to the mirror, turning it to face the wall.

Not a second later, a voice floats up to her: "Jadelynne Carr?"

Pell. He's here.

Jay backs against the wall, not breathing. Pell must've heard her talking, her lonely voice echoing as she pleaded with Amber. Her eyes dart to the center of the room. The two phones are lying in plain view. Before she can move, Pell arrives in the doorway, looking right at her.

He's panting from the exertion of the stairs. "Jadelynne?" he repeats.

She releases the smallest breath. He's addressing the spot behind her. He can't see her. He moves cautiously into the room. His foot hits Brandi's phone and sends it skidding a few inches: Pell stoops to retrieve it. "Well," he says. "Just what I was looking for." He slips it into his pocket, gives it a little pat. Jay swallows her panic. The others are going to be furious that she lost their only real insight into Brandi's mind. "I was hoping you could help unlock it."

The victory Jay felt in the police office is a joke now. He must have noticed her stealing evidence. And the fact that it's taken him

279

so long to come after her: there was a reason that the phone was lying on his desk, glossy and tempting, just within reach.

Pell hesitates, spotting Jay's phone now. He picks it up, tries a few passcodes. Jay wants to lunge forward and grab it. She clenches her fist so tight her fingernails cut into her palm. Pell looks around, smiling. "Should I take this? Seems like a fair trade. Phone for a phone."

"Fuck you," Jay says under her breath, knowing he can't hear.

Pell puts her phone back on the floor, like placing bait in a trap. He turns in a slow circle. He's close enough that Jay can smell the spice of his cologne, see the shaving rash along his jaw. She wonders if he senses her; how much does he know? A man who knew absolutely nothing wouldn't be in an empty room, talking aloud.

"Believe it or not, I really do want to help Brandi Addams. I know I've let that girl down in the past."

Jay doesn't move a muscle, even as she absorbs the realization that Pell has been mired in the same doubt and guilt. His role in everything is so interlocked with Jay's own, but she never considered the way she and Pell might carry similar guilt.

"This house," Pell muses, and raps on the wall. The vibration snaps Jay between the shoulder blades and she starts, and for a split second Pell looks her way again. "I know she cared about this place. Lots of places around town she cared for. Never could make sense of it."

Outside the turret windows, the sun is beginning to set in a bleed of orange and pink.

"You know what's crazy? I reckon if I could figure out what's going on with these houses, I'd know what happened to Brandi Addams." Pell scratches the back of his neck. "About six months ago or so, there was a fire at that little house along CR 334. Burned to the ground. Thank the lord, no harm to surrounding property. But it sure seemed like an intentional act."

The Truth House. He means the Truth House.

"We were never able to pin it on anybody. But the consensus, at the time? Around the station? Around the town?" He pauses for effect. "Was that Brandi Addams burned that place down."

Jay bites her lip till rust floods her mouth. She wants to pace, shake her head, scream. But she's stuck here, a fly on the wall, worried that any big gestures will attract his attention.

"Thought it was out of character for her," Pell says to the empty room. "Now, six months later, her friends are back, she's missing, y'all are sneaking into and out of these same old houses that Brandi herself always loved. There's something there, I reckon. Just out of reach."

He knows. He knows, he knows, he knows—and Brandi, Brandi herself, was the one who trapped the five of them here, who left Jay alone in Eternal Springs with only a memento of the place where truth once lived.

But there has to be a reason Brandi took the truth away. Jay lets herself think about this possibility without fear or dread or the belief that Brandi is punishing her. She stays open to it. There's a reason, and this town—the town where Jay was born, the place where Theodora spun her secret magic—will lead her to the answer.

Pell cocks his head and sighs heavily, then starts for the stairwell again. "If people have anything to say for themselves," he says, "I hope they'll speak up. I surely do. Because it's getting to the point where I'm wondering why y'all are sticking around, and—"

His radio crackles, spits out a staticky voice. Jay catches numbers, *nine-five-three*, and she doesn't exactly understand, but Pell's expression changes. He pales, stares around for a moment with an almost lost look, as if beseeching Jay to do something. Then he turns and leaves, hurrying down the narrow staircase, his tread shaking the mirrors on the walls.

When she hears the distant slam of the front door, Jay creeps forward for her phone. The screen lights up with a notification. Max. She hurriedly signs in, only to see his text: *EVERYONE. LUCK HOUSE. NOW!*

47

2000

THEN

Wednesday night. Their last night on earth. Their first night in another world.

At the entrance to the AIR House, Hilma stepped aside to let them enter. She wore a dress with a plunging neckline, deep bronze silk. A goddess, ready to lead them into the underworld. Goose bumps rose along Jay's arms.

"So where is the portal?" Iggy asked. "Will we need a car or can we walk?"

"You're already here, my darlings," Hilma said.

"What do you mean?" Jay, sticking close to Iggy, followed Hilma deeper into the house. Then Jay stopped, awestruck.

This house, always beautiful, had been transformed. Votive candles guttered and glowed in circles on the floor, on the bookshelves, on the mantelpiece. The huge dark windows caught the candles' reflections and amplified them until the flames twisted with the tree branches outside, joined with the stars in the sky. A thousand points of light.

Max and Charlie were waiting, arranged cross-legged on the floor. Brandi was standing, her backpack on her shoulders, as if she were already one foot out of reality.

"The AIR House *is* the Portal House?" Iggy asked.

"How did we not know that already?" Jay asked.

"Well, it makes sense." Hilma swirled across the room, skirts brushing dangerously close to the flames. "It's a large house. Not accessible to locals, which explains why nobody has accidentally slipped into another world. Located at a prime spot. Isn't it amazing? It's been right under our noses all along." She was manic, buzzing at a strange wavelength.

"Was this house built during Theodora's time?" Iggy asked.

"The year before her mysterious disappearance," Charlie said. He sounded determined and reckless, not quite himself—but they were all moving beyond the people they'd been.

Jay tried to quell her doubts. This house up on the mountaintop had gleamed with promise for as long as she could remember. Every time she was in here, she'd felt a pull of *something*. Why not another world?

"Where are your parents?" she asked the twins.

"Out of town," Max said. "All night. Up in Fayette to rub elbows with Arkansas's finest. We promised them we'd be good."

Jay imagined the Garnet parents walking into their house, finding it echoing and isolated, only these stubs of candles remaining. Her stomach fizzed with excitement and fear. "So how do we open the portal?" Jay asked, trying to prove she wasn't losing her nerve.

"The key, of course. We're going to recite the inscriptions," Hilma said, brandishing her notebook. "I have them all here. I'll do the honors, if that's all right with everyone."

"As if you'd let anyone else," Max said.

The candles turned the air hazy with heat, snapping against Jay's skin. Brandi was in her jacket, her boots; Charlie and Hilma had dressed too formally; Iggy was in his football jersey, athletic shorts; Max and Jay were dressed for a school day in jeans and sneakers. They had no idea what they'd encounter when they slipped into another dimension. Jay had a photo tucked inside her backpack, her and her dad and her mom, the three of them together when she was little. She wore her friendship necklace and saw that Brandi had its twin at her throat.

"Look, are we sure about this?" Charlie burst out. "We're potentially saying goodbye to our families and to—everything. All of it." He took a deep breath. "Even once we come back, everything could be changed."

"Well, Brandi and I aren't coming back," Jay said. It was time to come clean.

"Bluejay," Hilma said. "What are you talking about?"

"I decided on it. We're ready." She locked eyes with Brandi, and there was both a dare and a hopefulness. Brandi gave a half smile, and she was the old Brandi again, the other half of Bradelynne. They wouldn't be separated, not for anything.

"Wait, hold on, you didn't mention this," Max said, looking back and forth between Jay and Brandi. "Nobody ever talked about staying there forever. Shit. I would've gone in on that."

"No, you wouldn't have, Max," Hilma said. "Don't be absurd. I know it's a big moment, but we need to keep our heads. We'll go in, come back out. Nobody's staying behind for good."

"Are we even sure there is a way back?" asked Charlie quietly, but it seemed only Jay could hear him.

"Why not?" Max asked Hilma. "If Jay and Brandi stay, why can't we?"

"But Max, we have—" She stopped short.

"What?" Max asked.

"This world is different for us," Hilma said. "This was just supposed to be an adventure."

Something passed between the twins. *We have options.* That's what Hilma was going to say, Jay realized. They weren't like Brandi and Jay, they weren't like the Arkansans. It surprised her to see Hilma Garnet suddenly afraid of loosening her grip on the world that they'd all agreed to leave behind. Jay felt a sudden power—she could take this bold and life-shattering move that Hilma Garnet herself was too nervous to make.

"Let's vote on it, then," Charlie said. "We're all in this together. Do we go forward, or do we turn back?"

"Of course," Hilma said at last. "I wouldn't want us going headlong into a portal unless everyone was absolutely sure. Do we stay in this world we know or leave it behind?"

The silence felt heavy with meaning.

"We have to leave at some point," Jay said. "Everyone moves away from what they know, right? All the adventurous people."

Brandi added, "Everyone's going away right now."

"Yeah," Max said. "I mean, yeah. You know that rat-faced kid in AP lit? He's going to Auburn. That girl with the weird hair is going on some Tibetan self-discovery backpacking tour."

"Destiny," Brandi said, and Jay thought she was getting philosophical until she added, "Destiny already ran off to Hollywood. Amber was crying about it in class the other day."

Max's head dropped, as if mourning his lost chance. "See what I mean?"

"Everyone's leaving," Jay echoed. She saw her own resolve falling across the others' faces as well. "This is a chance barely anybody gets, and here we are. Whether we stay for a long time or not, we have to do this. We can't spend our whole lives wondering."

She looked at Iggy as she said it. She was asking a question, and he answered exactly as he'd hoped, stepping closer to her, kissing her cheek lightly. "I'm coming with you," he said. "I wouldn't miss it, Jay."

"Is everyone decided?" Charlie asked, and one by one they all nodded their assent.

Jay looked out the windows at the lacework of tree branches, the jewel-bright night sky, out here away from the streetlights. For a startling second she hoped that the world beyond the portal was as beautiful as Eternal Springs.

Opening the notebook, Hilma began reading. "'Truth is more of a stranger.'" Her voice was clear, sweet. "'One must live unseen. Oh, I am fortune's fool.'"

The candles guttered, some flames darting higher.

"'His words are bonds, his oaths are oracles. I taste a liquor never brewed.'"

The shadows cast their faces into unusual shapes, new profiles, like they were transforming into the people they'd need to be in whatever environment waited for them.

"'*Hypocrite lecteur, mon semblable, mon frère.*'"

Outside the window, there was a submerged movement, like glimpsing a fish in murky water. Jay's pulse quickened; the Garnet parents arriving home unexpectedly? But no, it must've been a white-tailed deer lurking, a raccoon.

Hilma was nearly to the last of the seven inscriptions. She paused, and Max gave the smallest nod, encouraging her.

"'And eternity,'" she said, voice lifting, trembling, "'in an hour.'"

Jay shut her eyes. She waited for the portal. A cold breeze, a lifting sensation. She waited for a new world to materialize beneath her feet, unrolling like a carpet.

But there was nothing. No noise. No change in the atmosphere. The heat of the candles kept pressing against her, sticky, and she wanted to scrape it off.

"Did it work?" asked Brandi.

"Fuck," Max said. "What happened?"

Slowly, Jay opened her eyes. The AIR House was unchanged. All the magic she'd felt earlier was a flat disappointment now. "Maybe it'll open in a second?" Jay said. "Or maybe the portal is somewhere else? We'll have to search the house. The houses don't always work instantly, we know that."

"Right," Iggy said. "Like, what did we think? That we'd just get transported right away?" He bumped Brandi with his elbow, a cheer-up gesture. "It'll be okay. We're stubborn."

Charlie seemed caught in a mix of relief and shock, hugging himself hard.

"All right," Hilma said. "Yeah. Of course. This is the trickiest house of them all, this is Theodora's greatest treasure. It won't be easy. We're going to look everywhere. My parents aren't coming back until morning, we have all the time in the world."

They looked everywhere. They searched the entire house. Every time Jay walked through a doorway or peered into a closet, every time she moved up or down a staircase, she was prepared to end up in a different world, but again and again, she was only inside the AIR House, its familiarity wearing thinner and thinner. Every time she passed one of the others as they zigzagged across the entire square footage of the AIR House like diligent ants, she saw the same edgy disappointment. The world itself felt old, uninspired, too tight around them.

Downstairs, the candles melted into crusted puddles, the flames slipping to nothingness, the wicks' little metal underpinnings exposed. Exhaustion tugged at the backs of Jay's eyelids, the comedown of the adrenaline rush sloshing with the disappointment.

Eventually they all ended up slumped across the white leather couches downstairs. It was two in the morning, the house growing ever dimmer. No portal. Hilma tried the inscriptions in a dozen different configurations; Charlie and Jay had recited them too, hoping to shake something loose with their own voices. Nothing.

"The key," Brandi said. "Maybe it was a real key."

They looked at her, bleary-eyed, confused.

"I been looking at the journal. I reckon there're different ways to read what she wrote. Like, why are the *sayings* the key? Maybe she meant a real key."

"Like a key you put in a door?" Charlie asked, tired.

"Yeah. Theodora was a builder. Why wouldn't a key just be a key?"

"Sometimes a cigar is just a cigar," Charlie muttered.

"Theodora wasn't 'just a builder.' She was also a poet, a traveler, a visionary," Hilma said. "If she was going to have a stupid key, like for a dead bolt, she wouldn't have bothered writing an entire journal in this intricate code."

"It's a good thought, Bran," Max said. "I like that. A key. Imagine how easy that would be."

"But Theodora clearly wanted us to collect the different engravings," Charlie said. "She returns to that idea again and again. The key is abstract."

"Maybe it ain't the right house, then," Brandi said.

"It has to be the right house," Hilma burst out, "there just aren't any other options, you fucking look at the journal if you're so smart," and she half tossed the journal to Brandi, who caught it carefully, reverently.

There was a sudden pounding at the door. Everybody jumped, electroshocked out of their sour sleepiness. It took them a second to locate the exact location of the sound: the back door, the one that led into the garage, inaccessible from outdoors.

At first no one moved. They eyed each other with a resurgence of hope. Could it be? Then Hilma, a blur of bronze, marched across to answer it—in the surreal gloom of the AIR House, Jay wondered if it was a visitor from another world. A guide, a mentor. Maybe the new world would be delivered to them like a package, she thought, her giddiness briefly revived.

Looking across the living room, Brandi made a strangled sound. Jay followed her gaze. Hilma backed up, tripping on the slippery hem of her gown. Framed in the darkness of the empty garage was Gene Stippley.

48

2000

THEN

"What are you doing here?" Hilma asked, all her anger and disappointment lashing out at Gene. He stood disheveled, red-faced, leery-eyed, like a living reminder of the ordinary ugliness of the world they were now stuck in. "This is private property." She started to slam the door, as if Gene were nothing, but he caught it in one hand, stronger than any of them. He pushed his way inside slowly, with a single-minded purpose that cut through their fog.

"I told you not to spend time here," Gene called to Brandi. "Why the fuck couldn't you listen? I'm supposed to stand back during this little sleepover?"

The six of them were half-dead with exhaustion and disappointment. With only a few candles still flickering, the room was strangely shadowed.

Max got up, holding out his hands toward Gene, but Gene

was homed in on Brandi and Brandi alone. "Shit, man," Max said. "How'd you get in? Did you keep a key?"

Gene didn't even respond. Jay saw Max as a kid, suddenly. He was half a foot taller than Gene, but he looked so young, completely unequipped for this, his eyes frantic and unfocused. He kept looking toward the door, obviously hoping his parents would come in and stop everything. All of it. Bring them back to the moment before, before, before.

Iggy grabbed Jay's hand. He began pulling her back, toward the AIR House kitchen, away from the living room, away from Hilma yelling and Charlie paralyzed and Max spitting out increasingly panicked and useless threats. Iggy was just trying to keep her safe, but Jay fought against his grip. She saw it all: the clear trajectory from Gene to Brandi.

And Brandi stood alone. Her face was pale but firm. Her chin was tilted up with a show of defiance. She'd known this was coming. This had been waiting on the other side of the failed portal all along. Brandi deserved to be safe right now, she deserved to be in another world. Free.

But she was here, and Gene grabbed her elbow. "You ask my permission," he said. "You don't sneak out at night. They're liars, Brandi, they're liars and perverts, and your mom'd kill me." He began pulling her toward the door, and Brandi was unresisting, her steps matched to his.

Jay ran forward. Brandi caught her eyes now and shook her head, a single fierce warning. *Stay back. Stay out of it.*

"You have no right," Hilma said, stepping in front of the door. "This is our house. You're intruding. She's eighteen, you don't own her."

"It's not your house," Gene said.

"It is—"

"Your parents let you fucking dress like that?"

Hilma's steeply plunging gown was slipping, a plain bra strap showing, and she flushed, tugging the strap back into place. "Fuck you."

"I know what you're doing," Gene said. "You think you own every house in this town, don't you? Little rich bitch, going wherever you want, taking what you like. But Brandi's not like you, and you won't get away with any of it. First thing I do when I get home is file a police report on all of you."

Hilma stood, her face too still, her eyes brimming with a mix of fury and shame. She managed a thin laugh. Gene let go of Brandi, attempting to shove Hilma aside. "Move."

"No," she said.

With a nightmarish quickness, they were grappling; his hands were on her arms, twisting and lifting. Hilma cried out, sounding like a child, and he threw her aside, the shock of it sending her careening into the side table, catching herself, her shiny dress bunched around her thighs, too bright against the panic and confusion.

Charlie and Max were frozen, Jay couldn't speak, couldn't move. Iggy stepped forward, but he seemed like he couldn't decide what to do next. There was a layer of surrealness to everything, as if instead of opening the portal to another world they'd only conjured a far worse version of their own.

As Jay watched, Gene turned toward Brandi, and he stopped. His face fell slack.

"Don't touch them." Brandi was wide-awake now, her daze lifting. Her body was the only clear line in this room, she was spring-loaded, coiled. She pointed a gun right at Gene. Her hands shook, and even Jay knew that she wasn't holding it exactly right, but Gene seemed silenced by it, his hands lifted, a new tension wrapping around the room.

It was Gene's gun; Jay knew that much. Brandi must've stolen the gun and brought it in her backpack. She anticipated potential violence in the other world in a way the rest of them didn't.

"Now, girl, I know you don't want to do that—" Gene began.
And then Brandi fired.

Jay and Brandi were running. Running. There were so many places
they could've gone, sheltering in the cradle of the Luck House, or
hiding unseen in the Mirror House. They could've run into the forest, found the Forever House, and never left again. But they went
to the shed.

The other four had stayed behind. Sobbing, Hilma had yelled at
the two of them to go, just go, and Jay hadn't needed any encouragement, she'd wanted nothing in that moment but to be Bradelynne, to erase everything that came before. Even Iggy wasn't on
her mind. He had a family. Brandi only had Jay.

It made no sense for them to go here, separated from Gene by
two thin panes of glass. This trailer park was the first place people
would look for them. There was no magic in the shed to protect
them. But without speaking, they knew it was the only place they
would feel safe. They huddled on the damp, cool floor, curled together. Brandi didn't speak. Her face was tearstained, her eyes too
big. A little kid again.

Jay didn't know if Gene was alive or not. In the movies, a man
got shot and he fell to the ground, neatly dead. But Gene hadn't
even fallen; he'd flinched, run, stumbled out the door, leaving a
sticky trail of blood. Also unlike in the movies, there hadn't been
some pointed close-up on his body, a direct diagram from the bullet to the wound. Jay thought the bullet had hit his shoulder or arm.
But there'd just been Gene, white-faced and reeling.

"It's okay," Jay whispered to Brandi, stroking her hair off her
face. "No matter what happens next, we're here. We're with you. I
promise."

49

2000

THEN

The next week would always exist in Jay's memory as a strange, twisted blur. The opposite of what happened in the Forever House. Everything moved too quickly, jerky and uncanny. There was no news about Gene, either good or bad. His pickup sat unused in the trailer park. Iggy called in sick every day that week to school, his empty desk a raw reminder. Brandi moved some clothes and a sleeping bag into the Mirror House and stayed the night—when Jay walked into the turret, she had to turn the mirror around to reveal her friend, bruise-eyed from tiredness, hair unwashed. Meanwhile, Charlie stopped talking to Jay in the school hallways, and she couldn't blame him. Hilma and Max instructed the others to "start cleaning up," erasing all evidence of their time in Theodora's houses, but no one was helping. Jay felt like time was caught around her ankle and she was being pulled along, helpless to avoid whatever came next.

When Max saw Jay sitting on the front steps of the Truth House, he smiled, confused. "What, Igster couldn't make it?"

Jay stood, dusting off her jeans. "Uh. He's busy." Actually, she hadn't even told Iggy about Max's request to move the borrowed furniture back into the AIR House. She wanted to be alone with Max.

A car drove past and they both froze, exchanging awkward glances once the car was gone. Gene's absence was starting to feel more suffocating than his presence. Jay didn't know if he'd dragged himself off like an animal to die in the forest. Or was he plotting their destruction? If he wanted to hurt them, it wouldn't be hard. They were broken, dazed. Instead of poring over Theodora's journal, Charlie was contacting every school he'd been accepted to, securing his place for the fall. Iggy had been spending more time with his family, and Jay caught him with a pamphlet for UCLA. It felt like they were all scrambling numbly for some consolation prize.

Jay knew they shouldn't give up on the portal. Theodora wouldn't lead them all this way—across time and space—just to abandon them with a broken promise—would she? But all the energy that had driven their quest had vanished.

"Well, thanks for helping a guy out, Jaybird," Max said inside the Truth House, examining the white chair that Hilma had transferred from the AIR House. "We cleaned everything up, but my parents know something is weird. They're having us bring everything back to the house before we leave town."

Jay grabbed one edge of the chair. Her heart was beating in her ears; maybe this didn't matter right now, but she needed to know anyway. "Is this it? The only thing you need to return? Like, the only thing missing from the AIR House."

"No," Max said, heaving up one side of the chair, forcing Jay to step back. He paused, gave an odd smile. "Shit, I forgot what it's like to be in here. Uh, no, it's not the only thing missing. You got me."

He'd meant to lie to her. "Because of that painting that your parents think Gene stole."

Max made a noncommittal noise.

"Did you steal the painting?" she asked levelly.

She could almost see the lies forming in his head. "Yeah. Okay, yeah. I did. I took it."

"I saw it in the Luck House," Jay said. "And you've done it before, haven't you?"

"What do you mean?" Max's eyes hardened.

"The first time we were here, Hilma asked if you'd left the doors unlocked, when all your mom's paintings got stolen." The moment was so clear to Jay, but she wondered if Max even remembered. "You managed to lie in the Truth House?"

"Oh, that. No. Not exactly. My sister didn't ask what happened to the paintings. She asked about the doors being unlocked. I would've told the truth if she'd asked."

"Because you'd have been forced to."

"Seriously, Jay. I took some of my parents' paintings. So? They have dozens of them."

Jay set her half of the chair down; it bounced on the hardwood floor. "I still don't understand why you did it."

"Because I wanted to. Because it's embarrassing to have your parents' vulvas all over your house. Because sometimes I like watching them worry about something they love." Max's cheeks were bright as he held his side of the chair, lopsided. "Shit. Don't ask big questions in the Truth House unless you want the truth, Jadelynne."

"What you do with your parents' work at home is your business. But you've seen how your parents are blaming Gene."

"Gene? Jesus, who cares? The guy didn't steal a painting, okay, whatever, but he tried to—he tried to kill us—"

"Brandi," Jay said loudly. "Brandi's the one who pays the price when you make Gene's life harder. Haven't you seen that now?"

Max stared at his feet. The leaves outside cast long, tattered shadows against the back of his neck. "I'm sorry," he said at last. "You're right. I've been an asshole. Brandi's great, she doesn't deserve that."

Tears stung Jay's eyes. "I'm scared. I don't know what's going to happen to her."

"Hey." Dropping the chair, Max wrapped her in a tentative, brotherly hug. "We've all gone through a major disappointment. It's shitty, Jay. Just be sad."

She could only nod, the top of her head not even reaching his chin.

"It's not the worst thing in the world to have a Plan B," Max said, voice buzzing above her. "I know we've been focusing on the Portal House, but there's more out there. I've seen it with my own eyes. The world beyond the Ozarks. You can still leave Eternal."

She managed a damp laugh, stepping back. "It's a little late for that."

"Not too late yet."

Jay smiled sadly, feeling the gap between his life and hers, the way things were always fixable for Max, the way chances darted by her so quickly and stayed suspended forever for him.

Max hesitated before he spoke again. "There's this scholarship my parents are always yammering on about. It's for artists who are 'financially underserved.' They've had trouble getting applicants so they're, like, extending the deadline. Would you be interested in that? You'd need to send in a portfolio of your work and everything."

She stared up at him. "Seriously?"

"Of course. I thought of you right off. The world owes you one, Carr."

"Yeah. I mean. Maybe if I can—if I can double-check my portfolio." The world crept back around her. A different version—cracked and patched—but something Jay could still use.

"I'll send you the info this afternoon, then. Perfect," Max said. "Look, if I have it my way, every single one of you will get out of Eternal Springs and never have to come back. Charlie and Igster and you and Brandi. You'll go big places."

50

2000

THEN

The morning of high school graduation, Jay sat cross-legged in the basement of the Mirror House, drawing pad on her lap. She drew as quickly as she could, withstanding the dry hunger of the mirror against her skin. She was hurrying to put together the portfolio, throwing herself into it with a scrambling, single-minded desperation. Max was right. If she couldn't find the portal, at least she could leave Eternal, the way she'd always planned anyway. Max had been true to his word; she was surprised at how eagerly he'd been helping her, making sure all her information was sent in, assisting her with the paperwork, like he knew how hard it was for her to focus during this nightmare.

Jay snuck quick, daring peeks into the mirror, drawing herself on this paper that was nibbled into lace at the edges. Her self-portrait was half-formed and ghostly, the faded outline of a person. One last image of herself as the unformed not-yet-woman she was in Eternal Springs.

She checked her watch and reluctantly got up. While Charlie and Iggy had rented their regalia earlier that year, Brandi and Jay had been forced to borrow the tatty secondhand robes and caps that the school kept around for the lazy or broke students. Jay was dreading the whole ceremony, the valedictorian speech and the weepy goodbyes and the promises for a bright future, but at least it was a recommitment to normalcy. It was ignoring the loss that hurt the most.

"... According to the dictionary, the word *valedictorian* comes from a Latin phrase that means 'to say goodbye, or farewell.' Indeed, that is what we are doing now. We are saying 'goodbye' to each other today, but we are saying 'hello' to so much more ..."

The six of them sat in the back row, right next to each other. They were all edgy, quiet. Jay scanned the crowd. She felt self-conscious, as if everybody here must know that they weren't supposed to be present at graduation. They should have already hopscotched over everyone else's plans. But of course other people couldn't know. Amber sat alone, conspicuous without Destiny at her side. Kenny and Judd were playing thumb wars, though their eyes were glossy with nerves.

And at the edges of her awareness, him. Jay jumped at every little movement in the crowd, thinking he might have appeared. Gene's continued absence was lodged in her like a thorn, pinching whenever she twisted the wrong way.

The valedictorian, Jessica Suarez, was still talking about optimism and hard work.

"We can't give up." Brandi's whisper sliced through the morning.

"What do you mean?" Jay asked.

"We ain't going to just give up, are we?"

"On what?" Max asked gently.

"On Theodora. On the Portal House." Brandi's eyes, bloodshot, darted from one of them to the other. "All this talk about—about going out into the world, but we're all staying here, right? We're gonna find it. We only tried *once*, that's nothing. We'll try again."

"Well, in case you don't remember, there are certain other things going on," Hilma said. The Garnets hadn't bothered with regalia; Hilma's dress was long even on her, trailing into the sprinkler-dampened grass as they sat on the football field in folding chairs. "Sorry that we haven't thrown ourselves right back into our little quest."

"I have plans," Charlie said quietly. "I accepted a position at Columbia. This is what I've worked for, and if I don't commit now, I'll lose my chance again."

"My parents are moving to California," Iggy said. They were officially opening a second location of Cozy's, and he planned to help his family out while he went to school. He'd discussed it with Jay tentatively, watching for her reaction.

Jay picked at a fingernail, sweaty beneath the borrowed robe. She could still take Brandi with her into the future. Maybe there was a way to have Brandi apply to the same scholarship, she should ask Max, she should—

"Yeah, but I been thinking," Brandi went on. "There's so much we still haven't done. What if'n we go to the Forever House again, and we get those letters?"

"Brandi," Hilma said. "You need to focus on your own life right now."

"But—there's still a chance—" Brandi was on the tender, humiliating verge of tears. Jay was horribly aware of the people around them, shifting, mumbling.

"I mean, knowing that you and Bluejay were going to make it a one-way trip? It makes me think you two were getting in way too deep," Hilma said. "I never wanted that."

"I didn't want that either," Brandi said, and Jay stared at her. "I was gonna come back. But I want to at least go through. I want to finish this quest, the way Theodora planned."

"You didn't want to stay?" Jay asked.

Brandi wouldn't meet her eyes.

Somebody behind them was standing up, the crowd's vague muttering growing to a roar, Jessica Suarez faltering over her speech at the podium. Jay turned her head—Gene. It was Gene, coming to find them, blood-soaked and furious, ready to reveal all their secrets, or it was—

Officer Pell's shadow fell over the row of them. He stared down at them, triumph and pity battling in his expression, like he'd expected to enjoy this more than he actually was. "I'm afraid Brandi Addams is under arrest," Pell said. "For shooting Gene Stippley."

51

2015

NOW

Jay hurries through the evening. Behind her, to the north, distant sirens thread through the twilight, growing steadier and louder. Probably Pell coming back for her, ready to make his arrest. She's the one who stole evidence, the one whose half of a necklace was found at the scene of Brandi's disappearance. It should be Jay in trouble, not the others.

Inside the Luck House, all four of them are waiting for her. They collectively wince when she lets the door slam, and she stops short. After her almost-encounter with Pell, after learning that Brandi herself burned down the Truth House, Jay's brimming over. But she sees their faces and she knows: there's a secret in their midst, and it's not hers.

The unsettling thing is that they're caught between joy and panic. Iggy's almost smiling, Hilma's almost frowning. Jay wonders if Brandi came back. If she's shown up at the last moment, ready to offer them the grace they couldn't give her—

"Where were you?" Hilma demands.

"At the Mirror House," Jay says. "Pell was there, he—"

"Yeah, I saw his cruiser outside," Charlie says grimly.

"It doesn't matter, because we're leaving town," Max announces.

"What?" Jay asks, trying to catch up. She looks around; no Brandi.

"I've bought tickets for all five of us. They would be first class, but it's a three-gate airport, so no luck. But we leave at seven a.m. tomorrow, earliest I could get. Have your carry-ons packed and ready, kids."

"Max," Jay says, "what's happening? Are you drunk?"

"He's not, apparently," Iggy says. "This is a sober decision."

"We're free," Max insists. "Look. Look at your arm."

There's a buoyant mania in his voice that Jay hasn't heard since he was a teenager. She drags her eyes from Max's grin and pulls up her sweatshirt sleeve. Her scar's gone. The skin's smooth, a small freckle blossoming, as if the scar—and the oath—never even happened. Jay's numb with the shock of it.

"Maximilian, what did you do?" Hilma asks, awed and terrified.

"I did what we should have done immediately. I burned down the Oath House."

Hilma's voice goes deadly. "You didn't."

The sirens are louder, expanding against the dusk. Jay doesn't know what to think. She should be thrilled, even ecstatic—if it's true, then the only thing truly keeping her here is gone. Her punishment has dissolved. But Jay's surprised by the grief she feels— for fifteen years, that little scar has been her only anchor back to Eternal Springs. Back to Brandi.

And also, Max destroyed one of Theodora's houses. Another one is irreplaceably gone.

"Max, that's illegal," Charlie is saying, body alive with tension. "That's vandalism, that's arson. Possibly murder?"

"It was empty. What kind of monster do you think I am? Whoever Red Art is, the insurance money will let them rebuild. Meanwhile, we don't have to be stuck to a promise we made as babies. God, I've never burned down a building before. It was easy. Gasoline. Matches. Old-school." He bounds to his feet. "I feel good. Why do I feel so good?"

Jay imagines the Truth House going up in flames: the strike of a match, everything gone. Their bond dissolving like nothing, as easily as electrical wiring and plywood and glass. Did Brandi feel this joyful power when she destroyed the Truth House?

"You've always thrived on destruction," Hilma says. "No wonder you went into finance." Her panic is shedding away, and it's like she's waking from a dream, taking stock of what's a real danger and what isn't.

Jay can almost feel the oath letting go of her, unraveling. It feels . . . bad. It leaves behind something small, slick, aching. The thought of the five of them scattering back to their own lives, escaping from Eternal, still knowing nothing about Brandi . . .

It's cheating. She's not ready to go. Jay hasn't found out the truth.

"And if Red Art comes looking for you?" Iggy asks Max. "If the cops find out it was you, isn't this worse for all of us?"

"We fly out in, what, nine hours?" Max says, consulting his watch. "We'll be long gone by the time they have any basis to arrest us, and once we're out of this place, we can operate from our home turf. Where we aren't sitting ducks surrounded by small-town vengeance."

"But Brandi—" Jay begins.

"Brandi's gone," Hilma says flatly, and Jay sees that she's shifted over fully to her brother's side. "She wanted us to come back and have our little moments of realizing what shitheads we are, which we've done." She looks around, and nobody corrects her. "There's nothing left here except whatever revenge Brandi Addams has cooked up for us, and I'm not exactly eager for that part. So yeah. We're going."

Jay's on the back porch when Iggy finds her, staring into the forest. Those pine trees, like pen strokes, rising impossibly tall and thin, slicing up the butter-yellow moon. The katydids and frogs are so loud that Jay doesn't hear him until he's right beside her. "So," he says.

"So," she echoes.

"What are you going to do now?"

"I have an almost-first-class ticket with my name on it. I guess I should use it before the cops find me."

"But that's not what you want," Iggy says.

He can still read her so well. Or maybe it's not even that, it's just that her doubt is emanating so strongly from her. "We're not done here yet," Jay concedes. "I'm not done here, anyway. I don't know about the rest of you."

"What, you want to go back to the AIR House?" Iggy asks. "Try the inscriptions one last time, see what happens?"

She hesitates. "What if we went to the Forever House?" He wasn't expecting this. Jay barely knew she'd suggest it until the moment she spoke. "When I talked to Amber, she said that she dropped Brandi off near the—near the old trailhead, remember? Asher Lake."

He understands at once. "But those forests are huge. There's no guarantee that she found the Forever House."

"It's the one place we haven't visited. And it's important to Brandi. To us."

"Are you sure you can handle going back there?" Iggy asks.

"I wouldn't feel right leaving Eternal without knowing why Brandi went there," Jay says. "I don't want it to be some big deal, Iggy, and I know everyone else is ready to go. But . . . what if I just go quickly? What if I can find it on my own?" She manages a smile.

"If we know one thing about the Forever House, it's that I can be back before anyone notices I'm gone."

Iggy gazes out into the tree line for a while before he answers. "I don't think it's safe for you to go alone, Jay." He keeps talking above her protest: "So I'm in. We'll go together."

52

2000

THEN

Brandi had been in the holding cell for twenty-four hours. Jay tried to piece together the full story. Gene's friends had noticed him missing; Pell, going by for a wellness check, discovered blood in the trailer, spattered throughout the bathroom. There'd been a few garbled calls from Gene left on a friend's answering machine, ranting about *that bitch*, something-something *with my own gun*. When Jay heard that, she crouched in her own bathroom for a long time, wishing she could throw up, wishing this panic would go away like a bout of food poisoning. No luck.

"What did she do with the gun after you two ran?" Iggy asked Jay when they met up. Based on the grooves beneath his eyes, he hadn't been faring any better than Jay.

"Didn't she leave it at the AIR House?" Jay said. She knew that if Pell found the gun, with Brandi's fingerprints, there would be no way out for her. "I hope the twins got rid of it."

The Garnet parents expressed their heartbreak about the whole thing. Jay hoped that they might intervene for Brandi's sake. But when Jay worked up the courage to talk to her, Ms. Garnet vaguely fluttered that the legal journey to vindicate Brandi could be long, and complicated, and expensive—and the Garnets were leaving in less than a week. "Anyway, darling," Ms. Garnet said to Jay, "I was worried that something like this might happen. We knew that he was mistreating that poor girl, and we should've stepped in sooner. But if she did in fact kill him—"

"What if she did?"

Ms. Garnet paused. "Then good for her, fighting back."

"But she might spend her life in prison," Jay said. "Because of fighting back."

"Even this backwards state can't do that without evidence. It would be a national outrage." Ms. Garnet squeezed Jay's shoulder. "Promise me you won't let this distract you from your postgraduation plans. It's not worth it, darling. You deserve a life too."

Jay finally broke; she needed to do something other than sit at home obsessing. She'd accidentally left her markers behind in the Mirror House. Iggy tagged along with her to retrieve them. "When did you last use them?" he asked.

"Uh. Graduation morning?"

"Well, I hope you left them on the stairs, 'cause if you left them in the basement, they're probably not around anymore."

"I have to finish the portfolio, it's due soon," she said as they descended the stairwell toward the basement.

"You'll get the scholarship," Iggy said. "Don't even worry."

His steady belief in her made something ache in her breastbone. "And you'll go to California," she said. "A whole fresh start."

"I guess so. Unless you . . . unless you want me to go with you."

"Come with me instead of going with your parents?" Jay said. "You'd do that?"

"I mean, maybe. I could apply to the same school. We could . . . get a place together."

A place of their own. A small apartment. A place where they could be together, build a small life. For a second, it shimmered with magic.

"I don't see the markers," she said, stalling on answering him. "Maybe—"

They opened the basement door. Iggy and Jay stood in the door-way, gone quiet. Jay's vision detached from her brain, leaving her mind scrambling to figure out what she was looking at. Dead center in the basement, a pile of gore. Half a man, the side of his body opened up like an old-fashioned anatomical illustration, organs exposed, rib cage jutting. His clothes were still recognizable. A sodden flannel shirt, blood-stamped. Jeans, a single muddy-cleated boot.

His face—what was left of it, this thing that barely counted as a face—was tilted toward Jay. One eye stared from the ruin of his skull.

Gene. As she watched, a mealy section of his lip drooped away, sizzling into nothingness.

Jay would never fully remember running up the stairs. She and Iggy were outside, suddenly, in the forest that encroached on the Mirror House. Iggy was throwing up. Somehow, seeing him vomit eased some of Jay's nausea, as if he had taken on her disgust for her. She gulped in one fresh breath after another.

"He's dead?" Iggy whispered at last. Birds sang overheard. The sunlight was crisp. An ordinary day. "He's dead. He's really dead. Why is he here?"

"Somebody dumped his body." The words sounded ridiculous in Jay's mouth, like she was reciting lines from a TV show. It couldn't be her life. "Someone knew what they were doing. That's obvious. Within a day or two he'll be totally gone."

"Brandi?" Iggy asked, wiping his mouth on his sleeve, a childlike gesture.

"Brandi's been in jail for two days already," Jay said slowly. "I went straight to graduation and Brandi was already waiting there. I would've seen if she'd dropped off the body then."

Iggy blinked, shaking his head. "So . . . she asked somebody else to do it?"

"Who would she ask? She doesn't trust anyone but us. She doesn't *know* anybody but us." Jay's mind was spinning, dizzying whirls, but as her thoughts slowed, she realized that she preferred the wildness to the cold clarity of the conclusion she landed on. "Iggy. It's not just that somebody else left him here. I think maybe somebody else killed Gene."

53

2000

The twins sat side by side on the white sofa, the other three—Jay, Iggy, Charlie—standing in front of them. Circling all five of the friends, like a tribunal, were the elder Garnets' paintings. Those women in their various half-finished states. Crooked teeth gleaming, overlapping, in their oblivious mouths, between their legs.

Jay almost faltered. Hilma and Max, their glamour clinging to them even in the strangest circumstances. After everything they'd been through, was Jay really going to accuse the Garnets? These visitors from another, better world?

"I found Gene's body," Jay said.

The twins didn't answer. They didn't respond at all. She'd tossed a grenade into their laps and they weren't even bothering to fake fear or shock. Jay's stomach sank.

"It—he—it was in the Mirror House basement. Brandi couldn't've put him there," Jay went on. That staring eye in the half-eaten face. "Whoever put the body there knows about the houses."

Jay had thought Hilma's anger would undo her, but it was the buried glimmer of heartbreak that made Jay stop talking. The silence stretched until it nearly snapped.

"All right," Hilma said. "What are you suggesting? Spit it out. Don't be coy."

"Hilma," Iggy said, desperate. "Please. Just tell us the truth. Did you have anything to do with Gene's death?"

"If you're going to interrogate us, shouldn't we be in the Truth House?" Max asked, in a pale imitation of his usual bravado.

"No," Jay said. "Because I know you'll tell the truth. Because we're friends. Aren't we?"

Hilma looked right at Jay, and a memory shifted between them: Hilma's vulnerability, the realization that she'd come here friendless and alone. The way the four of them had coalesced around her and Max. She wavered, and then Hilma Garnet began to explain.

Their parents had been gone again, another reception in Fayette, marking the quickly approaching end of their stint in Eternal. Gene must've waited for the twins to be isolated. Hilma was in her bedroom when he broke in, bleary with alcohol, half out of his mind, the gunshot wound in his shoulder festering. He was leaving town, he insisted. He was getting out of Eternal, this good-for-nothing place, but Gene wasn't going without exacting a price.

"He'd figured out the houses," Hilma said, staring at the floor, eyes glassy. "I mean, he didn't quite understand it all, but he'd watched us and eavesdropped enough. He was threatening to tell everybody about the six of us 'breaking into those places' if I didn't pay him. I was yelling for Max, he had his stupid headphones on. That creep was going to kill me."

"You could've called your parents," Jay said.

"Wow, thank you, Jay," Max said, too loudly. "Very helpful."

"What happened to him?" Iggy asked.

"I shoved him," Hilma said. She sounded like she was daring herself to say it, her voice touched with a pained wonder. Max didn't move. He was staring at Hilma as if she could cue him on how to react. "He was at the top of the staircase, and he was coming for me, and I shoved him away and—and he fell."

The AIR House. All around them, those lofts and their thin, swirling staircases. It had always thrilled Jay, this openness, but she pictured Gene's weakened, alcohol-dizzied body plummeting to the floor below. The crack of bone.

Hilma's eyes were haunted. "Max helped me get him out of there before our parents were home. We hid him and the gun in the storage shed until we could transfer him."

Jay was shaking all over. She'd had no idea. Hilma and Max had kept it so well hidden. Her head hurt, throbbing, as if it couldn't hold the new reality. Brandi was innocent. She'd shot Gene, but hadn't killed him. She was innocent, innocent, everything was okay—

"You need to tell the police," Jay said. "You need to let them know it was self-defense." This could all be solved, then. The Garnets would tell the truth; Brandi would be released.

"Cool, great idea," said Max. "Let's just walk the police down to the basement and show them the mirror that eats people. Here's the half-dissolved body of a dead guy! It was us."

More than half-dissolved by now, Jay thought. Gene was probably close to gone.

"We can't," Hilma said. "We're leaving town, we can't be pulled into some drawn-out legal trial. No, no, no. Arkansas was only supposed to be a year. It's not going to fuck up the rest of our *lives.*"

"This thing with Brandi is a hiccup," said Max. "They won't find his body or the gun—we dissolved that, too. They'll figure out they can't charge Brandi, she'll be set free, and we can all move on." He made it sound almost reasonable. "We can go. We never have to come back to this place. We're all eighteen, or close enough. Nobody's going to think it's strange if we leave."

"You're saying we let Brandi take the fall?" Jay asked.

Hilma answered this time. "We're saying . . . that we let it blow over. You know the only reason Pell is being hard on Brandi is because he's a piece of shit. It's his power play. Trust me, she'll be okay. Brandi's tough as nails. People will forgive her because they know her around here. What about us? You see how Amber and Destiny and Kenny act like Max and I are these monsters. If they knew that we were involved in Gene's death, people would want our heads."

"When's the last time you heard about a rich person convicted for killing someone in a trailer park?" asked Charlie. But he sounded more exhausted than interrogative.

"Okay, then also consider this. If we explain what happened now," Max said, "everyone will know about the houses."

Iggy and Charlie exchanged glances. Jay hadn't even thought about this before.

"If we let them think it's Brandi," Hilma said, "Gene'll just be another abusive drunk who disappeared from town, good riddance. But if I tell them what happened, they'll poke at every part of our friendship. They'll find out about Theodora."

No one said anything for a long time. Jay's mind felt like it was being tugged in a thousand directions at once, and none of the directions made any sense. Her eyes ached.

"I invoke the charter," said Hilma at last. "Let's put it to a vote."

"Brandi's not even here," said Jay, miserable.

"This isn't her decision right now," said Hilma. "It's ours. Do we tell the truth for no good reason and risk losing our whole futures? I vote no."

"I vote no," said Max, though he blushed as he said it.

The others didn't answer right away.

"Well, I'm not giving up my spot at Columbia because of white kids committing murder," Charlie said. "Absolutely no way. So I—I vote no."

Jay turned to Iggy, searching for his answer before he gave it.

"We didn't do anything," Iggy said, a plea. "I can't get my family involved."

"That's a no vote?" Hilma pressed.

After a second he nodded.

"Bluejay, it's up to you. I want us to be unanimous." Hilma searched Jay's eyes. "Be reasonable. That's all I ask."

The magic of Theodora's houses had already turned so strange and tangled, so different from the joy of when they'd first encountered it. Jay couldn't stand the thought of the houses becoming evidence, salacious gossip, something to gawk at. It felt like—if that happened—there'd be no more magic left anywhere in her life. Even Brandi would understand that. Magic just gone, ruined, and life a long stretch of meaninglessness.

"All right," Jay said. "I'll keep your secret. What do we have to do?"

54

2015

NOW

They step inside. Time rearranges itself. It's just tipping into darkness outside, and the silence falls as richly and completely as if someone dropped a curtain over them. That ancient, sacred smell of moss and mildew: Jay breathes deeply. Home.

"We found it so easily this time," Iggy whispers into the gloom.

"It must know we need it," Jay says.

The Forever House settles around them, welcoming them back. It's as if Jay's viewing a place from a history textbook, thousands of years gone by, instead of a house that she visited as a teenager. She turns on her phone light and wanders the living room. Everything is dust-thick, muted with age. The memories flutter like moths.

"Iggy," Jay says. She's been thinking, and it feels like the right time to broach this. "While we're here . . . we should undo the hold this place has on us."

She can sense his frown. "Are you going to burn this place down?"

The Forever House groans and creaks in protest.

"No, no, of course not. I figure . . . if this house gets under our skin, then maybe we can undo it. Fall out of love. We can stay here for however long we can manage, a few days at least. No one will come looking for us."

Iggy is quiet.

"We can be in here and not love each other," she says. "We can be deeply and truly not in love. We can let each other go. Just walk away free."

"I'll miss you," Iggy says.

"See, that's exactly the kind of thing we can't say."

"Jay . . . no. Listen, you're the one who wanted us apart in the first place."

"That's not fair, Iggy, I—"

"I wanted to stay with you," Iggy says fiercely, and Jay falls silent. "I would've followed you. You were the only good thing left from my time in Eternal. But you insisted on walking away, and I had to respect that. I've made a life for myself without you, just like you asked."

Jay reaches back into the murk of that May, looking for one clear, shining glint that matches what Iggy's saying.

"Do you ever think we give these places too much power?" Iggy asks. "We decided that what we felt for each other is because of the Forever House, but I don't know if that's true, Jay. We liked each other before what happened here. I don't want to deny Theodora's magic, but they're just houses. They're only houses. And it's like we've never left them."

Jay presses her hands into her eyes until bright spots bloom. "What about Brandi?" she whispers. "If she believed her addiction was fueled by the Forever House, maybe she never sought help. I didn't stick around to talk her through it. She was alone here."

"You're here for her now."

The Forever House stretches around them. Outside, the night

sky is unmoving, sharply glistening. Jay reminds herself why they came here in the first place. She forces herself to focus, push everything aside but this one final attempt to help her friend.

Jay's flashlight beam swings in a neat curve. Her heartbeat hiccups, and she retraces the swoop, more carefully. In the dust, barely visible, are the faint ghosts of footprints. Heading out of the living room, toward the staircase, and then looping back out. Disappearing over the threshold. "Someone else has been in here," Jay says. "Recently, I think."

"Brandi?" Iggy asks at once.

"I don't know."

Tension comes into Iggy's voice. "How do we know whoever it is isn't still here?"

The shadows prickle around them. When Jay starts walking toward the stairs, Iggy's footsteps follow her, his beam keeping pace with hers.

It's waiting halfway up the staircase. A white envelope, perched there, age-worn but still fresher than the house surrounding it. There's writing on the envelope. Jay picks it up with trembling hands. "It's for me," she tells Iggy. "It's from Brandi."

"Holy shit," he whispers.

It's the closest Jay has felt to Brandi since they arrived in Eternal Springs, and she can barely stand it. Iggy places a hand on her shoulder, steadying, and she opens the envelope. The letter is written on a simple piece of notebook paper, in scratchy pen strokes. Brandi's handwriting. Jay begins to read, the words floating, translucent, in the halo of light.

Dearest Jay,

You might not be the one to find this but I sure hope its you. Isn't it funny how we never cared much about the truth house? We acted like it wasn't important at all. We were only intrested in the others and what they could do for us. But the truth house was the most special. You dont find the truth much in the real world. Ive realised that now.

I watched them come back, Iggy and Charlie and Max. Even after everyone pretended like they were gone for good. I thought, maybe they <u>ALL</u> need to come back again and this time, they need to <u>remember</u> who we really were. And who we always will be.

I don't expect yall to get in trouble. Not even him. But I wanted you to feel what it was like for me, 15 years ago, when you didnt care at all. Thats why I burnt down the Truth House. I reckon youre mad over that, but it felt like youd taken the truth from me, so Id take it from you. I hope Theodora can forgive me.

If you are here, in the forever house, then you must know why my heart has broke. I reckon I am to blame too. I was too scaerd to come back to the forever House for a long long time. Maybe I could have helped. I am trying to help now, even if I worry its too late.

Here is what I have come to believe during my time in Eternal. Yall once said that we had to find Thedoras other houses first so that we could get used to magic. But I dont agree. I think that Thedora wanted us to love this world before we went to another one. I dont know that I always did a good job of that, but Ive tried. Ive seen the beautie in Eternal Springs, in every little thing. Now I finally feel ready for more. I hope you can understand.

I waited for you, Jay. I thought you would come back for sure.

Once yall take care of everything, come find me. Come find me. It was right under our noses all along. Theres so much Ive wanted to say to you. I cant wait to see you again, Jadelynne.

Your friend forever and ever,
Brandi

P.S. I was right about the key!!

Something falls out of the envelope, landing with a metallic clink on the floor. Iggy stoops to retrieve it before Jay can; he rises, holding the object into the light.

A small and perfect gold-plated key.

55

2000

Don't worry, Jadelynne," her father said. "Pell is on your side here. They're only trying to figure out what happened. It will help Brandi."

"How will it help her?" Jay asked, agonized. They sat outside the police station. Next to the car, a flock of birds took off from the telephone wire in a sudden ribbon. Her dad drove her here right on the heels of going to the post office to dispatch Jay's finished portfolio for the scholarship committee. Sending it express to a New York address: *Fancy*, the postal worker had said. And now they were at the police station, like it was just another errand.

As she walked into the station, Jay was a water balloon, tight with unshed tears. Pell waited for her in his office, smiling with what resembled kindness. His graying hair was combed back neatly. It both comforted and unsettled Jay to realize he saw her as an ally.

"I'm sure you know you're here about Brandi Addams and her father."

"Her stepdad."

"I need to know anything you might've heard or seen that could help us get to the bottom of this whole mess. Did Brandi talk to you about Gene? Did she have any conflicts with him?"

"I mean. Yeah. He was—he's a horrible person." The past tense just slid out.

"Have you ever heard or seen Brandi behave in a violent way toward Gene?"

"What about Gene behaving in a 'violent way' toward Brandi?" When Pell only smiled, she was confused. It felt like any way she turned, she'd be giving Pell what he wanted.

"I'd like to know about that too," he said. "Any violence you can relay is relevant."

Sweat chilled her armpits even as Jay felt feverishly hot. She tried to focus on the exact right words to say, a shuddering tightrope under her feet. Jay had to convince Pell to let Brandi go, but she also had to avoid implicating the Garnets. Hilma had gone over this with her, role-playing, but every time, Jay had dissolved into a mess by the end.

Jay was the last to be called in and questioned. In a weird way, it was the closest they'd come to being acknowledged as a friend group: all five of them bound together in suspicion.

"What do you think happened, Jadelynne?" Pell asked. "Do you believe your friend killed Gene Stippley?"

"She didn't kill him." This, at least, Jay could say with confidence.

"Why do you think he was talking about Brandi shooting him?"

"What?" Jay blurted, mouth dry. For a moment she saw Gene resurrected, his jawbone imparting all their secrets. Then she remembered the answering machine messages. "I—I don't know what he meant." The gunshot, the blood. The shove. Gene's body plummeting to the floor below. The images ricocheted too fast, some remembered, some invented.

"You doing okay?"

She nodded, tried to push her lips into what resembled a smile.

"Now, we drug-tested Miss Addams," Pell said. "It seems that she's on a high dose of opiates. Painkillers. Do you know anything about that? Were you two experimenting?"

"No," Jay said. "Those were—she was prescribed them. She was hurt."

"Hurt how?"

Jay chewed at her bottom lip. If she told him about Gene hurting Brandi, would it make Brandi seem more innocent, or less?

"Was it Gene who hurt her?"

Jay dithered, heartsick. "Yes. Yeah."

There was a click behind his eyes: Surprise? Recognition? Jay couldn't tell if it was bad or good. She just felt she'd nudged something closer to an inevitable conclusion.

"Can you tell me more about that?"

"I don't know a lot about it. Brandi didn't really— I just know he was violent with her." Pell didn't speak for a while. Jay had a compulsive urge to fill the silence. "There was a time she had a sling? For a fractured arm. We pretended it was an accident, but it—it wasn't."

Pell's face didn't move.

"Anyway, that's why she was—she didn't have a—a drug problem. It was prescribed."

"Okay. Well. These particular drugs weren't prescribed by a doctor, the ones she had. She's been behaving like someone with a history of addiction. She's dealing with withdrawal, saying some strange stuff. About houses. Houses making her do things . . . magical places, I suppose. Like those Narnia books, almost. You wouldn't know anything about that?"

"Um. No." Jay injected confusion into her voice. It wasn't difficult: She truly was reeling, a hidden depth charge expanding in her belly. Brandi had been talking about the houses. After everything, all their promises, she'd revealed their secrets to Pell, of all fucking people.

Jay was suddenly furious at Brandi. She knew it wasn't fair—what would it be like to be stuck in a prison cell for days, alone, scared, no way out, no contact with the rest of them? But Pell coming so close to understanding the houses felt like an exposure Jay couldn't bear.

"Well, it struck me as mighty strange. But Brandi has clearly been struggling for a while. She's acting . . . erratically. You know what that word means?"

"Yes."

"Unless you can clear up what she was talking about when she mentioned these weird houses. Do you have any idea what that was referring to?" Pell's gaze is gentle, intent.

"I—it sounds like she was—"

Pell waited. Jay tried to figure out how to phrase this, which statement would lead to which outcome. If she acknowledged that Brandi was out of her mind on drugs, would it make them more likely to let her go, or to prosecute her? Everything was sliding out of Jay's grasp. Brandi shot Gene, but didn't kill him. Hilma shoved Gene and *did* kill him. Brandi was addicted to those pills, but she wasn't lying about the houses. And Jay couldn't explain any of this.

"It sounds like maybe she's crazy?" Pell asked.

"Yeah," Jay whispered at last. "Maybe she's crazy."

56

2015

NOW

Jay looks up, eyes aching with tears, cheeks wet. Brandi is alive, *alive*, and she's brought them here on purpose, and she's waiting somewhere for Jay. Everything that's been building since her plane landed in Eternal Springs breaks open, finally. Jay cries, curled into a ball, snot sticky against her skin, kneecaps pressing into her forehead. Her clothes smell like Eternal now, pine and grass. Jay could be a teenager again. Iggy crouches next to her, arms around her, and she can feel the light shiver of his tears too.

But the relief isn't pure and complete. Not yet. When she stops crying and rereads the letter, the unanswered questions glow as if spotlighted.

"Where does this lead?" Iggy asks, examining the key. "Somewhere in the AIR House? If we go back, will we be able to go through the portal?"

"If Brandi went through the portal, wouldn't she still have the key with her?"

They both contemplate it, this small piece of metal nestled in Iggy's palm. Jay remembers how impatient they were with Brandi when she suggested an actual key. But Brandi had understood Theodora Trader, both her practicalities and her mysticism, better than anyone.

Iggy begins laughing, low and unexpected. "God. She must have duplicated it."

Jay waits a second before she joins in. She hopes he's right. This inventive mischief wipes away some of the grime that's been clouding Brandi in Jay's mind all these years. "The blood too," she says, recalling the stain in the Duplication House basement. "It could've been a single cut, but she got enough to fake the crime scene."

Jay takes the key from Iggy, slips it securely into the pocket of her jeans.

"I don't understand this letter," Jay says, voice still tear-damp. "Who does she mean here? 'Not even him.' Is that referring to Gene?"

"It couldn't be. Kenny? Pell?"

"Or Roy," Jay says. Clutching the letter, Jay looks around. The awareness that she's still in potential danger closes in, the darkness cinching tighter. Her eyes catch on an anomaly, down the stairs. "The cellar door has never been open," Jay says. "We never went down there."

When they descend the stairs and edge closer, they realize there's something left on the threshold of the cellar steps. Iggy bends to retrieve it.

"What the hell is this?" He turns it around and around, blowing the dust off. Chunky plastic, with indecipherable dials. "An—an EpiPen?"

"I think so," Jay says, squinting. "Or, no. An insulin pen, maybe?"

"That's bad, if somebody left that behind. Did we know anybody who needed insulin?" asks Iggy, but Jay remembers at once, and she sees from Iggy's expression the moment when he remembers too.

She looks again at the cellar. The stairway, descending downward into that tiny pocket of space, below everything, hidden from the outside world.

The flashlight picks up the dress first. She's lying curled in one corner, almost peaceful. Her dress is wrinkled and stiff, wound through with the curls of dried leaves, mouse droppings spattered like beads along the skirt. She's a skeleton—her bleached white skull, jaw hanging open, that look of perpetual wide-eyed surprise. Although death and time have scraped away her identifying features, Jay knows who it is. That dress, the sequins still glimmering. Jay last saw her smiling in the school gym, face illuminated with hope beneath the sparkle of the disco ball.

Jay falls to her knees, dropping her flashlight: the beam lands on Destiny's skeletal hand, draped over her hip. The smell of the earth down here is overwhelming. "I don't understand. She got out, didn't she? She got out of Eternal."

Iggy clutches his mouth, and she knows he can't trust himself to speak.

"She's been here since the Senior Ball," Jay says. "How did she get here? How would she have known to find the Forever House? She was supposed to be in California all this time."

There's something in the corner, a backpack. Neon-yellow Jansport. Jay goes to it, rifling through the belongings. Changes of clothes, striped cotton underwear, lip balm, maxi pads. An old printout of a Greyhound itinerary—three days, Fayette to Hollywood, stops in Joplin, Amarillo, Flagstaff. "She was leaving town that same night?" Jay says, checking the date. "Why is she here?"

"She must've known about Theodora's houses," Iggy says finally, hoarse. "We always knew we might not be the only ones."

"Or—or one of us brought her here." Little details of that long-ago night push through. She and Iggy had left the dance, gone back to their respective homes. Brandi, in her coat, had departed the gym alone. Where did the Garnets go? Where was Charlie? "So what if Destiny found her way here, somehow, and she didn't have her insulin pen, and she was stuck—"

"She wasn't stuck. She was trapped," Iggy says.

Jay stares up at his shadowy silhouette in the gloom.

"There were marks around the door," Iggy goes on. "She was trying to get out. Destiny would always keep her insulin pen on her. Her family couldn't afford to replace them constantly. And why wouldn't it have been in her backpack?"

"Trapped," Jay repeats. The truth comes circling closer. "By who?"

Destiny lies there like she's listening.

"Max," Jay says softly. She sees Destiny's hair flip, her gloss-pinkened smile. Would she have followed him somewhere, anywhere, after the dance? Everyone was taking last-minute chances that night, high on the possibility of endings and beginnings. Destiny was about to leave town forever.

The cellar. The scratches at the door. The pen, just outside. Realizing that by the time anyone noticed she was gone at all, Destiny would be long dead, beyond their grasp.

The moment they carry her over the threshold, Destiny changes. Flesh blossoms back onto her bones: the glistening layers of muscle, the webby nerves and veins, all building up in an eyeblink. Flossy blond hair sprouts from what was age-grayed bone just a second ago. Her face spreads across her grinning skull like clouds racing across the sky, and there she is, Destiny, her long lashes sticky with mascara, her face slackly peaceful.

She's heavier, suddenly, and Jay stumbles. They lay her on the forest floor. Jay kneels to feel for Destiny's pulse. Nothing. She's chilly, lips already tinged with blue, skin losing its temporary flush of newness as Jay watches.

"Did you think she'd come back to life?" Iggy asks gently.

"Maybe." Jay doesn't know the full implications of this place. Maybe the time inside the Forever House would peel off, and Destiny would wake up like a fairy-tale princess.

But she lies there, peaceful among the pine needles and the moss. Just a teenager. Her formal dress sparkles with sequins. Her limbs gleam with a spray tan. Her blond hair is curled and crimped in a style that Jay both recognizes as outdated and, on a gut level, as enviable. Jay's caught between times. She's a teenager in the year 2000, looking at this beautiful girl who always intimidated her, and she's a grown woman, staring at a dead child who will never reach adulthood.

"Fuck, we can't use her body as evidence now," Jay says, hugging herself, furious at this realization. "I didn't think of that before we brought her out."

"She was an ancient skeleton. That would be as hard to explain as Destiny being fifteen years too young." Now that she can see him in the moonlight, Iggy's dark eyes are pools of grief, rage. "She's fallen through the cracks, no matter what."

Jay examines Destiny, her press-on French manicure, the tiny details bringing everything else into focus. "Brandi wanted us to find Destiny. We owe it to her to solve this, after what we did with Gene. So. We're going to try to make things right."

57

2000

THEN

Brandi was finally free. There wasn't enough evidence for Gene's murder to keep her stuck in the cell, despite Pell's best efforts. No body. No weapon. They'd gotten her for the pills—illicit use of controlled substances. Pell had at least extracted that much personal satisfaction from the whole mess. The Garnets had paid bail for her, refusing any thanks. The least they could do.

The five of them—Charlie and Iggy, Hilma and Max, Jay—picked her up from the police station, then drove her to the Mirror House. It was a farewell party mixed with a welcome-home party, all overlaid with a desperate sadness.

They sat with cups of the expensive vodka that Hilma had provided, clear and tasteless as water. Jay drank too quickly, feeling her head float away from her body. She could barely look at Brandi. Her friend resembled the photos national newspapers used when they ran a story on the Ozarks. Tired, beleaguered, too old for her years.

Hopelessness. Maybe that's what it was.

"Catch me up," Brandi said, making a brave stab at their old camaraderie. "What are y'all doing? Where's everyone going?"

The silence bristled with everything they couldn't say. "She's better off not knowing about Gene," Hilma had said to them. "It will only complicate things more." And, looking at Charlie and Iggy and Max, Jay had seen the same thing in their faces that she felt. They couldn't tell Brandi. They couldn't reveal their own shame.

"How are you, Brandi?" Charlie asked instead. He sounded stiff, formal, like they'd gone back to being mostly strangers.

"Fine. It wasn't fun or nothing, but I'm—I'm okay." She hugged herself.

"Were you treated all right?" Hilma asked. "Were you—"

"Hey," Brandi interrupted. "I wanna talk about y'all. Please. Tell me about your plans."

"Um, I'm going to Albany," Jay said, the words scraping her mouth painfully. "I got the scholarship money, so it won't bankrupt my dad. Thank god."

Brandi broke into a grin that transformed her, briefly, back into the girl Jay knew. "Oh, Jay, you're gonna be the greatest artist ever. I can't wait to tell people I know you."

"Thanks." Jay took a drink, pressing her thigh into Iggy's. She couldn't bear this. She couldn't, but she had to, she had to—

"We may've put in a good word for you," Hilma said to Jay.

Jay blinked into Hilma's smile. "How did you—why would you—" Max had made the scholarship sound like an opportunity he just happened to know about. She didn't remember any specific ties to the Garnets.

"My dad's on the scholarship committee," Max said, not meeting her eyes.

"I didn't know," Jay said. "Wow. Thank you, then. Thank your dad for me."

"How about you, Brandi?" Charlie asked. "Any plans?"

"I dunno," Brandi said, staring down into her vodka. "I don't know what's gonna happen with these charges. The lawyer says I should plead guilty, but it's gonna cost a lot. And I got my work cleaning houses and all. Kathy didn't fire me or nothing, she—she understands."

"Well, of course," Hilma said. "None of this was your fault."

Brandi shrugged, miserable. "Isn't it?"

Nobody answered.

"Today, while I was waiting for y'all, Amber's cousin stopped and yelled at me out the car window, asking where I'd put the body. People think I killed Gene." Her voice dropped. "Maybe he is dead. But I'm just scared he's gonna come back. I don't know where he went. What if I wake up one night and he's just—he's waitin' for me?"

The alcohol rose in a sour bubble up Jay's throat. She was going to throw up.

"That won't happen," Hilma said. "That deadbeat left town."

A terrible flash of Gene's staring eye in the Mirror House.

Brandi didn't look comforted.

"Hey, I think you should leave town, Bran," Max said confidently. "You're smarter than any of us assholes. You should be taking on the world. How about it? We all leave, together?"

Jay doesn't understand what he's trying to do. He has that manic gleam to him, that fix-everything fervor, but it feels misplaced. Like a tinny echo of the people they were nine months ago. Brandi blinked, surprised and embarrassed.

"I ain't that smart, Max," she said. "No way. I can't leave town right now anyway, I got that trial and everything."

All the stereotypes Jay was trying to outrun had caught up with Brandi. Legal trouble, an addiction, an empty trailer. Jay sidestepped every one of those clichés and let them land squarely on Brandi instead. She felt the exact moment when they split apart—not Bradelynne. But Brandi Addams. Jay Carr.

"It's okay, really. I want to stay," Brandi said, and to Jay's surprise, she sounded like she meant it. Like this was a sincere decision. "I—I'm not ready to say goodbye to Eternal, I reckon. Probably one day."

"You're not serious," Jay said. "Why wouldn't you want to leave? We've always wanted to. That's been our big plan."

"You always wanted to, Jay," Brandi said. "And I wanted what you wanted." She wasn't angry. The way she said it, her wanting what Jay wanted was natural, inevitable.

"You're not at all curious?" Jay pressed, even as Hilma shook her head, eyes wide, signaling to Jay to drop it. And Jay didn't even know why she was doing this, but it came out of her in a rush. "About everything waiting out there for us?"

"I am," Brandi said. "But maybe it's not my time just yet."

For a second Jay thought of Theodora, choosing to stay in Eternal even after she stepped out of that sanitarium and into freedom. Brandi was stuck, and yet . . . on the verge of walking alone into the future, Jay felt a flash of envy, of wishing she could stay in the known world a little longer. This version of her felt so tired, so broken.

"When are y'all leaving town?" Brandi asked the Garnets.

"Tomorrow," Hilma said. "First thing in the morning. Listen, since this is our last gathering, what can we do for you, Brandi? Anything. I hate that you've been through this."

Brandi took a second to think about. "We can look for the key."

"Brandi—" Hilma began.

"I just know that the portal didn't work because we didn't have the key. I reckon that if we go back and we—"

"Why do you want to find that key if you aren't even leaving Eternal?" Jay asked, knowing she sounded bratty, not caring.

"Well, I want to see Theodora's other world," Brandi said. "Even if I ain't staying for good." Then she looked down, fiddling with the tarnished half of her friendship necklace. "And I want us to do something together, I guess. One last time."

"We're not doing that anymore," Hilma said.

Jay glanced at the scar on her forearm. It seemed so far away, the night when they'd sworn an oath to always be there for each other. As with the Portal House, the magic there hadn't worked, in the end. Maybe everything of Theodora's was just a cheap trick.

"I do have something for you, though," Hilma said. Reaching into her satchel, she produced the journal. Its pages of knotted code and beautiful sketches, the hints and clues that'd led them to house after house but never to another world. "You should keep it."

Brandi was on the verge of tears. She stretched her hands out, then withdrew them. "No, no, I can't. I can't, Hilma. I'm not even—I don't understand none of it, without y'all. I'd just lose it or—"

"Nonsense," Hilma said. "You've always loved this more than any of us."

Maybe it was an apology for something Hilma couldn't even say out loud. Or maybe it was simply because the journal was worthless now.

"Are you sure?" Max asked, uncertain, but he stilled when Hilma gave him a look.

Brandi cradled it to her chest. "Thank you," she whispered. "I'll take good care of it."

The next morning, Jay rode her bicycle to the AIR House. Even from the outside, she could tell it was empty of life, the windows thin and hollow, reflecting only the surrounding trees. Like a body with a missing heartbeat. It felt like the house itself had physically shrunk. Jay reached for the awe she'd always felt, seeing it high above the town, and found nothing.

The Garnets were gone, as completely as if they'd never been there.

2015

NOW

Jay stands alone inside the Luck House. It all seems obvious now, as if it's been written on the walls in a code she couldn't bother to decipher. Max showed up last to Eternal Springs, later than anyone else. Max has pretended to lead the charge, take control, fix things. But they've been stymied over and over. He's been using the Luck House to find Brandi, but that's led nowhere. He destroyed the Oath House.

Maybe—maybe because Max doesn't want Brandi discovered.

Jay hasn't been in the Luck House without Max Garnet, and it's not until she's here, all alone, that she feels the full, vital power racing through her. Every other time, Max's been blocking the source of the luck without the rest of them realizing it.

Iggy's distracting Max at the hotel—faking a mix-up with the plane tickets—but he's always been a bad liar. Jay has to work quickly. She flexes her fingers, calms herself. She thinks of Destiny's face, both long gone and right here. Destiny's family might never know what happened to her, unless Jay can be courageous.

Jay searches the Luck House. Methodically, carefully. There's not much furniture in here, but Jay looks everywhere. She trails her fingers above the doorframes, she crouches to examine the floorboards. Even when half an hour slides past, there's a shiny confidence wrapped around Jay like armor, so that each setback only strengthens her conviction that she's close.

And finally, her eyes land on it. The slightest raised scar on the wall, covered over by glossy paint. The old crawl space. Lucky's replicated body, the stolen painting. Jay gets a knife from the kitchen and begins scraping at the paint, revealing the old, familiar paneling beneath. She digs the blunt blade deeper, not caring that she's vandalizing this house, just wanting to know. She manages to get enough of the door's outline uncovered to press on the hinge, and it springs open, creaking, its sweet, mildewy breath still at the center of this sleek update.

In contrast to the spartan neatness of the renovated Luck House, this crawl space is a nest of chaos. Jay reaches inside, half shutting her eyes, letting her fingers brush against the edges of papers. She trusts she'll find what she needs. When she pulls a sheaf of crumpled papers out, covered in tiny print, dense legalese, she doesn't allow herself to panic. She sits back and decodes these words that'll guide her to the truth, as surely as Theodora's journal led them into the heart of magic.

As she reads, Jay begins to understand. She has to double-check, squinting at the small typeface. The current of luck hijacks her, guiding her attention like a hand at her chin. She gets it. And, following on the heels of her understanding, comes a simple desire: She wishes she didn't understand. She wishes she didn't have to.

Jay remembers Max the first time they ever entered this house, sitting on the floor, royal flush after royal flush. The way Brandi had looked at Max as if he hung the moon and the stars. Her trust in him would be so easy to rekindle. Tears rise into Jay's eyes, and with them, a deep rage.

She dashes the tears away quickly, a plan forming at the back of her head. Picking up her phone, she texts, rapid-fire, explaining as much as she can without leaving room to argue, knowing that at least for now, she has luck on her side.

Max walks into the turret of the Mirror House, and Jay turns from the window. Eternal Springs is spread out in front of them, warm and glittering in the dark. It's nearing midnight. Jay's overcome with love for this little town, the ribbons of the streets, the lit windows like bright seeds, each one cradling a separate life.

"Jaybird. What's all this about?" Max says.

He stays in the doorway, watching her. He's not giving any sign that he understands why she called him here: They could be friends again, meeting up for the last time before they depart back to their own lives. For just a single beat of her heart, Jay wonders if she can do this.

But of course she can.

"Hello, Roy," Jay says. Right before he smiles in fake confusion, she catches it: the flinch of recognition. "So you're the one behind Red Art."

59

2015

NOW

Did you kill her?" Jay asks. The two of them face each other, the whole of the Mirror House quiet around them. Now that it's the two of them, she can see his teenage self more clearly in those blue eyes, that almost childish blond of his hair that hasn't grayed like his sister's.

"No," Max says at once, forcefully. "I would never hurt Brandi. I love her."

"You love her? Like a friend, or like . . . ?"

"We'd been seeing each other. Yeah."

"Why didn't you let her know how you felt when we were kids?" Jay asks. "That would've meant so much to her. She adored you."

"I was stupid then. I couldn't see what was right in front of me. I wanted all the wrong things, the wrong . . . people." There's a small hitch in his voice at this. Jay probably would've overlooked it before, but now her stomach roils.

"What is all this, anyway?" Max asks. "You want us to miss our flights? I'm happy to stay in touch with you after we're home, we can keep discussing everything, but—"

"Where is Brandi now? You have to know. Max, please tell me." It's a strategic move, hiding the fact that she knows about the letter. It's not hard to channel her real urgency into this fake-out question.

"I'm as much in the dark as any of you."

"Yeah, but not really," Jay says. "You've spent more time with Brandi than anyone else has. You've been buying up the town from under her feet. How did you convince her to work for you, anyway?"

Because Brandi trusted Max Garnet. She always had, no matter what. Until she hadn't: but he doesn't know that yet, or not fully.

Max shrugs, uncomfortable. "She's a businesswoman at heart."

"Why have you been pretending you don't know what's going on?"

He looks around the turret, sighs deeply. "I'm going to disappoint you, Jay, because I barely know anything. Here's what I *do* know. I never let go of my friendship with Bran. We kept in touch all this time. Sometimes a phone call would make a big difference to her. The rest of you couldn't even do that, could you?"

Jay's startled by this. So many years of Max and Brandi's secret friendship, kept connected when the rest of them had—Jay assumed—stayed true to their separate bubbles.

"Bran caught me using the Luck House. At first she was angry that I'd come back. But she was . . . god, just so much herself. She was still Bran. I realized I had more fun talking to her than I did to half the assholes I worked with, or the flaky girls I met on Tinder. She's more . . . I don't know, more *real* than I appreciated as a dumb kid."

"And she called you Roy?" Jay asks.

"Her nickname for me. I think we, uh, both wanted to move on from the past. You can understand that, Jay." He looks at her, half-pleading. "You and Iggy. You haven't wanted a fresh start with him? The two of you, but different? Better?"

She swallows, the back of her neck prickling. Of course she's wanted that, but she's not going to let Max dig his fingernails into her vulnerabilities. "Roy for royal flush," Jay provides, and Max flickers with surprise. "The past was still right there. Anyway, I don't think it was about restarting. You didn't want anyone else to know that you were seeing Brandi. You were still ashamed of her."

"Believe what you like," Max says. "At least I had the integrity to tell her about Gene."

This knocks Jay sideways for a moment.

"We should've done it fifteen years ago. Don't try to tell me the guilt hasn't been weighing on you too. I know it has. We were so young when we let Brandi take on all the suspicion for Gene's disappearance. She grew up with that hanging over her, I've seen how it changed her. We've grown since then. And this way she didn't have to keep looking over her shoulder, wondering if he was coming back. I saved her from that. I couldn't make things up to her," Max says. "But I could give her the truth."

Jay's briefly seduced by this. There have been so many times she's nearly caved and told Brandi. In a letter, a call, a visit home. But always, her fear of Brandi's reaction outweighed everything else.

Still. Underneath Max's self-righteousness, something rings false. Max knew what a fragile reputation Brandi had, how protective she was of Theodora's magic. She wouldn't have gone running to the police once he told her. He must've been comforted by that. Jay has a vision of Max winning Brandi's trust: this peace offering to hide another, even larger betrayal.

"Working for Red Art was her idea, actually. She wanted to help me. She's more practical than you give her credit for. Little towns all over are being revitalized by people with the money in hand, it's a harsh reality—either that, or become a ghost town. Bran understood that Red Art was better than another option could've been."

"What about you? Were you going to profit from flipping these houses, or were you going to use the magic for yourself?"

"No, no," Max says, adamant. "Jay. Come on. I was always going to respect Theodora. That's never been in question. You know me. It was—in a way, Red Art was an attempt to keep other people from coming in and exploiting Theodora's houses."

"Max," Jay half whispers. "You burned down one of her houses a few hours ago."

He smiles at her, and she senses him deciding which direction to take this conversation next. "Is this like at the end of some cheesy movie, where the villain just explains everything to you?"

Jay swallows, not sure if it's merely a joke.

"That was for *you*," Max goes on. "So that we aren't held back by the oath. Charlie nearly died trying to leave town, I'm doing you clowns a favor. Not that you ever did anything for me."

"The main thing I haven't understood," Jay says, "is why now? Why was Brandi looking for the Portal House *now*? And I finally get it. It's because of you. You weren't happy with your amazing life on earth, Max. You had to find the other world too. You knew that Brandi would help you, and you couldn't do it on your own."

"Of course I wanted to find the Portal House," Max says, and the simple, heartbroken hunger in his voice nearly fells her, because it's what she's felt too. *Of course.* Who would ever want anything else, once they knew?

"We came right up to the edge of stepping into another world and then backed away." His voice breaks, fierce with longing. "You feel it too, Jay. I've seen it in you. Out of all of us, you get it more than the others. It's left its mark on you. Don't be mad at me, when I *know* you understand. Maybe Brandi and I should've reached out, or . . ." He shakes his head.

What would that have been like? Max and Brandi and Jay, back together, questing? What if they'd found the portal and the three of them went through together?

But this vision dies as Jay remembers what else she knows. The evidence that she's been hiding from Max. He doesn't yet realize that she's dug up the worst of his secrets. Jay has to playact as that clueless woman a little longer.

"Bran has a connection to this place that I never will," Max says. "She was born here. She's a local. She always loved Theodora. It made sense for her to look for the houses. Everyone in her life underestimates her, but this is what Bran's good at."

Jay lifts her eyes to his, his gray-blue irises, those lashes too fine to see except as a shimmer. "What happened? Why aren't you there yet? You should be gone alongside her."

They're so close. Nearly touching now. Jay imagines how they look through the encircling windows, these two old friends, her head tilted up, his shadow falling across her.

"I don't know," he says, and Jay exhales. "I thought everything was fine. More than fine. Bran told me she knew how to get through the portal, she knew where it was, she understood all the steps at last. That very night, I was due to fly out to Arkansas. Then I get a text from her: Deal's off, don't come, forget everything. She wouldn't give me a straight answer. After that, she stopped talking to me. She blocked my fucking number."

"But you aren't the type to give up easily," Jay says.

He smirks at his feet. "I just figured she hadn't found the portal after all. She was so hard on herself. I hunkered down and focused on my work for a while. Next thing I know, I got the letter, I came back, and found all of you here."

Jay braces herself for what comes next. "Max, the thing is . . . Brandi *did* find the portal."

He looks up sharply.

"She left us a letter. Well, *me*. She left me a letter. She's waiting on the other side. And I know how to follow her."

"My god," Max says, stepping even closer, taking her by the shoulders, his eyes shining. "Jay. Jadelynne. Then let's go. Let's go, my god. Fuck the tickets, fuck all of this, we'll—we can go through the portal, the two of us, we can meet Brandi, we can—"

"First I need to ask you one question, and I need you to answer me honestly. Even though we don't have the Truth House anymore."

"All right. Yes, anything, anything." He's brimming with joyful impatience.

"What do you know about Destiny Lautner?" Jay asks.

60

2015

Max instantly knows what she means. Every detail is pulled to the surface, the way that guilt moves together: one piece drags everything from its hiding place, a long trail of fear and regret and disgust that usually lies coiled, packed tight inside him. She's felt the same.

"Did Brandi find out?" he asks. "Is that how you know?"

She moves past this, homed in on what she needs. Her heart is racing. It's as if Destiny is in the room with them, the corpse in a hopeful gown. "Tell me everything, Max." He starts to protest, and she stops him. "Tell me everything, or I won't tell you what I know about the portal. It's the only way you'll ever get through it."

"It's history. It's nothing." But he gauges the steeliness of her eyes and knows that she's serious. "Fine. You want to know? I took Destiny into the woods that night. The Senior Ball. We'd been talking for a few weeks, but she was finally willing to hang out with me, I couldn't believe it when she accepted my invitation. We were drunk. I was just . . . so excited to be in the Forever House at all. That place never bothered showing up for me before I had Destiny with me. When I saw it, I thought I was dreaming. I was so excited, Jay."

She waits. The silence is shifting, bristling. Jay wonders if the Forever House showed up for Destiny because she was a local, and Max mistook that magic as his own.

"I told Destiny that the house was magic, but she didn't believe me." He gives a dry echo of his usual laugh. "We went inside. I wanted to show her this incredible thing we'd found together. But Destiny didn't care. She was bored and angry, worried about missing her stupid fucking bus. She kept insisting that the Forever House wasn't magic, calling me an idiot. A freak. Saying I was stupid for believing it." He appeals to Jay. "Just like Amber did to you, right? You and Brandi, with the Truth House."

She makes herself nod once, grudgingly remembering the ache of that. To stand inside magic with somebody and know she rejected its influence.

"She couldn't see what was right in front of her. This whole little town, they never appreciated what they had, right here. It pissed me off. No wonder Theodora didn't share it with the whole town, you know?"

"If someone dragged you into a dusty house in the middle of the woods and told you it was magical, would you believe them right away?" Jay demanded, voice trembling.

"Okay, so it was wrong of me. I know that. I regret it. Yes, I took Destiny to the Forever House, yes, she knew about the magic. Is that the problem?"

"It's not," Jay says. "I need to know how Destiny ended up dead."

The word feels as if it moves around the turret, glancing against the windows.

"Jay," Max says. His voice is hoarse. "You don't have to do this."

"But I do." The Greyhound tickets, all those hopeful stops, the bus winding across the country without her. "If you want the portal, we have to do this."

"We were fighting," Max says. "That's all. I told Destiny she could find out for herself. I told her she had to figure out how to escape. Right? It was the only way to make her *see*, because she'd get out, and she'd see no time had passed and she hadn't missed her bus, and she'd see that I was right. So, yeah. I—I locked her in the cellar. Just to show her. Prove it to her.

"I left. I stood out there in the forest for . . . I don't know. Twenty minutes. Maybe I didn't really believe how powerful it was myself. I'd never been in there."

Max had been steeped in enough of Theodora's magic by then to believe in it full-heartedly, to understands its beauty and its danger.

"I went back inside. I thought maybe she'd be older, I don't know. Maybe she'd be starving, or scared, or begging for company because she'd been alone for so long. But she was—"

"She was dead," Jay says. Clearly. As if to a jury.

"Not even—there was no question about it, Jay. I didn't have to check for a pulse. She'd been dead for a while. Her face was—she was—" Max hid his own face in his hands for a moment. "I ran. What the fuck else was I supposed to do?"

Jay inhales, exhales, aware of the windows all around her.

"It was an accident. God, Jay, you've got to believe me. I've hated myself every day for it. She was leaving anyway. She had her back-pack with her and everything. People just assumed that she'd left town. Wasn't it kinder to let them believe that? How would I even explain this—this corpse, when Destiny was alive a day before?"

Max had ensured she could never leave. That her world, just when she thought it would grow infinitely bigger, became as small as a dark cellar.

"If I could undo it, I would," Max says. "Jay. Please. I didn't—"

She opens her hand and holds out the insulin pen. He falls quiet at once. He looks at it quickly, just one glance, and then away.

"Why was it lying just outside the cellar door, then?"

He won't answer.

"If you want to go through the portal—"

"Motivation," Max says, low.

"What?" Jay asks.

"That's what I told her it was. Motivation for her to get out faster."

And then Jay knows that she'll never remember the Forever House as unending sunlight, or Iggy's heartbeat in her ear, or even the last few precious days with Brandi before the pills took hold. She'll only think of Destiny, and the impossible life dangled within arm's reach. "Were you proving the magic to her, Max? Or were you punishing her?"

"Both," he said. Then, as if remembering Jay's leverage over him, he whispers, "I wanted to hurt her. All right? In the moment, I wanted to hurt her. I didn't mean to—"

"You did mean to," Jay says. "Do you know what I just realized? I always thought I was at the center of Brandi calling us back. I thought it was targeted at me, more than the rest of you. But it was you, Max. Brandi forced you to come back to solve her disappearance. She caught you in a paradox. You thought you were getting out of here, into a whole new world, but she dragged you right back to the Ozarks, with us, and forced you to face up to what you did."

Max rubs his hands over his face, stretching the skin until he's unrecognizable. His skin is humid with nerves; he seems paler, as if the memory is sapping something from him.

"Didn't you worry that Brandi would find the Forever House?" Jay asks.

"No. No, Bran was terrified to go back. She was worried that it would make everything worse with her addiction." Max's voice is low, hoarse. Outside the windows, the sky is dark.

"Is that why you kept tabs on her? Is that why you—is that why you helped me get the scholarship? You wanted us all gone from here for good."

She expects Max to crumple, but he unfurls. There's a sudden energy between them, and Max grabs for her hands, his skin burning, his palms dwarfing hers. The insulin pen falls to the floor, rolling. "Jay. We should go."

"What?"

"You and me. Let the others fly back home, and we'll find Bran, we'll leave everything about ourselves behind. Jay, please. It's perfect. The two of us, we know what it's like to want to be in a new world and become new people. We can find Brandi. We can make it up to her."

The horrible thing is how much she wants to agree. She wants to let go. Just give in to Max Garnet. What if she walked away right now, what if she turned her back on this world, all the mistakes erased, every regret left behind? She feels the *yes* hovering on her tongue.

"No, Max," she says. "When she found Destiny, Brandi realized all over again that it doesn't matter what world she's in: if she's in that world with you, it will always become yours."

Max's face is blank now. He's disappointed, she thinks. And she's angry, so angry with Max for being infinitely careless with the riches he was given, furious on behalf of Destiny, who should've had her own imperfect, beautiful life, spun out with all its own mistakes. She's heartbroken for Brandi, her trust broken no matter how many times she patched it back together. Jay starts to step away from him.

"Where are you going, Jay?" he asks.

He hasn't let go of her hands. Her heart throbs at the way he's clinging to her, to this last, precious proof of their friendship. "Goodbye," she whispers. "I have places to be."

The room crackles. The rest of the Mirror House is so silent.

"Max, please," she says again, and gently pulls her hand back. He won't release her. His grip tightens around her hands, almost painful. She can't move unless he lets go. The awareness of how fucked she is by this arrives slowly, then too fast, a sinking weight inside her.

"Jay," Max says. "I'm so sorry. But you know what this means to me."

"What do you mean? What are you going to do?" She stops struggling, because it hurts, or maybe because she wants to avoid the proof that he's the one hurting her.

"You need to tell me where the portal is."

"I'm not going to do that."

"What was your plan? You'd confront me about Destiny, you'd taunt me, you'd go find Brandi, and leave me here?"

"Something like that. Yeah."

He shakes his head. Jay wonders if what she sees now, this flat, cool, almost regretful person standing in front of her, is what Destiny saw the night she died.

"You're going to tell me," he says.

"Or what? You're going to hurt me, like you hurt Destiny?" He doesn't answer. A chill passes through Jay. Max's grip tightens again. "What, you're going to take me to the Forever House?"

As she says it, though, Jay knows that they don't have to go to the Forever House. There's a source of power right here, beneath their feet. The basement. The mirror, its inexorable hunger. If Max brought her down there, locked her in, how long would it be before Jay buckled? How long could she bear having her body dissolved?

"You're not the friend I knew," she says to Max.

He reels slightly as he begins walking backward, still not releasing her, dragging her toward that long, twisting staircase. She catches the way he trips, something broken in his stride. Is it grief over what he did, or disgust over what he's about to do? She doesn't fight back: she follows, eyes locked on his. "The others will come looking for me," she says.

"They won't, Jay."

"No, they will. Even without the scars, they'll come when I call them," Jay says. "And I call them now."

They're in the room. Hilma, near the door, blocking Max's way, her face pale with fury. Charlie leans against the window, one hand clamped over his mouth. Iggy—Iggy has a look on his face Jay's never seen, an anger that transforms him from the inside out, every cell of his body quietly burning. Iggy hangs the oval mirror back on the wall, facing outward, so that they can all see each other now. So that they can see everything.

"They've heard every word, Max," Jay says. "They were with us all along."

As she watches—as they all watch—Max Garnet collapses to his knees.

61

2015

They tie Max up in the turret. They turn the mirror back to the wall, concealing him. He's surprisingly compliant. By now—after everyone's questions, after Max's delirious attempts at explaining himself—it's only two hours until their flights take off. Even through her anger, Jay feels a throb of grief. The six of them will never be back together, then. Not because of Brandi's absence, but because of Max.

"All right," Iggy says, straightening. "He should be secure." He's pitiless now, all empathy and patience gone.

"What's wrong with him?" Charlie asks, flatly curious.

Max looks worse than he did when he first arrived in Eternal. Waxy, loopy-eyed, posture sagging. Jay's stomach squirms as she notices that his sleeve is bloodstained, a sticky flower blooming on his forearm. Almost as if his scar has come back.

"Well, congratulations," Max says slowly. "The meddling kids have saved the day. Now what? You're going to leave me here to think about what I've done?"

"Yes, Max, that's exactly what we're going to do," Hilma says.

The four of them set off into the early morning, the predawn light gilding the world around them. The years have fallen away and they're hopeful, brash.

As Jay walks down the steep sidewalks, overhung with trailing branches, the drop-off plummeting into the wild forest at every step, she remembers what Brandi said in her letter. Theodora wanted them to love the world they already inhabit. Jay sees the town with the eyes of her childhood self. The forest presses in, the greenery so vibrant and eager to grow that it seeks out any tiny opening, alleyways and backyards and cracks in the sidewalk exploding with life. The dense, rocky forests spread out in every direction, the pines and bluffs, the deep, moss-damp caverns, the springs that burst forth from the earth, carrying ancient heat. The diamonds glittering in the aftermath of long-ago volcanoes. The houses that have persisted here, built in a burst of optimism, these little structures that survive in the face of tornadoes and storms, fires and floods, nestled trustingly among the trees.

They pause at a crossroads. "How are we getting into the AIR House?" Iggy asks.

"We aren't," Jay says. "The AIR House isn't the portal. We were all wrong. In the letter, Brandi said that it was 'right under our noses.'"

62

2000

THEN

Jay said goodbye to Iggy on a late May evening. They sat together on the porch of the Luck House, surrounded by the wild buzz of the insects, the heady perfume of the shoulder-high wildflowers. Their hips nearly touched, but she left a careful sliver between them.

"I can come visit you, at least," Iggy said at last. "During summer. We can email or talk on AIM. People had long-distance relationships when they had to travel by stagecoach. We can probably do it, we've got computers and phones." He paused. "Or I can still come with you."

Jay didn't answer. She'd made up her mind last night, and she knew it was the right thing to do, but to actually put it into words felt like too much.

Iggy finally pressed into her silence. "What's happening? Are you breaking up with me?"

"I don't want to say it like that."

"But you don't want to be together. So. That's breaking up."

"No, it's not about you or us at all," she said. "I've made up my mind that I'm never coming back to Eternal Springs."

"Never? What about your dad?"

"I won't be seeing anyone if I can help it. I'm starting a new life," Jay said. "My dad is considering moving anyway, once I'm not keeping him here. I talked to the others about it. They all agreed. Hilma, Charlie. Max."

"Okay," Iggy said, careful. "Then we'll keep in touch in our new lives, right? Easy."

"I mean, don't you want a fresh new start in California? Charlie doesn't want to exchange contact info. The Garnets are thrilled to stop talking. And—" She stopped short of mentioning Brandi; it hurt too much. "I think it's smart. All of us deserve to leave Eternal behind, and maybe that means leaving each other."

"Are you kidding? What if I don't want a fresh start? What if I want to stay with you?"

"What, you date me for two months and then you're stuck with me forever?" She tried to joke, but that word—*forever*—clung to the air.

"Yes. Maybe. I don't know. That doesn't feel so bad to me."

"It will, later on."

"I'll deal with it later on, then. Jay. Seriously? Don't do this."

"You knew we were going different places," Jay said. "You're going to go to Los Angeles or wherever, and I'm going to Albany." She would pretend that they never found the houses, never used them to turn their lives into something amazing, never used them to hurt each other irreparably. She would pretend they were just high school sweethearts, their puppy love always flimsy with the awareness that it wouldn't last.

"Jay, I don't want to break up—"

"It's the Forever House," she said, harsher than she intended. She took a moment, then tried again. "It's not even *us*, don't you get that? We weren't in love until we were in there. It all happened there. And what if we don't actually love each other?"

"We had sex for the first time in there, that doesn't mean we didn't like each other already." Iggy sounded like his heart was breaking, a wild sadness at the edges. She steeled herself against it.

"You didn't even really talk to me until we met the Garnets," Jay said.

"Yeah, but—"

"I'm doing it for you, Iggy," Jay said. "Think of all the people out there you'll meet. You won't even remember me soon."

Iggy leaned in close, breath warm against her. He kissed her cheek, and she had to shut her eyes and tell herself it wasn't the last time. "I would've gone into another world with you, Jadelynne," he said, almost too quiet for her to catch. "I wish we could be together in this one."

63

2015

Jay steps into the shed, and instantly everything makes sense. This location holds her clearest, deepest memories of Eternal. This is where she spent her time before the Garnets, before Theodora, before even Iggy or Charlie. Just her and Brandi, taking photos, drawing, talking for hours or comfortably sunk into silence. Jay wants to go back to those days, just for a moment. She wants to say to Brandi: *You were always the best part of me. If I could take back even one second of waiting for other people and other places and just be with you, I'd do it.*

"Are you sure about this?" Hilma asks, squeezing into the shed, rubbing her nose against the dust. "This doesn't fit Theodora's descriptions of the Portal House."

"I trust Brandi," Jay says. "You left her with the journal, Hilma. She saw something the rest of us didn't. I wonder if Theodora was—was tricking us. Do you know what Brandi said? That Theodora wanted us to appreciate our own world. This very town, in fact."

Charlie looks reflective. "You know, I did find something out. Someone at a party told me, when I mentioned where I'm from. Arkansas's state nickname used to be 'the Wonder State.' They nixed it after a decade or two because the Wonder State was too old-fashioned, it didn't draw enough economic growth."

"Wonder didn't sell," Iggy says, only half a joke.

"But Theodora saw that same wonder," Jay says. "So in her journals, she made up this ornate home. A place bigger and grander than anywhere else, the portal to another world, and . . . it was all a lie. It was this tiny place that nobody would notice. This shed."

With four of them in here, it's a tight fit. One of Jay's old drawings slips off the wall, fluttering to the floor. Iggy's hand presses warm to Jay's hip.

"How much time did you and Brandi spend here?" Hilma asks.

"Almost all our time," Jay says, and laughs softly. "We'd go through the window, it led into Brandi's bedroom." The window, clouded over with grime. Something in Jay's chest tugs, clear as a string pulled taut. She bends down, examines the small, defunct keyhole at the bottom of the windowsill. Jay reaches into her back pocket and produces the key that Brandi left for her. She's surprised at how steady her hand is, because her heart is beating so hard she could levitate, each pulse a wingbeat.

She doesn't let herself think about the night in the AIR House and the depth of that disappointment. She clings to the idea of Brandi, Brandi, Brandi. Her friend is both close and an entire world away. "Are we ready? Are we going through?" Jay asks.

"We have to," Iggy says. "Don't we? We've wanted this for so long."

"It's completely undiscovered territory," Hilma says.

"Undiscovered by *us*," Charlie adds.

"So do we say the inscriptions?" Iggy asks.

"I don't think we need to," Jay says. "We have the actual key."

Jay reaches for Iggy's hand; Hilma reaches for hers, and Charlie takes Hilma's hand, and they're intertwined, shoulder to shoulder, the four of them staring at the window. For a second Jay thinks they'll walk right through without second-guessing. They'll be reunited with Brandi, everything else erased. Exactly what Max so badly wanted for himself.

But then Iggy's hand in hers falters, and she feels a shift in the shed.

Charlie speaks first. "I have Damon. My boyfriend. I have a life in New York City. I want to go through, I do. God, I've dreamed about it for years. But I can't turn my back on what I've built here, not yet."

"I'm pregnant," Hilma says simply. "It's a girl."

Jay looks at Hilma with new eyes; she hadn't guessed. "Hilma—"

"No, no. I didn't want to tell the rest of you. I knew it would make things strange. But she can't grow up in a different world, away from her father." Hilma gives a slow, rueful smile. "Maybe my time's passed for this kind of thing, for a while."

"I have to make things right with Elle," Iggy says. "It's not fair to her, to leave her behind to deal with everything I've done to her." He squeezes Jay's hand once.

"Jay?" Hilma asks. "Will you be our delegate, then?"

Jay's left a small blank space at the center of her life, ready to replace everything. She hesitates on the brink, the dividing line between here and there. Then she reaches forward, letting go of Iggy's hand, and slides the key into the shadowy slot. She turns the key, and, like she has a thousand times before, she opens the window.

A cold wind brushes against Jay's cheek, electric with a scent she can't place. She gasps. Jay's had tiny moments like this, during the change of the seasons, when a stray breeze will brush against her neck and she'll have a sudden, intoxicating glimpse of adventure, her familiar patterns rearranged briefly. But this—this is a thousand times more powerful.

The window glows.

It's no longer the ordinary window frame that Jay's crawled through a hundred times, with the silt of dust at the bottom and the cobwebs in the corners. It doesn't look directly into Brandi's bedroom window with its flimsy curtains. Instead, the window shows a glimmering landscape beyond, a stretch of pure snow. The sky is a color she can't quite place, close to blue but shifting even as Jay watches, deepening and rippling like an ocean. The image wavers and flickers every few seconds like a mirage, like an old TV set changing channels.

They stand, the four of them, kids again, laughing and wonderstruck, and Jay is so high that she almost doesn't notice when the shed door swings open behind them.

64

2015

NOW

"Max," Hilma says. "Max. My god. What's wrong? You're—"

His looming presence fills the shed, dispersing the magic. Jay glances at the window again, and Max follows her gaze, his eyes unsteady, but his pupils dilate with sheer desire when he realizes what it means.

Jay's stunned, wrong-footed. She'd thought if he tried to follow them, he'd go to the AIR House, drawn back like a homing pigeon. Then she notices the blood.

"Of course," Max says, blinking as he looks around. "This place."

He's in bad shape: his shirt blotchy with damp patches, his face white. Around his wrists, the deep marks from the rope are a hot red, knotted, almost pulsing. Too severe to be the result of the half hour he's been tied up. Like some infection inside is nudging to the surface.

It feels wrong to see him like this. He's eroding quickly. "Brandi only found the portal because of me," Max says, voice strained, breathless. "She's waiting for me."

"She's not waiting for you anymore, Max," Jay says.

Iggy positions himself in front of the window, backlit by the shine of the other world. "You need help, man."

Blood drools from one nostril, and Max reaches up mindlessly, leaving a smear across his lips. He takes a step forward. Jay sees precisely how easy it will be for him to launch himself through and get what he wants. Even in this state, he can take them on. Brandi is waiting for Jay, and instead Max Garnet will emerge into whatever she's created for herself on the other side of this window.

"Well," Hilma says. "We can't stop him. Can we? Go through, Max. It's your right."

Even Max is startled by this. "What?" he whispers.

"Go through. Go on." Hilma's face is sphinxlike. "Just say the inscriptions."

In the silence, Jay makes a quick calculation. Max doesn't know about the key. Iggy and Charlie catch on too. The four of them move in front of the portal, forming a barrier. "All you have to do is say them. All seven of them. Nobody else is going to do that for you." Jay shrugs. "It's your quest, right? Prove to us that you want it badly enough."

It's a simple request. Max has been laying the groundwork to leave this world for a long time. As Roy, as the owner of half of Eternal Springs, he's had nothing but opportunities to piece everything together and prepare.

He opens his mouth. Nothing comes out. "'Oh,'" he tries, "'I am . . . I am fortune's . . .'"

"You needed Brandi to remember them for you?" Jay asks.

"I can't . . . who could remember all those?"

They've been written directly on Jay's heart, all this time.

"You don't even have them written down?" Iggy asks. "You can buy this entire place, but you can't remember a few lines of poetry?"

Max's gaze darts into every corner.

"You thought Destiny didn't deserve the magic," Jay says. "You think you deserve this town's magic all to yourself. But look at how careless you are with it."

"Say it," Hilma prods. "You can remember one, can't you?"

"Fuck, it's fine," Max says, bracing himself on the wall. He coughs, and blood lands at his feet. "I have time. I'll find them again. I know where the portal is now. I can—" He sways, and Charlie and Hilma rush forward, steadying him almost tenderly.

"What's happening to me?" Max asks, and he finally, slowly, brings his arm to the front of his body. Iggy winces, turning his head. The scar is back. Max's arm is eaten by the wound this time, the skin necrotic, a deep, bruising purple, almost black. His eyes are filming over.

"Do you remember the letters?" Charlie asks, making an effort to stay calm. "The ones Brandi found in the Forever House? Brandi mentioned something about a punishment, if you tried to go back on your promise."

"Burning down the house to get out of the oath," Iggy says. "That seems grim."

"Is there any way to fix it?" Hilma asks the rest of them.

"Maybe he could fulfill the promise," Jay suggests. "He could still help Brandi. Or he could help Destiny . . . he could admit to what he did. Tell the whole town."

"I don't know how to help her anymore," Max whispers, and Jay's not sure if he's talking about Brandi or Destiny or . . .

His eyes move to the portal. Jay can feel his longing, the way this body is giving out on him. The newness of that other world is just waiting to embrace him and change him back.

It happens so quickly. He launches himself at the window, using the last of his energy. Jay doesn't even think about it; she must have been planning it, on some level. She yanks the key from the keyhole and flings it into the snowy expanse of the other world. It spins, a dark speck, and then vanishes. Max lets out a strangled cry, and Jay slams the window shut right as his outstretched hand hits the glass, leaving an uneven indent in the pane, webbed with cracks.

Outside, a grasshopper bounds from the weeds, startled.

Because the window is just a window again. The glass, dewy with morning condensation, heated by the same rising sun they've known their whole lives. Through the windowpane come distant traffic sounds, the delighted warble of birdsong. The other world is gone.

Max sinks to his knees. He leans his forehead into the glass. Everyone else seems too stunned to speak.

"Jay," Iggy manages at last. "The key. You can't—you won't get it back."

The portal is closed now. A secret locked tight in plain view.

"It's all right," Jay says, and she means it: the melancholy is tinged with relief, a sense of rightness. "I know she'll come for me, one day. And I'll wait for Brandi. However long it takes."

Hilma kneels next to her brother. She holds him in her arms, not caring that his blood smears against her. Slowly, he softens. They rest their heads on each other's shoulders. Jay thinks Hilma's forgiving her twin, that maybe this bond between them is always going to supersede anything else. Then she realizes that Hilma is saying goodbye.

EPILOGUE

2019

J ay kneels in the garden, fingers dug deep into the earth. Behind her, the back door is open, so she can look over her shoulder and see the comfort of her home, waiting for her, the ceiling fan blades stirring up a lazy coolness.

The fourth anniversary of her move back to Eternal Springs, Arkansas, is approaching. The July air is luscious with humidity, insects shrieking and singing. Jay stands, wipes her hair back, leaving dirt damp against her forehead. There's something strange in the air; she's felt it all week. There are times the fine membrane that separates the two worlds—one world that she's learned to love, the other she hasn't yet met—feels thin. Right now, the barrier is almost nothing.

A rare breeze lifts the hair at the back of Jay's neck and she half turns; for a moment she had a funny feeling someone was watching her. Nothing. It's not time for Iggy to come back. He's with his family for the weekend, visiting his parents and brothers. He comes to stay with her frequently, for weeks at a time. Even with his travels, they rarely go longer than a month without seeing each other.

At its heart, their relationship has a question mark, but one they stare at openly now, examine between the two of them, unafraid. Iggy isn't sure whether he'll come with her, when—or if—Brandi returns to give Jay her second chance. Their romance has a timer on it. But then, Jay thinks, every relationship is like this, wound through with uncertainty.

True to his word, Iggy ended things with Elle, directly after everything happened in 2015. Freed from the Oath House, he had the complicated gift of breaking up with her on their own terms. Apologizing. Letting Elle walk free into her own future. The first time Iggy returned to Jay, they spent days in bed, both grieving and grateful. Rediscovering each other.

It was like a repeat of the Forever House, but a version that belonged only to them. Time moved at its normal pace—the sun rising and setting, Iggy and Jay curled up laughing and naked at midnight, woken by birdsong at dawn. By now Jay suspects that whatever is still trapped inside her and Iggy from the Forever House has loosened, finally making space for what they've experienced together in these completely ordinary rooms.

It was another letter that saved them. A letter from Brandi that showed up at Amber's place a week after Jay closed the portal. The letter explained that Brandi was fine—that she had left town of her own volition, that she was unharmed, happy, but sorry she couldn't explain more. That she missed Eternal Springs and her good friends there.

The bloodwork came back showing that it was Brandi's blood, nobody else's. Jay arranged with her Albany landlord to have her own half of the necklace sent, proving that the duplicate wasn't hers.

The evidence against the five of them dissolved, leaving them adrift again. Only their own consciences still tethered them to Eternal.

Charlie and Iggy left Eternal Springs as planned. Jay volunteered to stay behind. Max was in Eternal Springs' tiny hospital, fading out of consciousness. Hilma surprised Jay by staying too—not only for Max's sake, but for Jay's. For Brandi's. Jay had never seen Hilma Garnet like this, all her indomitable resolve directed toward undoing past wrongs.

It took Jay and Hilma days, weeks, to plead their case. Jay became more familiar with the police station than she thought possible as she and Hilma sat drinking tepid coffee together, reaching into the past from their perches in the plastic chairs. They took turns conveying what had happened.

Explaining Gene's fate was easier than explaining what happened to Destiny. Even though Destiny's death was more clear-cut, less blood and obfuscation, its very simplicity—a girl on the verge of escape, an act of petty vengeance amplified by too many years—left Jay mentally drained, her eyes hurting as if she'd been crying, even as she fought to stay calm.

The thing was, they couldn't explain without filling in the gaps. They couldn't explain without acknowledging Theodora Trader.

Being back in Eternal had planted the seeds. Judd's suggestion that the town was magic. Even Pell's unexpected sliver of belief in the Mirror House turret. It all connected with the tiny signs that Jay hadn't appreciated as a teenager. The rumors, the whispers, the people who moved out of houses too quickly, the people who saw beauty and strangeness inside Eternal's buildings. Little kids like Brandi and Jay, playing games that they didn't fully understand.

When she was young, Jay believed keeping Theodora's magic hidden was the most important thing she could do. That urgency guided every choice she made. She'd sat in Pell's office at eighteen and betrayed her best friend because the other alternative was to betray the magic, but the magic had never been Jay's to protect or hoard. The miracles woven into Theodora Trader's structures belonged to the town itself, and it was up to them to hand that wonder back. They'd failed once. They wouldn't fail this time.

Now Jay gathers up an armful of weeds and heads around the back of the house. The day stretches ahead of her, open and free. The air smells like wild onion, wildflowers, everything that grows freely and abundantly. Closing her eyes, Jay whispers the inscriptions like prayers.

There's a gallery in downtown Eternal. Jay's drawings are highlighted there. She's drawn the houses in all their intricacy, alongside blueprints that she sketched from memory. The gallery also holds Brandi's photos, re-created in gelatin silver print, a few images preserved as the original instant camera castoffs. In some photos, the Garnet twins are captured as shoulders, brilliant hair, a corner of a laughing mouth. Iggy's framed in half a dozen of them, and Charlie: Brandi captured Iggy's tenderness, Charlie's wistfulness.

But most of the photos are of Jay and Brandi. Jay's teeth shine, crooked and overlapping, pre-orthodontia. The two of them sit in the trees together, they perch on Formica bathroom sinks, arms around each other. Again and again, Jay smiles fearlessly.

Hilma's recompense for Gene's death has been complex. Jay's been able to see Hilma for what she was: young, scared, trying to defend herself in the middle of an unfathomable disappointment. Jay knows that their true crime has been—not Gene's death—but letting Brandi take the fall for it, leaving her alone with the ghosts of suspicion circling her. Whatever Hilma worked out with Pell in private, she came out and announced to Jay that she'd be handing Red Art's property back to the town.

Max is still a complex ache at the center of everything. His coma has lasted for these past four years, as if the destroyed Oath

House holds him in stasis, his broken promises pinning him to the parameters of his own body. When Hilma calls Jay—her daughter laughing and playing in the background—she still holds out a half-guilty and stubborn hope. She still believes that one day, somehow, Max will be given a second chance.

"What if Brandi comes back?" Hilma had asked, last time they talked. "What if she can forgive him, somehow? Do you think she could . . . ?"

"I don't know," Jay had said, quieted by the grief in Hilma's voice. "Maybe."

The Garnets have given Destiny's family money. It's a poor substitute for what the Lautners have lost, Jay knows. She passes by their house sometimes. She notes the way they've fixed it up, made it stronger, a better container for their lives as they grieve. That gives Jay the smallest sense of peace.

For the first year, Jay woke up every single morning praying that Brandi would be back. She watched out the windows, she turned at every unexpected footfall. Iggy teases her about it: "You'll never stop waiting for something, will you? It's just the way your heart is built." But as the years have passed and Brandi hasn't reappeared, Jay's settled into the Ozarks. She finds herself enjoying the particular formation of clouds in the mornings, the impossible expanse of the trees, the roads that knock the breath from her lungs when she runs in the mornings and evenings.

She's forced herself to admit that maybe Brandi won't come back at all. It's likely she's found a place in the new world, she's forgotten all about the distant dream of Arkansas. Maybe, when Jay didn't come through the portal, Brandi gave up on her yet again. Maybe, maybe, maybe. Whatever the case, there are worse things than waiting.

———

With the help of Hilma's legal machinations, Theodora's houses have gone to Jay. The five remaining houses are safe now. The Duplication House, the Mirror House, the Luck House, the High House. Somewhere in the forest, the Forever House, revealing itself only occasionally.

Jay tries to be a good caregiver for the surviving houses. She's let the Luck House lawn grow thick and lush again, she's restored the Duplication House. Otherwise, she's left the houses mostly alone. The people around Eternal know where to find Jay when they need Theodora's magic. When they crave a minor boost of good fortune; when all they want in the world is time, just a little more time. Jay has done her best to share the rules with them, as well as the warnings and the cautions. She respects the magic of the small worlds contained within those walls.

Even though the journal is gone, Jay retrieved the letters from the Forever House. They've revealed Theodora in a way her confusing, confounding journal never could. The journal was a game, but the letters are a quiet revelation. Jay sees Theodora's responses to the people of Eternal, the way she tried to weave ease and escape and strangeness into the fabric of Eternal Springs. And this guides Jay as she steps into Theodora's left-behind role.

With Charlie's occasional, long-distance help, she's also been tracing the town's history, looking into the other, previous owners of Theodora's houses, slowly working her way toward a full history of Theodora's legacy. People are eager to come forward with their own details and anecdotes and photos. Each house has become more complex, settling into its own history. Jay wonders why she ever kept these places all to herself. It's so obvious now that they always held the invisible marks of the people who walked those rooms. The long-ago residents of the High House who hosted lavish dinner parties during the 1940s; the woman who'd held séances in the Truth House. The child with leukemia, Lucy Braddon, who had briefly lived with her mother in the Forever House.

Her neighbors are less skeptical than she assumed they would be. They're open. These houses have existed as half-whispered stories for so long, and now Jay's able to help explain. There are still people around town who don't want anything to do with the woman who abandoned her best friend, and Jay gets it. She's an uncertain presence; she'll never be perfectly at home in Eternal Springs, maybe not anywhere. But she's here for the Eternal citizens if they want her—in her little house, the one where her mother spent time with her as a baby. Magicless in every way but the most important.

Today, Jay walks toward the side of the house, arms full. Her house beckons her, shaded and welcoming.

Someone calls her name, every syllable beloved: *Jadelynne*.

Jay takes a moment before she turns to see a woman walking down the road toward her, half-familiar, lifting a hand to Jay, her whole face open with joy. And Jadelynne Carr drops everything she's holding and she's running, running back into the arms of her best friend.

ACKNOWLEDGMENTS

First, thank you to the many Arkansans I've known throughout my life who've made this book what it is by being complex, interesting, hopeful, and ambitious individuals. I hope I've represented Arkansas and the Ozarks in a way that feels fair to many of you, though I can't capture everybody's experience of the area. Any missteps are my own.

Huge, eternal thanks to Daphne Durham, my amazing editor, for being such an incredible joy when it comes to creative collaboration! Thank you for pushing me to make the book more compassionate and enchanting, and for seeing *The Wonder State* for *exactly* what I wanted it to be even when I lost sight of that vision. I'm so grateful to you for nurturing the potential of this Ozarks town and its strange houses and rocky friendships. Thanks to Lydia Zoells, Brianna Fairman, and the whole wonderful team at MCD and FSG. I'm very lucky to work with you.

My agent, Alice Whitwham, has been such a believer in my work from the very start, and deserves all the heartfelt thanks I have to offer. Also, my gratitude will forever go to my mentor, Kathryn Davis, for your help and encouragement over the years.

Writing is very collaborative, so I have to honor some of my earliest readers: Thank you to Kate Broad for reading an early draft and taking this book seriously when it was uncertain and fresh. You helped me strengthen the shape of this book into something much more magical. Thank you to Franklin Sayre; I'm grateful for your opinions on the particular strangeness of living in a small town as a young person, even if you were far from the Ozarks. Thank you to my lovely writing group friends (Inna, Patty Barrué, and Jill Beissel). Your keen, spot-on insights helped me shape my drafts, and your wisdom and camaraderie sustained me through deadlines.

This is my third book, and the readers who saw beauty, magic, and fun in my previous novels have kept me writing and pushing forward to find that connection. I'm incredibly grateful to everyone who reached out, spread the word, or read one of my books quietly and granted me their time for a while.

Thanks to Karen, my mother-in-law, whose generosity gave me the free time I needed to write this novel more rapidly than my previous ones. And thank you to Karen and Tim both, for reading final drafts and getting as excited about these weird houses as I am.

My parents are the ones who raised me in Arkansas. Love to my dad, who used to tease me for being born in Arkansas as if I did it on purpose, and my mom, whose own restless spirit has shaped my own. Thanks to my siblings, who explored the Ozarks with me during our wild childhood. (I promise one day to write a book where the main character has siblings.) Thanks to my siblings-in-law, who are so supportive and wonderful.

Finally! I send all my love to Ryan, for everything, but especially for your willingness to brainstorm. My ideas never feel quite alive or quite right until we've discussed them in detail. Miles and August, you're my own beloved explorers who already obsess over portals, magic, and other worlds. I will try to make this world a little better for you. I love the three of you infinitely.